CROSSING THE LINE

Books by James D. Shipman

TASK FORCE BAUM

IRENA'S WAR

BEYOND THE WIRE

BEFORE THE STORM

A TIME FOR DEFIANCE

CROSSING THE LINE

Published by Kensington Publishing Corp.

CROSSING
THE LINE

JAMES D. SHIPMAN

KENSINGTON
PUBLISHING CORP.

kensingtonbooks.com

KENSINGTON BOOKS are published by

Kensington Publishing Corp.
900 Third Avenue
New York, NY 10022

All Kensington titles, imprints, and distributed lines are available at special quantity discounts for bulk purchases for sales promotion, premiums, fund-raising, educational, or institutional use.

This book is a work of fiction. Names, characters, businesses, organizations, places, events, and incidents either are the product of the author's imagination or are used fictitiously. Any resemblance to actual persons, living or dead, events, or locales is entirely coincidental.

To the extent that the image or images on the cover of this book depict a person or persons, such person or persons are merely models, and are not intended to portray any character or characters featured in the book.

Special book excerpts or customized printings can also be created to fit specific needs. For details, write or phone the office of the Kensington Sales Manager: Kensington Publishing Corp., 900 Third Avenue, New York, NY 10022. Attn. Sales Department. Phone: 1-800-221-2647.

KENSINGTON and the K with book logo Reg. US Pat. & TM Off.

ISBN: 978-1-4967-4778-5
ISBN: 978-1-4967-4779-2 (ebook)

First Kensington Trade Paperback Printing: January 2026

10 9 8 7 6 5 4 3 2 1

Printed in the United States of America

The authorized representative in the EU for product safety and compliance is eucomply OU, Parnu mnt 139b-14, Apt 123
Tallinn, Berlin 11317, hello@eucompliancepartner.com

Inspired by a true story.

Chapter 1
Grzegórzki District

Krakow
Occupied Poland
February 1941

Natalia Wajcblum dug the knife into her palm under the table, letting the sharp pain burn through her hand and up her arm. She had to do something, or she would scream. And her father never allowed outbursts at the table. She turned to him now as he concentrated on dipping a crust of bread into his soup. How could he eat, think, breathe right now?

"There is a new production of Chopin's work coming to Old Town," he said, turning to her mother. "What do you think, Aleksandra? Should I secure tickets?"

She smiled at him, the cracks and creases around her eyes and forehead rippling like lightning. "Do you know who will be conducting?"

"The paper didn't say, but it would be a nice evening for all of us. We could use the distraction."

A servant entered the room and looked over their bowls. He was a Pole, Thomasz, and had been with them since before the occupation. Natalia wondered what he would do next for employment, now that they'd received *the notice*.

"Should I bring the next course?" Thomasz inquired.

Her father nodded, not deigning to look up. "Natalia, what do you think? Would you like to attend a concert?"

"What kind of dream are you both living in?" she demanded, unable to contain herself any further. "Concerts? Social engagements? It's over. It's all over."

"Now that's enough of that, miss," her father interjected. "I won't have my table interrupted by—"

"We won't have a table soon enough, Father, or servants, or anything. They're going to shove us into the worst hole in Krakow. And you want to talk about concerts." She began to rise. She'd had all of this she could take.

"Sit back down," her mother ordered. "We are at our meal. And Wajcblums conduct themselves with discipline and decorum. I won't have you raging like you're the daughter of a baker or a garbage collector."

"Are we better than them now, Mother?" she asked. "Father lost his law practice a year ago. We've been hanging on here at the house, banned from work, banned from school, and now they're forcing us to move to some ghetto with the rest of the dregs."

"It's a Jewish Quarter," her father said. "And we'll make the most of it." He looked up, eyeing Thomasz, who had returned with their main dish. "Besides, this is hardly the time or place for a family discussion."

"I thought this was going to be an adventure?" her brother Stefan said. He was not yet thirteen and didn't fully understand what was going on around them.

"That's right, my boy. Don't you worry about a thing." Her father looked meaningfully at his daughter, his thick, peppered eyebrows furrowing sternly. "Natalia is just having one of her little episodes."

"When then, Father?" she asked. "We've had the eviction notice for a week. When are we going to talk about what's going to happen to us?"

"Not here, and not now," her mother said. "Your father will take care of things, as he always has."

"How? Like he took care of his job? Like he took care of my education? The Germans are the ones making the decisions. I'm supposed to be halfway through my first year of medical school, and instead, we've sat here doing nothing, waiting for every new regulation to crash in on us, every new restriction. And they've finally done it. They are stripping us of the last thing we have left. Our home."

"Don't worry about that," her father said, winking. "I've got inquiries out with friends. We will have something just as nice in the new district."

Aleksandra scoffed, pivoting on her husband. "How will that happen?" she asked. "The place they are sending us to is the worst. Full of workers and Jews."

"We're Jews, or have you forgotten?"

"Yes," her mother said. "Racially that's true but it hardly matters otherwise. When is the last time we celebrated a holiday? Even the major ones. Why would the Germans classify us based on our parents and grandparents? It's ridiculous. So is this move. I know you'll do your best for us, Jakub, but truly, you won't find something there that will compare to our home."

"I intend to secure the finest housing in the Podgórze District."

"How do you expect to do that?" asked Natalia.

"I'm going to go see Petre."

Petre Lendowski. He was a longtime friend of her father's. Petre was a Pole and had been a senior administrator in the old

4 James D. Shipman

government. "What can Petre do for us?" she asked. "Is he still even working for the government?"

"He is," said Jakub. "He retained a position after the occupation. When we got the eviction notice, I reached out to him. I have an appointment with him in the morning."

"Do you think he'll be able to help us?" her mother asked.

"No doubt he will. He has to have some power left."

"Why would he assist us?" Natalia asked.

Her father looked at her sharply. "For friendship, of course."

"What good has that done us this past year?" she asked. "We've lost everything except our house, and that's about to be taken from us. They quashed my acceptance to medical school. Where was Petre when they took my future away?"

"You shouldn't have been wasting your time with that nonsense in the first place," her mother snapped. "The one good thing that came out of the occupation was the derailing of your foolish insistence on a practical education. As if a woman in our circle would work a job. I would die if anyone found out you wanted to be a doctor."

"Mother, I worked my entire life to be able to study medicine. It might be enough for you and your friends to be *married* to someone who did something in life. But it's not enough for me."

"How dare you say something like that to me! You are lucky you—"

"Enough!" her father ordered. "We're not going through this again. It's a moot point. Medical school is closed to Jews now. Until the Germans are gone, Natalia won't be getting the education she wants, and you, Aleksandra, will not have to fight her over it. Now we have more important things to deal with." He looked at his plate, the uneaten food staring back at him. "I've indulged both of you tonight. You know the rules. We don't talk about problems at the dinner table." He gestured at Thomasz, who started clearing the plates. "I don't want to hear any more on this subject. I'm going to go to Petre tomorrow and straighten this out. The two of you have nothing to worry about in the interim. Now if it isn't too much, I'm going to enjoy my pipe and a good book. Make sure Stefan gets his homework done before bed."

"I want to go with you tomorrow," Natalia blurted out.

Her father, who had been halfway out the door, turned to his daughter in disbelief. "What on earth are you talking about?"

"I might be able to assist."

"How would you do that? By making cookies? This is hardly the place or time for a woman's—"

"He's a man."

"I know he's a man. What are you suggesting?" His eyes widened and an angry vein materialized on his forehead. "Do you think I would parade my daughter like a common streetwalker just to gain some favor?"

"Father, we need any advantage we can get. It's not the old days. You don't know if Petre has any power anymore. Even if he does, he may not be inclined to help you."

"Why wouldn't he? We go back two decades. All the way to the university."

"She's right." Natalia was surprised to hear her mother interjecting on her behalf.

Jakub turned on her. "Are you mad as well?"

"I'm not losing my mind, Jakub. I'm trying to be realistic. Natalia is right. Things have changed. When's the last time you saw Petre? Before the occupation? You don't know what has become of him, what pressures he is under. He stayed with the government. With the Germans. That's cause for concern in and of itself. If Natalia is with you, it might soften him up a little. He watched her grow up. He might feel more sympathy for our cause. And after all, she is very pretty."

"You'd have us prostitute our daughter for housing?"

"Of course not. I'm not suggesting she do anything more than be present. Perhaps a smile and a friendly word. At best, it will remind him of who we are and our histories together. At worst, it might give him another reason to help us despite himself."

"I won't," said Jakub. "My request stands on my friendship with Petre. I would never stoop to such antics."

"Jakub, you need to take her," her mother said. "I can't live in some hovel. We must use any advantage we have—Petre is a man and Natalia is a young woman. A smile could buy us a few extra rooms."

He hesitated and opened his mouth again to say something, but then seemed to change his mind. "Fine," he said at last. "But don't you dare flirt with him, Natalia. You are coming as my daughter, and a family friend. If that helps us in some way, so be it. But I won't allow anything beyond that. Do you understand me?"

"Yes, Father."

"Good. And now, if that's quite enough from the two of you, I'm going to go try to enjoy my pipe. Good evening."

He stepped out of the room.

"Thank you, Mother."

"No need to thank me. It will be nice for you to make yourself useful. You've moped around here for the past year, pining after school instead of finding yourself a suitable husband. But all will be forgiven if you can secure us decent housing. Now listen to me—don't you worry about your father. When the time comes, smile for all you're worth."

The next morning, Natalia set off with her father toward the Department of the Interior. It was more than a mile away, and they were both heavily bundled against the cold. Natalia shook her head against the bitter wind, amazed at how their life had changed. Before the occupation, they would have been whisked through town in their Mercedes, driven by a chauffeur to the shopping district or one of Krakow's many restaurants. But the Germans had impounded their car on the first day of the occupation, leaving them to walk from place to place like common workers. That had been the first of so many indignities the Nazis had inflicted on them. And now they were facing the greatest one—the loss of their beautiful house. The only home she'd ever known.

She mustn't think about that now. Instead, she watched the pedestrians as they marched along. The sidewalks were busy, with people heading into work or walking children to school. A long line snaked out of a corner grocery store, with people queued up for their meager ration of bread, an egg or two, and some vegetables. Meat was difficult, if not impossible, to get now. So were fruits, coffee, chocolate, all of the luxuries. Vodka was the only thing readily available. The Germans must have figured a drunken population would sit by more docilely while they stripped the country of everything else.

"Natalia, pay attention," her father said, turning back to her. "What are you doing?"

"Just thinking about what's happened to this country since the Germans came."

"Not so loud," he said, looking around. "You don't know who is listening."

"What difference does it make?" she asked. "What more could they possibly take from us?"

"Just do as I say. We're almost there."

He led her several more blocks until they reached a large, brick nondescript building taking up half of a city block. The Department of the Interior had stayed in the same location after the occupation, but some things were very different. A huge swastika banner adorned the space above the front doors, fluttering in the icy wind. At the entrance, a German guard, rifle in hand, stood at attention, monitoring the comings and goings of those entering the building. Her father paused as they reached the stairs, and she wondered whether he would have the courage to enter. Natalia wondered whether Jews were even allowed to come here anymore.

Jakub squared his shoulders and gestured for her to follow. Fortunately, the guard merely eyed them without any inquiry and nodded for them to enter the building. She followed her father through the glass double doors and into the interior. There were people everywhere, moving this way and that down the long corridor dotted with office doors of various departments. Natalia was alarmed at how many uniforms were here. Almost everyone was a German soldier of one kind or another, and they all seemed to be eyeing the two of them suspiciously.

"Can I help you with something?" a woman at a desk asked them. She was off to the right in the open lobby and served as the receptionist for the place.

"Oh, yes," said her father. "I'm here to see Petre Lendowski."

She raised an eyebrow. "Do you have an appointment, Mister . . ."

"Mr. Wajcblum."

Her eyes shot up even more. Their last name marked them as Jews. "I'm sorry, sir, but without an appointment I won't be able to help you today. Perhaps phone ahead and try another time."

"Can you please call him?" Jakub asked. "I'm a friend."

She looked skeptical of that, but after a moment she picked up the phone and hit some numbers. "Yes. There's a man here to see Mr. Lendowski. Yes. A Mr. Wajcblum. No. He doesn't have an appointment. Yes, I'll wait." She sat on the phone for a few moments, looking down at her desk as if it was distasteful to keep eye contact with them. Finally, a voice in the receiver caught her attention again and she nodded before hanging up. "You may go up," she said. "But you'll have to wait for an opening."

"I understand," her father said. He motioned for Natalia to follow him again and they continued down the hall and then climbed three flights of stairs, finally reaching the top floor. They moved down the tiled hallway, passing numerous departments until they reached Petre's office at the end of the corridor. They stepped inside. There was another woman here, another desk.

"Are you Mr. Wajcblum?" she asked.

Her father nodded.

"Please take a seat," she said. "Mr. Lendowski will be with you as soon as he is able."

Jakub gestured at a chair to his right. He leaned over and whispered to Natalia. "I told you I would get us in. It won't be long now."

But much to their embarrassment and dismay, they sat in the reception area for hours. While they waited, various officials came and went. The receptionist ignored them, answering the phone or typing up messages from a tablet of shorthand she must have taken. Natalia kept checking her watch, feeling her irritation turn to humiliation, and then to anger. "Let's just go," she whispered to her father. "He's making a fool of us."

But Jakub shook his head. "He's a busy man. We have to stay. This is our chance."

So they waited, and the morning turned to noon, and then afternoon. It was nearing the end of the workday when the telephone rang and the receptionist rose, gesturing for them to follow her. Natalia was exhausted and starving. At this point, she just wanted to go home. But she rose and followed her father into Petre's office. The space was large, a corner unit with windows looking down the long avenues of Krakow in two directions. He sat behind a rich mahogany desk, a looming picture of Adolf Hitler perched behind him. The eyes of the

German leader scowled down at them, as if he dared them to ask a favor. Petre was on his feet in an instant and stepped around the desk to take her father's hand.

"Jakub, my friend. You must accept my apologies. You wouldn't believe the volume of work I am forced to deal with these days." He turned and noticed Natalia for the first time. He smiled at her and his eyes wandered down her figure, just for the briefest of moments. "And can this be your daughter? Natalia, isn't it? I haven't seen you in years. What a lovely young woman you've become. And not yet married? Do you still live with your father and mother?"

She nodded. "Yes. I was going to study medicine, but they took—"

"Now, now, Natalia, we're not here to tell Petre our troubles. Well, not all of them at least."

"Why are you here?" Petre asked.

Natalia was surprised by the abrupt tone.

"Right to the point, then," her father stuttered. "I had hoped we could catch up a little."

Petre smiled again, but not with his eyes. "Another time. As I said, I'm simply too busy, even for old friends. But there must be a reason you've sought me out after all this time. What can I do for you?" He sat back down, glancing over at Natalia again, his eyes lingering.

"I'm sure you know about the resettlement to the Jewish Quarter."

"Know of it? I've been dealing with the details for a month. The Germans threw the whole thing in our lap with no notice. You can't imagine the amount of planning and paperwork it's taken to even begin the process."

"We're losing our home, Petre."

He looked up at Jakub, embarrassment flashing across his face for the first time. "Of course. I'm sorry, my friend. If there was anything I could do about it, I would."

"I came here today to ask a favor. To see if you could secure something suitable for us in the district. A townhome, preferably the same size and stature of our current place. I know the area isn't the best, but surely there must be something. Aleksandra has been positively panicked since we got the notice."

Petre leaned back and closed his eyes, pursing his lips for a moment. "I don't know how to tell you this, Jakub, but there is nothing like that available."

"No townhomes? How about a decent-sized flat?"

"You aren't listening, Jakub. There won't be any individual apartments in the ghetto. All spaces will be shared. Any space you receive will be shared with at least one other family, perhaps two."

Natalia was stunned. Sharing their housing with other people? Her father was evidently facing the same emotion.

"Petre, you can't be serious."

"I'm afraid I am. I'm sorry."

"But can't you make an exception for us? For old times' sake."

Petre shook his head. "There's just no way. The Germans will be monitoring everything we do. They will inspect the apartments once everyone moves in. Even if I arranged something like that, they would quickly discover the situation and take it away. It would be easier to hide you in the city than to arrange that."

"What about leaving us in our home?" asked Natalia. "Could you arrange it so we didn't have to move at all?"

Petre laughed. "I was joking, young lady. No, I can't do that either. They'd have my head in a noose."

Jakub leaned forward and whispered. "But perhaps you could arrange it, Petre? Yes? I don't mean for free, my friend. But what if we could pay you? What if our paperwork was lost somewhere in the shuffle and a new permit issued? We wouldn't tell anyone; I promise you that. We don't go anywhere; we don't do anything. We send our maid out to do our grocery shopping. We aren't causing anyone any problems."

"I don't know how that could be done, Jakub. And if it could, the cost would be astronomical."

"Then there *is* a price," Natalia said, leaning forward and flashing a smile. "Please, Petre. We would be so grateful."

He was lost in her eyes for a moment. "My, my, you've become such a lovely thing." He turned back to her father. "Go home, my friend. It's late and we're closing up for the day. I'll think about things and if there's something I can do, I'll send someone over with a message."

"Why not call?" Natalia asked.

"Not a good idea. They are always listening." He rose and gestured toward the door. Jakub stood up and reached his hand out. Petre looked down at the hand for a moment, and then took it. "Be well, my friend. I'll be in touch as soon as I have something for you." He turned to Natalia. "And you. Do you have a husband, a fiancé, something?"

She blushed and shook her head.

"What's wrong with the boys these days?" he asked. "If I was the same age as you, Natalia, I would have snatched you right up. If I was a Jew, of course."

"Those lines didn't matter in the past," her father said.

"They do now," he said. "In ways you don't understand, Jakub, they matter."

They stepped out of the office building and onto the street. It was already dark, and the temperature was dropping. They hurried as best they could back toward their house. "What do you think he meant that it matters we are Jewish in ways that we don't even understand?" Natalia asked.

"I'm sure he was just being sensational," said Jakub, although his voice belied the words. "Petre always had a flair for the dramatic."

"Will he help us?"

"We shall see, won't we?" He stopped and turned to her. "I thought I told you not to flirt with him. You disobeyed me."

"Father, he made us wait the whole day in front of his office. Then when we talked to him, he was different from the past. Even I remember what he used to be like, and I haven't seen him in years. Yes, I flirted with him. But it mattered. Did you see him keep looking over at me? It made a difference. As distasteful as that is, it might have turned the tides."

Her father looked at her for a long time. "You've grown up, Natalia. I guess during all this chaos, I've been so focused on my situation, on protecting the family, that I missed that. I am sorry about your education. Sorrier than you will ever know. If there was anything I could do about that, I would. I was so looking forward to you becoming a doctor."

"Mother is glad at least."

"Don't blame her. She's old-fashioned. In her time, a woman of a certain station, of our circle in society, wouldn't dream of having a job. But the last war changed that, and everything that has happened since. She's proud of you too, even if she won't let herself see it."

"But what will all of that do for us now?"

He shrugged. "We will see. I know Petre. He likes nice things. He's always been a little jealous of our life. He'll be motivated by money and that's why he dismissed us. He wanted to think about the number. You watch. By the end of the night, that messenger will appear, and we'll have an answer."

"How much do you think he will ask for?"

"It won't be a small amount. I'd guess twenty-five thousand zlotys."

"But do we have that, Father? The Germans have taken almost everything."

"Oh yes. When the war clouds rolled in, I was already watching. I knew if we lost, the Germans would enact the same laws against Jews here that they had in their own country. I took much of our savings out. I've got that much, with some to spare. We'll need all of it and more, I'm afraid, before this war is over."

"And when will it be finished, Father?"

"Who can say? The Germans have won. This is their world now. Unless England can pull off some miracle that I don't see. But at some point, I'm sure they'll lift these ridiculous restrictions against the Jews. What benefit could they possibly get from it? To scrape a swath through the doctors, lawyers, musicians, bankers. It's a self-inflicted wound. No, trust me. This is all theatrics. They want the Poles to blame someone besides their oppressors. But once our countrymen have properly settled into their new shackles, the authorities will come back to us Jews. They need us. They always do."

"I hope you're right."

He smiled. "How often am I wrong? I don't say that as a boast. But I'm a thinking man. And I know history. All of this mess will come to an end. Mark my words. Now, let's get home before we freeze to death out here. Besides, your mother will be frantic that something has happened to us."

They arrived at their town house a few minutes later. As Jakub had predicted, Aleksandra was half mad with worry. He settled her down and then sent Stefan to bed early so the three of them could talk over what had happened.

"But why did he make you wait so long?" she asked when he had finished. "Doesn't that mean something? Something bad?"

Jakub shrugged. "We can't worry about that. The Germans who observed us there knew we were Jews. He probably needed to ignore us for their sake. For his own protection."

"Will he help us?" Aleksandra asked.

There was a knock at the door. "There's your answer," he said, smiling at her. They'd dismissed the staff for the night, so Jakub answered himself. Natalia peeked from around the corner and saw a Polish man there, not much older than he, greeting her father with a handshake and an envelope. They spoke for a few moments and then he closed the door and stepped back into the library where they had all been talking. He took his favorite chair, resting against row after row of law books, and ripped open the envelope to examine the contents of the letter. His face grew pale.

"What is it?" asked Aleksandra. "Did he say no?"

Jakub looked at both of them. "He said yes. But he wants one hundred thousand zlotys. In twenty-four hours. The bastard."

"Do we have that much in cash, Father?"

He looked at Natalia and shook his head.

Chapter 2
Breslau, Germany

February 1941

Elsa Baumann sipped her wine as she listened to Erik's story of his training. The restaurant was busy, and they'd been seated at a tiny table near the kitchen. The banging of pans and shouts of the cooks beat against her ears, disturbing his words, and her evening. She pushed down her frustration. She wanted tonight to be perfect.

"Our stupid lieutenant. The new one. He decided instead of giving us the leave he had promised that we would spend a weekend in the field. While everyone else was in town drinking, spending their pay, we were marching up and down a mountain, conducting exercises. He wants us to be the best unit in the company. As if we need it!"

Elsa felt relief that his leave had been spent conducting exercises. She was apprehensive about what went on when he had these rowdy weekends with the boys. "All the extra training will pay off," she said. "When you go to the front, you'll be prepared."

"What front?" he asked. "Who is left to fight?"

"What about the English?"

"They don't fight on land. And I'm not a marine. I won't be battling Brits, unless our Führer decides to invade them after all."

"If there's no fighting left, then why do you even have to go?"

"Don't be stupid. My unit was called up. I go where they tell me to go, for Führer and Fatherland."

Elsa was stung by the words, but she held her tongue. "How long will you be away?"

He shrugged, gulping down his wine. He gestured to the waitress, a pretty little thing, and she rushed over to assist him. He ordered another bottle, and Elsa watched his eyes on her as she darted off to serve him. She almost said something, but tonight wasn't the night for fighting.

"You were saying?" he asked.

"I said how long will you be away?"

"It depends on the fighting. But I hear the English are close to making a deal. We may have garrison duty for a while in France or Holland, but I'll bet it won't be too long. No more than a year."

"A year!" She choked on the words. This was worse than she'd feared. Still, maybe that meant something. He'd invited her to dinner tonight for a reason.

"Maybe longer. But don't get that curly-haired head of yours in a fog, Elsa. It won't be so bad. It will be a grand adventure!"

"For you."

"Yes, for me. It is a man's job to go to war, and a woman's job to wait."

"Then you want me to wait for you?"

He started to answer but the waitress returned. She uncorked the bottle, her eyes lingering on Erik's uniform. She poured them both a glass and gave him a smile and a wink before scurrying off to another customer.

"Erik!"

"What?"

"Your eyes were all over her."

"Who? That waitress? Bah. You don't know what you're talking about. What were you saying again?"

"I was asking whether you want me to wait for you or not?"

"Of course I do. I'll need someone to write to, won't I?"

"Is that all I am? A pen pal?"

"Enough of the nonsense. We've been together now for how long?"

"Almost a year."

"Well, there you have it."

The waitress returned with their meal. Elsa had ordered schnitzel, and the plate could barely contain the serving. "Who does she think is going to eat all this?" she asked.

"Perhaps she looked closely at you before she brought it."

"Erik. That's a terrible thing to say."

"Come on now, I'm just joking. You know I like a little meat on my woman's bones."

"It doesn't seem like it tonight. You can't take your eyes off that little waif."

"If we're going to fight, I'm just going to go home now, Elsa. I have to leave in the morning and I'm not going to spend my last night like this."

"No, please! Please don't. I'm sorry. I know you were just kidding me."

He was placated, if just barely. They ate in relative silence. Elsa hardly touched her food. She felt her weight, her size, as she sometimes did when he called it to her attention. Her clothes seemed tighter, her skin stretched. She knew it was an illusion. She wasn't even particularly large. But she'd never been thin either. She'd been teased horribly for it when she was growing up, and the pain was constantly with her, clawing at her confidence, whispering lies to her that nobody would ever truly love her. She knew that wasn't true. Erik cared for her. Although the creature inside her that tore at her emotions told her if she'd been prettier, thinner all along, he would have treated her better—that he would already have asked for her hand. That was her hope for tonight. That Erik had invited her here for an engagement. Weren't so many of her friends freshly engaged and even married as their men went off to war? Why not her?

Finally the meal was concluded, and Erik was already glancing at his watch and looking around for the check. "Surely our night isn't over already?" she asked, a little desperation in her voice.

He checked the time again. "Honestly, Elsa, it's already half past nine. I have to report at seven tomorrow morning. Otherwise, I'd be happy to stay and have another drink at least. Besides, you seem mad at me. You've hardly touched your food. The evening just didn't turn out the way I thought it would."

Her stomach fell. What if he'd intended to ask her and she'd ruined it by sulking? She had to do something, say something. "I'm sorry, Erik. It's just been a long week. Please, please stay out a little longer."

"Let's have another drink, then," he said. "A stronger one." He gestured for the waitress to come back over and ordered double schnapps for both of them.

"Erik, I can't possibly drink that. My head will spin, and I'll fall to the ground."

"Perhaps that's what I want," he said, a slice of passion flickering in his eyes.

Elsa didn't know what all that meant, but she also didn't want him to leave, so she smiled and asked him more about his unit, his training.

Erik was more than happy to oblige. He explained what

they'd been doing the last few months when he was gone. The work with tank support. The weapon and tactics training. It was all lost on her, more so as she sipped away at her drink. Soon enough, her head was indeed swimming. But she no longer cared. She felt calm and warm. She wasn't upset anymore that he'd only asked to see her at the tail end of his leave—that he'd flirted outrageously with the waitress and continued to watch her as they drank. That he hadn't come to this dinner to ask for her hand, as she'd hoped and prayed. Right now, she just wanted to live in the moment, to be talked to, appreciated and loved.

"Let's have another," he said, as they finished their drinks.

"Erik, I couldn't." She could barely say the words now.

"Nonsense," he said with his hand already in the air. The second round was in front of them before she knew, and Erik was encouraging her to drink it, laughing at her words, kissing her hands. When they finished and rose to leave, she could barely walk. He put his arm around her, helping her out. He felt warm, and strong, and hers.

They reached the street, the cold air hitting her like a frozen hurricane. She blinked, sputtered, laughed at the searing feeling of it. "I'm drunk," she said at last, having never been so.

"So you are. And so am I. And now you've had your way, Elsa, for it's far later than I'd intended to stay out, and morning still stares me in the face."

"You can't leave me now," she whispered. "I can't go home like this."

"Just so. But I have a different idea, my love. Let's get a room together."

She tensed. She'd never been with him, not like that. Nor with anyone. It wasn't proper to be with a man before marriage. "I can't, Erik. You know that."

"But why? Look, I'm off to war tomorrow. I may never come back. We've been together a year. I love you; you love me. We'll be married someday, won't we?"

She staggered, the words hitting her like a welcome slap. "Will we, Erik? Will you marry me?"

"Of course that's what I intend. But I don't want to bind you like that right now. All of this training, the fighting, it's come too fast. And now I have to face it. But I want to go off to war with the memory of your kisses on my lips, of your body against mine. Love me tonight, Elsa. I ask it of you."

She couldn't think. She tried to consider, to decide, but the alcohol swam and swished against her thoughts. He loved her. He wanted to marry her. And she did want him. She had for a very long time. What could it hurt? She nodded slightly, not even wanting to say the words.

"Thank you, Elsa. Thank you. You've made me so happy. Come, I already got a room."

Already. He'd had this planned all along. She almost pulled away then, but she knew if she did, it would be the end of them. And she needed something desperately right now, needed him. Who else would come calling for her? She allowed herself to be led a few blocks to a little hotel nestled between a grocery store and a laundry. It was a seedy sort of affair, the kind that wouldn't require a marriage certificate. He led her past the front desk, a middle-aged man watching the two of them with an arched eyebrow. Soon they were in the room.

Erik kissed her. She kissed back, trembling, afraid, lost in the dark. The voice inside her whispered that this was all she deserved. The night was a fiery mixture of pain, regret, and passion. When he fell asleep beside her, his snores echoing through the space. Elsa's tears filled her pillow. She was violently sick in the bathroom. Then again. She lay there on the hard floor, her head splitting, stomach burning.

Hours later she woke, still lying on the cold tiles near the toilet. She blinked, wondering where she was, how she had ended up there. Then she remembered. Pulling herself up, she was sick again, freezing, her body shaking. She called to Erik, but he didn't answer. When she was finished, she crawled toward the bedroom and pulled herself up into bed.

He was gone. The room was empty. He'd left her without saying goodbye. Left her like that. Without a note, or a blanket, or a kiss. She lay there for long minutes after, then drew on her clothes and stumbled out the door.

Chapter 3
Podgórze District

Krakow
Occupied Poland
Under the Eagle Pharmacy
February 1941

Irena Drozdzikowska counted the pills out one by one, dropping them into a bag for her customer. The older woman, one of their many regular Jewish patrons from the neighborhood, smiled grimly at her and thanked her for her help. Irena smiled back, trying to put hope and security in the expression. She walked the woman to the door and locked it behind her. They were closed for the day, and perhaps they were closed forever. She turned back to the counter, where her two fellow assistants, Helena Krywaniuk and Aurelia Daner-Czortkowa, were standing.

"Is that it?" asked Aurelia. "Are we shut down for good?"

"Tadeusz hasn't decided yet, he wanted to talk to all of us," said Irena, speaking of the chief pharmacist, Tadeusz Pankiewicz.

"What is there to decide?" asked Helena. "The Germans want us out of the ghetto. Everyone else has already left, including the other three pharmacies."

"That does seem to settle it," said Aurelia.

Irena looked at the door. "And what about that customer I was just helping? What about all the rest of them, and all the Jews that are going to be packed into this neighborhood in the coming weeks? What is our responsibility to them?"

"We've already been through this, Irena," said Helena. "The Germans have made arrangements to supply the necessary medicines inside the ghetto."

"And we're supposed to trust them? To believe them?"

"If we stay, we're putting our own lives in danger. Think about it, Irena. How many intellectuals have we seen disappear in the past year and a half? It's not like the Nazis are above killing Poles. This ghetto will be a safe area for the Jews. The Germans don't want us here. I don't see how we have a choice in the matter."

"To stay or not to stay, that is the question," came a voice from the back. Tadeusz stepped into the lobby, a sad expression on his face. "I see you're thinking about the same problem I've pondered for the past two weeks now. What should we do? What is our responsibility to our customers, our friends of these many years?"

"We should stay," said Irena. "We owe it to them."

Tadeusz nodded. "That's my instinct, too. But how can we make that work? The Germans won't supply us within the boundaries of the ghetto. And they told me if we stay, we'll have to pay a big tax every month. Also," and he chuckled at this, "they won't guarantee our safety here."

"As if they would protect us anywhere," said Irena.

"We'd be far safer outside than in," said Helena. "They've offered us a location just outside the boundary. If we go, they will supply us everything we need. And we'd still be able to take care of our customers. At least some of them."

"Yes," said Tadeusz. "The Polish ones at least. But the Jews inside the ghetto would be on their own. Helena, what you say has much truth to it, though. It is the easier path, and I've been sorely tempted to take it."

"You should," she said. "Tadeusz, I hate this as much as you do. But what can we do about it? We didn't create this mess, the Germans did. How can we be better off by trying to fight them? With what? We are medical professionals, not soldiers. If we stay, we won't even have the supplies we would need to help the people inside the ghetto. And from the sounds of it, the population here is going to go up by three or four times with an influx of Jews from the countryside. How could we help them when we have nothing to do so with? How could we even get to work? Would the Germans let us in every day, and back out after? We have family, Tadeusz, obligations on the outside. We can't simply stay here."

"What do you think, Aurelia?"

The woman blushed, turning away. "I will do whatever you think, Tadeusz. Whatever the group decides."

"Irena?"

"I vote we stay. We can figure something out, some way to help the people here. If we don't, do we really trust the Germans to supply them? They'll cut off all medicine to the population. We know how they feel about the Jews."

"I agree with that," said Tadeusz. "The Germans are not honest brokers. If we leave, the population will suffer the worst for it."

"It would be hard to let so many people we care about just fall into the hands of our enemies without any protection from us," said Aurelia.

"Well, Helena, it sounds like it is three to one. I do value your opinion, and frankly, we may risk all of this to our great detriment. But I don't want us to leave. I want to take care of these people, whatever may come of it. I don't have answers right now about supplies, although I have an idea. I do want to see if we can make a go of it. If you choose something different, I'll understand, and you'll have only the very best reference from me."

Helena looked at them one by one. Irena could see the anger and the frustration in her friend's face. Yet Tadeusz had given her the perfect opportunity to disengage. Irena felt the same way. They would be running tremendous risks, perhaps the ultimate risk, and if Helena didn't want to be part of it, she certainly understood.

"I'll stay," she said, surprising Irena. "I think we may all come to regret this decision, but I'm not going to abandon all of you, if this is the will of the entire group. But Tadeusz, there is no point if we cannot bring in supplies. You said you had an idea of how we could get them. What do you mean?"

Tadeusz set his shoulders and gripped the counter. It was clear that he was going to propose something momentous, something they would have never considered before. "We'll have to go to the underground," he said.

"You mean black marketeers?" Helena asked. "They're the scum of Krakow, preying on the poor, withholding goods that would otherwise be properly rationed. And they are criminals, Tadeusz. They would as soon slit your throat as help you. What will stop them from just taking our zlotys, and giving us nothing in return?"

"That's possible," said Tadeusz. "We will have to choose carefully. But I can think of no alternative. The Germans control all of the legitimate medicine. If they will not supply us with what we need if we stay, and if we are in fact determined to remain, then the only thing we can do is go outside their line of production."

"If we're caught, we're dead," said Helena, launching a final objection. "The official punishment for smuggling is death—and we would assuredly be smugglers."

Tadeusz nodded. "Yes. You have it just right." He looked at all of them. "Knowing this, do you still want to try? Do you still want to remain here in the ghetto?"

Even Irena hesitated now. It was one thing to talk theoretically about helping their customers. Even defying the Germans a little on paper was digestible. But directly breaking the law, with your life on the line, was something else entirely. "Isn't there anything else we can do?" she asked.

"Yes. We can move out of the ghetto as Helena has suggested, and as the Germans desire of us. If we do, she is correct, we can still help some of our former clients—the Polish ones, at least. And we wouldn't be running any real risks. The Germans would provide the space, quite nearby in fact, and they would supply us with everything that we needed. We wouldn't be running any more risk than any other Pole under German occupation—which, of course, is uncertain in and of itself. But staying in the ghetto is a magnitude riskier, perhaps several."

"I still want to stay," said Irena. "It all comes back to our Jewish friends here. If we leave, they will have nothing. No protection, no access to medicine. I can't call myself a Christian and simply leave them to their fate."

"I agree," said Aurelia, although she looked even less sure than before.

"Then we go to the smugglers and see what is what," said Tadeusz.

"I'll go with you," Irena found herself saying. She was stunned by the words. Tadeusz didn't need her help, and she was increasing her own risk at the outset. Still, she settled into the words, gritted her teeth, and waited for his response.

"I think I'll take you up on it," he said at last. "I must admit, I'm a little nervous about this process myself. It will be nice to have some company, and I would think they will conduct themselves more appropriately around a woman."

"If they don't rape and kill her," said Helena.

"Now, now, let's not borrow trouble. And Helena, you may get your way in any event. If we can't convince the smugglers to help us, and if we can't afford their help, then we will be forced to move regardless of what we would like to accomplish here. We will simply have to wait and see what happens."

She merely grunted in return.

"When will you go?" asked Aurelia.

Tadeusz checked his watch. "I have an appointment tonight, in just about an hour."

"So, you were going ahead with this no matter what we said," accused Helena.

"No. If we'd voted against it, I would have cancelled the meeting. But we haven't, and I won't." He looked at Irena. "Can you come tonight? And are you sure you want to go?"

She nodded. "Yes, I'll come."

"Well then, let's all of us have a little dinner here, and then Irena and I will be off."

A half hour later, Tadeusz and Irena left the pharmacy and headed north, crossing the Vistula River by bridge and heading into the Wesola Zachod neighborhood. Irena kept checking her watch, realizing they would have to hurry if they intended to have a meeting and be back to their respective homes before curfew.

"Who are we meeting?" she asked.

"Someone named Mietek," said Tadeusz. "That's all I know for sure. That and an address." He waved a piece of paper he was holding in his hand.

"How did you find them in the first place?"

"A customer, who knew someone who knew someone."

"Is this safe?"

Tadeusz laughed. "You know as much as I do, Irena." He paused, looking at her. "I wonder if I made a mistake inviting you. In the safety of the pharmacy, it seemed more logical, but now, out here, I wonder if I should go in by myself."

"No," she said, shaking her head. "I want to go with you. Whatever this is, let's face it together."

"You're a good friend, Irena," he said. "Now let's hurry before they give up on us. We're running a bit late."

They continued on a few blocks, Tadeusz periodically checking the addresses against his crumpled slip of paper. Finally, he paused at a warehouse situated about two-thirds down a block. "This must be it," he said.

Irena frowned. There were no lights on. "Are you sure?" she said.

"There's only one way to find out." He reached up and banged on the door. The metal rattled and shook. They waited there long moments before Tadeusz repeated the gesture.

"I think we might have the wrong place," Irena whispered. It felt like a whisper was correct here in the darkness.

Tadeusz checked the paper. "No, this is right."

"Are you sure you have the right night?"

"Positive. I confirmed this morning."

"There are footsteps, somebody is coming."

From the door there was the sound of a heavy metal latch sliding free. The door opened up and a figure stood in the darkness, staring at them, saying nothing.

"I'm Tadeusz Pankiewicz," the pharmacist said. "I'm here with my assistant, Irena. We're supposed to be meeting Mietek. Is that you?"

The figure grunted and turned around, gesturing for them to follow. They stepped forward into the building. If it was dark outside, with the wartime regulations dimming all the lights, it was impossible within. Irena could barely see Tadeusz a foot in front of her. She reached out and grasped his shoulder. He was swaying as he worked his way forward, feeling along the pathway.

"Can you still see him?"

"No. But I saw the direction he was going."

"What if this is a trap, Tadeusz?" The thought had suddenly occurred to her in the midnight dark of the space. There could be a squad of Gestapo waiting for them. She braced herself, fearing the lights would suddenly come on, and she would be seized by the authorities.

"Let's just keep moving," he whispered, shuffling forward again.

They heard a sound in front of them and, to their relief, a door opened, showing a little light. They moved more quickly now, and soon were at the entrance. They were looking into a bare room. A man sat at a table, smoking a cigarette. He had a dark moustache and was in his midthirties. He gestured for them to come in.

"Are you Pankiewicz?" he asked.

"I am, and this is Irena. Are you Mietek?"

"The same." He looked over at Irena. "Why did you bring the skirt? This was a meeting for just you."

Irena was alarmed to see that Mietek wasn't alone in the room. In both corners behind him, lurking in the shadows, were two more men. "He brought me, but why did you bring them?" she asked, nodding toward the two of them.

Mietek stared at her for a moment and then burst into laughter. "I like her. Is she your lover, Pankiewicz?"

"Of course not. We work together."

"A shame. You should consider it. A spicy girl like that."

"If you're only here to insult us, we will take our leave," said Tadeusz. "I won't have you say another word about Irena."

"Fine. What do you want then, pharmacist? I'm used to stealing from people like you, not helping them."

"We need medicine."

"Don't we all."

"Can you provide it?"

"What's wrong with the Germans?" Mietek asked. "Too busy killing everyone to provide what you need?"

"The Nazis won't give us what we need anymore."

"And why is that?" Mietek was interested now, Irena saw.

"Because my pharmacy is located within the boundaries of what will become the Jewish Ghetto."

Mietek laughed again. "Only that? I thought you'd poisoned a Gestapo agent or something worthwhile. We can't help you."

"And why not?"

"We're not interested in the Jews. Let the Germans deal with them. We have our own problems."

"I'm not asking for charity. I'm here to make a deal."

Mietek leaned forward. "And what, good doctor, would you have that I would be interested in?"

"Zlotys, of course."

"Well, if we even consider it, you'll need plenty of those."

"What's the price?"

"Ten times wholesale."

"You've got to be kidding me," said Tadeusz. "Black market rates are double, perhaps triple at best."

"Ah, but that's for bread and cheese. Medicine is another matter entirely."

"Four," Irena said, surprising herself.

"I'm not talking to you," said Mietek. "It's ten."

"Four," she said again.

The smuggler laughed. "Fine, let's call it eight."

"Five."

"Seven."

"Six."

Mietek pounded the table. "A deal." He turned back to Tadeusz. "You really should be sleeping with this girl, my friend. She's got real spirit."

"I told you; I won't have you insult her."

"I can handle myself, Tadeusz." She turned to Mietek. "When will we expect deliveries?"

"Deliveries? You amuse me again. Six gets you the supplies for pickup. If you want it sent to you across the river, the price is back to ten. The Germans are all over that district. It's damned dangerous."

"Let's call it eight, and you bring the supplies to us."

Mietek spat in his palm and extended his hand. "Deal."

Irena looked at the extended hand. "I'll pass on the hand-shake. But yes, we have a deal."

"What do you need? For the initial shipment?" he asked.

"We'll send a list tomorrow," said Tadeusz.

"Fine. But one more thing," said Mietek, leaning forward. "If you're caught with goods, you didn't get them from us. If you betray us to the Germans, they won't find us here, I can assure you of that. We've eyes everywhere. But after they come looking, we will find you. You'll be dead the same day you squeal. I can promise you that. Your families too."

"I understand," said Tadeusz.

"Good. We look forward to your list. Now get out of here."

The sentry, or whatever he was, led them back out the door and through the dark room, depositing them onto the street. They walked to the end of the block, and then took a moment to collect themselves.

"Well, that was an adventure," said Tadeusz. "I didn't know if we were coming out of there alive."

"I wasn't sure they weren't Germans, at least not at first."

"I had the same thought. But we've done it, Irena. We've made contact." He took her hands. "I have a lot to thank you for. You handled yourself well back there. Better than me."

"It wasn't so hard," she said. "That Mietek is more mouth than anything—not that he couldn't do what he threatened. Is eight too high?"

"It's worse than I thought, certainly, but to have the goods in hand, delivered by them? It will have to do." He checked his watch. "We better part ways here. We have to get to our respective homes before the curfew starts, and there is little time to spare."

"Those supplies are going to cost us a fortune," she said. "I had no idea you had that kind of money, Tadeusz."

He stared at her for a moment, wringing his hands.

"I don't."

Chapter 4

Grzegórzki District

Krakow
Occupied Poland
February 1941

Natalia and her parents sat in the library, a fire licking at the wood in the hearth as the light flickered and danced off the books and the paneling.

"A hundred thousand zlotys," said Aleksandra, repeating the sum. "Can it be done? In a day?"

"Not with what we have here," said Jakub. "I've got thirty thousand in cash, and another twenty thousand in jewelry, but if we spent all of that, we would have nothing in reserve for the future. And it's an uncertain future at that."

"Where would we get the rest?" asked Natalia.

"We'll have to ask our friends and family."

"But they're in the same boat as we are! At least the Jewish ones. How can they give us what they need for their own survival?"

"You're right," said Jakub. "So, we can only ask our Polish friends."

"Do you think they'll give it?" asked Aleksandra.

He nodded. "I think so. It's an enormous sum, but I have plenty of people to call. Some may be a gift, others a loan, but I think I can get it together."

Aleksandra gave out an audible sigh of relief. "Oh Jakub, you always take care of us. What a joy to be able to stay here, away from the wretched ghetto. To imagine sharing a tiny apartment with some unwashed strangers. I don't care what else happens to us, if we can just remain here and ride out the war, I know we'll be okay."

He nodded. "I think so too. The key for us is to keep out of that ghetto. Inside, there is no place to maneuver, there are no options. We are directly under the thumb of the Germans. But here, with official permits to stay, perhaps we can quietly exist— and escape their notice."

"But for how long?" asked Natalia.

"Until the Germans are driven out, if such a thing is possible. If not, until the storm passes and they realize the Jews—at least the better ones—are too important to the economy and the infrastructure to simply flush down the drain."

"How will we survive until then?" Aleksandra asked.

"I intend to get the full hundred thousand from others. Then we can use what we have in reserve to get by. I won't lie to either of you. Our movements have already been restricted. If we pull this off, we will have to limit trips out of our home to the absolute minimum. It will be a drab existence, but we can't risk alerting the Germans to our position—permit or no."

"That sounds dreadful," said Natalia. "We can't sit cooped up in here for months or years on end."

"We won't have a choice. It's that or the ghetto."

"We'll make do somehow," said Aleksandra. "Anything to avoid that."

"It's settled, then," said Jakub. "In the morning, I'll start calling my contacts."

Natalia went to bed, feeling better than she had since they'd received the notice of eviction. She'd never realized how much their home meant to her. It was the only thing they had left, besides each other. If they could only stay here, they'd be safe from whatever the ghetto was to be. She had her university books. She could keep studying, keep dreaming. With any luck, the Germans would lose the war, or as her father predicted, relax the regulations, and she could return to school. For the first time in a long while, she felt some hope that her dreams would be reached again someday.

The next morning, when she rose and went down for breakfast, her father was already at his desk and on the phone. She stepped in and watched him for a few minutes. He had a pad in front of him with a long list of names. Several at the top were already crossed off, but one had a number next to it. Five thousand. Her father had already secured some funds this early morning. She stepped behind the desk and put her hands on his shoulders, giving him a squeeze. He was her rock, the center of her universe. Her father, one of the top lawyers in Krakow before the war, had wielded wealth and influence, providing her and Stefan a childhood she hadn't even understood at the time. No matter what came their way, her father had always been there with a solution, just as he was now.

As she stood there, Stefan ran into the room, a wooden airplane in his hands. He whipped the model back and forth, obviously trying to get his attention. Her father waved at him to go away, but he persisted. Natalia stepped swiftly around the desk, taking him by the arm. "Not now," she whispered, pulling him away.

"Leave me alone!" Stefan shouted.

She grabbed harder at his arm, pulling him into the other room.

"Father is doing something very important. You need to stay out of his room."

Stefan pulled away and ran back upstairs. Natalia shook her head. Her brother was a handful. Of course, she couldn't blame him. Robbed of the ability to spend almost any time outside, he was full of energy and bored to death. She realized just how difficult their enforced solitude was on him. And if they succeeded now, things would get worse. They'd be cooped up full time in their townhome. Well, she couldn't worry about that today. Today was about securing their future.

She ate her breakfast with her mother and Stefan, and then went up to her room. She pulled out her medical books, daydreaming about her future and trying to concentrate on anatomy terms and not on what was happening downstairs. She struggled mightily, wanting so desperately to know if her father was going to be able to raise the funds in time. In the early afternoon, she bundled up Stefan and took him for a walk in the park. There was a little danger in this, as Jews were not allowed access to the public parks any longer, but they didn't look particularly Jewish, and besides, they would be stuck inside soon enough. When she returned to the townhome, she saw that her father was in the dining room talking to her mother. She rushed in, inquiring how he had done.

"I've got it," he said. "I had to use every name on my list, and even a few stretches beyond that. But I have commitments on paper for the full one hundred thousand."

"Did you call Petre?"

Her father nodded. "I didn't tell him anything on the phone, except that I had news for him. He's going to drop by after work."

She checked her watch. It was already nearly four. Petre would be by in no time. Jakub gave the staff the evening off. In these times you didn't leave anything to chance, regardless of relationships they'd had with some of them for years now. Anyone could betray you. It was enough of a risk to involve Petre. Jakub served them all a little glass of brandy, and they waited, sipping and talking, dreaming about their future here, safe and secure.

At six o'clock sharp there was a rap on the door. Jakub rose and swiftly answered. It was Petre, and he was alone. He stepped into the house and followed her father into the library, where he took a seat. While he spoke to Aleksandra briefly, Jakub poured him a glass of brandy that he accepted gratefully, and then he topped off their own glasses. It was a time to celebrate.

"What news?" Petre asked, at an appropriate time in the conversation.

"The best kind," said Jakub. "I've raised the funds."

"Do you have it all now?"

"No, but it's all committed. It won't take any time to get it together in cash, a day or two at most."

"Splendid. I'm impressed, Jakub. That is no small feat. I expected you'd called me to say the funds were simply not available."

"It is a large amount, Petre," said Aleksandra. "Is there nothing you can do for less? For old friends."

His eyes fell on Natalia for a moment, and he smiled at her, before turning to her mother. "I'm sorry, Aleksandra. You are right. But you have no idea what it takes to move these Germans. These funds aren't for me, I assure you. They are bribes for my superiors. You won't believe their stubbornness when the Jews are involved. It's like they have some kind of blind spot to their own best interests. And it comes from the top down. It's almost a religion with these people, this Jew baiting and Jew hating." He turned back to Jakub. "And I'm afraid I have yet worse news."

"What now?" Jakub asked. "Has the price gone up in one day?"

"No. But I'm afraid it can't be done."

"What do you mean?" Aleksandra said. "You said for a hundred thousand zlotys you could secure the permit."

"And so I thought. But I've spent the day trying to obtain the commitments from my sources and superiors, and they're telling me it's too risky. Beyond that, I've been told there's no point. There are to be no exceptions—regardless of influence or favor. So even if you received the permit, any passing policeman or other official, unrelated to my department, might call you out. The second you were identified as Jews outside the ghetto, your permit would be useless. You would be forced to move, regardless of what we secured you. But," he said, leaning forward, "I may have better news."

"What is that?" Natalia asked. She was wondering whether this *better news* would have a bigger price tag on it, after the seeming ease that Jakub had raised the funds.

He turned to her, giving her a wink. "The best news of all, my dear. My superiors told me that if I really wanted to help you, the solution is not to hide you here, it is to get you out entirely."

"What do you mean, get us out?" Aleksandra asked.

"Just that. To secure you visas to Sweden. I would get you permits and arrange train transportation to Gdansk. From there, you would board a Swedish iron ore transport and ride it up to Stockholm. You would have an official visa to stay in Sweden, and if you wished, you might be then able to arrange transport to England, although I must tell you that would be risky, because of the U-boats and bombers. Still, if you chose, you could get all the way there and ride out the war in Britain, or even that dream of dreams, the United States."

"But not for a hundred thousand zlotys, am I right?" asked Natalia.

Petre looked back to her. "Such a bright young woman you are, as well as pretty. But you're right, of course. I can't do this for a hundred thousand."

"How much, then?" asked Jakub.

"Well, there is an answer to that too, my friend, and I'm glad you're sitting down. It would be half a million."

"Why are you wasting our time?" shouted Jakub, angry now. "A half million? Why not just ask for the moon? It took everyone I know and everything I had in me to secure a fifth of that. I went beyond the bottom of the well. It can't be accomplished."

"I understand that feeling, my friend. If it can't be done, it can't be done. But you still have six weeks until you have to report to the ghetto. If you can raise the funds before that, I can get you out of the country. Instead of moving to the Jewish District in a month and a half, you could be sitting in a hotel in Stockholm drinking to my health and free of the Germans for good."

"I guess we don't really have a choice, do we?" asked Jakub.

Petre shook his head. "You don't, unless you just want to go to the ghetto. If you decide that, I'll do everything I can to get you the best accommodations, but you'll be sharing space with others, and you'll be in the heart of the cauldron, subject to whatever the Germans might be intending."

"I appreciate you coming to see us," said Jakub, rising and shaking Petre's hand.

"You're welcome, of course. And Aleksandra, it is wonderful to see you again, and also you, Natalia."

"Thank you again," Natalia said, not fully meaning it. Jakub escorted Petre to the door and then returned.

"Well, that was unexpected."

"More than unexpected, it's impossible," said Aleksandra.

"Perhaps not. If we have six weeks, I may be able to pull it off. I raised a hundred thousand in a day, why not a half million in forty-two?"

"To what end?" said Natalia.

"What do you mean?"

"He can't be trusted. I think he's a rotten liar. He saw how fast you raised that money and now he's giving you more time to bring him a bigger sum. He's going to milk us for everything we can give him, then betray us to the Germans."

Jakub shook his head. "I've known him all my adult life, Natalia. Petre is many things perhaps, but he's no traitor. If he can't do what he promised this time, it's because it's truly impossible. And think, Natalia, what he's offering now. Not a temporary reprieve, but freedom, life. An escape from all this oppression we've lived with for the past year and a half."

"How would we be better off in Sweden or England?" asked Aleksandra. "We won't be able to take enough money with us. We'll go from poor conditions here to poor conditions there. If I have to choose a rat-filled tenement, I'd rather go with the devil I know."

"I disagree," said Natalia. "I'm gravely concerned about Petre, but if he is being honest, if we could raise the money, we would be far better off out of Poland." She was already thinking about England, and the opportunities it presented to her. Opportunities to fulfill her dreams.

"What else can we do?" asked Jakub. "If we can't raise the money I suppose we will have to relocate to the ghetto, and take our chances. But if I can pull it off, we have to risk it."

Aleksandra and Natalia agreed.

The next six weeks passed in an anxious blur. Her father rose early every morning and spent the entire day on the phone. He'd started with his original list, upping his request. Then he moved on to other people, vague relatives, distant acquaintances. Every night he would come to the dinner table exhausted, sometimes defeated, but ever so slowly, the number rose.

During this time Natalia's fears eroded. Perhaps it was the promise of a better life, of the chance for all of her dreams to finally come true. Perhaps also, it felt impossible that her father's hard work and faith could be rewarded with a betrayal. He had, after all, been a figure of prominence in Krakow for so long, known even in Warsaw for his legal skills and influence in the business and financial community. As the zlotys piled up, she felt more confident by the day. They just had to make it to Sweden and all would be well.

One night, just a few days before the deadline, her father appeared at the table with an exhausted but satisfied grin. "We've done it," he said.

"I knew it," said Aleksandra. "You're our savior, Jakub. You always have been."

Natalia took his hand across the table. "I'm so proud of you," she said, and she meant it.

"Papa, does this mean I'll get to ride in the boat?" asked Stefan.

"Yes, my boy, the boat and the train. It will be a grand adventure."

"What do we do now?" asked Aleksandra. "Do we wait until the deadline is up?"

"No need," said Jakub. "I called Petre, and he'll process us through tomorrow."

"Will you have all the money together by then?" her mother asked.

He nodded. "I just have to collect a little bit in the morning. But we can walk over by noon. Petre said it will take the afternoon to get through the visa process, but we'll be on a train to Warsaw and then Gdansk tomorrow. He is securing a sleeper car for us, first class, leaving at six. Can you be ready to depart tomorrow by noon?"

Aleksandra nodded. "I've been ready for weeks. I thought we might have to depart suddenly, and I wanted to be prepared."

"Remember, one suitcase each, and the lighter the better. I will need to spread some of our jewelry out in each bag, and some zlotys from our savings, so leave a little room."

Natalia spent the evening putting her things together and also helping Stefan. Her brother was sad, not wanting to leave their house or his friends. He also had comic books and a soccer ball he wanted to bring. She tried to explain things, why they had to leave, why this would be better for all of them, but he wasn't really listening. He seemed to want to cling to their past—to games, toys and fun. It broke her heart, but there was nothing she could do. She kept telling herself that he would adjust more quickly than any of them to the new country, even learning the language. And the alternative, as uncertain and unpleasant as it was, was not worth contemplating.

The next morning, her father left early and collected the rest of the money. He was back and ready for all of them to depart by eleven. "I've arranged for a taxi to take us to Petre," said Jakub. "We can't lug these bags all the way through town."

"How many sleepers did he arrange for us?" asked Aleksandra. "And is that included in what we're paying him?"

"It better be," said Jakub, but lightly. "I'm sure he got us two, and if not, we can survive cramped quarters for a night and a day."

They rode in the taxi over to the Department of the Interior. Petre was on the sidewalk waiting for them and had two young men to assist with the luggage.

"It looks like we are getting the royal treatment," said Jakub. "We should be, at the price he asked."

Natalia couldn't help but notice the young Polish men were very attractive. She smiled at one of them, not even sure why she did so. She'd never see him again, that was for sure. Seeing Petre at the street had calmed her fears. She hadn't known whether they could trust him, or what might await them here as they pulled up. Having him present felt safe, felt authentic. She gave him a smile as well, and he returned it. No hurt in greasing the wheels a bit.

They followed Jakub's friend into the building, and he led them quickly to a large room that was full of people. At the far end of the hall, there was a row of barred windows, a person sitting behind each one. Each was talking to a family, checking paperwork and stamping documents.

"This is where you will get your passports stamped and your visas," he said.

Jakub looked around. There might be a thousand people inside the cramped space, and no place to sit. "Will we have time to make our train with all this?" he asked.

Petre laughed. "Do you have my special suitcase, Jakub?"

Her father handed him a battered leather satchel. Natalia recognized it as her father's old work case. Her mother had hated the thing, and even bought him a brand-new one to use in court. But her father had refused. He'd had it throughout his entire practice, a gift from his parents on his graduation from law school. It was his lucky case, and he'd won huge cases with it. Natalia just hoped it carried a last ounce of luck now for all of them.

"You have the total?" Petre asked.

"Would you like to count it?"

"No, no. That won't be necessary. Your word is good with me. And let me answer your other question. No, you certainly would not have time normally. Some of these people have been coming for days, months even, trying to get the authorities to issue them a visa. But this is not a normal situation. Let me show you what I mean." He motioned for them to follow, and he walked them up to the front.

Natalia could feel eyes on them, and some murmuring among the crowd. Let them complain. Her family had paid heavily for this privilege. Petre took them to an open window and spoke for a moment with a gentleman who waved them forward. Jakub handed him their four passports and the man hardly examined them. He stamped each in turn, then pulled out a folder that Natalia saw had their name on it. He tore open the top and removed four documents with official seals. "Your visas," he said.

Jakub took the documents, thanking him, then turned to Petre, who ushered them back out of the enormous room. "What's next?" he asked, when they were back in the hallway.

"Next is the station."

"But it's so early," said Aleksandra. "I don't want to sit in a common area for hours."

"It's fine," said Jakub. "We will make do."

"No need, my friend. Once I saw everything was in order, I changed your tickets." He handed them an envelope. "Here are first-class sleeper tickets from here to Warsaw, and first-class regular seats for Warsaw to Gdansk. Your train leaves in an hour, and I have a private car to take you. Your train arrives in Warsaw at two a.m. Sorry about the time. Your next train leaves at seven o'clock, so there will be plenty of time for you to have a little breakfast and get to the next platform. I'm afraid you'll have to wait at the station in Warsaw for a time, but there is a first-class section so it should be comfortable."

"What about our luggage?"

"All taken care of."

Natalia was impressed. Petre had taken care of every detail. He kept them moving out the front door and back to the street. Their luggage had been moved to a private car.

"Well, this is where I get off." He took Jakub's hand. "Godspeed, my friend. I hope to see you when this is all over."

"Only if you come to England," said Jakub. "I won't be coming back here, no matter what happens."

"Deal. By the time this war is over, I have no doubt you'll be living in some grand country estate. I'll be happy to come for a few days."

"If we are in a country estate, you can come for the summer," said Jakub. "But for now, I just want to get us to Stockholm."

"You'll make it," he said. "The hard part is already over."
He reached into his coat and pulled out an envelope.

"What's this?" Jakub asked.

"Five thousand zlotys. A personal gift from me. I know
you'll need money where you're going."

Jakub shook his head. "I couldn't take it. Don't worry, we
have a little with us. We will get by."

"Are you sure?"

Jakub nodded. "You've already done enough."

Petre stepped forward and hugged Aleksandra, then Stefan.
Finally, he put his arms around Natalia. His hands lingered on
her back, a moment too long. She stiffened and pulled away. "I
wish you the best too, Natalia," he said.

She smiled, forcing the expression, and then stepped into the
car. She was glad she wouldn't see Petre again for a good long
while. The family joined her, and the vehicle lurched into motion. Within a few minutes they were at the train station, and
their bags were loaded onto a porter's cart.

They hurried into the station, Jakub checking his watch.
"We're cutting it a little close," he said.

"Better than sitting here waiting," said Aleksandra. "And we
have five minutes still. We'll make it."

They moved through the ticketing area and out onto the
platform. Jakub kept checking their ticket against the signs,
making sure they were going the right way. They found their
train with a minute to spare. Marching as fast as they could,
they found the correct car and showed their tickets to the conductor.

"Ah, the Wajcblums," he said, smiling at them. "We've been
expecting you. You have our finest spaces. I hope you enjoy
them."

"Thank you," said Jakub. "We're looking forward to the
trip. It's been a long time."

"It will be a long time indeed," said a voice behind them.

Natalia's blood froze. She turned to see three men marching up to them. They wore suits and, on each lapel, there was a swastika.

"Please arrange for their baggage to be taken off the train," the lead man told the conductor in broken Polish. "The Wajcblums will be coming with us. They have a different trip to take."

Chapter 5

Breslau, Germany

March 1941

Elsa thumbed through the letter from Erik again, keeping an eye out for Herr Weber, her boss. She pored through each word, looking for anything she had missed. But there was nothing. Her boyfriend—was he a fiancé now?—wrote in detail about his travel to France, about visiting Paris, about new people he'd met and their accommodations and advanced training. He discussed everything, in fact, except he said nothing about their relationship, about missing her, about their future together. In six weeks, this was the first she'd heard from him, and she had rushed to her room to tear open the envelope. Only to find . . . nothing. She'd shed some tears and then stuffed the letter into her coat, deciding she would read it again when she had calmed down. Surely, she'd missed something, some subtext or undertone to what he was writing to her. But now, having gone through the entire document meticulously three more times, she had to conclude he'd said nothing personal at all. He could have written this letter to his parents, even to a town newspaper. It was all about him, and his experiences, and nothing about them.

The door jangled and she jolted. She thought for a second her boss had caught her red-handed. But it was a customer, coming in to retrieve his vehicle. This was a problem of another kind. She recognized the man immediately. He came every six months or so for regular maintenance, and the occasional repair. But this was the first time she'd seen him since Herr Weber had instituted his new billing practices.

"Good morning, Fräulein," the customer said. "I'm here to pick up my vehicle."

"Right away," she said, reaching into a drawer and removing his invoice. She felt her insides twisting as she handed him the folder. "Here you are."

He scanned the invoice, his eyebrows arching and a scarlet wave washing over his cheeks. "There's been some kind of mistake," he said, trying to hand her back the paper.

"There's no mistake, sir. I'm sorry. But that is the price. I went over it with Herr Weber this morning because I knew you were coming in."

"This is outrageous!" the customer shouted. "It's five times what it should have cost. Where is Herr Weber? I want to talk to him now!"

"There are wartime expenses," she explained as she'd been told to, knowing under no circumstances was she to let him talk to her boss. "Parts and labor have increased tremendously."

"Give me my keys!" the man shouted, throwing some Reichsmarks down on the counter. "You'll never see me here again; I can promise that, missy!" She handed him his keys and he stormed out of the store, slamming the door behind him.

"Elsa, what's going on out there?"

She cringed at the sound of her boss's voice. He'd heard everything.

"Nothing, sir. I have everything under control."

"Get back here now!" he demanded.

She rose, stepping through a back door and down a narrow hallway to Herr Weber's office. It was a ramshackle space with the smell of dust and stale cigarettes. Smoke filled the room and as she entered the office, her boss shoved a butt into a tray already overloaded with extinguished ends. He looked up at her with his dark, beady eyes, mopping sweat from a greasy, bald forehead.

"Well?" he asked.

"I don't know what you're asking me," she said.

"Stupid as always. I don't know why I hired you in the first place. I was asking why my customer just stormed out of here and slammed the door?"

"He was angry about the prices, sir."

"Did you explain our costs have gone up?"

"I did, sir, but he wasn't listening."

Herr Weber rose, storming around his desk. "Sit down!" he ordered. "What on earth are you good for? You have a simple job: schedule appointments, give out invoices, collect the money. Yet you don't seem capable of doing it."

"But sir—"

"But what? You just lost me a lifelong customer, who can't be replaced. And all you had to do was give him the simple explanation I told you to give."

"I did, sir. He just didn't listen."

"Then you didn't do it right!" He raised his hand and for a moment Elsa was terrified he was going to strike her. But he stopped an inch from her face.

"What am I supposed to do with you? You're useless!"

"I'll . . . I'll do better next time."

"You'd better. Or that day will be your last!"

She lurched to her feet and sprinted toward the bathroom. Rushing into a stall, she vomited violently. She'd felt ill all morning, since she'd seen Erik's letter. She sat there for some time, finally pulling herself back to her feet, washing her mouth out at the sink, and then returning to her desk. She hoped and prayed that was the end of their discussion.

"Baumann, get back in here, I wasn't finished with you."

She froze. She didn't know what to do. She still felt ill, and sicker still in contemplating a return to his office. Still, she couldn't afford to lose this job. Her family depended on her. Steeling herself, with a hand still on her stomach, she stepped back down the hallway and into his office.

"And just what do you think you're about?" Herr Weber asked. He was still standing near the doorway, and as she entered, he stepped closer. His breath was fetid and there was a stale, sweaty stench about him.

"I'm sorry, sir. I'm just feeling ill today. I'll do better with the customers. So, if you'll excuse . . ."

"I wasn't done with you," he said, taking a step forward. He put his arm around her back, pulling her close to him. "I've been waiting for this for a long time," he mumbled, his words slurring.

She realized with horror he'd been drinking. Panicked, she tried to pull away from him, but he was gripping her tightly. "I'm sorry, sir, I need to get back to the front desk."

But he wouldn't let her go. He reached forward, his lips brushing her cheek. "I know just what will make you feel better," he said.

She shoved hard, knocking him away from her. He crashed into the desk, falling backward over it.

"Get back here, you whore!" he shouted.

She turned and rushed out of the store and on to the street. Not stopping there, she hobbled down the sidewalk and around the corner. She fought back the vomit again, and the tears. It was over. She'd lost her job and could never come back. Fighting the nausea, she stumbled along a few blocks until she came to a little corner café she knew. She sat down at a table and ordered some tea and a little bread. She closed her eyes, breathing in deeply, trying to calm her nerves and her stomach. Sipping at the tea and nibbling at the bread, she managed to diminish her upset stomach a bit. A few minutes later, she was able to think again and begin considering her situation.

What was she going to do? The thought rippled through her mind. Her father had been unemployed for years. Her mother did a little sewing, to try to make ends meet, but the family primarily lived on her salary. They had no savings, and at times could barely pay the bills. She couldn't afford to miss a single day of work. She would have to find something, today if possible. She laughed at herself. The job interview process could take days, weeks even. How on earth would she find something in a few hours?

She spotted a newspaper at a vacant table nearby and stepped over to grab it. A stabbing pain pierced her stomach. What was going on with that today? She retrieved the paper and returned to her seat, closing her eyes to calm herself again. A few minutes later she was able to leaf through, looking for the want ads. She ran her finger down the columns, looking at the various postings. Nothing was sticking out to her until she came across a secretarial job.

Interesting. She had never worked as a secretary, but she had taken typing in school and been the top in her class. One of the reasons Herr Weber had kept her around as long as he had was her ability to type. Desperate, she decided she would walk down there today and see if the position was still available. The address was only a few blocks away, and in fact was closer to her family apartment than the auto repair shop had been. It could be perfect.

She paid and started on her way. She had to stop frequently and lean against a building. She willed herself to keep going. She had to find a job. She couldn't let her stomach get in the way of that. She made it another block but then fell to her knees, vomiting on the pavement in full view of the cars and pedestrians all around her. A man rushed to her assistance, asking her if she was all right.

"I'm fine," she said. "I'm just feeling a little sick. I'll be able to get up again in just a few minutes."

"I don't think so," said the voice, and she looked up, realizing he was a policeman. "I'm going to get you to the hospital," he said. "You need to be checked out. You're as pale as a sheet of paper."

She didn't want to go to the hospital. She couldn't afford another bill, or to go another day without a job. She shook her head, but he ignored her. Helping her to her feet, he escorted her into the back of his car. She wanted to protest further, but she was weak and dizzy. He was right, she couldn't go on. Whether she wanted it or not, she needed medical attention.

The officer drove her a few blocks to a nearby hospital. She heard him speaking to someone outside, and then the back door was opened. A medical orderly was there with a rolling gurney. He helped her out of the car and laid her down. Rolling her into the hospital, she was taken into a room and the door closed behind her. A few minutes later a nurse came in.

"Hello, Fräulein . . ."

"Baumann."

"What seems to be the problem today?"

"I've been throwing up and I can't stop. It's made me very dizzy and weak."

"Let me check you out." The nurse took her vitals and then drew some blood. She asked if Elsa wanted anything to eat, and when she refused, the woman left, telling her she would return as soon as she had results.

Elsa lay on the table, under a blanket, fighting back the nausea. She was there a long time, starting to drift in and out of sleep. She was abruptly awakened a while later by a doctor standing over her in a white lab coat. He was clutching a piece of paper and peering at her with a disapproving look on his face.

"What is it?" she asked.

"Well, Fräulein, it appears you are pregnant. And unmarried at that. Shame on you. What will your parents say? And who is the father?"

She lay there stunned. She thought she had food poisoning. To be unmarried and with child. She would bring shame on herself and her family. *Oh, my Lord, what am I going to do?*

Chapter 6

Podgórze District

Krakow,
Occupied Poland
Under the Eagle Pharmacy
March 1941

The woman at the counter rifled through her bag, searching for payment. She wasn't from the neighborhood, but instead was one of the thousands of new deportees, shoved into the confines of the ghetto by decree of the Nazi government. Irena stood patiently, waiting for payment of this item that was now five times what it had cost before the Jewish Quarter was formed.

"I'm sorry," the woman said, her face reddening. "I thought I had a little money left, but I just remembered I had to use it last night for some milk. We have a baby in the house. My daughter's. She's so hungry."

Irena heard variations of this story multiple times a day now. The population within the ghetto was already starting to starve.

The Germans weren't only restricting medicine into the district, but food too. They'd promised this would be a haven for Jews, a safe place where they would not be subject to racial discrimination and violence from the Polish population. But the Germans had lied. It wasn't a haven; it was a prison. She smiled at the customer and excused herself for a moment. Walking to the back, she found Tadeusz at a table, counting tablets and dropping them carefully into a bag.

"Ah, Irena, how are you this afternoon?" he asked, his eyes smiling kindly at her, despite the fatigue.

"I have another one," she said. "A woman who can't pay."

Tadeusz sighed, squaring his shoulders. "And why this time?"

"She says that she spent the last of her money on milk for her daughter's baby."

He nodded. "I'm sure that she did." He shook his head. "We are a few weeks into this, and the people are already running out of money, running out of food. What on earth are the Germans doing? How can they behave like this?"

"I don't know. It's like they want to starve these people to death. To deprive them of every necessity."

"Perhaps that is their plan."

"But they are civilians, innocents, women and children."

"Not to the Germans. I thought all of their rhetoric was merely bad propaganda. And when the Germans first came here, they seemed much more interested in eliminating Poles than Jews. I lost a lot of friends in the intellectual community along the way. But now, they've turned back to their pet project of Jew-baiting with a vengeance."

"What do we do about her?" Irena asked, referring to the customer.

"We give it to her for free."

"Tadeusz, how many times can we do that? We're giving half of our product away at no cost. But the black marketeers— they won't help us."

"Indeed, they've already raised their prices again. Something about supply problems."

"Our supplies are dwindling down to nothing. What are we going to do? In a few days, we will be out of medicine. The Germans will have eliminated this pharmacy as effectively as if we'd moved in the first place."

Tadeusz nodded. "Yes, I've been watching our supplies closely. I can still inject a little more into the process, but I won't be able to keep up forever."

"You're using your savings to keep the pharmacy open?"

He nodded. "What other choice do we have? These people need us. The more I see what the Germans are up to, the more I'm certain we made the right decision, and that we have to keep this pharmacy open."

"I have a little money stashed away," said Irena. "I'll bring it in tomorrow."

"No. I won't ask that of you or the others."

"You don't have a choice, Tadeusz. I won't let you sacrifice everything for this while we continue on as if nothing has happened. I'll talk to the others. I know they will feel the same way. We'll bring everything we can tomorrow. That should keep things going a little while longer."

"Thank you, Irena. I'm sorry to trouble you with this."

"We're all in this together."

The women all agreed and brought in their savings the next morning. Altogether, it promised to provide another two weeks of supplies. "But what are we going to do after this money runs out?" asked Helena. "I think we still must think about moving. We can't make medicine out of nothing. I propose that we continue operating until we are out of supplies, and then we relocate. We will have done everything that we can. Besides, it's getting harder and harder to come into the ghetto. The Germans are getting aggressive with us. Aurelia agrees with me."

Irena looked sharply at Aurelia, who stared down at the

counter and wouldn't meet her gaze. So, Helena had been working on her behind the scenes. Aurelia hated confrontation and would go along with the will of the group. She could feel her anger stirring at Helena, but she stopped herself. Was she wrong? The Germans *had* become more difficult over the past week or so. They were spending more time combing through their paperwork, asking questions about why Poles were coming voluntarily into the ghetto. And they were almost out of money, with no way to replenish their supplies.

"There has to be some other solution," Irena said at last.

"But what?" said Helena. "What will we do when we are out of medicine?"

"I've been thinking about this for a while," said Tadeusz.

Irena turned to him. He hadn't discussed anything with her about another plan. "But what could it be?" she asked.

"I'm going to try the Judenrat."

Irena was surprised by this. The Germans had recently formed a ruling council of Jewish leaders within the ghetto. But their authority and resources were uncertain and limited.

"How could the Judenrat help us, Tadeusz?" asked Helena. "They have nothing, no power, no money. And a teeming population on the brink of starvation that needs their help. The last thing they are going to want to do is contribute to a for-profit pharmacy that quadrupled their prices on the population."

"We have to try. I agree with you, Helena, it is difficult to ask for money from the council. We will be begging from the beggars. An unfair thing to pursue. But I firmly believe this pharmacy must be preserved. If we fail, then the only medicine they will receive will be at the whim of the Germans. We've already seen that they are not honest brokers. But it's more than that. This population is increasingly cut off from the outside world. We are some of the few people who can come in and out. We have sources of information, contacts with Polish Krakow. We are more than just a dispensary for these people."

Irena nodded. "I agree with you, Tadeusz. We should go to the Judenrat. We have to try. There's nothing else we can do."

"It's a waste of time," said Helena. "They won't help us, and even if they do, it won't be enough. We should take the offer the Germans have given us, while they are still willing to make it. Yesterday, I ran into one of our former customers outside the ghetto. A Polish customer. He told me that he has to walk a kilometer now for his medicine. There is nothing else nearby. He's eighty years old, Tadeusz! We have a responsibility to all of our customers from the old days, not just the Jewish ones. We should leave now, while we still can."

"Aurelia, you haven't spoken up. How do you feel about this?" Tadeusz asked.

She went red in the face and looked at each of them before she spoke. "I want to help these people," she said. "But Helena is right. The Germans are getting more aggressive. The person directly in front of me in line this morning was arrested by the SS and hauled away to who knows where. I'm worried one day they will take me away. Or worse, I'll come into work and one of you will be gone, perhaps forever. The Germans won't take lightly that we are defying them. They will want revenge at some point. If we can only stay open a little while longer, does it make sense for us to try to do so? Shouldn't we consider whether we could do better from the outside? You should go to the Judenrat, Tadeusz. But what if you arranged for them to take shipments of medicine from us? We could still provide supplies into the ghetto but let them dispense it. Surely there are Jewish pharmacists amongst the population. We could be suppliers, but still take care of our old customers, and keep ourselves safe."

The concept caught Irena off guard. She had not considered moving and their pharmacy acting like a wholesaler, in essence. Would the Germans allow it? It wasn't much different from what was happening right now. Of course, the wagons coming in currently had paperwork signed by Tadeusz, and the pharmacy was still officially tolerated by the authorities within the ghetto. She felt a glimmer of hope. It would be a great relief to get out of the ghetto, to not have to walk by the gauntlet of German guards each morning and night to pass back and forth through the boundaries. "Is that possible, Tadeusz?" she asked. Even as she made the inquiry, she felt the guilt sinking in. What terrible choices this war made them consider.

"My instinct is that it wouldn't work. That the Germans would cut us off, or simply confiscate the goods without delivering them to the Judenrat. But Helena, I will consider your words. I do intend to go to the Judenrat. I will discuss my idea and also yours. After I have more information, I'll report back, and we can decide what to do."

The next morning, Tadeusz opened up the pharmacy and made sure everything was ready for the day. When he was finished, he drew on his winter coat and prepared to travel the length of the ghetto to the Judenrat headquarters.

"I'm going with you," said Irena.

Tadeusz looked at her in surprise. "I think not. We have a busy day, and there's no reason for us to both go."

"Look. I went with you when we talked to the black marketeers. I was helpful then and I'll be helpful now. And unlike that situation, there is nothing to be afraid of in talking to the Judenrat."

"Don't be so sure about that," said Tadeusz, but he was half joking.

"Besides, it will help to have a woman with you as well. It takes away from the idea they might have that you're trying to earn a profit from the request."

"A profit! I'll be lucky to leave this war with the shirt on my back."

"Yes. I know that, and you know that. But they don't. Think about it, Tadeusz. They've been battered around by the Germans since the occupation. By Poles too. They've learned not to trust anyone. It's understandable if your request is going to seem odd to them. At best they will be worried you are taking advantage, and at worst they may see you as a threat—as a German agent even?"

"I would never work for the Nazis. How could the Judenrat think that, with everything the enemy has done?"

"I don't think they will believe you are a German spy. But they will naturally be concerned. My presence will help with that."

"Because you're a woman? I didn't realize there was a limitation on who the Germans might use as agents."

"That is true. But women are less suspect, certainly. And the fact that we are there together, two people making this request, it cannot hurt, and it will likely help."

"Fine. If the other two are willing to man the shop while we are gone, I will take you with me."

Irena cleared things with the other two pharmacists and a few minutes later they set out from the pharmacy. They crossed Plac Zgody, the square adjacent to their location, and then walked down Jozefinska Avenue past the Jewish Aid Agency. They took a left on Wegierska and then a right on Limanowskiego, finally coming to the Judenrat offices at the other end of the ghetto. The entire trip was only about five blocks and took hardly fifteen minutes. Irena was aware of the looks they received as they walked along, some by people who nodded in recognition, but many more peering at them with suspicion and fear.

"Do you see, Tadeusz?" she asked. "Even here, just out on the street, they are afraid of us. Inside the Judenrat, when we make this presentation, they will feel the same, if not more so."

"You're right, Irena, as you always seem to be."

The Judenrat building was a modest affair, set on the corner of a block. There was a long line weaving out the front door.

"Should we wait outside?" Irena asked.

"I don't think so," said Tadeusz. "These are individuals waiting for services from the Judenrat. We have a different agenda." He marched up the stairs, Irena following, and entered the building. There was some grumbling within the crowd about line cutting, but when it became clear they were not Jews, they were allowed to pass to the front. A woman sat there at a rickety table, right before a staircase. She had a tablet and what looked like a calendar.

"May I help you?" the woman asked, eyeing the two of them with suspicion on her face.

"Yes, hello. I'm so sorry to interrupt things here, but I am hoping to speak to a member of the Judenrat. I am Tadeusz Pankiewicz, and I am—"

"The pharmacist," the woman said, her face softening. "I know who you are."

Irena heard murmuring behind them as the people in line realized who they were. It made her feel strange, like a celebrity almost.

"Is there any way we could meet with a Judenrat member?" Irena asked.

The woman looked down, checking her schedule. "It would be difficult," she said. "The schedule is full. But still . . ." She looked at both of them and then stood up. "Excuse me for just a moment."

She climbed the stairs and disappeared down a hallway. When she returned a few minutes later, she waved for them to join her on the second floor. "You're in luck," she said. "I have a member who can meet with you. But we are pushing back other appointments. So, you can only have a few minutes."

"A few minutes is all we need," said Tadeusz. "Thank you so much for the accommodation. Your name is . . . ?"

"Kasia Rosenthal."

"Thank you, Kasia."

She led them down the hallway and then paused at a door to her left. She knocked and then led them inside. There was a man sitting at a desk, wearing a sweater. He was in his late forties or early fifties, with hair just beginning to pepper. A bushy moustache threatened to consume his mouth. He looked like a college professor and perhaps might have been in his former life.

"This is Mr. Henryk Badowski," the woman said by way of introduction.

"I'm Tadeusz Pankiewicz and this is Irena Drozdzikowska."

"Please come and have a seat," he said, motioning to two folding chairs in front of him. They took their seats, and the woman closed the door behind her.

"What can I do for you?" Mr. Badowski asked.

"As I think you know, I operate the Under the Eagle Pharmacy nearby."

Badowski nodded. "Yes, and on behalf of all of the Jews in the district, let me thank you for your decision to remain here. I don't know what we would do without you."

"That is too kind of you. You may or may not know that the Germans refuse to supply us here in the ghetto."

"We prefer 'Jewish District.'"

"My apologies. In any event, we have had to secure medicine and supplies from other . . . shall we say unorthodox sources."

Badowski leaned back and whistled. "I did not know that. And it must be costing you a pretty penny."

"That's what we've come about."

Irena could see the color drain out of the Judenrat member's face. "Whatever do you mean?" he said.

"We have increased our prices to try to keep our pharmacy stocked. But many of the Jewish community members have run out of money. I've dipped into my own savings, and so have my assistants, but we are running out of resources. It won't be long, and we'll have to close down, I'm afraid. So, we are coming here to talk to you."

"Are you suggesting we pay you?" Badowski said. He shook his head. "You must be dreaming! You have to realize we have almost nothing to give to these people. We are strained and beyond with housing, food, everything. And now you're telling me we are going to run out of medicine. What you ask is impossible, Pankiewicz. You'll simply have to do better."

"Do better?" Irena said, her anger up. "We have sacrificed everything to stay here in the ghetto."

"District."

"Whatever you want to call it. We were offered a new pharmacy location out of the district, and supplies at market rate, supplied by the Germans—"

"So, you would collaborate with the Nazis?"

"Certainly not. But they are the government, and they control the supply of everything. So, instead of taking the safe path, the easy path, the profitable path, we chose to stay. We are the only lifeline you have to medicine, and if we don't obtain some assistance, you will lose us."

"Perhaps the Germans will supply more—and for free?"

"Now who is dreaming?" asked Tadeusz. "Of course you're welcome to leave it to the Germans, and if that is the position of the Judenrat, please let me know. It will make my life and the lives of my assistants much easier. But I think we both know you can't let that happen. I assure you, Mr. Badowski, it pains me beyond measure to make this request. If I had any other alternative, I would take it. You must know that. But I don't. We need assistance, and we need it now, otherwise we will have to close within the month."

"That may be what you have to do," he said. "We can't help you."

Irena rose. "I think we've exhausted the possibilities of this interview," she said. "Let's go, Tadeusz."

"I agree," he said. He stood up, turning back to Mr. Badowski. "I understand your position, given your resources. But I hope you will reconsider. Talk to the rest of the Judenrat. It's not so much money that we need, but we do need assistance."

"I'll see what I can do, but don't get your hopes up, Pankiewicz. Times are hard and we must all take care of ourselves."

They headed to the door. Irena was out first, and she was surprised to see the door close behind her. She thought of going back but realized that Mr. Badowski must have wanted to speak privately with Tadeusz. She heard the murmuring of voices for a few more minutes, and then Tadeusz came out, nodding to her and heading back downstairs. When they were outside and a block down the street, she asked him what had happened.

"We got our money," he said.

"How can that be?"

"He wanted something in return."

"What do you mean?"

"He wants ten percent of the zlotys to be diverted back to him. Privately. Not to the Judenrat, to him personally."

"How horrible. I'm sure you refused."

"I accepted."

"But—"

"But we don't have a choice in the matter, Irena. I agree with you that his demand is reprehensible. But we still get our money. In these times, we have to take what we can get."

"I still think we should refuse."

"I know. And I appreciate you for it. You may place this entirely on my shoulders. I am choosing to work with this thief, this liar."

"Of course I don't mean it like that," she said, feeling a little guilty for her attitude. "You're right. It's not like we're accepting a bribe, and it's not like we're working for the Germans. We already associate with black marketeers, and they're hardly any better than this man. This is the right decision. Thank you for seeing it more clearly than I did."

"You didn't see it because fundamentally you are a good person, Irena. And for that, I am forever grateful. Now let's go tell the others the good news."

They arrived back at the pharmacy a few minutes later. They were surprised at the grave and sorrowful expressions on Aurelia and Helena when they walked through the door.

"Success!" shouted Tadeusz, his arms in the air. "We can make our next order for shipment to us—and we can make it a big one. We are back in business."

"No, we aren't," said Helena.

"What are you talking about?" Tadeusz asked.

"Look at this," she said, handing him a pamphlet.

Tadeusz read the document, his face paling. He handed it to Irena. She was shocked by what it said.

By order of the German authority, construction will begin tomorrow on a wall to surround the Jewish District. The Jewish headstones from the nearby cemetery will be utilized to the greatest extent possible to build the structure—so they will finally have a useful employment. Nobody is to interfere with the workers, or come near the construction, on pain of the most serious consequences. Also, from this moment forward, no Jew is allowed in or out of the district without a permit. Any Pole working within the district also must have a permit. Under no circumstances will any unauthorized materials or supplies be allowed

to be transported into the district, effective immedi-
ately. Further, any Pole caught directly or indirectly
assisting a Jew will be severely punished.

She couldn't believe it. All of their hard work for nothing.
The Germans were walling off the ghetto, and they had prohib-
ited their ability to bring in supplies. The trip today, their savings,
their sacrifice was for nothing. The Germans were starving them
off, and the ghetto with it.

Chapter 7

Breslau, Germany

April 1941

Another two weeks had passed. Elsa lay in bed, staring at the ceiling. It was a Saturday morning, and she had the day off from the job she'd found in the clothing shop downtown. She still felt ill, and she was starting to show. It was just a matter of time before one of her parents noticed.

"Elsa, it's breakfast," her mother shouted from the other room. "Are you going to sleep the day away? I have a big sewing order to deal with, so you'll have to make lunch and supper. I've got a long list of cleaning jobs as well."

She sighed. So much for a day to relax. Since she'd found out the news, she'd twisted and turned her mind, wanting to tell her parents, even more wanting to tell Erik. But she hadn't been able to bring herself to do so. Her mother, a fiercely devout Lutheran, would be mortified when she learned what had happened. Her father . . . well, nothing seemed to impact him these days. Elsa climbed out of bed and straightened her sheets

until there were no creases. She set her pillow in the exact center of the headboard, making sure there was an even amount of
space on each side. Then she stepped around her room, adjusting a picture here, a book there. When she was finished, she
took a deep breath. It would pass inspection when her mother
came through later. As for the rest of their flat, she would have
to see what the list was. But if this was a regular weekly cleaning, and her mother was too busy with sewing to help, then
Elsa's whole day would be taken up.

A wave of nausea hit her. She paused for a second, wondering if she would have to rush to the bathroom, but thankfully
she held it down and after a minute was able to move into their
main room. Her father sat in his favorite chair, smoking a pipe
while he pored over the Saturday paper. He glanced up and
nodded to her before returning to his reading. "It looks like the
invasion into Yugoslavia is a smashing success," he said. "The
Führer was right to punish them for throwing in with the English. The fools."

Her mother was at the kitchen table. She had already eaten
and was behind a sewing machine, busy at work. She nodded
toward the counter and Elsa stepped over to find some bread
and a little cheese. They used to have cold meats for breakfast
every day as well, but rationing had severely limited the amount
they could purchase each week. She helped herself to a little of
the bread and stepped over to the table. She wasn't hungry, but
if she didn't eat anything her mother would notice immediately. She sat down across from her, and broke off a little crust,
nibbling on the edges.

"You eat like a mouse now," her mother said, eyes apprais-
ing her. Her narrow nose twitched like she could smell something wrong. "You'd think you'd lose some weight—the way
you pick at your food. But I suppose not."

Elsa ignored her mother's jibe. There was a reason she wasn't
losing weight, and it wasn't something she wanted to talk about

right now. "Work has been busy," she said, trying to divert the subject.

"How busy can you be, showing customers to a dressing room?" Her mother snorted, looking back down at her work. "If only you had some talent with a sewing machine, I could find you some real work."

"What were you saying about Yugoslavia, Papa?" she asked.

"Nothing important," he said. "The invasion is going well, that's all. Is that boyfriend of yours involved?"

"No, thankfully. He's in France."

Her father grunted. "In the first war we didn't hide in occupied territory and avoid fighting."

"Papa, that's not true. Erik is brave. He would never shirk his duty." The words hit her, even as she said it. He had another kind of duty now. And how would he react to that? She realized she had to tell him. She'd known the answer to that for weeks now, she'd even started to write to him several times. But she couldn't delay any longer. She prayed he would do the right thing, that he would decide to marry her. Surely his commander would give him a short leave so they could have a ceremony. If he went through with it, then everything would be fine. It was scandalous to become pregnant out of wedlock, but if the man stepped up and you were married, well, then all was all right. It might even make for a saucy story for their children someday.

"Excuse me," she said, getting up. Now that she'd made her decision, she wanted to write him immediately.

"And where do you think you're going?" her mother asked. "I told you I have chores for you. You can start with the breakfast dishes."

Elsa realized she couldn't just disappear into her room right now. It would be too suspicious. So, she started on the dishes, washing and hand-drying them. She then dusted the front-room kitchen, and the two bedrooms, and cleaned their bathroom. By the time she finished all of this, it was time for lunch, and then the cleanup after. It was midafternoon before she knew it.

The mail. She'd almost forgotten. She left the apartment and went down to the ground floor. Opening their mailbox, she retrieved a handful of items. Thumbing through the envelopes, she felt an electric jolt up her spine. There was a letter from Erik! How perfect. Perhaps he was going to tell her he had some leave. If he was coming home, she could even wait to tell him about the baby. Or perhaps she should tell him anyway, because then they could arrange for a little ceremony at the church. Would her pastor allow her to be married there now? Given her situation? Well, she would cross that bridge when it came to it. One problem at a time. She returned to their apartment and dropped the rest of the mail off with her father. Taking her precious letter, she escaped into her bedroom, closing the door behind her. Thankfully, her mother left her alone. Perhaps she'd completed her tasks for the day?

She sat on her bed and tore open the envelope, beginning to read.

> *Dearest Elsa,*
> *I'm sorry I haven't been able to write you recently. Our training has been even more intense here in France. I miss you. I often think about our last night together. I will treasure that always. We received important news. Our unit is being moved out for the front. By the time you read this, I will probably already be there. As I head into danger, I'm thankful I have you at home waiting for me, and that home is unchanging—even with the chaos that I will face in battle. If I do not survive, know I will always love you.*
> *Yours, Erik*

He missed her! He loved her! She couldn't believe the words. But oh, how terrible that he was heading into battle. What if he was killed? The baby wouldn't have a father. And how could she tell him? How could she put this all on him, at the moment he would need every ounce of his attention on the task at hand? Worse yet, she thought again, what if he rejected her, or claimed the child wasn't his? All her feelings of unworthiness overwhelmed her.

She decided there was nothing she could do. She had to tell him. She took out her pen and wrote to him, telling him about the baby, how she was as shocked as she knew he would be. She told him she hesitated to tell him now, but she was beginning to show. She loved him so much, she wrote, and wanted him to be safe, particularly because they now had this child together. She poured all of her hopes for the future into the letter and expressed her hope that he would soon be home, so they could all be together.

Life went slowly on as the days continued to pass. She kept her hours at the new job. If she hadn't felt ill, she would have enjoyed this new line of work so much more than the last. Here she got to feel like a woman, as she worked amongst the fashionable clothes and the chatty customers. When young mothers came in, she smiled at them and their babies, dreaming of her life one day not so far away. She imagined the war over, and Erik and her married, perhaps buying a little cottage outside of Breslau where they could begin raising their family. But then the fears would crowd in again, and with each passing day without any correspondence, she felt the tension more and more.

Then one afternoon, it was there. A letter from Erik. She didn't return to the apartment. She wanted this for herself only. She went down the street to a café and ordered some ersatz coffee and a little bread. She was hungrier now, the morning sickness slowly receding. Her stomach was swelling little by little each day, and she could feel her bump under her dress. For once she was happy with the extra weight she had always carried, because it had prevented her parents from knowing the truth. Although now each day, she expected them to notice. Her coffee arrived and she took a couple little sips. Closing her eyes for a moment, she prayed to God that he would be excited by the news, that perhaps he would even ask her to marry him right in this letter.

> *Elsa:*
> *You could not have sent me more disturbing news. How could you think that something like this is the right thing to tell me, when my life is on the line every day? How can this child even be mine? We were together one time, and one time only. We had so much to drink that night, I didn't even think anything actually happened. I must wonder who you have betrayed me with—whose child this really is. You must get rid of it in any event. I won't wonder for the rest of my life whose bastard is in my house. If you want any chance with me, you will do the right thing. I must go now. We had a short break, but now it's back into danger. Don't write to me again if you keep this child. I won't want to hear from you.*
> *Erik*

Elsa stared at the letter in complete humiliation. She had no idea what she would do now. She was alone.

Chapter 8

SS Prison

Krakow
Occupied Poland
April 1941

Natalia was rushed down the corridor, a guard jabbing her in the back with his pistol. She was out of breath, weakened from lack of food and exposure in her frigid cell. She looked this way and that, trying to comprehend what was happening to her, fearing the worst. A door opened and she was shoved outside into a courtyard, surrounded on all sides by a three-story building. Her eyes squinted beneath the bright light, her breath puffing into mist in the frigid air. There was snow on the ground and her bare feet burned at the touch of the stuff.

"*Schnell!*" her guard shouted, shoving her. Natalia fell forward into the dirty, packed snow, crashing hard against the pavement. She sputtered, her hands clawing at the ground, trying to find her balance. The guard grabbed her hair, pulling her to her feet. "Move it!" he ordered.

Natalia stumbled into the middle of the courtyard where a few other women were standing, huddled together. "What's happening?" she whispered, looking around in terror.

"We don't know," one of the women answered.

A door swung open, and a squad of German soldiers marched out, carrying rifles. They stopped in a line and lowered their weapons, aiming at Natalia and the rest of the group.

"They're going to kill us!" one of the women shouted.

Natalia couldn't believe it. Her life was ending, here and now. Without an explanation of why, of what she'd done wrong. She would never know what had happened to her family, or if they were safe. She would never finish her schooling, meet a man, marry and have children.

A sergeant stepped forward, calling for the soldiers to take aim. Natalia, who spoke German fluently, understood the command. She closed her eyes, waiting for the end.

"Fire!" the sergeant shouted.

She winced, hearing the click of the triggers. She fell to her knees, sobbing, waiting for the bullets to hit her, to end her life. But moments passed and there was nothing. No gunshots, no impact, no sounds but the wailing of those around her. She opened her eyes. The soldiers were laughing, clapping each other on the shoulder. The sergeant stared at the women with an arrogant smirk.

"Get up, you Jewish whores!" he shouted. "*Schnell! Raus!*"

The soldiers moved forward, rifles raised again, shouting at them to rise up. They were herded together out of the courtyard and down a tiled hallway. In moments they were outside the building, on the snowy sidewalk of a street, joining a crowd of other women, children, and even a few men. The entire group was surrounded by soldiers.

Natalia heard a rumbling and around the corner a convoy of trucks emerged. They were huge affairs, with open backs, and they pulled up in a line in front of them on the street. Even as they stopped, soldiers rushed forward, unlatching the back gates. The Germans motioned to the crowd, screaming, ordering them into the vehicles. Natalia moved forward, numb, disoriented. She craned her neck, looking this way and that, searching desperately for her family. For any of them. But she saw nothing. She climbed into the back of one of the trucks. There were hard wooden benches on both sides, and she took a seat against the cab. Another woman sat down right next to her, and the bed was quickly filled until she was wedged so tight she couldn't move. She hated the claustrophobic feel of it all, but at the same time, the press of bodies provided a little warmth against the biting cold.

The truck lurched into motion, moving down the street and turning left. Natalia looked around. After a few blocks she recognized where they were. They were traveling through Old Town and headed toward the Wawel castle district. They must have been in the north part of the city. As they proceeded, she watched the periodic pedestrian stop and stare at the column, no doubt wondering what was going on and who these people were. But the wind was too biting, and craning her neck was difficult, so she turned her head back toward the bed of the truck.

She wished she could talk to these other people, women mostly, and ask them who they were, and if they knew where they were going. But there was a German soldier with them, rifle by his side, staring sternly forward. She was sure any words from her would bring a swift reproach, perhaps something worse. Her mind flashed back to the courtyard, to the firing squad. She had been so sure she was going to die. She realized now, as uncertain as the future was, as miserable as she felt, she was elated. She had survived. She was breathing, living another day. She had never realized until now just how precious her life was to her, how much her body and mind screamed for her to live.

The trucks crossed the Vistula. Now she knew where they were going. They were headed toward the Podgórze district that contained the ghetto. She'd rarely been to this blue-collar, industrial part of town. After all, there was no reason to go there. Nothing for her affluent family to wish to see. As they grew closer, she was shocked by what she observed. There was a wall up, surrounding what must be the ghetto. She was sure that had not been there before. The Germans must have constructed it to keep in the Jews, and recently. So, they were doing more than merely forcing them into the confines of a few streets. They intended to isolate them there, cut them off from the rest of the world. Still, after weeks in a cell, the ghetto would feel like a luxury. If she survived, if she could just get away from these Nazis and into the crowd where there might be a measure of safety.

The truck halted at a gate. There were SS here, holding submachine guns slung over their shoulders. One of them stepped up to the driver, checking papers. Then he walked around the back of the truck, inspecting the human cargo. He wore a look of hatred and contempt she'd never seen on another human before. At least not toward another person. No, it was the glare one gave to an unpleasant bug, right before you squashed it.

The truck rested for another minute and then rumbled forward again, and Natalia was able to get her first glimpse inside the ghetto. The initial thing she noticed was the sheer volume of people. The district was packed with humans, more by far than she'd ever seen in one place. The sidewalks were full of figures, shuffling this way and that. She also noticed the tattered clothing, the dirty and hollow cheeks, and that few people even bothered to look up and watch them as they moved along. What had happened to these people? And how had it occurred so quickly? She felt her fear returning. Is this what was going to happen to her? To her family—if she ever found them again? How would they survive in this place, hemmed in by an enemy who despised them? She shook her head to clear her thoughts. She couldn't consider these things right now. She had to get off this truck, and then get her bearings and try to find her family.

Finally, the vehicles stopped at the edge of a city square. She'd been here before, just once. Her father had bought her ice cream at a little stand nearby. But she could not remember the name of it. A door opened and then slammed shut. She saw a soldier run around to the back of the bed and unlatch the gate. "Get out, Jews!" the man yelled. The soldier inside the truck started pushing and screaming. The Germans seemed to operate that way, all shouting and hitting as if that sped things along somehow. The panic they created had the opposite effect, with people stumbling and crashing into each other in their haste to get away. Natalia wanted to do the same, but she willed herself to stay put for a few seconds, until there was room to move. Then she pulled herself up and dropped out of the truck. She was still barefoot, with no coat. The tattered skirt they'd given her in prison barely covered her thighs.

She wanted to look around, but not so near the Germans. She stepped away, her feet burning painfully in the dirty snow, until she was a half block down a side street, away from the vehicles. Here, she stepped over to a building and put her head against it, closing her eyes, trying to gather her breath.

"Are you all right?"

She looked up. There was a man there, an Orthodox Jew from his appearance, with a long beard and tassels dangling from under his coat.

"I'm looking for my family," she said. "Have you heard of anyone here with the last name Wajcblum?"

The man shook his head. "I haven't. But look at you, you're freezing, and where are your shoes?"

"I've been held by the Germans," she said. "We were betrayed and my family is missing."

"You better come with me," he said. He removed his coat and covered her with it. Helping her hobble along, he led her several blocks until they reached a building. He led her inside, to find a space packed with people, many with blankets on their shoulders, some with cups of hot liquid in their hands. "This is the Jewish Aid society," he said.

"I'm not Jewish," she responded automatically. But then that wasn't really true, was it?

"Rabbi, what can we do for you?" a woman asked, approaching them.

"This woman was just dropped off at Plac Zgody Square with many others. She has no shoes, no coat, and she doesn't know where her family is. She was in prison apparently. She needs assistance."

"Of course she does," the helper said. She hurried away and then returned back with some socks, shoes, and an overcoat. She helped Natalia to a bench and then assisted her in putting on everything. As her feet started to warm up, she felt an overwhelming itchiness, and a burning pain. She prayed there wouldn't be any lasting effect from her exposure to the cold.

The coat she put on was for a man, and a number of sizes too big, but it was woolen and thick, and she luxuriated in the warmth of it. She'd been frozen for so long now—since the day they'd departed their home on what they thought would be their road to salvation.

"Thank you," she said at last, the words slurring out of her mouth. She felt an overwhelming weariness coming over her. "I'm . . . I'm sorry. I'm getting so tired."

"You're exhausted," the rabbi said. "You need rest."

"We'll see to it, rabbi. I'm sure you have other things to attend to."

"You'll take good care of her?"

"Certainly. We'll get her to bed, and tomorrow we'll feed

her and then find out where her family is—and see to her housing assignment."

"Shalom," the rabbi said.

"Shalom."

Natalia didn't remember any more. When she woke up, she
was under covers in a bed. She thought for a moment she was in
her room at home, that she'd woken up from some terrible
dream, but she quickly saw that was not the case. She was lying
in a ward of some kind. There were at least a dozen other
women here, all in bed, some with bandages wrapped around
arms or their head. She worried for a moment that she, too, was
sick, that there was something wrong with her, but she gave
herself a check and realized she was all right—other than her
exhaustion. Then she remembered the day before, the horror of
the courtyard, the freezing truck ride, the ghetto. She was there
now, she realized—in some bed provided for her. She wondered who that rabbi had been. Why had he helped her?

She checked herself again as she became more alert. She was
wearing the socks from yesterday on her feet. The coat was
folded at the foot of the bed, and the shoes were resting on the
floor next to her. She dressed quickly and made her way downstairs. As soon as she arrived, she was confronted by a woman.

"You're up, I see. I was hoping you would recover quickly.
It looks like all you needed was a good night's rest. I was worried about frostbite, but you avoided the worst of it. Your
youth helped you there."

Natalia stared at the woman for long moments, wondering
who she was. Then she remembered the person from yesterday
who gave her the coat and shoes. Yes, this was the same person.
"I'm Natalia," she said. "Natalia Wajcblum."

"I'm Katerina Grabinska," said the woman. She was a little
older than Natalia, perhaps close to thirty, with raven hair and
a twinkle in her eyes. "Now that introductions are over, I need
to get you something to eat."

Natalia shook her head, wanting to protest, but she quickly relented. As much as she wanted to search for her family, she knew she had to have her strength. Katerina led her into a makeshift meal hall. It was small, not much bigger than her dining room at home, but there were a half dozen tables crammed into it. She had Natalia take a seat, then she brought her a metal tray with a cup of soup and a small loaf of bread.

Natalia thanked her and dug into the food. She hadn't realized how hungry she was, and she devoured the contents in a matter of minutes. When she was finished, she located where the trays were placed, and then sought out Katerina again in the front hall.

"Well, did you get enough to eat?"

"As much as I could expect. Thank you for helping me. Can you point out to me the direction of the headquarters?"

"Headquarters?"

"For the people in charge. I have to tell them what's happened to my father, to my family. My father is an influential lawyer, with connections to the government, but we were terribly betrayed by one of his friends. He has to be brought to justice. They will want to know."

Katerina looked at her for a moment in surprise, as if she thought Natalia was joking, then she seemed to change her mind. "You will want to go to the Judenrat," she said. "You need to visit there in any event. They give out the housing assignments."

"Thank you, which direction is that?"

Katerina pointed. "Be prepared for a long wait."

Natalia nodded. "Thank you again." She didn't bother to tell her that she hardly expected to wait in any line once she had identified herself. She stepped out of the building and headed down the street toward the direction Katerina had indicated. She had to ask a few times, but she eventually made it to the Judenrat building. There was indeed a lengthy line winding out of the building and down the street. But Natalia marched right past it and into the building.

She stepped up to a table where a woman sat, checking people in. "Hello," she said.

"May I help you, miss?" the woman asked. "I'm afraid I saw you come in through the door. There is a line that everyone must wait in."

"Yes, I'm certain that's true for others, but I'm Natalia Wajcblum. My father is Jakub Wajcblum. He's one of the most prominent citizens of Krakow, and I have urgent news about him I must report to the authorities."

The woman looked her up and down. "I'm sorry, miss, but I cannot help you now. You'll have to wait your turn like everyone else."

"But my father—"

"Is like a lot of people here. Doctors, lawyers, business owners, musicians. Many people here, many people *in that line*, were prominent people. You are just going to have to queue up and we will attend to you when you arrive back here."

"I don't—"

"Get in the back of the line, you stupid girl."

Natalia was shocked by the words. They had come from behind her. She turned and saw a man, standing at the front of the line.

"You heard the woman. Get in the back of the line before I drag you there myself."

Natalia felt her anger surge. Perhaps it was everything she had been through, her weeks of helplessness. She desperately wanted to lash out at this man. To tell them all that she wouldn't stand to be treated this way. But she stopped herself. She realized it would do no good. Taking a deep breath, she turned around and marched out the door. She heard laughter behind her as she left, and the humiliation nearly overwhelmed her.

The wait in line was every bit as long as she had feared. She didn't have a watch, but by the time she reached the doors again, it had been several hours. She was inside for another half hour before she finally made it back to the front. The woman at the table smirked at her, her eyes defiant, daring Natalia to say something out of line.

"I am here to see the authorities about my father. Also, I have no place to stay. I need a housing assignment. You have housing for the professional classes, I assume?"

"You assume a lot, young lady. No, we do not have special housing. Everyone gets what is available, first come, first served." The woman flipped through a folder and drew out a piece of paper. "Here is a housing assignment."

Natalia looked at it. "But this is for one person. I need an apartment for four. I told you, my family is—"

"Not yet here. At least we have no record of a Jakub Wajc-blum registering for housing."

"But they'll be along anytime."

"Have you looked around? This district is teeming with people. We can't give out spaces for people who aren't here. If they show up, then you can resubmit for a new assignment. Although it is not a guarantee."

"This is outrageous. I want to speak to someone else. Someone with authority."

"You won't be doing that today. I can assure you of that. I already checked. There are no appointments. If you want to speak to a member of the Judenrat, about your father or any other topic, I can schedule something for you. Right now, the wait is three weeks."

"Three weeks!" Natalia shouted. "Did you not listen to me? My family is in prison. We were betrayed by the Poles. I demand somebody speak to me now!"

The woman looked past her and nodded. Natalia felt her arms seized on both sides. "Let's go, miss," a gruff voice said from behind her.

"Release me immediately!" she shouted. But he wasn't listening. Natalia found herself half dragged, half pushed out of the building. Once outside, she was spun around to face the man who had grabbed her. He was a rough-looking character, in his early thirties. He wore an amused expression. "Here's your assignment, miss. Take it and go away before you end up sleeping on the street. You have an appointment in three weeks with the Judenrat. You can come back and lodge your inquiries or complaints at that time." He waved a finger at her. "And not before, do you understand?"

She didn't answer, but she didn't complain either. He looked at her a few moments longer, and then turned on his heels and marched back into the building. Natalia glanced down at the scrap of paper in her hand. She had been assigned to an apartment on the third floor of a building on Krakusa Street. She had to ask where that even was, but was happy to find it was only a block away. It was starting to get dark, and at this point, with everything that had happened in the last couple of days, she just wanted to get to her flat and go to sleep. She would think about things tomorrow and decide what she was going to do next. As she walked along, she wondered what kind of apartment they had assigned her. Was it furnished? She was horrified by the prospect that she might find a completely empty space. And what was she going to do for food? Well, she would have to go out and figure the issue tomorrow.

After a few minutes she'd arrived at the apartment building. It didn't look too bad. A little dumpy perhaps, but that was the entire neighborhood after all. She stepped inside and climbed the stairs. It took her quite a bit of time to make it up as she was still weak. Natalia finally made it to her door. When she arrived, she realized they hadn't given her a key. But to her relief, the door was unlocked.

She stared inside the apartment in shock. There were six people inside a single room. They looked up in surprise, staring at her. There was a mother and father, and four children, all around a tiny table. There was a bathroom but no bedroom. Mattresses were laid on the floor, almost up to the table. On the other side, there were a few cupboards, a sink, and a stove. There was a pungent aroma of unwashed bodies and cooked food that was almost overpowering.

"I'm sorry," Natalia said. "I must have the wrong apartment." She looked down at her paper again, but this was the correct address.

The husband, a thin man in his thirties with brown hair, a clean-shaven face, and a firmly set jaw stood up. "No, you do not," he said. "We were told to expect another person in our space."

Natalia abruptly remembered the discussion her family had long ago. That the housing within the ghetto would be shared. All of her worst nightmares were coming true.

Chapter 9

Breslau, Germany

April 1941

Elsa marched through the streets of this lower-class section of Breslau, her steps wooden and mechanical. She stared down at the address in her shaking hand, checking now and again at the numbers on a door. Many of the little shops were boarded up, and the foot traffic was light and unsavory. Several men looked her up and down as she walked by. One even whistled in her direction, catcalling her. She increased her step.

Finally, she arrived at the property number, a nondescript door attached to a warehouse. She knocked, waiting a few minutes for a reply. The door opened and a middle-aged woman was standing there. "What do you want?" she asked, frowning.

"Are you the nurse?" she asked.

"Who wants to know?" She could see the distrust in the sallow lids, her frown creasing across her cheeks and forehead.

"I'm Elsa Baumann. I called you. About the . . . the procedure."

"Keep it down," the woman warned her. "Get inside."

Elsa stepped into the building. It was indeed a warehouse, with boxes and crates stacked and strewn about like the wreckage of some monstrous battle. The woman led her farther into the space, weaving through the flotsam and jetsam until they finally arrived at the back. In the extreme rear of the structure, surrounded by boxes stacked almost to the ceiling, there was a cramped space with a rickety hospital bed. A tray of instruments sat nearby, and a cold white light shone down from a bare bulb. The linens were faded and there were spots that looked like faded blood.

"Step right up," the woman said, cackling gruffly.

"Is this where we will do it?" Elsa asked, backing away a little.

"Well, what do you expect, deary? This is the best I can do and the best you'll get. You had your naughty fun and didn't have the sense not to get yourself with child. Now it's time to take your medicine."

Elsa steeled herself. There was no other choice, nothing else she could do. She couldn't wait any longer. Her mother had started looking at her stomach. She knew she would be confronted soon. And Erik. Oh Erik, if she was going to be with him, she knew what she had to do. "All right," she said at last. "I'm ready." She didn't feel it, but she knew she had to go ahead.

"I won't be doing nothing until I see the color of your money."

Elsa reached into her purse and drew out an envelope stuffed with Reichsmarks. It was her life savings, everything she'd scrimped and saved together for her future. She had wanted to use this to set up her new little apartment with Erik someday, but now it was gone—wasted on a procedure she didn't want, to save something she wasn't even sure she had.

The woman snatched the envelope and rifled through the notes. "Hah. Hardly enough here to pay for the ether. But you're lucky, you little hussy, because it's been a slow month. So, I'll take this on for almost free. Now get your clothes off and get on the bed."

Elsa stared in disbelief. "Isn't there a gown or something?"

"I don't have the time or money for that, deary! Now get naked and get on the cot or get out."

Elsa slowly removed her dress and then her undergarments. She'd never undressed in front of a stranger like this before. She covered her breasts with one arm and her private area with her other hand. The warehouse was unheated, and her body shook from the cold.

"Well, look what we have here," said the nurse. "Getting along already, aren't you? Or is that just your natural padding? Well, no matter, I'll fish that baby out in no time." The woman laughed to herself and then roughly took Elsa's hand, pulling her over and shoving her down on to the bed. She stepped over to the instruments and picked up a cloth. Grabbing a nearby bottle, she uncorked it and poured some liquid onto the rag. "Sniff this now hard, girly, it's nighty time."

She shoved the fabric against Elsa's nose. She gasped, fighting for air. The liquid was cloying, and she felt as if water was being poured over her head. Her eyes fluttered and she tried to fight, tried to remove the rag, but she was already fading, and soon the darkness overwhelmed her.

Voices. She heard loud, almost violent shouts. She struggled to awaken, to learn the source of the noise, but she couldn't, even as she vaguely felt a rattle from the hospital bed.

A stabbing brightness jarred her out of the anesthesia.

"She's waking up," said a voice she didn't recognize. Where was she? And what had she been doing? She lay there for how much longer she didn't know. Slowly, she remembered why she was under, what she had undergone to do. But none of what she was feeling now made any sense. She'd heard multiple voices, and the sound of a male. She kept that way for a long time, drifting in and out of consciousness, until finally she was able to blink her eyes painfully open.

When she adjusted to the harsh light, she looked around the room. It was all white. She was still in a hospital bed, but this one was larger, and she wore a gown under the blanket. Her arm was connected to an IV, the tube extending up to a bottle to her right. At the end of the bed, a nurse and a doctor stared down at her with what seemed mixed expressions of relief and concern.

"You're with us again, I see," the doctor said. He was an elderly gentleman, in his sixties at least, with short gray hair and kind eyes.

"Where am I?" she asked.

"At the hospital," he said. "We almost lost you. Your abortion went terribly wrong. That old witch botched the procedure. Fortunately for you, she has some scrap of a conscience still, because she called an ambulance. You were near bleeding out by the time they got you here."

"Am I going to be all right?" she asked.

"Yes."

"And the baby?"

"Your procedure worked," the nurse said, a little angrily. "You managed to kill the child."

"That's enough," said the doctor. "Why don't you go check on the next patient and I'll finish things up with Fräulein Baumann here."

"But that's *my* job," said the nurse.

"And that's an order."

She frowned at the doctor, then at Elsa, and marched out of the room.

"My apologies," he said. "Some of our staff have rather strong opinions about some of these things. She is a wonderful nurse, but a little harsh at times. She's married and doesn't understand that women get themselves in trouble at times outside of wedlock, and don't have any option but to seek a solution—illegal or otherwise."

Elsa nodded through tears. Her heart wrenched that the baby

was gone. She knew she would carry this guilt for the rest of her life. "How long have I been here?" she asked.

"Almost a day. And you'll be here for a long time to come. Two weeks at least. Do you have any family you would like us to contact?"

Elsa hadn't thought of that. She couldn't imagine her parents coming here, her mother who'd never made a mistake in her entire life, reading scripture to her and pointing out her many faults. She couldn't take that, not now. "No," she said at last. "At least not yet."

The doctor seemed to understand. "Well, get some rest." He started to leave and then turned back around to face her. "I have something else to tell you," he said, and she saw the sadness creep back onto his features.

"What is it?"

"The police were called after you were brought here. I'm sorry, I would have stopped it if I could, but there are mandatory things we must do, and the penalties for failure to report are severe."

"I understand," she said, fear tearing through her. She'd known what she was doing was illegal, but the woman she had gone to had a reputation for success, and for discretion. "What's going to happen to me?"

"I don't know," the doctor said. "In the old days, you would have received social services and a fine. But in these benighted days, they aren't so lenient, I'm afraid."

"What will they do to me?"

"It depends. I'm not a lawyer so I can't really — "

"Do you know the worst?" she asked.

The doctor looked away, but finally nodded.

"What is it?"

"The official penalty for an illegal abortion is death."

Chapter 10

Podgórze District

Krakow
Occupied Poland
April 1941

Natalia stood on the pavement, watching the trolley pass by. It was full of people, Poles and a few German soldiers, most staring ahead, indifferent to the teeming mass of humanity within the ghetto. It was so strange to her that this little car rumbled through the Jewish Quarter multiple times a day, but she couldn't use it. There were no stops. Nobody was allowed to get on or off. It would have been better if the Nazis had rerouted the tracks. Instead, the clacking noise stood as a stark reminder of the freedom of the outside world, something that was lost to her and everyone else inside, perhaps forever.

She'd had no news of her family. She'd attempted to return to the Judenrat, but the woman at the table, that bitch of a gatekeeper, had recognized her and ordered her to leave immediately. She'd tried to talk to some of the people on the street, but everyone had their own problems, and nobody had any news. None of them had even heard of her father before, which was a surprise to her. Of course these were lower-class Jews for the most part, who wouldn't have had any reason to mingle with the upper crust of Krakow society.

The light was starting to dim in the sky. Soon she would have to return to the little one room flat. She tried to stay out all day as the quarters were too cramped, the smell almost unbearable. The family was nice enough. Their children were sweet, and the mother always inquired into Natalia's needs. But they were so different from her. The father had been a mechanic. They'd lived close to the ghetto, in a little tenement by the river. Neither had attended a scrap of university, nor were they interested in books or the arts. They were concentrating on keeping food on the table for their family now, which was fair enough. They were kind to share what they had, since Natalia had no money, no way to contribute. She was grateful, but she yearned for her own family, for a little space of her own in the ghetto. If they arrived, she could go back for a new housing assignment. She could obtain some books, a little furniture. Her father would find something, likely an important assignment, and they would make it somehow.

She wandered into Plac Zgody Square. The place was full of people. There were garbage cans with little fires burning inside, and she could catch snippets of conversation as men and women discussed the ghetto, missing family members, the daily struggle for food, for medicine, for some employment that would keep everyone alive and safe for another month.

As she was walking along, she glanced over and saw a two-story building with faded yellow walls and white windows. The first story had a sign. It was a pharmacy of some kind. She'd spotted it before, a few days ago, but she'd been too consumed with her thoughts to visit it. Natalia checked her watch. She had a few minutes to spare before she headed back for dinner. She decided to go inside.

She pushed through the doors and entered a lobby. There were oil paintings of pleasant landscapes on the walls. A few chairs dotted the waiting area, leading up to a long counter that was waist high and extended the length of the building, save for a small gate leading behind it. Behind this were shelves full of endless bottles. The area was empty except for a blond woman behind the counter. Her hair was pinned in a severe bun, and she wore a gray lab coat buttoned in the front. The woman was working away at an order, pouring powder carefully into a glass container, her forehead creased with concentration. "I'll be with you in just a moment," she said, not looking up.

Natalia waited until the woman was finished. "This is a beautiful store," she said.

"Thank you. I don't think I've ever seen you before. Are you new to the district?"

"I am. I'm Natalia Wajcblum."

"I'm Irena Drozdzikowska."

"How did you get everything set up so quickly?" Natalia asked.

"We were already here," said Irena.

"How lucky for you, that you didn't have to move."

"We're not Jews. This pharmacy is operated by Poles."

Natalia was surprised by that. She didn't think there were any Poles left in the ghetto. She said the same to Irena.

"Yes, we get that a lot. Our principal pharmacist, Tadeusz Pankiewicz, has operated this store here for many years. His father was a pharmacist as well. When the Germans announced they were turning the district into a Jewish Quarter, we were offered the opportunity to move, but we declined."

That was surprising too. "Do you live in the ghetto, then?"

Irena shook her head. "No, we come in and out each day by the gate. It's very close."

"I don't think I've seen that entrance. I thought there was only one?"

"No, there are three. One is just a few paces from our building."

Irena and the other staff members could come and go every day as they desired. A thought occurred to her. She didn't even know this woman, but perhaps she could help? "I'm wondering if there might be something you could do for me. I apologize, it is very bold for me to ask when we've just met."

"Not at all," said Irena. "If there is a way we can help. What is it?"

"My family and I were all arrested by the Germans. I was in prison for a few weeks, and then abruptly released and dropped off here. Since then, I haven't been able to find out anything about them. Is there any way you, or your chief pharmacist, could make some inquiries outside the ghetto for me?"

Natalia could tell that the woman was taken aback by the request.

"You've caught me off guard, I must admit. I just don't know how we would possibly do that."

"But you are able to leave the ghetto each day. Isn't it possible that there is someone you could contact?"

"Do you know where they are?" she asked.

Natalia shook her head.

"I'm sorry, I just don't know what we could do. But write down their names, and I'll take this to Tadeusz. Check back in with me in a day or two, and I'll let you know if there is anything we can do for you. But please don't get your hopes up. We are just regular people. We don't have connections to the government, and certainly not the Germans. In fact, we are rather out of favor with our occupiers."

"Why is that?"

"Because we were supposed to move. They don't want us here."

"I've studied a bit of medicine."

"Really? In what context?"

"I was preparing for medical school. I'd already been accepted and was about to start when the Germans invaded. Of course, when they took control, they banned all Jews from that profession."

Irena nodded. "Pharmacy school too. It's a stupid, foolish tragedy that makes no sense whatsoever. How can a whole race of people be collectively responsible for whatever it is the Nazis think you did?"

"I couldn't agree more. It's funny, we weren't even practicing Jews. I've never seen the inside of a synagogue. We had a rabbi, a friend of my father, come over and conduct a Passover dinner for us one time, but that was more a social event, a curiosity, than anything."

"There are plenty of Jews here who have never practiced. We hear about it all the time. Even children of one Jew, and grandchildren of one Jew, who haven't been part of the faith in generations."

"When will it end?" asked Natalia.

"I don't know. But the Germans are winning everywhere. The newspapers in Krakow say they've overrun Yugoslavia and are pressing in on the Greeks as well. Nobody seems able to stop them. Of course, it's hard to say if the papers are reliable. They are all organs of the Nazi party now, so we only hear the biased news."

"We don't even get that news in here. There's a paper, but it mostly just lists proclamations from the Nazis."

"You might be blessed by that. It's quite depressing to read of German victory after victory and their new world order. But you were saying, about your studies?"

"Oh yes. I have, or should I say had, some medical books. I was keeping up on them, in case my circumstances changed. Of course I lost those in the arrest. I suppose everything we owned is gone forever now."

Irena stooped down behind the counter, not speaking for a second. When she rose again she had a hardbound book in her hand. She offered it to Natalia.

"What is this?"

"It's a basic book on pharmacy. Kind of the initial primer when you first start school. Would you like to borrow it for a while? I don't need it."

Excitement rippled through her. She took the book with trembling hands, leafing through the pages. It had been so long now since she'd had a book, any book in her hands, and now to have something in the medical field . . . "I don't know how to thank you!"

"Think nothing of it. But do please be careful with it. It's my first book from school, and I do treasure it."

"Of course, I will take the very best care of it."

She was preparing to leave, when a man stepped out of the back. He was of medium height, with peppery short hair and sunken cheeks. Irena motioned for Natalia to wait, and then she stepped over to the man and held a whispered conversation for a few minutes.

"Miss Wajcblum, it is so nice to meet you," said the man, coming to the counter. "I am Tadeusz Pankiewicz."

"Nice to meet you as well."

"Irena was just telling me about your problem."

"Yes. I'm so sorry to even ask anything of you. I don't know you at all. But I don't know who else to turn to. I have an appointment with the Judenrat coming up, but I have no idea if they will assist me, or if they even have the ability to do so."

Tadeusz nodded his head. "I may be able to do something. I don't want you to get your hopes up, but I have some contacts in the Polish government. Poles, mind you, not Germans. I will make some inquiries, but it could take a while, and it may come to nothing."

"That would be wonderful. Thank you so much!"

"Think nothing of it. We are here as pharmacists but the unique situation the Germans have placed everyone in means that, at times, we are a bit more. Check back in with us in a few days, and Irena will let you know if we've heard anything."

Natalia thanked them and strode out the door. It was almost dark now, and she needed to hurry because of the German-imposed curfew. But there was a spring in her step as she moved through the streets, clutching the book. She had something to read now, a new subject matter to devour, and more importantly there was a lifeline to her family, at least a potential one. She hoped that when she returned in a few days they would have news. For now, she would relish the little victories she'd had today and look forward to the possibility of a better future.

Chapter 11

Breslau, Germany

April 1941

The two weeks in the hospital passed slowly for Elsa. Each day she felt a little better, even as the terror threatened to overwhelm her. The police had come and interviewed her. She'd been honest, explaining everything that had happened and why she had made the decision she chose. They'd taken notes and then departed, giving her no comfort but informing her they would be in touch. The doctor told her it was a good sign they did not leave an officer behind to guard her. The longer they left her alone, the more likely it was they might do nothing at all. She clung to that hope, and with each passing day the idea set more firmly in her mind that they might miraculously just let the circumstances slide.

But she was alone. On the second day, she had relented and given her parents' information to the medical staff. They'd called them immediately and informed them of what had happened. Elsa had spent the day in trepidation, waiting for the terrible confrontation. But there was nothing. That day had passed, and the next, and still they hadn't come. Now, two weeks later, she reconciled herself to the fact that they were never coming—that they had decided she would face whatever was in front of her, on her own. She could never have imagined them abandoning her like this. She was their only child. Yelling, yes. Judging, certainly. But never this. The fear of the future, and the loss of any family support left her feeling like she almost wished for the authorities to kill her. What did she have left?

Certainly not Erik. She had written to him about what happened, the steps she'd taken. And just like her parents, there was nothing in return. Here at least there was hope, perhaps just a fantasy, that he was in combat and unable to respond. Perhaps they hadn't even been able to get her letter to him yet. The last string of life she clung to was that he would be there for her, that her act of heroic love would finally make him see the light—and they would be together forever. If that happened, she wouldn't need her parents anymore. She would have her own family, with other children to come someday. And surely at some point, her mother and father would forgive. Yes, that was what she needed, to just hear back from Erik, to learn that everything was going to be all right.

The door opened and Dr. Zimmerman was there. "How's my patient today?" he asked, with a warm smile.

"Alive still—perhaps not much more than that."

"I understand," he said. "Have you heard from your parents, or your boyfriend?"

She shook her head, fighting back the tears.

"Well, none of them deserve you, then." He pulled her chart up and reviewed the information. "I have a good piece of news for you, at least. You're healthy enough to be released today."

Released. At least that was a little something. But released where? What was she to do? She realized she didn't have any choice. She would have to barge into their home regardless of the consequences. If they were dying of shame, fine, if they refused to speak with her, fine again, but she would at least have a place to lay her head at night while she tried to rebuild her life. "What time will I be able to go?" she asked.

"In the next hour or so," he said. "Do you have anyone to pick you up?"

She shook her head.

"Well, to hell with that. I'll drive you home. If home is where you want to go."

"Thank you, Doctor, you've been so kind to me."

"You're welcome. I think when I take you, I'll have a word with your precious mother and father as well."

She was mortified. "Please, no. I'll handle things."

"I think I insist. There are things that must be said to them. I've rarely watched something like this unfold, and I won't have it."

She was warmed by his words. She'd never felt protected before by anyone, even her parents. "Thank you. Thank you for everything."

The next hour passed quickly. Nurses came and went, checking her vitals and having her walk around the room while they observed. She signed a number of forms, and then one of the orderlies brought her a bag. She looked inside. It was her clothes from *that* day. She trembled as she was brought back to the event and all the relief, anger, fear, regret, and guilt associated with it. The medical staff left the room, and she pulled herself together, drawing on her clothing. She still felt weak, but she could walk on her own. She was apprehensive about what the doctor would say to her parents, but at the same time, she wondered if it might do some good for her. She decided this would be a new phase for her, a new life. If her mother and father continued to reject her, she would simply move out. Let them support themselves. She might find a roommate or two and have her own life for once. Yes, this was a chance for something new.

The door opened and the doctor was there. "Are you ready?" he asked.

"I am."

"My car is out on the street. Let's get you home, shall we?" He looked at her a moment, realizing she didn't have a coat. He removed his own and placed it over her shoulders. Then leading her down the long hallway, they went through the waiting room and out onto the street. The light was bright and the morning air still crisp. His car was already running, and she looked forward to the warmth on the way to her home.

"Excuse me, Fräulein Baumann."

She froze as a uniformed policeman stepped up to her.

"What is this?" the doctor asked.

"I will need to take it from here, Doctor. Fräulein Baumann is under arrest."

"On what charge?" he asked, stepping in front of Elsa.

"On obtaining an illegal abortion," the officer said, growing angry. "And if you don't watch it, Doctor, you'll be brought up on obstruction charges as well."

"This is ridiculous. Look at her. Nineteen years old. She didn't know what she was doing. Why bother with her when there are plenty of real criminals out there?"

"Be that as it may. The Führer has laws, and this is one of them. There's been a crackdown lately. Germany will never meet its destiny if the women of this country refuse to contribute to our future population. Killing a German baby is a greater crime than you think."

Elsa had stood terrified during this entire exchange. But she knew there was nothing the doctor could do for her now, and he was risking everything by trying to defend her. "It's all right," she said, putting a hand on his arm. "Please, don't say anything more." She turned to the policeman. "I will go with you."

The officer nodded and stepped forward, taking her firmly by the arm.

The doctor turned to Elsa. "I'm so sorry," he said. "If there's anything more I can do for you . . ."

"You did so much," she said. "I can never thank you enough. You saved my life, and you gave me back some dignity."

The officer scoffed. "Dignity indeed. Let's go."

Elsa sat in a cell in the basement of the downtown police station in Breslau. They'd removed the doctor's coat and her shoes, and she was shivering on the hard wooden plank that apparently served as a bed. There was a rusted sink and toilet shoved in the corner of the space, and nothing else—not even a blanket or pillow. She'd been here for hours now. The officer had driven her to the location and brought her directly to this cell. They hadn't interviewed her, had her sign any paperwork, or anything else. She still couldn't believe this had happened. The fear of arrest had faded in the hospital with each passing day until she'd forgotten it was even a possibility. But now she was here, and her parents didn't even know what had happened to her. But of course, they would, she realized. Her doctor would have called them after the arrest. That gave her a flicker of hope. It was one thing for her to be in the hospital. But in jail? Surely her parents would make contact with her now.

A figure appeared at the bars in front of her space. He wore a suit and tie, with a crisp white shirt and black-rimmed glasses. He was middle aged, trim and quite good-looking. "Fräulein Baumann, I see that you've settled in."

"What am I doing here?" she managed to ask. "What is going to happen to me?"

"You're under arrest for an illegal abortion as you already know," the man said. "In the morning, I will escort you up to the courtroom and you'll be tried." He looked at her and she saw just a trace of sadness on his face. "I'm afraid the penalties are rather severe for your actions, Fräulein."

"The doctor at the hospital told me that I could face the death penalty. Is that true?"

He nodded. "That's correct. The woman who performed your abortion was already executed."

Elsa felt the fear ripple through her. "Then they're going to kill me," she whispered, almost to herself.

"I don't know. But it's not guaranteed. We'd been looking for that abortionist for a long time. Her fate was sealed when we arrested her. Your little emergency finally brought us to her. I was surprised she called for help. She saved your life and it cost her her own. Examples have to be made, after all. But a girl like you? It's hard to say. I must tell you that when you are brought up, you should tell the truth, all of it. And only answer the questions you are asked. If you defy the judge at all, or irritate him, things will go badly for you. Your life hangs in the balance."

"Why are you telling me this?" she asked.

The man shrugged. "I don't know. Perhaps I wanted to see the woman that helped me solve an important case. Or perhaps because I have a daughter of my own, and would want to give her a chance if something like this happened. I don't always know why I do things. But understand this, I'm not your friend. If they sentence you to death, I can't help you beyond my words of advice, so don't ask." He looked at her. "I suppose there is a little something more I can do for you." He left her for a few minutes, returning with a blanket and a loaf of bread. "Here you are. At least you will have a little food and a little warmth tonight. Try to get some sleep if such a thing is possible in your position."

She nodded by way of thanks. After he departed, she wrapped herself in the blanket and ate a little of the bread. She had no appetite, but she forced the food down, knowing she would need her strength. It wasn't long before the lights flipped off and a guard walked down the hallway, ordering everyone to sleep. Elsa lay back on the hard plank, putting an arm under her head as a kind of pillow, and tried to rest. It was impossible. She was going on trial for her life tomorrow. She might be dead by this time the next day. And if not? What would happen to her? Was there any chance that they might simply let her go? Why would they? If they were truly cracking down on abortions—wouldn't she be the perfect example to set? How had all of this happened to her? And where were her parents? Where was Erik? The thoughts rushed across the landscape of her mind, along with flickering images of a lonely gallows.

She was surprised to wake up as the lights flipped on in the morning. At some point, somehow, she had actually fallen asleep. She started to rise and noticed the warden was there again, or whatever he was. He was standing at her door, staring at her as she struggled to sit up.

"It's time," he said.

So soon. She wasn't prepared for this. Still, perhaps it was better. The waiting was so much worse than whatever was about to happen.

A guard appeared next to the man and fumbled with some keys until he was able to unlock the cell door. The iron bars swung open, and she stepped out, still barefoot. The guard took her by the arm, and she was led along the row of cells. She caught sight of other vague figures in some of the spaces, staring up at her with fear or curiosity. She was taken up several flights of stairs and out into a long corridor with cold tile flooring. About halfway down the hallway, the guard turned to his right and led her up to a set of double doors. Pushing through, she was brought into a courtroom. There were six rows of wooden benches facing a raised platform with an enormous desk at the front of the space. The room was empty except for a woman seated near the desk at a table with a typewriter on it. She glanced up at Elsa and then quickly down again. The guard led Elsa to the front row of benches and motioned for her to sit. He then stepped back to the doors themselves, and stood in front of them, apparently to prevent Elsa from fleeing.

In spite of everything, she couldn't help smiling to herself.

Just out of the hospital, barefoot, what did they think she was going to do?

The door at the front of the courtroom opened and another guard came out, followed by the judge wearing judicial robes. He glanced at Elsa for a moment and then took his place behind the raised desk.

"Rise," ordered the guard.

Elsa stood up. She was shivering now and doing everything she could to hold it together.

The judge flipped through a folder at his desk. He looked down at her. "Are you Elsa Baumann?"

"Yes, Your Honor."

"And you were arrested for receiving an illegal abortion, is that correct?"

"Yes."

"Tell me what happened. Tell me everything."

Elsa started talking, her words in a rush. She explained her parting dinner with Erik and their night together. She talked about her morning sickness, the surprise pregnancy, and the letter from Erik heading into combat. Tears streamed openly down her cheeks while she explained but she left no detail out, following the advice of the warden. When she was finished, the judge stared at her for long minutes, looking down and flipping through his folder now and again.

"You understand that the official penalty for your actions is death?"

She nodded, unable to speak.

He flipped through the folder again. "Well, Fräulein, when I entered this room, I had intended to execute you. But now that I've heard your story, I've decided to be lenient. I'd like to have your boyfriend here. That alcohol business was a mean trick. So was his letter."

Elsa sputtered and leaned forward, her hands on her knees. She sobbed for a few moments, unable to control herself. Finally, she was able to pull herself back up and look at the judge. "Thank you, Your Honor."

"You may not thank me when you hear the rest. I cannot simply let you go, Fräulein. The directives from Berlin require that I be harsh with any abortion-related crime. I will spare your life, but I must sentence you to ten years of hard labor. To begin today." He looked down at her, giving her a sad smile. "I wish you the best of luck, Fräulein. If there was more I could do for you, I would. But this is the best I can do under the circumstances."

She was stunned. Ten years in prison. A lifetime. What would she do, how could she hope? She would lose Erik, she realized. Lose her whole future. She was led out of the courtroom before she could even compose herself to think. The guard led her back down the stairs and to her cell. A few minutes later the warden showed up, carrying a plate of hot food.

"I know you must be devastated right now, Fräulein, but you have to remember they could be dragging you out for execution as we speak. Take this blessing for what it is. And remember, ten years may or may not mean that much time. Who knows what the future might hold? I brought you some food. You need to eat while you can. I don't know when they will come for you."

She nodded, thanking him. He pushed the tray through, and she set it next to her on the bench. She couldn't tell him, but there was no way she could eat right now.

"Oh," he said. "There's something else. A letter came for you." He handed her an envelope that she took. She saw at once her mother's handwriting. They had reached out to her at last.

"Thank you," she said, taking it.

"You're welcome. If they don't take you away before lights out, I'll check in on you again."

She didn't answer, too focused on the paper she had in her possession now. With trembling hands, she tore open the envelope. There was another smaller one inside, with the top torn off. She saw immediately it was from Erik. But scanning the inside, there was nothing else. No letter, no note, nothing from her parents. They had simply forwarded one from Erik, and they'd clearly opened it. She fought back tears that her parents hadn't written her. At least she had something to read. She pulled out the letter.

> *Elsa:*
> *I received your letter at the front. It was wise of you to make that decision, but foolish to get caught. I don't know who the father was, but at least you won't have the burden of carrying a bastard. If the police do decide to intervene, you will have to face whatever justice they give you. After all, these were your mistakes. All is well here on the battlefield. I've been awarded the Iron Cross, Second Class for bravery, and promoted to corporal. The fighting is almost over, and I may be home soon. I must think of my future now, Elsa. I am a decorated soldier. You are a disgraced woman, perhaps a criminal. I cannot follow through with our discussions for marriage. It would not be in my best interests. Besides, I have been writing to Henrietta. I believe you know her from school. Her father is a butcher, and he will have a spot for me when I come back home. Henrietta and her family are well established. We've grown fond of each other in the last few months. She is an upstanding woman—not the type who would allow something to happen to her like you have. This is the last letter you will receive from me. I wish you well, and Heil Hitler.*
> *Erik*

She read the letter again, then another time. So everything she had done was for nothing? She was heading to prison because she'd tried to save her relationship with Erik, tried to save her family honor. He'd rewarded her by dumping her, for his own future, his own best interests. Her parents wouldn't even bother to write her, to visit and tell her they would be there for her, support her. She had ten years of prison in front of her. She couldn't even imagine what that might mean, where or when they would take her. Her life was caving in from every direction. She wanted nothing more than to just end it all, to take her own life. She wished they'd just executed her. Better that than to face this horrid future alone.

She heard footsteps coming down the corridor. Two guards appeared, one of them pulling out keys to unlock her door.

"Fräulein," said the other. "It is time."

Chapter 12

Podgórze District

Krakow
Occupied Poland
April 1941

Natalia stepped into the Under the Eagle Pharmacy. She tried to only visit every three or four days, because she didn't want to be a pest. But when the youngest daughter of the family she was living with had come down with a fever, she took it as the perfect opportunity for another trip.

The month was nearly spent now, and the snow was gone from the ground. In little pockets and places, she could spy spring budding. The hope of a new season was on the faces of the people she passed as well. It had been a hard winter for all of them, and there was a feeling in the ghetto that things would assuredly get better with the coming of the new season.

Despite that, there was plenty of suffering as she walked along. She passed a mother with two children begging for food. The younger child couldn't have been more than one, and was lying in her arms, eyes open, not moving. Natalia had the sinking feeling the child was already dead. She passed another block and several young girls, no more than thirteen, were standing at the corner, soliciting men as they walked by. She wanted to go up to them, to tell them not to give themselves like this. But what right did she have? What could she provide to them other than judgment?

She pressed on, entering the square and finally stepping through the doors of the pharmacy. She saw Helena behind the counter, helping a customer. At least she thought that was the woman's name. Yes, Helena and Aurelia. She'd not really talked to either of them. Even as she thought this, Irena, obviously having heard the bell of the door, came through the back and up to the counter. She saw Natalia and gave a smile, gesturing for her to come up to the counter.

"Didn't I just see you yesterday?" she asked.

"Yes. But I'm not here to bother you today. I have real business."

"And what could that be?" she asked. "A healthy young woman like you?"

"I'm here for the family that lives with me. Their youngest daughter has a fever. I was hoping you might have something that would help with it."

"Of course I do, give me just a moment." Irena stepped into the back, returning a few minutes later with a brown paper bag. "Here you go," she said. "The instructions are inside as well. This should help within a half hour of the first dose."

"Wonderful, thank you again so much." Natalia started to go, but she couldn't stop herself. "I'm sorry I—"

"You want to know if we've heard anything about your family?" Irena smiled. "Of course you do, and you are not being a pest. I'm sorry but we haven't heard anything yet. However, I know Tadeusz is trying hard to get some information, and as soon as I know something I will immediately get in contact with you."

Natalia was disappointed, but she knew this woman was doing everything she could for her. That she was taking risks even. "Thank you, Irena. I appreciate you." She left the building and took the medicine back to her apartment. She checked her watch. She had a half hour until her appointment. She felt the anxiety rushing over her. She'd waited weeks for this, and today it was finally happening. She left her apartment a few minutes later and marched the short distance to the Judenrat building.

She skipped the line again but this time when she approached the secretary at the desk, the woman checked the calendar and then rose, escorting her up the stairs. They didn't discuss the last incident. Natalia wasn't even sure the woman remembered. She was led to an office. A gentleman sat at his desk inside. He stood and smiled at her, extending his hand. "Ah, you must be Miss Wajcblum. Is that correct?"

"Yes, and you are . . . ?"

"Mr. Badowski. I'm a member of the Judenrat here in our lovely Jewish District. I understand you made this appointment weeks ago, and you wanted to talk to somebody with authority here about your family. I'm not sure how much power we actually have, but I am here to listen. Please, come in and have a seat."

Natalia stepped in and sat down.

"Now tell me, what has happened to you?"

"My family lived in our home in Krakow. My father was a prominent lawyer here. We are Jewish, but only racially—you might be sorry to hear it, but we haven't practiced the faith in my lifetime."

"Nor has my family. You have nothing to apologize for."

"Thank you for that. In any event, we were served notice that we must relocate to the ghetto by mid-March. We didn't want to move, and my father had a Polish contact in the government. He met with him and—"

"Let me guess, he demanded a huge sum of cash to assist you."

"Yes."

"How much?"

"One hundred thousand zlotys at first."

"Let me guess again, you raised that and then he wanted more?"

"Yes. How do you know this?"

"We've been hearing a lot of these stories. Poles setting up Jews with false promises. A lot of them friends, or should I say former friends. They start with one price, and then change the circumstances and ask for more. When they've collected it all, they turn the Jews over to the Germans, sometimes collecting another reward from them."

Natalia was stunned. That was exactly what Petre had done to them. "What can you do about it?" she asked.

Badowski laughed. "What can a Jew in the Jewish ghetto do against a Pole who cooperated with the Germans against us? Look around you, Natalia, we're at the ends of the earth. We've nothing left. If I could help you seek revenge, I would gladly do it. But I can't."

"What about my family? Can you find out where they are? If they are all right?"

He put his hands up in the air. "I'm sorry. I just don't know how I could possibly do that. I don't have any way to leave the ghetto. The only Germans I deal with here would sooner take me out and put a bullet in my head as answer a question or do me a favor. If you need something within the ghetto, I will do what I can for you. You have only to ask." He looked at her, his face serious. "See, I know your father, Natalia. Only slightly, really. But I worked with him a little on a project back in the day—before all this madness, when we hardly knew we were Jews, and our influence, education, and connections meant something in the world. If I can help him, or help you, I will."

They were interrupted by the door crashing open. Natalia jolted, expecting the worst, but it was a young woman, perhaps her age. She rushed in, laughing, and then saw Natalia sitting there.

"Oh, no. I'm sorry, Father, I didn't realize you were—"

"Not at all. I'm just finishing. But let me introduce you to the daughter of an acquaintance of mine. This is Natalia Wajcblum. Natalia, this is Sylwia."

Sylwia was freckled with reddish curly hair. She was about the same height as Natalia, but rail thin. She smiled at her and nodded. "So nice to meet you," she said, before turning to her father. "It's teatime, Father, and you promised you would finish work early and spend the afternoon with me."

"So I did." He turned to Natalia. "Thank you again for coming to see me. As I said, if there is anything I can do for you, just—"

"There is one thing."

"What is that?"

"My housing. I had asked for an apartment for my family, but they refused, and put me in a one-room space with a family of six. They are nice people. I mean, they try their best, but . . ."

"But you'd prefer a space of your own? Something a little bigger, a little nicer?"

"Yes. If that's possible."

"Consider it done." He drew out a piece of paper and began writing. A moment later, he tore the paper off and handed it to Natalia. "Give this to the woman downstairs. She will provide you with a better assignment."

"I hope so," said Natalia. "She's not very fond of me."

"That was before. Now you have me on your side."

Natalia felt a rush of gratitude. "Thank you, thank you so much!"

"Think nothing of it." He looked at his daughter. "But you can do something for me as well."

"What's that?"

"When you have time, come back and take my Sylwia out

for lunch or some tea. It's very hard for her to find friends here. People of the same—"

"Class?"

He smiled. "I knew you would understand. Thank you again, Natalia, and if I can think of some way to inquire about your family, I will certainly do so."

"I can't thank you enough!"

"It's nice to do a favor for a connection from the past."

Natalia stepped out of the office and back down the stairs to the woman at the desk. "I have a new housing assignment you are to give me immediately. On Mr. Badowski's orders." She relished the look on the woman's face as she handed over the paper. The secretary stared at the document for a moment, her face flushed. "Make sure you provide what was directed," said Natalia.

The secretary dug into her folder, flipping through page after page. "I don't have much," she said. "But I see something here that might work. It is a one-bedroom unit."

"Two. I want two bedrooms."

The woman glared at her. "Fine. Let me see." She looked through the stack again and found one, handing it over without looking up.

Natalia snatched it out of her hand without saying thank you. She examined the paper to make sure it was what was promised, then marched out of the building in triumph. She decided to go directly to the new flat before returning to the other apartment to take her few things and to say goodbye.

Natalia found the new location easily. It was in a corner building only a block away from Plac Zgody Square. She climbed up to the top floor and found the number. Opening the door, she couldn't believe what she was seeing. The flat had a large central room that included a kitchen. There were good-size windows looking out over the street. She could even see the

rooftop of the pharmacy in the distance. Two spacious bedrooms and a bathroom filled out the rest of the space. If she'd
been brought here directly from their real home, she would
have turned her nose up at these humble quarters, but after the
prison cell and almost a month crammed into a small room
with six other people, this seemed like a palace. She laughed,
tears spilling down her cheeks. She could make this work. Now
if she could bring her family here, everything would be all
right. She had gained a potential friend too in Sylwia, someone
who had a shared background, shared experiences.

She left the apartment, locking it with a key she had found
on the counter. She thought about heading back to the other
apartment to say goodbye, but she was so close to the pharmacy she decided to drop in on Irena and tell her the good news.
She stepped through the doors and was surprised by Irena's reaction. The Polish woman rushed from behind the counter and
took her arms. "I'm so glad you're here Natalia, I have news!"

"What kind of news?"

"The very best kind, Natalia. Tadeusz has heard back from a
friend of his who works for the Germans. Your family is in the
Montelupich jail in Krakow. It's an SS prison, and I'm afraid it
has a nasty reputation."

"How can that be good?"

"Because Tadeusz's friend was able to learn about their condition. They are all doing well, although your father had been
ill for a time."

"That's something, at least. Did he learn anything more?"

"Yes, and this is the best news of all. They are to be released.
Within the next couple of weeks."

Natalia felt a burst of joy. "Are you sure?"

"Yes. This source is very reliable. If he says they are going to
be released, then that's the truth."

Natalia couldn't believe her fortune. She took Irena's hands.
"Thank you. I don't know how I will ever be able to repay you."

"Well, there is a way."

"What way?"

"We've all talked it over, and we want you to come work for us."

Natalia was stunned. "But I don't have any experience with a pharmacy. Really even with medicine. I was getting ready for medical school, but the Germans stopped me before I could begin."

"That doesn't matter, Natalia. You're bright. We've all seen that. You've studied medical books for the past year. And you're tenacious, as we've discovered from your many, many visits."

Natalia blushed. "I'm sorry about that. It's just—"

"If my family was in prison, I would do the same thing, of course. Don't apologize for that. In any event, we think you'd be the perfect assistant for us. We need more help, with all the people in the ghetto now. And we can train you on everything that you need to know. So will you accept?"

"Yes, with all my heart, yes!" She couldn't believe this opportunity. To be able to work in the medical field. To have something to do each day, away from the streets, spending time with other professionals. It was a dream come true.

Irena smiled. "That is wonderful. We are so excited, I assure you. When could you start?" she asked.

"Tomorrow. I'll be back here tomorrow morning."

"Wonderful, just come over when we open, and we'll get you all set up. Tadeusz said he would work directly with you for the first few days, and then I'll take over. I'm afraid I'll be a boss of sorts."

"I wouldn't want anyone else, Irena. Thank you again!"

Natalia strode out of the pharmacy in a daze. New housing, a new job, her family to be released. After the arrest, she thought their lives were over, but now they would all be together, and she would have an important role in the ghetto. Once her father was here, perhaps there would be another opening on the

Judenrat. They must be looking for leaders with his background and connections. They could make a life for themselves here, perhaps a better one than what they'd been living since the Germans occupied Poland. The ghetto was walled off, but in a sense, this protected them from predatory Poles like Petre. Yes, with any luck, they could make this work and hopefully ride out the war until life improved again. Perhaps her father was right. Maybe the Germans would lose, and they would be free, and if not, surely when things settled down a bit, they would realize the gold mine of Jewish talent they were wasting? Yes, all would be well. If she could just get her family here, safe and sound.

She returned to her old apartment and gave the news to her host family. She thanked them for their support over the last weeks and took her meager possessions. She couldn't believe that everything she owned could fit into a small paper bag. She had picked up her pharmacy book, a spare dress, a couple of pairs of wool socks, and some mittens. She wished she could go back to her real home for just a half hour. If she could just retrieve one suitcase of items, she would be so much better off, but she supposed that was impossible. She wondered what had happened to their home, to their things—probably it had been occupied by some SS officer or something. Well, that was all right. With her wages from the pharmacy, she would be able to buy some more things—items for the apartment, clothing, food. Yes, they would be all right. She realized just now that her new place was unfurnished. How had she not thought of that? No matter, she'd slept on a hard floor before. She could rough it for a few nights and then find some furniture and a couple of beds. Zlotys were hard to come by in the ghetto. Once she'd been paid, all would be well.

Arriving back at her new apartment, she took her belongings and set them in the bedroom with the better view. She would share this space with Stefan when he arrived. She felt a twinge of guilt about securing the larger, better room, then thought better of it. She'd done the work to get this space, and she should reap a little bit of the reward.

She realized suddenly that she was starving. In the excitement of the day, she hadn't eaten a thing. She had a little money, and she decided she would go out for a meal at one of the cafés in the ghetto. She would have a celebratory meal and splurge a little. Meat was difficult to get in the ghetto, but she should be able to purchase a hearty soup, some bread, and a little vodka or wine. Alcohol was something that was still in abundant supply. Perhaps the Germans, like the Jews, were in a semi-stupor to hide what they were doing to them. Natalia headed toward the door when she was surprised by a knock. Who would be coming here? Nobody knew she lived here. Perhaps it was a neighbor desiring to welcome her into the building? She felt a flash of fear. Could it be the Germans? But why? She had done nothing wrong. She shook her head, scolding herself. No sense in chasing shadows. She stepped up to the door and opened it.

Mr. Badowski was there, a grin on his face. He was holding a loaf of bread and a bottle of wine. But she hardly saw him. Behind him were her mother and brother. She gave out a scream of joy as they rushed into her arms. She held them tightly, tears blinding her eyes. "You're alive," she whispered at last. "You're home."

"We should step inside," Mr. Badowski said. "No need to create a ruckus out here in the hallway."

Natalia welcomed them all into the bare space. "But how did you find me?" she asked. "How did you get here so fast?"

"What do you mean fast?" Aleksandra asked.

"I have friends at the pharmacy," Natalia said. "I had asked them a while ago if they could find anything out about you. I was told just a few hours ago that you might be released within a week or two. But not today, not now. And where's Papa?"

"I don't know," said Aleksandra. "I haven't had word of him since we were arrested. I had hoped he was here."

Natalia shook her head. "He's in prison, the same one you were in. But he's supposed to be released as well. I'm afraid he's been sick, Mama."

"Sick? What kind of sickness? Is he all right?"

"I don't know anything other than he was not doing well, but has recovered, and he's being released."

"Thank God for that!" Her mother looked around the room. "What is this place?" she asked.

"This is our new home, Mama."

Stefan immediately tore into the bedrooms, exploring the space. Her mother glanced around, frowning. "It's very small," she said. "Was nothing else available? And why are there no furnishings?"

"I can answer those questions," said Mr. Badowski. "I just gave this space to your daughter today. I know it feels humble compared to what you were used to, but this is as good as the ghetto can provide. Normally there would be three families assigned to a space this size. But I have a little discretion on what I do. So I am giving this to your family alone. And I can do more. I'll solve the furniture problem for you. We have a warehouse with items. You can come down tomorrow to the Judenrat and I'll send you over with a few men to pick out some items. They'll deliver everything and you'll be all set up by the end of the day."

Aleksandra didn't seem convinced that this was the best the ghetto could offer, but she smiled. "Thank you, Mr. Badowski. I appreciate all you've done for us."

"Of course. As I said, your husband is a good man, and I am delighted I can do something for his family. Now, if that is all, I'll drop this little housewarming present off on the counter and let you get reacquainted. In a few days, I'll send someone over to interview you about the prison. We are gathering as much information as we can about German operations, so your knowledge will be invaluable to us."

"Of course, I'm happy to help."

The Judenrat member dropped the items off on the counter and then took his leave. Natalia stepped over, tore the bread into three equal parts, opened the wine, and they sat on the floor there in the fading light of the day, sipping at the wine and eating the bread. Although the loaf was stale and the wine poor quality, Natalia felt she'd never tasted better. She was happier than she'd ever been in her entire life.

They shared stories about their prison experiences. To Natalia's surprise, none of them had ever been tortured. They'd barely been questioned. "Maybe they saved all of the questioning for Father."

"I hope they didn't do anything to him," Aleksandra said. "And you've set my mind to worry with talk of his illness. Why didn't they release him at the same time as Stefan and me?"

"I want to see Papa," said Stefan, finishing his bread. "And I'm still hungry."

"Don't worry, I'll go get us some more food tomorrow. I have enough money for a little feast. We will celebrate your freedom." She told her mother about the pharmacy, about Irena, about the job.

"A job? Working as an assistant for some Poles at a shop?" She shook her head. "Well, I guess it can't be avoided, at least until your father gets settled in."

"I'm not going to give this up when Father arrives. He will need time to get oriented to things here. And we will need every zloty we can make."

"We shall see."

There was another knock at the door. "It must be Papa!" she shouted, pulling herself up and rushing to the door. She unlatched and pulled it open. She froze at the threshold.

An SS soldier stood in the hallway. "Are you Aleksandra Wajcblum?" the man asked.

"No, I'm Natalia. My mother Aleksandra is right there."

"I have this document for you," the soldier said, handing an envelope to Natalia.

"But what is it?"

"That is not for me to say. Heil Hitler!" the soldier said, saluting her stiffly and then marching away. Natalia closed the door and walked to the window, tearing the paper to reach the letter inside. It was nearly dark now, and she could barely make out the writing. "It's about Papa," she said, as she made out the words. "It's informing us . . ."

"Informing us of what?" Aleksandra asked.

Natalia dropped the letter to the floor. "He's gone."

"What do you mean?"

"The letter informs us that he died in prison. They claim from typhus. There is no apology, no additional information. Just one sentence: Jakub Wajcblum *ist tot.*"

Chapter 13

SS Women's Prison

Outskirts of Berlin
June 1942

Elsa stood at the sewing machine, running the seam of the uniform under the needle a third time to ensure the tunic would handle wear under combat conditions and the brutal coming winter. The Germans had learned the hard lesson this previous winter about conditions in Russia, and they were making sure the cold weather gear issued to the troops going forward was warm enough, and durable for another year fighting the Soviet Union.

Elsa wondered about all of that. Last summer, when the Germans had first invaded, all the talk was that the war would be over before Christmas. Since then, they'd heard about victory after victory, and yet still she sewed, still they prepared for another winter of combat. Was the war not going as well as the authorities said? And how did she feel about Germany losing or winning the war? That was a hard issue for her, she realized. On the one side, she had grown up loving her nation, the German people, and the Führer. She had felt such intense pride when they had steamrolled Poland, and then won their miraculous victory against France. But Germany had also betrayed her. The Nazis had prosecuted her and put her in prison, over something that shouldn't even be a crime.

She thought of her parents. There was the true betrayal. Fourteen months now and she'd heard nothing from them. At first, she had written them almost daily, telling them of the prison, her new life, her pride in adjusting to the difficult circumstances—but there had been no response. A few months in, she received a huge stack of letters. It was everything she had written to them, unopened, and returned to her. That had nearly broken her, but what choice did she have? She had endured, moved on, day after day.

She'd never have made it in this place without Rachel. Rachel Schlectly was her cellmate and only friend. She'd arrived a month after Elsa, yelling and spitting at the guards who dragged her in. She'd been part of a theft ring in Regensburg, a true criminal who was tough as the streets. Elsa was terrified of her at first, and the woman had said nothing to her for days at a time, but when another woman tried to take Elsa's lunch at mealtime one day, Rachel walked up and punched the woman in the mouth, pulling her to the ground somehow despite her own tiny frame and beating her mercilessly until she promised to leave Elsa alone. And she had. Everyone had. After that, they'd become best friends. Rachel knew prison. She knew the seedy side of everything, and she feared nothing.

"How much longer?" Elsa said to her friend, who was standing beside her at another machine.

"It can't be long now," said Rachel. "Look at the light. It's dimmer by the minute. Look at Hansen over there," she said, referencing their guard. "It looks like he's about to tear the clothes off the new girl. I wouldn't mind if he did some tearing on me."

"Rachel!"

"Well, I wouldn't. I thought prison would be a lot of that. We're helpless in here, after all. These guards are too proper by half."

"I can't believe you sometimes."

"And I can't believe you. Sex one time and you don't want it ever again? You shouldn't be in a prison; you should be in an abbey."

Elsa laughed. "I don't know what I'd do without you."

"You're just lucky, that's all." Rachel leaned in, whispering. "Do you have the stuff?"

Elsa swallowed. She knew what Rachel was talking about. She nodded slightly, then turned back to her work, trying to look inconspicuous.

"How many?"

"A dozen."

Rachel nodded. "That should do. Are they well hidden?"

"Well enough."

The whistle blew, blaring through the factory floor. Four hundred women took a collective breath, and began to shuffle out of the space, walking past SS guards and German shepherds on leashes, scrutinizing them closely as they headed toward the prison cafeteria for their meager evening meal.

Rachel and Elsa lined up with the others and took a bowl of watery cabbage soup and a handful of bread that was half sawdust. They moved over to one of the tables and sat down across from each other.

"Have you heard from your folks yet?" Rachel asked.

Elsa shook her head.

"When we get out of here, I'm going to pay them a visit. I promise you they'll write when I'm done with them."

"Rachel, please, I could never let you do that." But she was secretly delighted that her friend would stand up for her.

"You may not be able to stop me. I'll be out of here in a year, if I don't make my own arrangements beforehand. I won't leave you in here with no help, no communication. I'm going to give them a piece of my mind."

"Talk is fine, but no fists," said Elsa.

"We shall see. We've plenty of time to sort that out."

"Have you heard from *your* family?"

Rachel laughed. "What family? My mom died of the Spanish Flu. Never knew my dad. If you're talking about my gang, they aren't much for writing. Probably afraid our friends in charge here would read the mail. But we're square."

"Will you go back to them when you're out?"

Rachel shrugged, tearing off a hunk of bread and dipping it in her soup. "If nothing better comes along. But we shall see. Perhaps Hansen and I will run off together."

Elsa almost spit out her soup. "You're impossible."

"You wouldn't have me any other way. Now, where is my little package?" Rachel asked.

"Shouldn't we wait until we are back in our cell?" she asked.

Rachel shook her head. "No, I need it now."

Elsa looked around nervously. There were guards watching, but they were in a hall with hundreds of other women. Taking a deep breath, she reached down into the inner lining of her skirt. Feeling along the seam, she felt a hard space. Working her fingers back and forth, she drew out the items. "Ouch!" she said, poking herself with one of them.

"Quiet now and be careful."

Elsa retrieved the rest of the items and pulled them up to the table. She lay the twelve sewing needles down on her tray.

"Perfect," said Rachel. Reaching down, she retrieved them and concealed them in her palm. "I'll be right back."

"You're doing it now?"

"Sure. No better time than the present." She stepped away and walked down the long line of tables until she was at the end. Looking both ways, she turned to the right and approached a female SS guard. They spoke for a short time, and then the guard led her outside. She returned a few minutes later.

"Everything all right?" Elsa asked. She didn't know how Rachel could take the risks she did.

"No problem at all." She reached into her dress and drew out a little silver flask. "I've got plenty for both of us, and we can sell the container. This will keep us warm tonight, and we can celebrate your fourteen months in this hole."

They returned to their cell a little later. Once the bars were closed and lights were out for the night, they huddled on Elsa's bottom bunk, taking sips of the schnapps, and whispering quietly to each other.

"What am I going to do when you get out?"

"Don't worry about that. I'll toughen you up in the meantime."

"I miss Erik," Elsa said suddenly, tears welling in her eyes.

"Elsa—we've been through this a dozen times."

"I know. I know we have. But he broke my heart, Rachel. Maybe if I were like you, I wouldn't care. But he took everything from me."

"Maybe while I'm visiting your parents, I'll get a chance to run into him. But he won't get words out of me, he'll get a knife to the brain."

"You wouldn't do that," laughed Elsa. "You've never killed anyone."

"Hmmm."

Elsa wasn't sure what Rachel had meant by that response, and she didn't pry any further. She just let the schnapps go to her head and listened to Rachel's stories of life on the streets. They sat that way long into the night, until she finally faded off to sleep.

The next day the whistle blew at dawn as it always did, seven days a week. They rustled out of bed and lined up for some ersatz coffee, laced with a tiny bit of sugar—all they would get until a crust of bread at lunchtime. Elsa felt the sides of her dress. She could pinch a few inches on each side now. The prison had finally done for her what she'd never been able to do for herself: she'd lost all of her weight. What she'd first found a blessing, she now worried about, as everyone here did. Would they starve them to death? She'd noticed a few women simply disappear since she'd been here. But she didn't know the reasons why. How much could a body handle? How many months of twelve-hour-a-day labor could a person endure before they finally collapsed?

She looked at her friend Rachel standing beside her. She had come in rail thin and seemed exactly the same. She also never seemed to tire, and nothing could bring her down. She remained strong, defiant, with a bitter and fiery wit. She loved her for it and wished she could be the same.

They finished their coffee and were marched to the factory. Soon they were at their machines, working on a new set of uniforms for the men at the front. She couldn't help but think of Erik as she labored, wondering whether he was fighting the Russians, and would need this cold weather gear for another winter on the Eastern Front.

The guard, Hansen, stepped over to them and leaned in, whispering something in Rachel's ear. He pulled her out of line, and they disappeared. Elsa wondered what was going on, hoping her friend was all right. Rachel returned a half hour later.

"What happened?" she asked.

Rachel smiled. "Nothing to be concerned about."

"You didn't?"

"I did. But that doesn't matter. What does matter is he wants another dozen needles today, and a couple spools of thread. I told him we would get it for him, but I wanted not only some drink but also some fresh fruit and a pound of sausage."

"Did he agree?"

"He did."

Elsa couldn't believe it. At Christmas last year they'd received a little stringy meat. She didn't even know what kind. That was the only time she'd had anything like that during her term. "Do you think he will really deliver?"

"Well, he just delivered, in a way."

"Rachel!"

Her friend gave a throaty laugh. "Yes, he's always been reliable. And if he wants a repeat of today, he'll need to make sure he holds up his end of the bargain."

Elsa worked hard the rest of the day. In the midafternoon, when the guards grew tired and less attentive, she excused herself and stepped over to the supply station. There was supposed to be someone here watching over the table, but whoever was on duty today had wandered away, perhaps to catch a nap in some remote corner of the factory. Elsa reached out and took a spool of thread and a needle. She took a breath, looked around, and grabbed three more spools and a pinch of needles. Moving quickly away, she headed back toward her machine. She was sweating, and felt dizzy and panicked, but she kept her steps and made it back to Rachel.

"Did you get them?" her friend asked.

She nodded, not looking over, not wanting to draw attention to herself until she had calmed down again. She took a few breaths, and then returned to her work, as if nothing had happened. The hours passed. As time went on, she drew calmer, and the fear of being caught faded away. There would, of course, be the gauntlet at the end of the day, when they must pass the guards on the way out of the factory. But in the many months she had been here, she had never been searched. She always brought the items through. Rachel, with a conviction as a thief, was regularly searched, but nobody suspected that Elsa, guilty of an illegal abortion, would be involved in anything like stealing.

Finally, the whistle blew. They stepped into the line and started out of the factory. As they approached the guards, Elsa froze. They were patting down each person as they stepped through. She'd never seen this before. What was she going to do? "Rachel," she whispered.

"Quiet. Just keep calm. Go through the line as if nothing is happening."

"But they will find it."

"You don't know what you don't know. Don't say anything more."

What did Rachel mean? She realized her friend wasn't taking any of the risk. All this time, she'd been the one subject to a search, the one who would be caught. Had Rachel manipulated her? Perhaps even befriended her for just this purpose? There was nothing she could do. She looked around. Could she go to the latrine? Could she step out of the line and drop the items? But they were being watched too closely. There was no place to go. And if she asked to go to the bathroom, she would assuredly be searched.

They moved forward, one at a time. Now it was Rachel's turn. She stood at the front, petrified, knowing it was moments before she was caught. She was pulled over by a woman SS guard, who started to pat her down.

"I'll deal with this one," said a voice.

She looked over. It was Hansen. He stepped up and roughly pulled her aside. "I've suspected her for some time," he said. "Time to find out if this little whore is hiding something." He searched her roughly, laughing as he did so, turning her this way and that. His hand went up to her crotch, where she was hiding the spools and needles. His hand passed over them. Certainly he felt their weight. He glared at her, and then gave her a wink. Pushing her away, he shouted after her, "You're clean this time, but I'll catch you, just wait and see!"

Elsa stumbled forward, relieved. She couldn't believe her

luck. She scolded herself for her thoughts about Rachel. Of course her friend had prepared for this eventuality. She'd been protected all along. She caught up with Rachel a few minutes later. They laughed together and moved on to dinner. At the meal, Rachel took the goods to Hansen. She returned later, empty-handed.

"Did he just take it with nothing in return?"

"No, he has everything I asked for. But he can't pass me that much right here in the open. He said he will bring it to our cell later."

"Are you sure you can trust him?"

"Why would he betray us? He would lose his access to the goods he's selling, and of course now he has extra reasons to keep me employed."

"I still can't believe you did that today. How did you even pull it off?"

"This is a women's factory," she said. "But there is a men's room for the guards. It was empty, at least before we got there."

Elsa was repulsed at the thought. Still, it had been so long since she had been with anyone. And then, just that once. For the first time since everything fell apart, she felt a tug of desire. They finished dinner and made their way back into the prison and to their cell. A little while later the lights were out. They sat there for some time, waiting in the darkness. "Do you think he forgot?" asked Elsa.

"No, he'll be here." And even as Rachel said that they heard footsteps coming down the corridor. Hansen materialized in front of them. He took his key and opened the front of their cell, before stepping in with them.

"Good evening, ladies," he said. There was a strong smell of alcohol on his breath.

"Good evening. Did you bring our stuff?" Rachel asked.

"Certainly, I wouldn't back away on a deal." He sat a sack down on Elsa's bunk.

Rachel stepped over and rifled through the contents. "It's all here," she whispered.

"And we're all here," said the guard, his words slurred.

"What's that supposed to mean?" Elsa asked.

"I just thought that we might make a little party out of it. Rachel, me, and you."

Elsa was terrified. The guard was drunk. They had smuggled goods in here. She couldn't call for help. Hansen reached out, putting his hand on her shoulder. She tried to pull away, but his grip was tight on her.

"Enough of that," ordered Rachel. Grabbing his wrist and ripping it away. "She's not part of the deal."

"Come on now, you're not going to deny me a good time? Think of the consequences."

"There won't be any," said Rachel. "And you're not to touch her. Or you can forget about getting another smuggled item from me. Or anything else that might be part of our arrangement."

He stared at her for a second, his mouth opening and closing as if he was going to say more. Then he seemed to change his mind. "Fine," he said. "A deal is a deal."

"Good night," said Rachel, by way of dismissal.

The guard stared at her for a moment longer, then departed the cell, clanging the door hard behind him.

Elsa started to cry.

"Stop it," said Rachel. "You weren't in any danger. I won't let anything happen to you."

"But won't he do something now?" she asked. "He seemed very angry."

"Boys always act that way when they're mad. But he'll get over it. What I'm providing him, on several levels, is more important that his hurt feelings. He'll go back to his room tonight and take a cold shower. He'll drink more, threaten, rage, pass out, and tomorrow he'll come back to me like a whipped dog. Don't you worry. Now let's feast."

And so they did. There was a pound of SS sausage, three oranges, and another flask of schnapps. They tore into the feast like ravenous beasts. Elsa had never tasted anything better in her entire life. She enjoyed the oranges even more than the meat, but all of it was delightful, particularly washed down with the peppermint liquor that blurred her mind, taking away her fears and the dreary forever of her life—at least for a while.

The predawn whistle screamed cruelly at her in the morning. She had a blazing headache and thought she might throw up. Rachel stood as if nothing had happened, as always impervious to everything. "Let's go," she said to Elsa, extending a hand for her friend to stand.

"I don't know if I can make it."

"You have to. You can't go to the sick ward. They'll know you were drunk. Besides, they say that once you go in, you never come out again."

Elsa had heard that too, and Rachel was right, she had to get up and go back to work, as if nothing was wrong, and nothing had happened. She battled to her feet, shaking her head, fighting down the nausea. She would struggle through somehow. She could hear the clang of keys as the guards moved down the line, opening up the cells. She heard footsteps in front of their cell. She was surprised by Rachel's gasp.

Elsa looked up. The prison commandant was there, along with Hansen and another guard. The commandant stared at them for long moments. "Smuggling, is it? And bribing my guards. You two have much to answer for."

Chapter 14

Podgórze District

Krakow
Occupied Poland
June 1942

Natalia headed home from the pharmacy as the evening shadows fell across the ghetto. She was meeting Sylwia that night at a café, and she couldn't wait to tell her friend about what she'd done today. Tadeusz had let her compound a complex medicine for coughing. This was the first time he'd fully entrusted her to such a duty, unsupervised, and she'd done the work perfectly. This wasn't medical school, but she was getting to help people and doing it directly. She also knew if she could survive this war, and if things returned to normal someday, she would be ahead of the game with the knowledge she'd secured here, and from the medical books Irena and Tadeusz had loaned her.

The war. They had no idea what was going on out there in the world, but there were rumors. Rumors that the Germans had suffered their first setbacks this past winter in front of

Moscow. That they were bogged down in Egypt, that the Americans were coming to save them all. But this might just be a fool's hope. The official German news told only of victories, of the impending collapse of the Russians, the fall of the British, the finalization of Hitler's new Europe.

She shook her head. Mustn't think about those things. They only drove her mad. There was nothing she could do about the war, about the Germans. She could only take care of herself, her family, and try to endure the ghetto. As she walked the few blocks to her apartment, she glanced around her. The people shuffling along were thinner than ever, with sunken cheeks and hollow eyes. She passed the corpse of a small boy, crumpled up against a building, a victim of starvation. Nobody paid him any mind. There were too many deaths in the ghetto.

She arrived at their apartment building and climbed the steps to her unit. Unlocking the door, she stepped in, looking around her as she did so. The space was fully furnished now, with a table and chairs in the main room, and beds with mattresses in both bedrooms. Natalia stepped into her bedroom and took off her coat, placing it on a rack in the corner of the room. After the news of her father's death, she had kept this room for herself, and her mother and brother stayed in the other one, when her brother came home, that was. She sat on her bed for a moment, her fingers running along the spine of one of her medical books. She would have liked to have dug into it for a few minutes, to have immersed herself in the pages for a while. She loved becoming lost in the science. But she had other duties to attend to before her own dinner.

She rose, steeling herself, and stepped into the other bedroom. Her mother was there, sitting in a hard wooden chair, facing a window. "Good evening, Mother," she said.

Aleksandra nodded but did not respond.

"How was your day? I had the most extraordinary time at work today. Tadeusz gave me new responsibilities and I performed them perfectly." She waited for her mother to say something, but as usual, she just kept staring out the window. She'd been this way these fourteen months, since the moment she'd received news of her husband's death. "I have dinner here for you," Natalia said, carrying the conversation. "I'm going out with Sylwia tonight, so I'll get your supper together now." She put a hand on her mother's shoulder. She grimaced at how thin Aleksandra had become.

Stepping back into the kitchen, she put a half loaf of bread and a little cheese on a plate, along with a glass of wine. They were the lucky ones, she knew. Her income from the pharmacy gave them access to food, clothing, furniture. Not only that, but the staff members often shared their food with Natalia, sometimes giving her some eggs, milk, and precious fats. She took some of this for herself, she had to maintain her strength after all, but she also brought things home for her brother and mother.

"Have you seen Stefan today?" she asked.

"No." Her mother's voice was barely a whisper. Natalia assisted her mom out of her chair and led her into the kitchen. She sat her at the table and placed the plate and glass in front of her.

"Eat up, Mama."

"I'm not hungry."

"You have to eat. If you don't, you'll die."

"I want to die."

"Don't say that, Mama. I need you. Stefan needs you. We're going to get through this. I promise you that."

Her mother picked at her plate, taking a bite of cheese and a little bread. But Natalia pushed her, forcing Aleksandra to eat all of the food and drink the glass of wine. "There you go," she said. "Now you'll be all right. I have to leave now. But I'll be back in a couple of hours. Do you need anything while I'm gone?"

Her mother shook her head.

"Do you want to stay here, or back in your room?"

Aleksandra nodded toward the bedroom, and Natalia helped her back to her chair. She pulled a coat off a hanger nearby and placed it on her mother's shoulders. "Take care of Stefan when he gets home. All right?"

Her mother nodded, but said no more. Natalia, fighting back tears, stepped out of the apartment and onto the street. She met Sylwia a few minutes later at a café. It was a strange reality in the ghetto that in the midst of all the poverty and starvation, there were still places where one could dine if one had the resources. The cafés catered to a mixture of former Jewish industrialists, Judenrat members, smugglers, and Nazi informants. Gestapo agents even came by now and again. The food was not much better than that available to the average citizen of the Jewish Quarter, but you could buy it in abundant supply. If you paid a fortune, you could secure vegetables, fruit, even a steak. And, of course, there was alcohol—quality Polish vodka and German fare.

Natalia spotted Sylwia at a table. Her friend was dressed in a fashionable wool skirt and coat. She was leaning back, puffing on a cigarette, enjoying the music played by a pianist and an accompanist on a violin. The musicians of the ghetto had found employment in these cafés, helping them to stave off the specter of starvation, at least for a little while.

"Ah, my precious friend," said Sylwia, spotting Natalia as she moved over to the table. "How are you this evening?"

"Not too bad," she said, and she told Sylwia about her day at work.

"I still don't understand why you spend your days in that pharmacy," said Sylwia, taking a drink from her glass. "If you didn't, we could spend our days together. I grow ever so bored during daylight hours."

Natalia laughed. "I'm not so privileged as you—at least not

anymore. I don't have a father on the Judenrat, to pay the bills. I have to take care of things myself now. For me and my family."

"How is that brother of yours?"

Natalia shrugged. "I hardly see him. He's gone feral. He spends his days running around with a gang of teenagers. Some nights he doesn't come home at all. I have begun to wonder if he's doing some smuggling on the side."

"Aren't you worried about him?"

"I am, but I don't think I could stop him if I wanted to. And I can't sit and babysit him all day. I have to work. But I'm more worried about my mother."

"Is she still the same?"

Natalia nodded. "It's been more than a year now. I understand her grieving. We all grieved. We still do, but you have to go on with life. I thought she would begin to recover. When she didn't, I understood it might take her longer than me. But it's been so much time now, and she's still the same."

"Maybe we should get her a job."

Natalia laughed. "That would be the day."

"I'm serious. If she had something to do, a place to be during the day, it would occupy her mind. Also, I think it's dangerous to be without employment."

"What do you mean?"

"Nothing. Well, nothing for certain. Father has heard rumors that the Germans may be cracking down again. They may want to take more people away for resettlement. If they do, it will be the unemployed, particularly children and the elderly."

"My mother isn't elderly."

"No, but she's not our age either. The Germans want young, strong workers. People in their twenties and early thirties. For everyone else, they are at risk of being taken away."

"The Germans say those who have been deported are better off. Where did they take the last round again?"

"Bełżec was the name of the camp."

"That's right. And remember, there were all those postcards sent back to families. That the new camp was better, that they were healthy and had plenty of food to eat."

"Yes, but is that trustworthy? I've heard other stories."

"I have too. That they're killing people there. Shoving them into rooms and pumping in gas. But surely that can't be true."

"Who knows what these Germans are capable of? I say that we are safer here. We know this ghetto; we have control here. Which is exactly why your mother needs a work permit. Your brother too."

"How will we secure those?"

"I don't know, but let's go see my father in the morning and find out what can be done."

The next day, Natalia visited the pharmacy early and informed them she needed the day off. Then she set out with Sylwia for the Judenrat, in the wind and rain.

"This morning is strange, it reminds me of the winter that will come again too soon," her friend said.

"Yes, these poor people." Even as she said that, Natalia had trouble with the words. The old prejudices still clawed at her. Her family had come from privilege, because her father had battled for what they needed. She had done the same. She had secured the job at the pharmacy. She had pushed at the Judenrat for better housing. Certainly, her father's connection had helped, but if she had not insisted on meeting with Sylwia's father, nothing would have happened. At times she felt that if these people around her, those starving in the streets, would only choose to fight, they wouldn't be in the position that they were in. She tried to sympathize, tried to understand their plight. But what could she do for them? She did help at the pharmacy, and beyond that, she had to take care of her family and herself.

They kept moving along, weaving through the pedestrians. The ghetto had thinned out from the deportations, a merciful blessing for those who remained behind. It would have seemed this would also mean there would be better conditions, more food, but the Germans had just cut back further, leaving everyone within the Jewish District to fight for whatever calories they could borrow, beg, and steal.

They arrived at the Judenrat. As always, a line extended out the front door, but they strode through and right to the front. The woman at the table was the same, and they passed right by her, Natalia giving her a knowing smirk as they moved up the stairs without her permission. They arrived a few seconds later at her father's door. Sylwia paused, listening outside. "We're in luck," she said. "He's alone." She knocked.

"Who is it?" came her father's voice from within.

Sylwia opened the door. "It's me, Father." He looked up from his desk, a tired expression twisting into a pleasant grin.

"My daughter and my favorite friend of hers. Come in!"

They entered, closing the door behind them.

"To what do I owe this pleasure? Are you two bored? Looking for something to do?"

"No, Father, we have serious business today."

He laughed. "Serious business, is it? And what could that be?"

"Natalia needs a work permit for her mother and her brother."

His face changed. "You've been listening to the rumors, I see. How old is your mother, Natalia?"

"She's forty-six."

"And her health?"

"She's well enough," said Natalia, stretching the truth just a little. She hoped her mother would be better if she only got back on her feet as Sylwia had suggested.

"Does she have any skills?"

Natalia wanted to laugh. Her mother? She was good at throwing a social party or attending the opera. But she kept her composure. "She knows how to sew and cook." This was true, her mother occasionally had made them dinner back in the day, and she'd taught Natalia how to sew, almost as a novelty.

"Hmm. Cooking doesn't help us much. But perhaps something in the garment industry."

"Couldn't you get her something with Herr Schindler?" Sylwia asked. "He has the best reputation in the ghetto."

"That would take more time. I'd have to wait for him to come through. He doesn't visit often. Besides, he makes enamelware. He doesn't need someone who is skilled with a needle."

"Madritsch, then?"

Her father nodded. "Yes, Julius might use her. I should be able to check in with him in the next few days, a week at the most."

"What about her brother, Stefan?"

"How old is he?"

"He's fourteen, but he looks like he's sixteen."

"That's tricky," Badowski said. "The Germans are cracking down on permits for children."

"Can't you find something, Father?"

"I'll certainly do my best. I'll need a little while to tackle both of these issues. Let's say that you come back three days from today, all right, Natalia?"

"Certainly."

"And bring my daughter with you. I hardly see her anymore. She thinks she's the social director of the ghetto."

Natalia laughed. "I will, sir."

They departed, taking the stairs two at a time. Natalia was happy. She would get permits for her family, and hopefully her mother would have not only protection, but something to do, a way to give her life purpose again.

They skipped along the sidewalk, chatting away about things, but something was wrong. The streets were almost deserted. Those who did pass them had terrified looks on their faces. "What's wrong?" Natalia asked an elderly man, who was hobbling away. He nodded behind him at a poster on the wall.

Natalia stepped over and read it. She felt the blood draining out of her face.

> *By Order of the German Authorities: all Jews are to report tomorrow morning for inspection. They must be issued a new permit, a Blauschein, in order to continue working and living in the ghetto. Only those with a current work permit will be considered. Not all current work permits will be honored. After the inspection and the issuance of the new permits, any Jew in the district without a Blauschein will be resettled to a new camp in the East, where they will find new work, and new accommodations. Failure to comply with this requirement is punishable by death. Jews to report to the old Polish Savings Bank for the new stamp.*

The Germans had spoken. This Blauschein was required the next day. And there was no way to get one if you didn't already have a work permit. It was too late.

Chapter 15

Podgórze District

Krakow
Occupied Poland
June 1942

Irena stood in the long line to enter the ghetto at the Lwowska Street gate. She stared straight ahead, trying to assume a calm, even bored expression. The truth was that in her bag, under a lunch and some clothing, were precious medicines, and two large salamis. She'd been smuggling items into the ghetto now for eighteen months. They all had. Once the district was walled off and gated, it had proved impossible to bring black market supplies in by any other means. So every day at least one of them transported the goods in the only way they could possibly provide them, by hiding the items in their clothing or their bags.

There had been searches. But in this they'd been lucky. Most of the time when they were pulled out at random, the individual pharmacist didn't have anything on them that day. Tadeusz had been searched twice with actual items, but he'd managed to talk his way through it, with guards unfamiliar with what the pharmacists were allowed to bring in, and not bring in. Of course, each trip through was a miracle. If they were caught with identified contraband, they would at best lose the pharmacy, and at worst they might lose their freedom or even their lives. They had accepted the risk, taking it at least once a week each, until the process was so routine it almost felt normal. Almost.

But today was different and Irena wasn't sure why. The guards at the front were shouting. The Germans were more agitated than she'd ever seen them. They had their weapons brandished, and they seemed to be meticulously searching each person as they came through the line. She felt cold droplets of sweat on her forehead. What was she going to do? She could explain the sausages perhaps, but the medicine? She had penicillin and morphine. There was no way she could explain them away for personal use. She looked around for some sort of cover, anything she could do to avoid the search, but there was no place to go. She was only a dozen people from the front, and one of the guards was keeping a close eye on the line.

The minutes passed in agonizing slowness. Finally, she was at the front. She had hoped she would recognize the guards, that she could charm her way through, but she'd never seen any of these men before, and that too was disconcerting.

"Your papers!" an SS sergeant shouted at her, stepping up so his face was barely an inch away from hers. Trembling, she reached into her coat and pulled out her identification.

"You're a Pole!" he screamed. "What are you doing in the ghetto?"

"I . . . I work here," she explained,

"Liar!" He started to grab her.

"I-I'm not lying," she stammered. "Here's my permit." She managed to push the document into the sergeant's hands.

He glared at her, then at the paper. He looked her up and down, his face red. Irena was terrified he was going to strike her. "What do you have in the bag?" he yelled.

"Just my lunch, and some personal items."

"Search her!" he ordered, and one of the other guards stepped forward, tugging her out of line. The soldier ripped the bag out of her hand, opening the top and inspecting the lunch and the blanket.

"There's nothing here," he said.

"Take everything out, you idiot!"

The soldier huffed, as if he'd already had a long morning, then set the bag on the ground. He pulled out her lunch bag and the blanket and stared at what was underneath. "Sergeant, you need to come see this," he said.

The NCO stepped over and inspected the bag. "And what is this?" he said, pulling out a sausage and a vial of morphine. "Drugs and contraband food. I'll have your head for this."

"They aren't contraband," she said, trying to make it believable. "I told you: I work at the pharmacy. This is medicine that we sell to the population. We're authorized to bring it in." That wasn't true, but she prayed that this man didn't know it.

He stared at her for a moment. "And the sausages?"

"Food for our lunchroom. I bought it with my ration card. I've been saving up for a month."

"You are lying, bitch!" he shouted. "Take her into custody. We'll see what song she sings after she spends a few days in the interrogation room."

The private seized her. She tried to pull away, but there was no use.

"And what do we have going on here?" said a voice.

Irena looked up and saw an SS lieutenant stepping up to the gate. He was one of the regulars and she felt a glimmer of hope.

"This Polish whore was trying to smuggle in medicine and food," the sergeant explained. "She said she has the right to bring it."

"She's telling the truth," said the lieutenant. "Didn't she inform you she works at the pharmacy?"

"She did but—"

"But what? Do you think their medicine grows on trees?"

"But the sausages!"

"I bought them with my ration cards," said Irena, desperation in her voice.

The lieutenant eyed her for a moment. "Let me see those." He examined the two hefty logs of meat, whistling. "This must have cost you a lot of points." He placed one in the bag and kept the other in his hand. "Let her go," he ordered.

"But sir—"

"Now, Sergeant!" The lieutenant gave her a wink, and walked away, carrying the spare sausage with him.

Irena gathered her things and walked swiftly away from the gate. She held her composure, marching with back straight and a purposeful stride, as if nothing in the world was wrong. She turned the corner and made her way to the pharmacy. Only when she'd unlocked the front door, let herself in, and bolted it again beside her did she collapse.

"What's wrong?" shouted Tadeusz, who had been at the front counter. He hurried through the little gate and across the space before kneeling beside Irena.

"The gate. They searched me. An SS sergeant wanted to arrest me. They were more aggressive than I've ever seen them. I . . . I thought I was dead."

"I'm not surprised."

"What do you mean?"

He handed her a piece of paper. "This was delivered to me a few minutes after you left last night."

Irena read the paper. "What is a Blauschein?"

"A new work permit. I managed to track Spira down out on the street and asked him what it was about. He said the Germans are going to vastly reduce the ghetto. They are deporting all of the children and the elderly. They are only keeping young adults and healthy middle-aged workers. Everyone is required to show up today, starting in less than an hour, and line up with their old work permit. If you don't have one, you won't get this Blauschein. And according to Spira, they are only going to give a fraction of the permit holders the new document. Even if one is gainfully employed, it is no guarantee."

Spira was the head of the Jewish Police Force. He was a shadowy character who collaborated with the Germans. But he also was known to help out Jews, to protect certain people with influence or for whom he felt sorry. He was a frequent visitor to the pharmacy, and had befriended Tadeusz, although the pharmacist was merely polite, and careful what he said around the man.

"I don't understand," said Irena.

"What do you mean?"

"Why would they get rid of workers who have jobs?"

"Who can comprehend these Nazis?" said Tadeusz. "They make no sense to anyone but themselves, and at times it feels like one hand doesn't even understand what the other one is doing."

Just then Helena and Aurelia came through the front door. Aurelia took one look at Irena and gasped. "What's wrong?" she asked.

"Not so much," said Tadeusz. "But our friend here has had quite the scare." He explained to them what had happened.

"So they are cracking down now?" asked Helena. "Is that finally enough for you, Tadeusz? Can we please take our leave of this hell? We've been lucky. Perhaps we've even been blessed by God above. Each trip through the gate has been a mini miracle, but if they are going to search everyone from now on, then we will have no choice but to close."

"Now's not the time for that discussion," said Tadeusz. "In a few minutes we will open and think of the rush. We'll be swamped from open to close. People will be looking for our hair dye, our cough suppressant, and for their medicines in case they are taken away."

Irena understood what Tadeusz meant. Hair dye helped disguise the age of a person, and people had been stockpiling cough suppressant in case they had to go into hiding. The liquid would quiet a child, even put them to sleep for a time. Otherwise, a family in hiding might be inadvertently betrayed by the crying of an infant or toddler.

"Tadeusz, you know I only bring this up because I care about you, about all of you."

"I know it, Helena. We must get through today, but you're right. Until further notice, when we come through the gate, we only bring our meals for the day and any extra clothing. No contraband whatsoever."

"And when the medicine runs out?" Helena asked.

"We will cross that line when we must," he said.

Irena could tell that her friend wanted to say more, but there was already a line forming outside the pharmacy, and they still had much to do before they opened. She pulled herself to her feet and joined the others as they scrambled to the back, bringing forth as many of their supplies as they could store at the counter. A few minutes later, Tadeusz opened the front door, and it was as if he'd released the gates of a mighty ocean.

They'd never been busier. The morning passed in a blur. Tadeusz had been right—everyone seemed to want hair dye and their cough suppressant. And there was a new request, more disturbing than the rest. People were asking for poison, specifically for cyanide.

"We don't have any," Tadeusz kept saying over and over, shaking his head in disbelief.

By noontime they were all exhausted. They closed up the pharmacy for a short break, so they could catch their breath. Aurelia, particularly, seemed ground down by the storm of customers, with their desperate pleas.

"What's wrong?" Irena asked her, handing her a crust of bread and a slice of sausage.

"I've never seen them like that," she said, her eyes filling with tears. "And the cyanide. How can we live in a world where people are asking for poison for themselves, for their children? How could it come to this?"

Irena shook her head. "I don't know, Aurelia, but we have to try to keep going. I understand what Helena is saying, and it might be true that we will have to close. But what will these people do without us? How would they survive?"

"That's why we have to be here," said Tadeusz, overhearing her. "That's why I have to stay. These people need us. More than ever. I don't know what the future holds. I don't know what the Germans will do to us, but we have to survive, somehow."

A sudden thought came to Irena. She'd been so frightened when she came in this morning, that it hadn't occurred to her. And then, they'd had a mad rush of customers. But now she'd had a moment to think. "Where's Natalia?" she asked.

"I don't know," said Tadeusz. "I've been worried about her all morning. But we mustn't lose hope. She has family to take care of. And she must register, just like the rest of them. I'm sure we'll see her before the end of the day, and if not, then tomorrow."

Irena could sense that perhaps he was not as confident as his words suggested. But there was nothing to be done about it. It was already time to open the doors again, and the mad rush continued. It was all she could do to meet person after person, to try to have compassion for their panic, for their stories, and to help them as best she could out of their dwindling supplies.

It was late afternoon when Natalia appeared, her mother and brother in tow. Her face was more distraught than Irena had ever seen before. She opened the gate and let all three of them behind the counter, whispering for Natalia to take them to the kitchen. She finished the order she was taking, and then excused herself and hurried to the back.

"Irena, I'm so glad to see you," said Natalia, rushing into her friend's arms. "It's chaos out there."

"What's happened to you?"

"I'm sure you've heard of the Blauschein."

Irena nodded. "Tadeusz told me about it this morning."

"I took my mother and Stefan this morning. I was worried about them, because they don't have permits, but I was hoping my status with the pharmacy might help us. We stood in line all these hours. As we got closer to the front, my fears increased. Person after person seemed to be arguing with the officials, screaming and crying. Some had to be taken physically away by guards, a few driven away by blows."

"You must be joking."

She shook her head. "I've never seen anything like it. We finally reached the front of the line. I handed the officer my permit, and then started explaining about my mother and brother—that the Judenrat has work permits for both of them, but they won't be available for a few days. He didn't even look up. He just waved us aside."

"How horrible. But if things are going that slow, Natalia, there still may be time. If you have a couple more days, perhaps Sylwia's father—"

"You don't understand, Irena." She reached into her coat and pulled out her permit, handing it to her to review.

"They denied you. But how can that be? You're an essential worker, employed by Poles, in an essential business within the ghetto! I don't understand."

"I don't either. But he rejected me. Maybe because of my mother and brother, maybe not. But here we are. None of us have permits. They are going to take us away, and there's nothing I can do about it."

"They won't take me away," said Stefan. "I'll hide, or I'll fight. The bastards aren't going to touch me."

"Watch your tongue," said Natalia. "You're living in a fantasy, Stefan. You and that little gang of yours. You would hide where? Fight with what? This isn't a game. You need to stick with Mother and me. That's our only chance. If you go out there, playing around, you'll get yourself hurt, or killed, and then what would happen to Mother? What would happen to me?"

Irena expected Aleksandra to react, but she was sitting down at the table and staring straight ahead as if she couldn't see or hear what was happening. She was going to ask Natalia about it, but realized now might not be the right time.

"Mr. Badowski. You have to go to him. Surely there is something he can do for you?"

"He already said it would be a few days."

"But did he say that before he knew about the Blauscheins?"

"Yes. I haven't talked to him since then."

"Things have changed. Surely he can do something for you. You're his daughter's best friend. You just need to see him."

"I can manage that. But what do I do with Mama and Stefan? It's not safe on the streets without the permits. Who knows when the Germans will begin the roundup."

"You can leave them here," said Irena. "They can stay in Tadeusz's room until you return."

"Oh, that would be a lifesaver, Irena! Are you sure Tadeusz wouldn't object?"

"I wouldn't," said Tadeusz, who had just come in.

"Thank you, you've always been so good to me," said Natalia. "I'll go right to the Judenrat and see if anything can be done."

Irena settled Alexsandra and Stefan in Tadeusz's bedroom. The room on the second floor had originally been a closet but once the wall was built the pharmacist had converted it into a place for him to stay the night so he didn't always have to travel back through the gate in the evenings. Tadeusz used the room several times a week, and Irena had even slept there a time or two when she worked late. The space had a small window near the ceiling that let in a little bit of light. There were shelves with various supplies on them, for this was still a storage area for the pharmacy itself. Tadeusz had stuffed a single bed into the room, and a small nightstand with a lamp.

"Will you be all right here until the end of the day?" she asked Aleksandra. The woman looked at her for a moment and then turned away, shuffling over to the bed and sitting down.

"Don't you worry about Mama," said Stefan. "She doesn't say too much these days."

"Is she all right?" Irena whispered.

"She's just fine," said Stefan, a defiant glint in his eyes. "You lose everything and see how you're doing."

"I'm not trying to offend," Irena said. "I'm just concerned about her."

"You don't know her, and you don't know me."

"We're just trying to help."

"If my sister had listened to me, we would be safely out of the ghetto already."

Irena was surprised by that. She hadn't heard anything about leaving the ghetto. "How would you do that?" she asked.

But Stefan only stared back at her. "Is there anything else?" he asked.

Irena didn't press the point. She handed him a liter of water and a loaf of bread. "You'll have to make this last," she said. "I may be able to bring a little more when it's closing time."

"This will be fine," he said, snatching the articles from her.

Irena stepped out of the room, down the stairs, and back to the busy counter. There were even more customers packed into the waiting room than there had been that morning, if that was possible. She stepped up to the counter and took the next order, which turned out to be a request for penicillin. She was grateful for the request. This was something she could handle— far easier than requests for poison. She stepped to the back and pulled down a bottle of antibiotics, carefully measuring out the proper number of pills.

As she did so she heard a noise coming from the lobby. Her blood froze. Something was wrong. She rushed back to the front and saw to her horror that the SS sergeant from that morning was there. He was shouting, forcing customers out of the lobby and back into the square beyond. Helena was trying to talk to him, explaining that they had the right to be there, but the man was not listening.

Tadeusz appeared from the back. "What's going on in here?" he asked.

"Shut your mouth!" the sergeant shouted. Irena noted there were two privates with him, and they were pushing all the customers out of the store. In just a few minutes they were alone in the lobby with this madman.

"I see we meet again," he said, spotting Irena. "You thought you were pretty smart out there, talking your way out of things. Who do you think you are? We are the SS, and we won't be mocked. Now I'm going to conduct a thorough search of this pharmacy. And if I find anything, or anybody, that isn't supposed to be here, I promise I'm going to rain terror down upon you."

"Of course, why don't you come with me?" said Tadeusz. Irena was shocked at the steady lilt of his voice. How could he be so calm? They *did* have people hiding. As she watched, Tadeusz opened the little gate at the counter, and the sergeant and his men stepped around. "Can I get you anything to drink?"

"Are you trying to bribe us?" the sergeant demanded.

"Of course not, but it's been a cold day. I presume you've been outside for a long time. I have a little vodka in the back. Perhaps you'd like a drink before we conduct the inspection.

Irena, why don't you go pour them a drink?" Tadeusz looked meaningfully at her.

"Certainly, sir," she said, starting toward the back door.

"Halt!" the sergeant shouted. "Do you think we're stupid? If you wish us to have a drink, we may indulge you, but we all go back together." The sergeant stepped forward and grabbed Irena's arm. She grimaced at the tight grip. "I'll bring this one with me," he said.

Irena was dragged through the door by the sergeant. He pulled her down the hallway and into the lab. "What's this?" he demanded.

"This is where we do the compounding," said Irena. "We turn chemical compounds into medicines. I can show you an example if you'd like."

"And give the rest of your staff time to hide things? I think not. Private!" he barked, gesturing at the nearest soldier. "Inspect everything in this room. If anything is out of order, I want to know immediately." He turned back to Irena. "All right, my little Polish slut, take me to the next room."

Irena led him to the kitchen. The shelves contained a little bread and butter, two cabbages, and the rest of the sausage from that morning. The sergeant let her go for a moment and stomped forward, opening cupboards and rummaging through the contents. Irena was relieved they didn't have more. They'd distributed food yesterday and hadn't built back the supply. They had no more than a meal or two for the staff here.

The sergeant pulled a bottle of vodka down from the shelf. "Where did you get this?" he demanded.

"I brought it," said Tadeusz, catching up to them. "Is there something illegal in our possession of vodka?"

The sergeant stared hard at him. "I suppose not."

"Why don't we have that drink now?"

The private appeared in the room. "I don't see anything out of order, sir."

The sergeant stepped over and took a glass off the shelf. "I'll have that drink now."

Aurelia and Helena led the other private into the kitchen, and the three of them sat down in chairs. Tadeusz poured them each a healthy glass of vodka, along with a drink for himself.

"To the Third Reich," the sergeant said, taking a deep drink. The others followed suit. Irena and the others stood behind them. She was petrified and unsure what to do. She wanted to get out of the room and to the bedroom, so she could lead Aleksandra and Stefan to safety. But she was sure if she tried to leave, the sergeant would stop her.

"What are you really doing here?" the sergeant asked Tadeusz.

"My pharmacy was here before the war. When the ghetto was formed, we stayed behind."

"Making a mint off these Jews, is that it?" he asked, his eyes assessing Tadeusz shrewdly. "So that's what this is all about. And here I thought your little Polish skirt over there was trying to aid them. You must be making a killing."

"We do what we can," said Tadeusz.

"And selling a little food on the side too, I think, aye?"

"You have us all sorted out, Sergeant."

He slammed his fist on the table. "I knew it! What did I tell you boys?" he said, speaking to the privates. "No Pole worth their salt would help the Jews. But making a little money off them, why not?"

As they sat there and continued to drink, Irena observed the sergeant more closely. Now that he was calm, he seemed like any other man. He was a young one at that, perhaps not much past twenty. He had blond hair and a pale complexion, his face marred by a scar on his right cheek. In other times, at another age, she might have found him attractive, but with his conduct, with the uniform he wore and the words spewing out of his mouth, she had nothing but contempt for him. He glanced up at her, catching her look.

"What's your name, girl?" he asked.

"Irena."

"Irena, is it? A pretty enough name for a pretty enough girl. I suppose I owe you an apology. I was rough on you today. Out there and in here."

"Think nothing of it," she said, forming the words without meaning them.

"Maybe I'll make it up to you sometime." He flashed her a grin and her stomach churned.

"Well, we should be getting back to our customers," Tadeusz said, polishing off his drink. "Do you have other duties today, Sergeant . . . ?"

"Klaus. Klaus Zimmerman."

"Thank you for visiting us, Sergeant Zimmerman," said Tadeusz, starting to rise. "If there's anything more we can do for you?"

"A hundred zlotys a week."

Irena froze. What was this man saying?

"I'm sorry," said Tadeusz. "What do you mean?"

"For your protection. We'll make sure everyone else leaves you alone, but it will be a hundred zlotys a week."

"But sir, we can't afford that," said Tadeusz. "You must understand our circumstances here."

Klaus laughed. "Now who is kidding who? The profit you must be making on the backs of these poor Jews. Don't make me laugh, and don't make me double it." The sergeant rose and the privates with him. "We'll be back each Friday for payment. And keep the vodka stocked. You're right about one thing, it's plenty cold out there."

Tadeusz rose with them. "We certainly will," he said. Irena could see the fatalistic desperation in his smile. "Thank you again."

"You're most welcome," Klaus said, with a mocking bow. He laughed, clapped one of his men on the back, and led them back down the hallway.

They stood there in the kitchen, stunned, not sure how to

even think about what had just happened. How could they come up with that kind of money? And every week. Besides, they would have these Nazis inspecting them, nosing around, disturbing the delicate boundaries of their operations. Well, they would have to adjust.

"We can't worry now," whispered Tadeusz. "Let's just get back to work and we'll figure this out tonight."

"Figure what out?"

Irena turned, shocked to see Klaus standing there, staring at her. "There is one more thing," he said, smirking at her. "Clever girl that you are, I couldn't help but notice that you led me to every room in this building, in the downstairs, but what's on the second floor?"

"There's nothing in there," said Tadeusz. "Just some storage. I have a little bed up there I use to sleep over sometimes."

"A bed, aye? For you and Irena?"

Irena could see Tadeusz bristle from the comment, but he kept his composure.

Klaus smiled. "I'm just kidding you. But come, indulge me. Show me the upstairs quickly and I'll be out of your hair. At least until our payment comes due."

"I'll do it," said Irena. She couldn't let Tadeusz take the blame. If there was going to be an arrest, it would be her, if there was anything she could do about it. She moved past her employer and led Klaus down the hallway and up the stairs. She showed him the storage areas and then took him to Tadeusz's bedroom. She knew she was moments from revealing Natalia's mother and brother, moments from arrest. Reaching the door, she took a deep breath and opened it.

The space was empty. Her eyes darted to the bed, the shelves, the squished spaces in between. There was nothing, nobody. The sergeant walked past her. He pulled a flashlight out and turned it on, moving the light over the shelves. He ducked down, checking under the bed. He stood up and turned to

Irena, running the light over her thighs, her stomach, her waist. "You're a fine woman, Irena. I look forward to getting to know you better." He started to walk out, and then flipped the light up to the ceiling along the wall. "You have a window open there," he said, yawning, "I'd close that. You're wasting precious heat."

With that, the sergeant marched out of the building and life began anew at the Under the Eagle Pharmacy.

Chapter 16

SS Women's Prison

Outskirts of Berlin
June 1942

"Do you know what the penalty is for theft in an SS prison?"

Elsa and Rachel stood in the commandant's office, flanked by guards. Elsa could barely breathe. What was going to happen to them? She was already serving a long sentence. But now this?

"Speak up!" the commandant shouted.

"You give us a box of strudel and a stern warning?" asked Rachel. Elsa couldn't believe the words had just come out of her friend's mouth, and even more surprising was the stifled grin on the commander's face. He pointed at Rachel.

"You have a lot of spunk. I've heard rumors about you, and I've watched you. Sometimes it has felt like you were running the prison, and the guards were your employees."

"Naturally. Now what did you have to say about our penalty?"

"Well, the answer is death. Death is the penalty for theft in an SS prison. But I think I have a better use for you."

"What would that be?"

"We're increasing operations in some of our units in the east. Requests have gone out for us to comb the prisons for certain individuals that might have the right temperament for it. If you accepted, we would bring you into the SS, you would get a uniform, an assignment, and you would have pay, food, and shelter for the duration of the war. I don't need to tell you the other benefits of belonging to our organization. We are the elite of the Reich. After the war, if you served with honor, your record would be expunged, and you would be free. You might even have a lifelong career if you played your cards right."

"Easy," said Rachel. "Sign me up."

"Don't agree yet," the commandant said. "There's a reason we're looking in the prisons. The duty will be . . . unpleasant at times."

"More unpleasant than running a sewing machine twelve hours a day? I doubt it. Sign me up."

The commandant looked pleased. "You've made the right decision."

"What about her?" Rachel asked.

The commandant looked over at Elsa, who had sat through this entire interview too terrified to speak. "I'm willing to forgive her transgression. After all, *you* were the one we wanted. So, she goes on as if nothing else happened, and you join us."

"No. *We* join you."

"What do you mean?"

"You take both of us, or I don't go."

"That's preposterous! You're not calling the shots."

"I think I am."

The commandant was growing angry. "She's not suited for it. We want you; we're not interested in Baumann."

"We're a team, it's both or neither."

"If you reject this, you are going to die. Do you understand that? You and your friend both."

"That won't happen. You might yell and scream. You might even hit me before you're through. But in the end, you'll give in and let me take her with me."

He took a step forward as if he might do just that. But then he exploded in laughter. "*Mein Gott,* girl, you've got some spunk! Fine. You both go. I don't know what they'll do with your friend here, but I'm sure they'll find something for her."

"When do we leave?"

"Well, you'll have to be sworn in. There's paperwork, uniforms, it's not as easy as you might—"

"When?"

"Tonight. We're putting you on a train to Krakow. You'll ride overnight and report for duty in the morning."

"We don't get any time off?"

The commandant sputtered. "Time off? I'll give you time off! You should be executed right now!"

"Fine. No time off, but we need breakfast before we do anything else. You kept us in a cell all night with this nonsense."

"Your tongue is going to get you in trouble someday."

"Perhaps, but not today." She turned to her friend. "Elsa, let's go get something to eat." She turned back to the commandant. "Where is the SS mess hall?"

"You're not going in there. You're not in the SS yet." She stared at him for long moments. "Fine, the SS mess hall it is. But you'll need to be fitted for uniforms first."

Rachel nodded. "Come on, Elsa." She led her friend to the door, but then stopped and turned back to the commandant. "Good doing business with you. Tell your guard Hansen he's not nearly as good as he thinks he is. And by the way, he's stealing from the SS, so you might want to look into that."

They were led out of the office. Elsa was finally able to

breathe. "I can't believe what just happened," she whispered as they were marched down the hallway. "I thought we were dead."

"I knew we were all right when they took us to the commandant's office. He wanted to talk to us. If they'd wanted to execute us, they would have just dragged us out into the yard and been done with it."

They were introduced to a woman in a small office. The guards departed. The woman had them stand up, and she measured them. A few minutes later she returned with uniforms. There were black wool coats, brand new, with a white blouse and a matching black skirt. There were also small leather boots. "I'll leave you here so you can change," the woman said. "Then I'll escort you to breakfast." The woman departed, closing the door behind her.

They began changing. Elsa felt strange donning the uniform of her oppressors. Still, the material was sturdy and warm. She felt like she'd been cold for so long. Soon they were dressed. "Let me look at you," said Rachel, sizing her friend up. She stepped closer and tugged at Elsa's blazer, then smoothed a crease in her skirt. "You look perfect," she said at last. "The uniform suits you."

"I don't know how to thank you," she said to Rachel. "You saved my life. And more. You fought for my future. You didn't have to do that. You could have left me here, but you put your own life at risk to help me. I will never be able to repay you."

"Nonsense," said Rachel, giving her a crooked smile. "He was never going to punish me. At least not seriously. Men are all bluster and blather. And as easy to read as a poster. I owned him from the moment he opened his mouth."

"I don't know how you understand everything," said Elsa. "I don't know anything."

"The streets teach you quickly. You learn or you die. Don't envy me too much, Elsa. I would have traded you for your little warm flat, with a mother and father, and supper on the table."

"A mother and father who want nothing to do with me?"

"True enough. I wish we had a little time before we had to go. We could take a train down to Breslau and I'd sort them out."

Elsa laughed. "I know you would. Oh, Rachel!" She stepped forward and hugged her friend, tears flowing down her face. "To be free. To have survived this. And now to have a future again!"

That evening they boarded a train to Krakow. Elsa was surprised that they were afforded seats in the first-class car. They were the only people in uniform and the other people traveling treated them with awe and respect. She'd never experienced anything like that before. The waitstaff in the dining car took their order first and returned often to make sure they had everything they needed. When it was time to pay the bill, the waitress thanked them for their service to the Reich and informed them that the meal was paid courtesy of the Reichsbahn.

"How about that?" said Rachel. "We're moving up in the world, it seems." Elsa could almost see the wheels turning in her friend's mind, calculating, assessing their new status and how it could be used to their advantage.

"I wonder what we will be doing when we get there?" asked Elsa. "I'm nervous about what the commandant said. What could be so unpleasant that they would pull us out of prison for duty?"

"Who cares? We're out, and that's what matters."

"I'm not you, Rachel. I am worried."

"Just stick by me as always, and we'll see what we see."

The train rattled along for the rest of the night. They stayed up late, talking about their experiences together, about their unknown future. Elsa caught a few hours of sleep before they rumbled into the station in Krakow.

As they departed the train, there was an SS officer waiting for them. "Are you Privates Baumann and Schlechty?" he asked.

"*Ja*," said Rachel, stepping up to the lieutenant. He was perhaps thirty, with blond hair and a chiseled face. And you are . . . ?"

"Lieutenant Schueller," he said. "I'm here to fetch you and take you to your new quarters."

They followed him out of the station. Elsa noticed that if they were received with a certain appreciation on the train, here in Poland they were treated with absolute awe. There weren't many Poles in the building, but those who spotted them stared with wide eyes, some taking a step back or turning to walk quickly away.

"They don't seem too keen to see us," noted Rachel.

Schueller laughed. "They've had time to grow used to the SS. You'll find your time here pleasant. We go where we want, take what we want, and we brook no bad behavior from the Poles."

"And the Jews?" Rachel asked.

"Certainly not from them. But you'll find a lot more out about that today."

"What do you mean?" asked Elsa.

"Didn't they tell you? You've been assigned to duty in the Jewish District. That's why you're here. We have a bit of an operation starting, and we needed more help—hands of those who don't have too many scruples and can manage a little bit of rough behavior."

Elsa didn't like the sound of that. Whatever did he mean? She started to open her mouth again, but Rachel pinched her arm and gave her a meaningful look. *Let me handle this*, she said with her eyes.

"What are the quarters like?" she asked. "And the food?"

"A seasoned campaigner, I see," said the lieutenant, nodding his head in approval. "You won't believe the quarters, you two will be sharing a room in a building adjacent to the castle. There isn't a lovelier spot in the city. And the food, well, you'll have the best available, gleaned from the farms and the stores all around this area. The SS gets the first pick, willingly or no. You'll find you have access to the best of everything."

"I'd like to have access to *him*," whispered Rachel, eyeing the lieutenant's backside.

"Rachel, you are impossible," said Elsa, laughing. Her friend's banter set her mind at ease, as it always did.

The car ride to the castle took only a few minutes. They weaved through the narrow, medieval streets of Old Town before rumbling up the long hill and into the Wawel Castle complex.

"This will do," said Rachel, eyeballing the majestic medieval structure. "This will do nicely."

"Hans Frank runs Poland out of that castle," said the lieutenant. "The SS has offices in there as well, although you won't be going into the castle itself very often. Your quarters are this way," he said, gesturing toward a building to the right. He led them through the massive courtyard and into a two-story building. They climbed to the second floor, and he moved down the hallway, consulting a piece of paper now and again. "Ah, here we go," he said, reaching one of the doors. "Your new home away from home."

Elsa and Rachel stepped into the apartment. She couldn't believe it. She'd expected bunk beds in a dorm room–like setting, but instead they had a two-bedroom flat with a full kitchen, a bathroom, and a living room. The space was entirely furnished, including all the kitchenware. Best of all, both bedrooms contained windows with views looking out over the city.

"This is delightful!" Elsa said.

"Nothing but the best for the SS," the lieutenant said. "I'd love to let you take a few days off to get acclimated, at least a day to rest, but I'm afraid you're needed for duty immediately, so please take a few minutes to get freshened up and then meet me back down in the courtyard."

The lieutenant excused himself. After he left, Elsa and Rachel screamed in excitement. After their tiny cell, they were going to have a beautiful apartment with their own individual living spaces. Not only that, but they would be paid, and they were part of something important in the Reich.

"This is a dream," Elsa said to Rachel.

"Yes, my friend. A new beginning for both of us. We must both make the most of it. Our pasts have been wiped clean, and we have a chance not only to exist, but to thrive here. If we do our duty, whatever it is."

"We could win promotion."

"I'm more interested in winning an SS man."

"Rachel! Is that all you ever think about?"

"No, but I do think about it, and so should you."

"I don't know, Rachel. After Erik—"

"I don't want to hear his name ever again. This is your chance to start over. You are in a new place, with a new future. This city will be crawling with German men. You can find someone worthy of you and start looking at a new future."

Elsa realized her friend was right. Enough was enough. It was time to look to her future, to enjoy this new duty, this new chance. "I'm ready," she said at last.

"Finally. Let's go see what this new world has in store for us."

They strode back down to the courtyard where they found a dozen other women standing around, visiting. They introduced themselves and were just starting to chat when Lieutenant Schueller reappeared. He led them over to a covered truck and assisted them into the back of it. Soon they were rumbling out of the castle complex. The bed had wooden benches on both sides and Rachel had grabbed a spot for them near the front. It was a little cold inside and once the vehicle was moving, it smelled of diesel, but they were comfortable enough.

"I wonder where we are going?" Elsa asked Rachel.

"To the ghetto," a woman answered.

"What does that mean?"

"The Jewish ghetto. It's across the river just a few minutes from here. Some of us have already been down there a couple of times. You should prepare yourself."

"For what?" Elsa asked.

"The smell, for one. The whole place smells like a backed-up sewer."

"That's not the worst of it, though," said another woman.

"We've seen plenty already," said Rachel.

"Street tough, are you?" the woman asked. "Well, this is something else entirely."

Rachel shrugged, ignoring the comments. Elsa felt her apprehension grow. What were these women hinting at? The minutes seemed to drag by. They rumbled across a bridge and the truck lurched to the left. They must be getting close. They slammed to a stop and Elsa could hear voices, then they moved forward again. She could see a gate behind her now, swinging shut again as they passed through it.

"Is this the ghetto?" Elsa asked.

"You got it," said one of the women.

Elsa couldn't see much from within the truck, just buildings and a few pedestrians. It looked the same as the rest of Krakow, really. She hoped these women were just giving them a bad time, an initiation of sorts like the ones that happened in prison. Yes, that must be it. Even as she thought this, she realized they were starting to slow down. They bumped and then halted. Lieutenant Schueller appeared behind the truck and pulled down the gate. They climbed out and he brought them to attention in a line, facing him.

"All right, ladies, you've all been called here from various points in the Reich for this special duty. Some of you have had training already. For the rest, don't you worry. We will bring you up to speed with regular drills soon enough. For now, we need bodies and you're here to help. As I'm sure you know, we are currently inside the Jewish Quarter, known by some people as the Jewish Ghetto. You are looking out at the Plac Zgody Square. It's the only space like this within the quarter, so it's the best place to gather people."

Elsa noticed there were long lines of people standing out in the frigid air. They were formed behind tables that sat at the end of each queue. The tables each contained an SS uniformed person, sitting in a chair, with a set of documents in front of them. "What is that going on over there?" Elsa asked.

The lieutenant glanced behind him. "Ah, yes. That is the heart of our current operation. This quarter is home to more than sixteen thousand Jews. We are stuck feeding them, and providing them with housing, clothing, medicine, everything you can think of. It's terribly expensive and a burden on our resources, as I'm sure you can imagine. Some of these Jews are employed productively in essential war industries. Those Jews are helping offset their expenses. But like all Jews, they are crafty. There are many others here who are doing nothing. The old, the young, those with false papers, they are sitting back in their apartments, reading books and stuffing their faces with bread that should be feeding our brave soldiers at the front.

"We are doing something about this. We've issued a new permit called a Blauschein. We are carefully scrutinizing the current paperwork of each one of these Jews, and only providing a permit to those who are young, healthy, and already working in an essential job. By doing this, we hope to cut the wasteful population by half, if not two-thirds."

"Where do the rest of them go?" one of the women asked.

"They will be resettled in other camps."

"But won't they still be a burden to the Reich at these new locations?"

The lieutenant smiled. "Don't worry about that," he said. "There's a plan to resolve all of those details."

Elsa felt a tug at her heart with these words. What was the

lieutenant saying? How could these people just magically become productive? Or did he mean something else, something more sinister? She wanted to talk to Rachel, to ask what her friend thought, but there was no time as the lieutenant was continuing.

"Your job today is to keep watch. I will position you around the square. You might think this is useless work, boring work, but I assure you, it is critical. You will be freeing up my men for other duties within the ghetto."

"What are we to do?" Rachel asked.

"Observe, report. If you see any suspicious activity, you are to let me know. Also, you can take an active part if you wish." The lieutenant gestured and a corporal stepped up. He was carrying an armload of yard-length wooden clubs, as if he was bringing in kindling for a fire. Schueller gestured at the women. "Come on now," he said, "collect a truncheon."

Elsa stepped forward with the rest of them. She took a club off the stack and moved away. It was heavy, perhaps two pounds, and grew fatter on the end. The handle near the end had some kind of tape on it, presumably to increase the trip? Rachel stepped over. She was whipping the club around with some skill. The wood whistled through the air when she flipped it back and forth.

"This would ruin someone's day," her friend observed.

"We're not expected to use these, are we?" Elsa asked.

"They're probably for show," said Rachel. "But don't be such a ninny about it. Remember, they told us this duty wouldn't be pleasant. We must be Germans. We must have hearts of steel. Remember our future, Elsa, and just stick close to me. I'll do the hitting if it comes to it."

The lieutenant gestured for them to follow him, and he positioned them all around the square, about twenty yards apart. Elsa was near the road, the wall not far behind her. There were a few buildings nestled near the square, including a pharmacy.

She settled into place, holding her club. Her feet were soon freezing, and she stomped them trying to keep warm. Her hands were worse. She realized the first order of business would be to order some gloves.

At first, the long lines of Jews at the tables had sickened her. Periodically someone would scream or cry, and at times a family would be pulled away, led through the crowd and off to some unknown future. After a little while, though, she grew numb to it all, and finally bored. The day dragged on, slower than anything she'd ever experienced. She'd thought that prison was tedious, but as long as the hours had been in the sewing factory, she'd been busy, working hard at the uniforms. Here she had nothing to do but stand, staring, not able to talk to Rachel, who was too far away to chat with.

She was jarred from her daze by a scream. A Jewish woman at the front of the line was out of control. She kept pointing at the officer at her table, shouting and gesturing. He was holding a piece of paper or a small card, and she kept lunging out, trying to grab it. A couple of guards were moving forward quickly to apprehend her, but as they grew close, she lunged forward, knocking the table over. She landed hard on the SS officer, and they tumbled to the ground together. Pulling herself to her feet, she evaded one of the guards who reached out to grab her. The woman sprinted away, shoving the other man and heading directly at Elsa.

"Stop!" she shouted, holding her club in the air. But the woman kept coming on, turning slightly so she would run past her. "I told you to stop!" screamed Elsa, but the woman wasn't listening to her. As she passed, Elsa, without even thinking, brought the club down. The wood slammed into the side of the woman's head. Her head snapped to the right and then she crumpled to the ground.

Elsa stood in horror. The woman wasn't moving. The whole thing had happened so fast, and she'd reacted out of instinct.

Rachel rushed to her side. Taking the club out of Elsa's hands, she put her arms around her. "It's all right," she whispered. "You did well. It's all right."

Lieutenant Schueller was there. He knelt down by the woman, taking her pulse. "She's alive," he said. "She'll be just fine." He arose and stepped over to Elsa. "That was good work, Private . . ."

"Baumann," answered Rachel. "This is Private Elsa Baumann."

"Corporal Baumann, I'd guess by tomorrow. But we shall see. I'll make my report to the major, and see what he wants to do, but we need someone to lead this unit, and I think we just found her."

Elsa was horrified, and didn't know what to say. She wanted to throw up, to run out of here and never look back. She'd never hurt anyone in her entire life. Even in prison, she'd never been in a fight—thanks to Rachel, if for no other reason. She'd never struck anyone, and never wanted to.

The other women were gathering around now, congratulating her. Rachel kept close, laughing and clapping Elsa on the back. "We'll go out and celebrate tonight. To Corporal Baumann!"

The other women gave out a cheer. Elsa could only stand there, ready to throw up, stunned, wondering how she would last here another moment. There was nothing she could do.

Chapter 17

Podgórze District

Krakow
Occupied Poland
June 1942

Natalia rushed from the pharmacy, leading out into the square. The space was filled with people, all lined up to obtain their Blauscheins. Others were lined up at the old Polish Savings Bank, doing the same. Natalia had to be careful here. Her work permit was stamped with a denial. The SS were milling around. If she was stopped here and required to show her paperwork, she might be marched off immediately and her family would never know what happened to her. Squaring her shoulders, she moved along the edges of the square, eyes on the pavement, avoiding the Germans as much as she could. She was going against the stream of the crowd, and she felt horribly exposed, but, by some miracle, nobody called her out, and soon she was out of the thickest of the throng and back on a side street, heading toward the Judenrat headquarters at the other end of the ghetto.

She had to cut to the left one block when she spotted a couple of soldiers standing on the corner, rifles in hand, checking the documents of a family. She kept working her way down the sidewalk, eyes darting left and right, and eventually made her way to her goal. She was shocked when she arrived. The line extending out the headquarters was longer than she'd ever seen it. Thankfully, she was able to circumvent it and go directly up to Mr. Badowski's office. Or so she thought. As she approached the doors, a man leaning against the wall put out his hand.

"Where do you think you're going, missy?"

"Upstairs to see Mr. Badowski. He's a friend."

"You can't go up."

"What do you mean?" she asked and started forward again. The man grabbed her by the arm, stopping her in her tracks.

"I mean you can't go up today without waiting in line."

"But I just told you, I know him personally. I don't have to wait in lines."

"Today you do. You know what's going on out there. We're scrambling here to do anything we can to help our people. And the word came down from high. No special circumstances, no exceptions, everyone waits in line today."

Natalia wanted to argue further, but she could see there was no point. She was almost frantic. She didn't know how long her mother and brother would be safe. Still, there didn't seem to be anything she could do about it. Taking a deep breath, she turned and headed to the back of the line, ignoring the smug glances and the murmuring from those already in the queue.

She was in the line for hours. Not only was it bigger than ever before, but it seemed to be taking much longer to process each individual request. Natalia wasn't sure what to do. Should she get out of the line and try to go through the front again? She peered forward and could just see the front. The man was still there, leaning against the wall. It would do no good to try, and she would lose her place in the line.

The morning turned to noon, and then afternoon. She advanced slowly, dogged step by step toward the front. Finally, she made it through the doors and then after another hour, to the front of the line. There was a different person manning the table today, a man. "How can I help you?" he asked, nicely enough.

"I'm Natalia Wajcblum," she said. "I'm a friend of Mr. Badowski's. I need to see him immediately."

"Do you have an appointment?" he asked.

"No. I just told you I'm a friend. I've never needed an appointment to see him. I can just go up?"

"You certainly cannot. We have rules from—"

"Yes, from up on high. I heard about that earlier. I just told you: I don't need an appointment."

"I can't help you today with meeting with Mr. Badowski. Is there something else you need?"

"Listen, I've been in line for hours. My mother and brother are in hiding. If they are caught, the Germans are going to take them who knows where. I know Mr. Badowski will help me. You have to let me see him."

He shook his head. "I'm sorry." He looked past her to the next person in line. "Can I help you?"

Natalia darted to the left around the table and sprinted up the stairs. She could hear shouting, and heavy steps pounding up behind her. She ran as fast as she could, arriving at Mr. Badowski's door even as heavy hands seized her. "Help me!" she screamed, even as they started to pull her away.

The door opened and Mr. Badowski was there. "Natalia! What is the meaning of this?" he asked.

"This woman came upstairs without an appointment. We told her she had to leave, but she ignored us."

"She doesn't need an appointment, now let her go."

"But the mandate, we're not—"

"The mandate doesn't apply to her. She is a personal friend, practically family. Now release her and get back to doing the job you were ordered to do."

Natalia rushed into his arms, burying her face and sobbing. He patted her on the back, letting her calm down, then led her into his office, closing the door behind him.

"What's happened, Natalia?"

She took a deep breath, and then told him everything that had transpired since she last saw him—the Blauschein decree, their failure to obtain the new card, including the denial of her own permit, hiding her family at the pharmacy, and her ordeal in the line today.

He shook his head. "I'll talk to the people downstairs. And I'll give you a pass, so you always have immediate access to me." He reached down and pulled out a piece of paper, writing on it furiously. After a moment he handed the document to her. "Keep this on you at all times," he said. "Any time you need to see me, this will get you right through those nosy bureaucrats downstairs."

"Thank you," she said. "But what am I going to do about my family?"

"I have good news on that score as well. I've managed to secure them Kennkarte." He reached into his desk and pulled out two passes. "This gives your mother the right to work at the Madritsch textile factory. It's in the ghetto, so she won't have far to go, and she can put those sewing skills to work. And I have another permit for Stefan, working at the Deutsche Emalia Fabrik with Schindler. This requires him to leave the ghetto every day, but that is actually a bonus, because he will be able to trade with the Polish workers for a little extra food. Both of these factories are known for benevolent owners. They treat their Jews decently and their soup has real substance to it."

"Thank you so much. But these are Kennkarte, not Blauscheins. What good will these do me? And my own permit has been denied."

"That is easy to solve. You just need to bring them down here and I'll take you to get your Blauscheins. I can get you right to the front of the line, no wait, and no chance they will deny you."

"Oh, Mr. Badowski. I don't know how we could ever thank you!"

"I told you, you're my daughter's dearest friend, practically family. And I still care about connections from the past. When all of this is over, there will be Jewish survivors. We will need leaders, members of our class. The more the better. Now go fetch your family and let's get you those little blue cards."

Natalia reached over the desk and took his hands. "You're a savior," she said. "I don't know how I will ever repay you."

"There is a way."

"How is that?"

"You work at the pharmacy. You have penicillin there, morphine, and a few other things. I might ask you to bring me some, from time to time, just for our own family's safe-keeping."

Had she heard him right? Was he asking that she steal from the pharmacy? "I don't know how I would do that," she heard herself say.

He frowned. "Not even for me? After everything I've done, everything I will do?"

He was right. How could she say no? "I'll figure something out," she said. "Just let me know what you need."

"I knew I could depend on you," he said. "Now, go get your family."

She stepped out of the office, hurried down the stairs and back out on the street. She nearly exploded in joy. They were going to be saved. He was going to take care of everything as he always did. She felt guilty for her initial reaction to his request. All he was asking was for a little medicine. And in return, he was saving all of their lives. She would ask Tadeusz about it. She was sure he would agree. And if not, would it hurt them if a little medicine went missing? They were giving people doses for free every day. How was it any different if she gave some things to Mr. Badowski? Well, she would think on all of that later. For now, she had to get back to the pharmacy and find her family.

She arrived back at Under the Eagle a few minutes later. Walking this way, she was in no danger of the Germans stopping her. After all, everyone was to report to the square and there were far too many people moving in that direction to notice one more young woman in the crowd. She walked around the outside of the square and entered the pharmacy. It was full of customers and she had to maneuver through them to make her way to the counter. She made eye contact with Aurelia as she got closer to the front, and the pharmacist moved over to the little gate, unlatched it, and led her through.

"I made it," said Natalia, with some relief.

"Natalia, you need to go see Tadeusz."

"What is it?"

"I'm sorry," Aurelia said. "I've got too many customers. But Tadeusz is in the back, he'll tell you what happened."

What happened? She could feel her blood freezing. What might have happened in the short time while she was gone? Did it involve her family? She rushed upstairs to the door of his bedroom and whipped it open. There was nobody there. More alarmed now, she hurried to the kitchen. Tadeusz wasn't there. She moved into the lab and found him at the counter, mixing some components and grinding them into a fine powder.

"Tadeusz!" she shouted, rushing to him. "What's happened?"

"Natalia, you're safe," he said, taking her arms. "We had some visitors while you were gone."

"What kind of visitors?"

"SS."

"They arrested my family!"

"No. Thank God, no. They cleared everyone out of the front and then inspected the back. We were able to keep them busy for a while and then they were leaving without even checking my bedroom. But at the last minute they demanded to inspect it. When we went inside, there was nobody there, but the window was open, you know the one high up at the end of the closet? Your brother must have got up there somehow and helped your mother to safety."

"From the second story? How could they have done that and where are they?"

"We don't know. They haven't come back. But the Germans didn't find them here."

Natalia took a deep breath. "He must have taken her home. I'll go find them."

"I don't know if you should go," Tadeusz said. "It's not safe out there. Perhaps you should just stay here, help us out, and I'm sure they will show up before the end of the day."

"I can't. I can't, Tadeusz. I've got to go find them. You have to understand."

"Of course I do. But please, be careful."

"I will."

Natalia rushed out of the pharmacy as quickly as she could and turned down the sidewalk toward her apartment. She was sure they were there. She checked her watch. It was three. She didn't know what time the Germans would shut down the operation for today, but if she hurried, she should be able to collect her family and get them back to the Judenrat, and then return to the square to obtain their new Blauscheins. She hurried, barely paying attention to the Germans, knowing that time was against her.

She made it safely to the apartment. Hurrying up the stairs, she reached her door and fumbled with her key, finally opening into the flat itself. She rushed from room to room, calling for them, but nobody answered. They weren't here. Where might they have gone? Had the Germans seized them after all? After everything she'd secured, was it going to be too late? She sat down on the bed, taking a deep breath, unsure what to do, then she rose and stormed back onto the street, calling their names.

Chapter 18

Podgórze District

Krakow
Occupied Poland
Under the Eagle Pharmacy
June 1942

Irena stood at the door, helping the last customer out before closing and locking it behind her. She leaned against the wall for a moment, shutting her eyes, catching her breath. She was more mentally and physically exhausted than she'd been in her entire life. The pharmacy had been a crush of customers all day. And it was not just the volume, but the desperation of these people, who'd become friends, who relied on them for comfort, a little information here and there, a bit of food. And now many of them would be going away to an uncertain future — out of this neighborhood, deeper into the throat of the Nazi monster. She felt the tears welling up in her eyes and she slid to the floor, tucking her head into her knees, weeping for those they couldn't save, who would pass out of their aid forever.

"It's all right," said Tadeusz. "You've done everything you can for them, Irena. I'm so proud of all of you. We've given everything we can give, and now it is in God's hands."

"What will become of them?" she asked.

"There is no way to know. I pray that they go to the camps that the Germans have promised they would be. Locations with food, and jobs, and shelter."

"Do you believe the Germans?"

Tadeusz shook his head. "It's hard to do so. Everything they've said so far is a lie. But we are in the midst of a war. A war that maybe now is not going as well for them as they'd imagined. They have all of this free labor available to them. Why waste it in some kind of meat grinder? It's not logical."

"When have the Nazis shown any common sense?"

"Yes. That's my concern. They have this blind focus on the Jews, as if they were the source of every problem the Germans have ever had. I don't understand it. I've lived around Jews my entire life. I've served them and so did my father before me. Sure, there are some individuals who may not be the best of character, but not to a degree different from what I've seen from the Catholics we live with. And a far sight better than these occupiers who profess their superiority over us. But you are right, Irena, I fear that despite what is in their best interests, they might still have some sort of diabolical ending planned for the people here. More in line with the dark rumors we've heard."

"Have you heard anything from Natalia or her family?"

"Not since she left here. I hope they'll be all right."

"Isn't there anything we can do for them?"

Tadeusz shrugged. "I've thought of that myself. I can talk to Spira to see if he can help. But I don't know if he will listen to me, and even if he is willing, would the Germans care? He's told me before that when it comes to these deportations, they won't take his advice."

"Do you think he's being truthful?"

"It's hard to say. He plays his own game. But I don't know why he would lie to me about that. And at the end of the day, I think all of them are in danger: the Judenrat, the Jewish Police, the lot. How can any of them be safe if the Germans continue on whatever mad course they are charting?"

"Will you speak to him?"

"Yes. Certainly, I will. I thought of trying to track him down today, but we've been so busy, and he hasn't stopped by. With all the chaos, and the visit from our German friends, I haven't had the time to seek him out."

There was a knock at the door. Irena froze. Who could be coming here after hours? She looked at Tadeusz. "No sense in trying to pretend we're not here," he said. "If it's the Gestapo, they won't let a door stop them." He stepped over and unlocked it. Opening the door, Irena could see his shoulders relax. A figure stepped in, closing the door behind him. He shook Tadeusz's hand. She recognized him. It was Dolek Liebeskind, the leader of the Jewish resistance in the ghetto.

"Good evening, Tadeusz," he said.

"Good evening, Dolek."

"A difficult day today."

"Indeed."

"Have you heard anything from Spira, or any of the Germans?"

Tadeusz shook his head. "I haven't seen Spira today or that sergeant who comes in every week. I'm not sure either of them would tell me anything even if they did come in. Have you heard anything?"

"I've heard they are going to clear out the ghetto. Get rid of everyone who didn't get their precious blue stamp."

"Do you know when?"

Dolek shook his head. "It's hard to say. It could be a day, it could be a month."

"Can I get you something to drink?"

Dolek nodded. "Sure, a little vodka if you have it." He looked over at Irena. "Is she safe to listen to this?"

Tadeusz looked over at her. "Irena? Sure. I would trust her with my life. And your life too."

Dolek grunted and stood there silently while Tadeusz went into the back, returning a moment later with a bottle and three glasses. He poured some vodka for each of them. Irena drank hers quickly, thankful for the harsh, bitter burning in her throat and the warmth that spread over her body, helping to fight down the tension of the day.

"So, what can I do for you?" Tadeusz asked at last.

Dolek glanced at Irena again. "Even with your words of assurance, I'd rather we talk in private."

"I told you, she's entirely trustworthy. She smuggles in food and medicine every week. She risks her life for the ghetto as much as you do."

"Fine. Have it your way. I need a favor from you, Tadeusz. A dangerous one."

"What favor is that?"

"It's about this *Aktion* that we are sure is coming."

"What about it?"

"We need to make arrangements with our friends in the Polish resistance. We are planning on getting some people out through the sewers, and we need to arrange exit points and safe houses for them."

"Why do you need me?" asked Tadeusz. "I thought the reason you worked at an outside industry was so you could keep contact with our Polish friends?"

"I have, and so have many of our members. But the Germans have shut down all of that—at least temporarily. Nobody is getting out or in. So, we have no way to get to them to make arrangements."

"What about those sewers?" asked Irena.

"True enough, the sewers could work. But we would be highlighting our escape route at the moment we need it most. The Germans and the Polish police are already aware of that potential. They periodically patrol them or set booby traps up near the exits. If we had someone arrested in the next few days down there, they would double or triple their guards. We need to keep those routes open, to the greatest extent possible."

"If they catch Tadeusz with documents, they'll kill him," Irena said.

"Yes. Like I said, it's dangerous. But we need that communication. It's up to you, Tadeusz. We all count on you in your role here. But we need you right now to do something different. Something perhaps more important, even."

"I'll go," said Irena. "I can do it."

"Absolutely not," said Tadeusz. "If the risk has to be run, it will be me."

"No, if they arrest you, they'll shut down the pharmacy. That would be the end of all of this. If they catch me, you can distance yourself from the situation. With a few bribes in the right place, they'll let you keep operating here. It has to be me."

Dolek nodded. "The girl is talking some sense, Tadeusz. She is a better risk than you are. Assuming you have as much confidence in her as you claim."

"I trust her implicitly," said Tadeusz. "Only I don't want her to take this risk. Still, she's right. As much as I hate it, we have to consider the good work we are doing here. Irena, if you're willing to take this risk, then I am willing to let you go."

"Good, it's settled, then," she said. Now that there was agreement, she felt the icy fear rising up inside her. She'd just signed up to risk everything—and just at the time when the Germans were the most vigilant. But if she could get there and make it back, then she would have done something critical for the people in the ghetto. She would have directly been responsible for saving lives. "What do I need to know and when do I go?"

"You just need to take this to the address written on the front," he said, handing her an envelope. "And you need to go now—and be back before curfew sets in."

"Why so soon?" Tadeusz asked.

"We don't know when the Germans will come. It could be as soon as tomorrow. We don't think so, because there were still people in line at the end of the day today. We think it will take at least until tomorrow to process all of the Blauscheins. But we can't take that risk. We must pass on the information to the Poles and receive their instructions in return."

"I'll go. I'll go now," Irena said.

"Good. It's not so far that you have to go. Just over the bridge. It's a twenty-minute walk. You should be there and back in ninety minutes, long before the gates to the ghetto close."

Irena made her way out of the ghetto gate without any difficulty. The SS guard, whom she knew, didn't even check her papers. A few minutes later she was at the bridge over the Vistula. This was also guarded, but again, she passed this way every day. She did have to show her pass here. The guard looked her over, and she feared he would search her, but after a few moments he motioned for her to continue, and she made her way across and into Krakow itself.

It was getting dark now, even on this June evening, and Irena was concerned that she wouldn't be able to trade information and make it back in time. She hurried along, shuffling by a pedestrian here and there. Compared to the cramped spaces in the ghetto, she was always struck by how deserted the Polish city felt to her. As she moved along, the castle loomed on her left. She turned right on Miodowa Street, looking around before she removed the envelope to check the address. Memorizing the number, she continued on until she came to a building on her right, next to a little grocery store. She knocked on the door and waited. Nobody answered. She knocked again. Still nobody. She looked at the intersection and saw a German soldier who was operating as a traffic guard. He was watching her. She felt her pulse quicken. She knocked a third time. To her relief she heard footsteps, and the door opened. There was a woman there, in her sixties, her face wrinkled and worn by the years.

"What is it?" the woman asked.

"I'm here from the ghetto," Irena whispered. "Dolek sent me."

The woman eyed her suspiciously. "I don't know you. I've never seen you before. Dolek who? We don't know anyone from the ghetto. Contact with them would be illegal." She started to close the door.

"Please," said Irena, taking her arm. "I have an envelope from Dolek. It's the routes they need for the sewer."

She looked Irena over again. Finally, she waved her in. "All right, come inside."

Irena followed her and they walked down a narrow hallway and then up some stairs to a single door. The woman opened it and led her into a dingy, poorly lit apartment. There was a man sitting on a sofa, smoking a cigarette. He looked up and spotted Irena. He reached inside his coat.

"No," said the woman. "It's okay. She's with Dolek. This is Jurek."

"Who are you?" Jurek asked.

"I'm Irena. Irena Drozdzikowska."

The man's eyes widened in surprise. "The skirt from the pharmacy?"

"You know of me?"

"We know of all of you. Tadeusz has been a big help to the Jews, and to us from time to time. Why are you here? I didn't know you worked with Dolek."

"I don't. But they've closed the ghetto. None of the workers are allowed out right now."

"I hadn't heard that," Jurek said, leaning forward. "Why?"

"They've issued a new work permit. They are denying it to anyone young or old."

"Ah, then they are culling the ghetto. I take it Dolek is expecting a new *Aktion*?"

"Yes."

"Funny we haven't heard anything about it on this side. The Germans must be very tight-lipped about this operation. Usually, we get some notice. Well, you better show me what you have."

Irena handed Jurek the envelope. He opened it and pulled out what turned out to be a medium-sized map. There were drawings on the map, and markings at a number of locations.

"He wants to use the sewers to get people out, I see." Jurek shook his head. "I told him it's too dangerous. The Germans know about it, and they've stepped up their counter measures. Dolek must be desperate if this is what he thinks must be done."

"He didn't tell me. He did mention the Germans were patrolling them more frequently, which is why he needed to coordinate with you."

"Well, desperate times call for desperate measures. Yes, we can accommodate this. Give me a few minutes here and I'll mark out times and exits."

Jurek set to work on the map. He was drawing a series of symbols she didn't understand. He marked a number of new locations. He checked the map several times, adding another item here and there, then folded it and handed the whole thing back to Irena.

"What were those symbols?"

"Those are addresses and times. But in code. That way if you're caught and killed, the Germans won't be able to decipher what we are doing."

"Also, if you're a spy, you won't be able to give the Germans any more than Dolek already has, by trusting you," said the woman.

Jurek laughed. "Yes, there's that too. Do you want something to eat or drink before you go?"

Irena shook her head. "I have to get back tonight."

Jurek checked his watch, whistling. "Dolek must think the *Aktion* is coming tomorrow."

"He told me he thought it wouldn't be then. But it could be the next day."

"Well, you'd better get moving, then. And tell Dolek we'll be watching, starting tomorrow, regardless of what he thinks."

"Thank you," she said.

"No, thank you. And thank Tadeusz. Tell him that the resistance is watching. We know what he's done, what he's doing. If he needs our help, we'll be here for him."

Irena nodded, and then turned and left. She was back out on the street a moment later. To her relief, the traffic guard was gone. She made sure the envelope was secure in her pocket and then hurried back down the street, heading toward the Kazimierz district and the Vistula beyond. She made it over the bridge and reached the gate into the ghetto just as it was about to close. The guard looked at her as if he was making up his mind whether to let her in, and then he jerked his thumb at her. She hurried toward the square, exhausted and relieved. She'd made it. She hurried toward the door and fumbled with her keys, the darkness making it difficult to find the right one. Finally, she got the door opened and stepped inside.

"Where have you been, my busy little bee?"

The man's voice came to her out of the darkness. A light flipped on. She was shocked. Standing at the counter was the head of the Jewish Police, Symche Spira.

"I was running an errand," she explained, battling to keep her face calm. "Where is Tadeusz?"

"Gone," said Spira.

"What do you mean 'gone'?"

"The Gestapo took him for questioning an hour ago. And I'm here to arrest you."

Chapter 19

Wawel Castle

Krakow
Occupied Poland
June 1942

Elsa stared in the mirror at the single silver diamond on her collar. She reached up to touch the insignia, still in a daze over her promotion.

"Unterscharführer Baumann, who would have thought it," said Rachel. "I told you if you stuck with me, you'd be all right. And now you've been promoted over me."

"It's a terrible mistake," said Elsa. "You should be the one with the promotion. The first chance we get, I'll talk to Schueller."

"Don't you dare," said Rachel. "I'll make my own promotions, thank you. And I wasn't the one who thumped that terrorist."

"She wasn't any such thing. She was just a woman trying to get away."

"You don't know that. And it doesn't matter. You performed admirably on your first day of duty. I couldn't be happier for you."

Elsa glanced again at her uniform. The silver flashed on the dark background. She smiled, admiring her curly hair, and her thin figure. The uniform was striking. And with the weight she'd lost in prison, she'd never looked better. Perhaps Rachel was right. Perhaps this was the best thing that could have happened to her. She glanced at her watch. "It's getting close to seven, we'd best be going."

"Look at you," said Rachel, laughing. "Five minutes in the new uniform and you're already giving commands. I'll make a leader out of you after all."

Elsa grunted, but she couldn't help smiling in return. "I just hope today is better than yesterday."

"Don't count on that. I'd say it will be the same, or worse. This selection they are conducting is going to mean something once they've sorted everyone out. Mark my words."

Elsa looked out the window. From her bedroom, she could see southward toward the Vistula. The ghetto was just over the bridge, a few minutes' drive from here. She wondered what the day would bring, and she said a silent prayer that she wouldn't have to be involved in anything like yesterday's events.

They stepped out into the courtyard, finding the rest of the women already there. They gathered around Elsa, admiring her new insignia and clapping her on the back. She felt like a fraud. She was no hero. She'd acted out of instinct, out of self-defense, the day before. And now she was expected to lead these women. There was nothing she could do other than do her duty, and hope for the best.

Lieutenant Schueller stepped out into the courtyard. He gestured for the women to gather around him. "All right ladies, today is going to be more of the same. This is the second day of the Blauschein operation and we're hoping to wrap up this portion of our operations by sunset. Be aware, things could be more difficult today. Yesterday, we had the most compliant members of the population—those who either had Kennkarten and expected to receive the little blue sticker, or those who follow the rules no matter what. Today we will be dealing with the more desperate and defiant portions of the population. You will still be posted on the outskirts of the processing area, but our men will be conducting building-to-building searches. We may have to use more coercive methods to bring the population in for review. So, expect to see some things that might be a little more unpleasant. Remember, these Jews aren't truly human—not the way we are. They are more like animals—cunning, vicious, quick to strike when they see any weakness. We must be strong, for our people, our nation and our Führer. Can I depend on you?"

The women shouted an emphatic "*Ja!*"

"Good. Our new unterscharführer will assign you your positions when we get there. When I'm not around, Elsa is in charge."

With that the lieutenant dismissed them and they scrambled into the same truck as the day before. As they rumbled toward the ghetto, Rachel and Elsa shared a cigarette. She hadn't smoked before prison but had taken up the habit with her friend's encouragement. The ones available in jail had been the worst kind of ersatz tobacco, but now, as members of the SS, she was entitled to better. The cigarette had a rich flavor, and the smoke went to her head, causing her to be a little dizzy but also steadying her nerves for the day ahead.

They piled out of the bed on arriving at the ghetto gate and marched into the Plac Zgody Square. "Peace Square" it translated to, an irony since there was nothing like tranquility here this morning. The tables were already out and lines beginning to form. But it wasn't the square itself that caught Elsa's attention. It was the sounds in the distance. There were shouts everywhere, and she could see down the streets the sight of men, women, and children being herded toward her by soldiers. A sharp crack broke the morning air, and another. Gunshots she realized. She looked around, alarmed. Why would anyone be using firearms in the operation?

"Elsa, you're supposed to be placing us," whispered Rachel, coming up to take her friend's arm.

"Do you hear that?" Elsa asked.

"Of course I do, but that has nothing to do with us. Get everyone into position, the lieutenant is watching you."

Elsa's face flushed. She shook her head, trying to drive the thoughts from her head, and then turned to her unit. "Follow me," she ordered, and began walking around the outskirts of the square, posting a woman to guard the perimeter every dozen yards or so. She kept Rachel with her until they were all the way around the square, and then posted her friend right next to her. She checked her watch; it was half past seven. They hadn't had breakfast, and she wondered if they would have to wait until lunchtime. It was colder out this morning, and she already felt miserable. It was going to be a very long day.

And so it proved. For the rest of her life, Elsa would remember this day. The hours dragged while endless lines of people were herded into the square. At least half of those who came in left without a Blauschein, including all of the children under fifteen or so and most everyone older than forty. The soldiers were free with their rifles today, using the butt end of their weapons to prod people along.

There was one highlight for Elsa. She'd noticed an SS sergeant amongst the soldiers, a striking young man with blond hair. He was leading a squad of men, ushering people back and forth into the square, issuing orders in a deep-throated voice. He caught her looking at him, and she turned away in embarrassment. When she looked back, he had stopped what he was doing and was staring at her. He stood that way, his square jaw set. Then he winked at her and gave her a quick grin, before returning to his duties. Throughout the day, she found herself watching him, wondering who he was, where he was from. For the first time since Erik, since the awful operation and the life-changing ramifications of it, she found herself looking at a man with interest, even longing. Amidst the misery, the terror of this day, he was a lifeline, something to cling to.

Finally, the light began to fail, and the lines dwindled down to a trickle, and then stopped altogether. The officious SS men at their tables packed up, and the lieutenant reappeared and ushered them back to their truck. When they were back in their apartment, Elsa rushed into the bathroom. She'd fought back her stomach throughout the day, managing to keep it together. But now that she was finally home, she couldn't contain her emotions any longer. She vomited violently into the bowl, her stomach heaving over and over. She lay there long minutes, even after she was done. Her body weak, shivering.

She heard a knock at the door. "Elsa, pull yourself together. We need to go out and celebrate."

Celebrate. What was there to celebrate? They'd stood there while a whole people were intimidated and brutalized. There had been killings, there was no doubt about it. The gunshots had gone on all day. Fortunately, from their vantage point, she had seen nothing, witnessed nothing worse than the terrified families lining up to watch their fate be decided by a little blue sticker.

Another knock. "Hurry up. You're going to want to come out here."

"I'll be just a moment." She pulled herself up and then walked up to the sink, putting some toothpaste on her toothbrush and scrubbing her teeth and mouth. She looked at herself in the mirror. The uniform was still there, but now she felt awful to be wearing it. Her face was pale, her eyes sunken. Taking a few deep breaths, she adjusted her clothing and stepped out into the main room.

Rachel was standing there, a grin on her face. She had one arm hidden behind her back. "I've got something for you," she said. "Something that is going to make you feel much better."

"If it's a drink, you can forget it," said Elsa. "I need a few minutes."

"It's not a drink, silly, although we will be drinking tonight. It's something much better." She pulled her hand out from behind her and flashed an envelope in front of her.

"What is that?"

"It's a letter. A letter from your parents."

Elsa froze. She couldn't believe it. How could that even be? "I don't understand. They don't even know I'm in the SS."

"They do. I wrote them the moment we found out we were being transferred. I will admit, I'm surprised at the speed of the post. But we are in the SS after all, and of course Breslau is not so far away."

"What did you write to them?"

"I told them what we were doing, and I threatened them a bit."

"Threatened?"

"Only a bit."

"Oh, Rachel, what would I do without you?"

"That's what I am always saying. But now, I'm going to go down to the mess hall and get some coffee. You take your time with that, all right?"

"Thank you," said Elsa, taking the letter. "Thank you so much."

Her friend departed and she took the letter with trembling hands. She recognized her mother's handwriting immediately. She tore open the letter and began to read.

> *Elsa:*
> *We were so delighted to hear from your friend Rachel, and amazed to learn the news of your enlistment in the SS. Your father is so proud. I know we*

haven't written to you, and I hope you can forgive us. We just didn't know how to handle what you did. It was the scandal of the season at our church. I couldn't show my face there for months. Your father sunk deeper into himself, barely leaving his chair. He wouldn't talk to me, wouldn't let me talk about you. I was so relieved when I learned that your sentence had been commuted to prison. I started to write you several times, but I just couldn't bring myself to send it.

But now, all that is past. You've been exonerated and you are serving in the SS! Now my friends at church are simply abuzz with the news. They asked me to write you and find out everything there was to know. And your father—it's brought over the most wonderful change in him. He's up and about, Elsa, and believe it or not, he's started to look for work again. He said that if you could do something like that, he could start again as well. You've inspired him, Elsa. You've inspired both of us.

We couldn't be prouder of you. You are serving the Fatherland. You have a future again, and so do we. I can't wait to hear from you about your posting, what your duties are, and everything else. I'm also hoping you will eventually get some leave, and you could come and visit us so we can be a family again. Please write back right away. And please, Elsa, won't you forgive us for not writing to you before? I pray you will understand, and that you can be a part of our lives again.

With love, your Mother

Elsa read the words several times through, tears splashing on the paper and smearing some of the ink. Her family had forgiven her. They were proud of her. They wanted her to come and see them. She'd thought she'd lost them forever but now they wanted to be a family again. She felt her pride swell. She marched back into the bathroom, using some tissue to wipe away the tears. She stood up straight and smiled into the mirror. She was a member of the SS, a soldier of the Reich, a proud young woman with friends and family.

Rachel arrived back a few minutes later. "How was the letter?" she asked. "If they were rude, I'll catch a train out there right now and finish the both of them."

"Oh, Rachel," said Elsa, rushing into her arms. "Thank you so much!" She handed her the letter and her friend read it over.

"Good enough," she said, her voice cracking with emotion. "I suppose I shan't despise them quite so much from now on. But they better keep writing."

"They will, they will. And when we get leave, I want you to go with me. I want you to meet them, to stay with us. Unless you want to go home, of course."

Rachel gave a bitter smile. "I don't have a home, my friend. But I'd love to come to yours. We'll set Breslau on fire." She checked her watch. "But come, some of the women are getting together at a nearby bar. It's supposed to be dripping with German men. I promised them we would be there tonight."

Elsa hesitated. She'd planned on staying home this evening—trying to process what she'd seen today. But that all felt different now. Why shouldn't she go out? Why shouldn't she have a drink to celebrate the letter, and her promotion? Didn't she have plenty to celebrate now? "Yes. Let's go, Rachel, and the drinks are on me tonight."

"Oh no, I think not. A promotion and a reunion call for me to pay. And I won't take no for an answer. You'll pay plenty when I get promoted over your head. And don't think it won't happen."

"Of course it will happen, and it should have happened already."

Rachel shrugged. "Such is life. Let's go my *meine freunde*."

* * *

They arrived at the bar a half hour later. It was in the Old Town district, looking out over the main square. The spire of St. Mary's Basilica towered in the distance. Normally lit up, the church was dark as night under the wartime regulations. Their destination itself was small and vaguely seedy, a few tables and a little floor for dancing. A woman stood in the back, playing mournful tunes on a violin. The bar itself had no stools, with one server. But what stood out the most in the space was the number of uniforms—it was filled with Germans. The space roared with Elsa's native tongue, harsh, loud, and staccato over the sounds of the stringed instrument beyond. The soldiers were mixing with Polish women, some of them startlingly beautiful.

"Over there," said Rachel, nodding to the left. There was a table with several of their unit members sitting, glasses of beer in their hands. They stepped over and took a seat.

"Quite a place," said Elsa, trying to get her bearings. The smoke was so dense it felt like she was sitting inside a chimney. Her lungs, never strong, struggled to breathe in the thick stuff.

"I'm Anna," said one of the women at the table, a dirty blond in her late twenties. "And this is Hilma." She pointed at a brown-haired woman slouched in the corner, who was glaring at both of them. "We're both from Hamburg."

"How long have you been here?" asked Elsa.

"Not much longer than you," said Anna. "We arrived a couple of weeks ago."

"Had you been to the ghetto before we got here?"

"A couple of times, but not to work, just to get oriented. They told us they were waiting for the full unit to arrive before we started our official duties."

"And what made you join the SS?"

"Mind your business," said Hilma.

"And you mind yours," said Rachel. "If you have a problem, I can solve it for you."

Hilma stared hard at Rachel, starting to rise.

"Sit down," Elsa found herself saying. "Sit down right now. And that's an order."

The woman looked over at her, her mouth open as if she was going to say something. But then she slumped back down into her seat.

"Don't mind her," said Anna. "She had a rough time of it before we got her."

"Were you in prison?" Elsa asked.

Anna's eyes opened wide. "How could you know that?"

"We were too. We were offered a way out, if we joined."

"The same with us. Hilma wanted to refuse. She spit in the commandant's face. I thought we were dead after that, but they just carted us off and shoved these uniforms on us. The next thing we knew we were here."

Rachel laughed. "You spit in his face? I take back what I said. The next drink is on me. In fact"—she raised her hand and the bartender scurried over to her—"I want drinks for the table. It's on me, and keep them coming."

"Thank you. What is your name?" Anna asked.

"Rachel Schlechty, and our young corporal here who is finding her voice is Elsa Baumann. I'm from Regensberg and she's from Breslau, although lately we're from a prison installation outside Berlin."

The bartender brought their drinks. Elsa sat back, listening to the conversation. She was basking in this moment. She'd asserted her authority over this Hilma, and the woman had backed down. She'd never had power over anything, over anybody. The feeling was not like anything she'd ever experienced before. The horrors of the day were receding under the influence of the beer, the letter, and her newfound authority.

"Excuse me," came a male voice.

Elsa looked up in surprise to see an SS sergeant standing over them. He had a glass of schnapps in his hand, and he was smiling at them. He was about her age, with short-cropped blond hair and a scar running down his right cheek. She realized it was the man she'd seen in Plac Zgody Square.

"And how is your evening going, ladies?" he asked. His voice was rich and lilting, dripping with confidence and a touch of humor.

"We're doing fine," said Anna, giving him a smile. "What's your name?"

"I'm Sergeant Klaus Zimmerman. And who are you?"

Anna gave the introductions, and he nodded to each of them. Elsa thought his eyes lingered on her for a moment, but she was sure she was just imagining things.

"May I join you?" he asked, putting his hand on an empty chair.

"Aren't you more interested in the Polish whores?" Rachel asked, glancing at the women milling around in the sea of uniforms behind them.

Klaus glanced behind him. "Certainly, many of my countrymen indulge for a bit of sport in the local flora and fauna, but I'm not interested in Polish skirt."

"Have a seat, then."

He took the chair and then threw back his glass, finishing the rest of his drink. "Ah, to be with German women again. It is an honor and a privilege."

"Where are you from?" asked Anna.

"Aachen," he said. "My family has been there for hundreds of years. Since the time of Charlemagne. Or so they claim."

"How long have you been in Krakow?"

"More than a year now. I was in the Waffen SS before. I was part of the group that invaded Poland in the first place. I fought in France too. But I was approached with the opportunity for a promotion and a transfer here, and I took it."

"So, you've seen combat?" asked Anna, leaning over the table.

Klaus pointed down at his uniform. There was an Iron Cross pinned to his tunic. "Yes indeed, and the medal to prove it. But truly, it wasn't as much as all that. War in thirty-nine and forty was more sport than death. The Poles, English, and French hardly fought us at all. They didn't like our tanks too much. But the Russians? That's been something else entirely. I wasn't sure at first that I made the right decision in switching over, but now I'm certain I did. Out of my company of a hundred and fifty men that left for the Eastern Front, there are only thirty left."

"But surely we are winning the war," said Anna.

"Who knows? We thought we would have victory by Christmas last year," he said. "We almost made it to Moscow, but then they stopped us cold. Or rather the winter did. But with luck, we'll finish them off this year. We shall see."

"What about the Americans?"

"What about them? They don't have an army. Or not much of one. By the time they get themselves ready for war, it should be too late."

"That's enough talk about war," said Anna. "Why talk about fighting, and ghettos and Jews, when there is dancing to be done?" She gave him a direct look.

"You're right," said Klaus. "It is time to dance." He turned to Elsa. "Shall we?"

She was caught completely off guard by this. She'd watched Anna's actions with a hint of dread. The woman was beautiful, and clearly interested in the young sergeant. But he'd turned to her instead.

"Well?"

She felt Rachel's fingers digging into her back. "Yes," Elsa managed to say. The sergeant stood and then reached his hand out, pulling her up. He kept his hand in hers and led her through the smoky throng to the dance floor. There was no one else out there right now, and when she saw this, Elsa pulled back.

Klaus turned. "What is it?"

She motioned toward the floor.

"Ah," he said, smiling at her. "But we don't wait for others, do we?" He took her hand again and led her into the middle of the little space. Facing her, he took her left hand in his and put his right arm behind her, drawing her close. He smelled of musk and leather, an intoxicating fragrance. His closeness made her dizzy. They swayed this way and that, in time with the music. Elsa felt the eyes of the crowd on them. The beer was going to her head—she'd never been able to hold her alcohol. The smoke, the smells, the music all swirled around in her mind as she moved around with him.

The song ended and she started to pull away, but he kept her there. "No, another." The violinist started up again, and they continued. He leaned even closer now, his lips near her ear. He reached a hand up and took a curl in his fingers. "Your hair is so dark, so dense. I love it."

Elsa didn't know what to say but she loved his touch, and she put her head on his shoulder, closing her eyes and relishing the rhythms of the music. He pressed her tighter still and she could feel his chest against hers, the rock-hard stomach. She was overwhelmed with the feeling of excitement within her. She felt more alive at this moment than she'd ever felt.

"Would you like to leave with me?" he whispered.

She felt a cold sting at those words. The past washed over her. Flashes of Erik, of their one night together, of his abandonment. But another part of her didn't care. It had been so long, she'd gone without any love, any touch. Without saying anything, she nodded. He took his hand and began leading her back through the crowd. They passed through and neared the front. Elsa glanced over and saw Rachel. She wasn't sure how her friend would react, but she was smiling at her, and gave her a wink, raising her glass in a silent salute.

They stepped out into the square. She thought that Klaus would take her to a hotel, but to her surprise, he led her out into the empty space itself, and they went this way, hand in hand, slowly through the darkness.

"It's so much nicer out here," he said, his fingers running over her palm. He looked up into the sky, the stars rippling and twinkling above them. "Will you walk with me for a bit?"

"Yes." He wasn't taking her to a room somewhere, she realized, at least not yet. They continued their stroll, walking closely to each other. He talked about his childhood, a private school education, and the house they'd lived in. They were on the edges of aristocracy, his father the grandson of a baron. But their family had fallen on hard times. The little company they'd owned had gone bankrupt during the depression. He'd been forced into public school. They'd had to sell their home. Moving to a humble flat near the cathedral, Klaus had left school early and joined the SS, to help support his family. Rising slowly in the ranks, he had been a source of pride and resources for his family ever since. His younger brother, inspired by Klaus, had joined the SS as well, and was serving with a unit on the Russian front.

"Do you worry about him?" Elsa asked.

"Certainly. I've encouraged him to transfer. It would be easy for me to arrange it through one of my superiors. But he's stubborn about it because I served in combat before transferring. He told me he will come here someday, but not yet, not until he has seen some action. I only hope he lives long enough to change his mind."

"Is it that bad in Russia?"

"Worse than you can imagine from everything I've heard. It's a whole different war. The Russians play for keeps. I would never say this to anyone in my unit, but I sometimes wonder if it will be worth the price, assuming we prevail."

"Is there any chance we won't win?"

"Anything is possible. If you've studied much history, you'll know that Russia has been the graveyard of many a western army. But I shouldn't talk of such things. We drove deep into the country this past year, and we'll go farther this summer. Perhaps it will all be over by this Christmas."

He stopped and turned her to him. Reaching his hand out to her chin, he pulled her close to him and kissed her. Elsa felt an electric ripple through her entire body. It had been so long. She put her arms around him and pulled him closer, kissing him passionately. They stood there for a long time, alone in the darkness of the square.

"Should we go somewhere?" she asked, surprised by her own words.

He pulled away, looking at her. "I would love to, Elsa, but I want to honor you too. We've been drinking tonight. For this evening, I'd love to escort you back to your apartment but then make my retreat. I want to see you again. Again and again, at that."

She couldn't believe his words. She didn't feel rejected—she was honored, cherished. She took his hand again and they kept walking, chatting and sharing. She told him about her own life, at least a little of it. She didn't explain about Erik, or her dishonor, or jail. That would be for another day. They strolled back through the old city and up the long road to the castle. Outside her building, they stood for a long time, holding each other.

As they departed and Elsa made her way up the stairs to her room, she knew today had been the best day of her life.

Chapter 20

Podgórze District

Krakow
Occupied Poland
June 1942

Irena, Aurelia, and Helena spent a sleepless night in a cramped holding cell at the Jewish Police headquarters. Irena had expected to be interrogated, if not worse, but after Spira had brought her in, he'd simply dropped her off in this cell with the other two. She had tried to talk to him on the way over to the building, but to no avail. He'd told her to be silent, and that was that. Overnight the three of them had sat, discussing the situation, feeling the helplessness pressing down on them. Now this morning, they continued the conversation.

"What are we going to do?" Aurelia asked.

"There's nothing we can do," said Helena. "This is exactly what I've been warning about all this time. I knew at some point they would turn against us, no matter how cautious we were. Now it's happened, and I fear it's the end of us."

"Hush now, Helena," said Irena, although she wasn't sure her friend was wrong. "Let's focus on what we can control."

"And what would that be? We've lost all power, Irena. Now all we have left is our fate."

"It could be worse. Think of Tadeusz. He's in some Gestapo jail. At least we're here, amongst our Jewish friends."

"Friends," said Helena, spitting on the floor. "Some friends. These OD members are as bad as the Nazis, if not worse."

"That's not true," said Irena. "Sure, some of them are corrupt, even Spira, but they are also caught in an impossible situation. Think of the demands that the Germans put on them, the requirements for deportation and arrest. Many of them have tried to soften the blow, to serve as a buffer between the Germans and the people."

"A buffer, all right," said Helena. "They protect their own families and sell out everyone else."

"And would we do different, if we were them?" asked Irena. "We have to have some grace."

"We'll see how much grace you have when they put us on one of those trains, headed to a furnace."

"Can't we just talk about something else?" said Aurelia. "I don't want to think about it. And Irena is right, we should be worrying about Tadeusz, not about ourselves. Isn't there some way we could find out what's happened to him?"

"Spira would be the only one who would know," said Irena. "And I don't know why he would tell us anything."

"I would tell you something, because the pharmacy is vital to the ghetto," said a voice. Irena jolted and looked up. Spira was standing there, staring at the three of them. She wasn't sure how long he'd been there.

"Do you know what's happened to Tadeusz?"

"I do. They took him to SS headquarters. But he's not been tortured. I've seen to that. They're questioning him, but nothing else has happened . . . so far."

"Why did they arrest him?" Irena asked.

"Because that fool Dolek was seen going into the pharmacy after hours, that's why. Do you think there haven't been eyes on your pharmacy all this time? The Germans have found it quite convenient to let your little operation go along in the ghetto, because they've been able to watch and listen. Not every customer of yours has been an innocent Jew. Oh no. There have been agents, even a German one or two. The Gestapo has had plans to arrest the lot of you for months now. But I've been standing in the way. I've talked them out of it several times. But this blatant action of letting the leader of the resistance come to visit—well, that was too much for them. Fortunately, I was able to get them to just take Tadeusz in, because I told them I would interrogate the three of you."

"But why do you care? Why would you help us, or Tadeusz?"

"Like I said, you are something vital to the ghetto. You provide medicine the Germans would never provide if left to their own designs. And your pharmacy is a haven. A place that Jews can go and feel safe, even for just a few minutes. And too, I've known for some time that Tadeusz was working with the resistance—that he was carrying messages now and again out to the Poles. He'd been very careful in the past, and that helped him too. But I couldn't help him this time."

"What's going to happen to him?"

"Who knows," said Spira, taking a bite of an apple he pulled out of a pocket. "I have a little influence with the Germans, but not much. I've been able to protect him from any physical harm so far, but I don't know how long that will last." He leaned in, looking at them. "You should be concerned about yourselves."

"What are you going to do to us?" Irena asked.

"I'm not going to do anything to you. I'm going to tell the Germans that I interrogated all of you thoroughly. That you knew nothing, that you weren't involved in anything that Tadeusz would have been involved in. In a few hours, I'm going to release you, and you're going to get that pharmacy up and running again."

"Without Tadeusz?"

"Without Tadeusz. At least for now. If there is a way I can secure his release, I will, but you must not hold out hope. If necessary, you will have to go on without him."

"How could we do that?" asked Aurelia. "He is the pharmacy."

"Things change. In the ghetto, more than anywhere else. You will have to adapt, as we all have. Even Poles have to bend to the winds of fate."

"Is that it, then?" asked Irena.

"Yes. At least for now. But you will owe me."

"What does that mean?"

"It means, my dear, that I just gave you all back your lives. So, if I need something from you in the future, whether it's medicine, zlotys, or a place to hide—I expect you to deliver."

"And if we refuse?" asked Helena.

Spira laughed. "You won't. But if you did, I would just send the Germans for you, and you can take your chances with them."

"We will help you if we can," said Irena, speaking for the rest of them. After all, what choice did they have?

"Your reputation as the smart one is well earned, Irena. Now, I can't let you go yet. But I will in a few hours. I'm afraid the pharmacy is going to have to be closed for today. But don't worry, my people are there, taking an inventory of things. And I'm collecting my first payment out of what's there. In the afternoon, you'll be released, and you can go about your business."

"What about Tadeusz?" asked Irena.

"What about him? Like I told you, if there's something I can do, I'll let you know, otherwise, I'm afraid your friend may be *kaput*."

With that, he left them.

"The bastard," said Helena. "We should have told him no."

"I'm surprised by your attitude," said Irena. "You're always arguing that we should save ourselves, and now you want to take on the Germans."

"I value my life as much as any of you. But we shouldn't have given in to him. We shouldn't do him any favors."

"For once, I have to agree with Helena," said Aurelia.

"To what end, though? If they cart us off to the Gestapo, what good have we done? Then Spira would take the remaining medicine and close us down. Either way he wins. But by giving a little, we preserve the pharmacy and can still help our Jewish friends. Not only that, but then there's a chance to save Tadeusz."

They continued on that way for some time, but finding no further insight, they lapsed into silence. At noontime they were given a little bread and water, and a couple hours later, a guard came to the cell, unlocked it, and ushered them back out onto the street. A few minutes later, they were back at the pharmacy. Spira's men were nowhere to be seen. Irena was relieved to observe that they had not made a mess of things. They must have been under strict orders. But a quick review of their inventory revealed that the men had made off with half of everything they had.

"What are we going to do now?" asked Aurelia. "We already were down to practically nothing."

"We will make do with what we have," said Irena. "For now, let's go home and get some rest. Tomorrow, we'll start anew."

"And Tadeusz?" Helena asked.

"There's nothing we can do," said Irena. "His fate is with Spira—for good or for evil."

Chapter 21

Wawel Castle

Krakow
Occupied Poland
June 1942

Elsa woke up feeling a little hungover. But despite her headache and the squeamish feeling in her stomach, she couldn't help but spring out of bed to face the day. Because today Elsa had a family again, she was a corporal with authority, and she had a man in her life for the first time in more than a year.

Rachel was still asleep, and she stepped into her friend's bedroom to nudge her awake. "It's half after six," she said. "We have to be downstairs at seven."

Rachel looked up at her, yawning before crinkling her nose. "You're bright-eyed today. That wouldn't have anything to do with the charming sergeant you left with last night, would it?"

"It might."

"I was frankly surprised to hear you stumbling in at midnight. I thought you might be coming home this morning."

"I wanted to go to a hotel with him," she admitted, a bit sheepishly. "But he said we'd been drinking too much, and he escorted me home instead."

"A gentleman, I see. Not really my style, but probably good for you."

"Rachel!"

"In any event, I'm happy for you, Elsa. I can't believe what's happened to you these past few days."

"Now it's your turn for some good fortune."

"I make my own luck. Although I wouldn't mind finding my own sergeant, or a lieutenant for that matter. A little rougher perhaps, but something in that category. I wonder if our Lieutenant Schueller has anything he'd like to share with me besides orders?"

"You're impossible. It's not allowed to fraternize between officers and enlisted."

"Like it's not allowed for a prisoner to sleep with a guard?"

Elsa laughed. "Well, you'd better be careful if you go that route, or they'll be shipping you back to Germany."

Rachel sat up in bed and shrugged. "We shall see. What are we doing today? I'm exhausted. Why can't we have the day off? It's a weekend, after all."

"There's more duty around these Blauscheins, I guess," said Elsa. She reached over and threw Rachel's tunic at her. "Now get dressed or we'll be late."

They had time to go down to the mess hall and grab a cup of coffee and some bread before they had to report to the courtyard. But they were running a few minutes late when they arrived outside. Lieutenant Schueller was there, and glanced at his watch when they appeared, a frown on his face. "Any time now, ladies," he said.

"Sorry about that," said Rachel. "I was running late. Don't blame the corporal." She flashed the lieutenant a smile. He stared at the two of them for a moment, and then continued.

"I was about to discuss our operations today. As you know, the last two days, we assigned new work permits to those workers that are young to early middle-aged, fit for work, and who already were working in what are considered essential jobs here in the ghetto. Today, we enter a new and more difficult aspect of our operation. There are approximately seven thousand members of the ghetto who are not eligible for a Blauschein. Today, we are going to ferret them out and deport them out of the ghetto. I want you to understand the details of this. We will be moving out children, parents, brothers and sisters of those remaining behind. Some may resist us; some will come willingly. Certainly, a number of people will try to hide, to avoid this process. You are going to see things today you've probably never witnessed. The men will be doing the job of searching homes. But you will be observing and reporting. And you'll have your clubs as a last resort, in the event anyone tries to run. We'll be using the Plac Zgody Square to concentrate groups of people. Once the square is full, they will be marched off to the trains. Your job will be to keep everyone concentrated in the square and maintain order there until the groups can be channeled out. Do you understand?"

They all nodded in agreement. Elsa felt alarmed about their orders today. It had been hard enough to watch these families when they weren't given the new work permits. Pulling them out of the ghetto and taking them away from their families was something else entirely. Her stomach was feeling worse. She wondered if she could report sick today and leave this to the others. But she knew that wouldn't do. She was in charge of this group of women. She was expected to set an example. She would have to steel herself for what was coming. And why shouldn't she? She was a proud German woman. She was serving her country in an organization that was elite in the Fatherland. She knew it would be difficult, but Rachel would be there with her. She could do this.

* * *

The scene in Plac Zgody Square was chaos. These weren't orderly lines of individuals waiting to learn their fate but rather groups of terrified individuals, knowing they were being deported to who knew what sort of end. There were masses of individuals tightly packed on the cobblestones. The sun was already up, and it was growing warmer by the minute. Elsa was assaulted by the smell of unwashed bodies and fear. Children were wailing, clinging to their parents. SS guards and Ukrainian auxiliaries walked among the Jews, shoving and kicking.

"This is so bad," she whispered to Rachel. "What are we supposed to do?"

"We do our duty. Now get everyone into position."

Elsa repeated yesterday's walk around the square, setting women into place to guard the outskirts. She had just finished when she heard a commotion down the street. She looked over and saw a man running away from the square. As she watched, an SS private raised his rifle and fired. The bullet struck the man in the middle of the back, and he stumbled forward, slamming hard into the ground. The body quivered and bucked for a few moments, and then was still.

"*Mein Gott*, he shot him," she said. Elsa turned to Rachel but even as she was about to say more, she heard another shot, then the staccato ripple of automatic fire.

Rachel stepped over to her, taking her by the arm. "Calm down now," she whispered. "Remember, people are watching."

"But what's going on?" Elsa asked.

"They're clearing the ghetto."

"Why are they shooting people?"

"We were told this duty would be unpleasant. These are Jews. There must be orders to be harsh with them. It's not our concern. We need to do what we're told."

"But I can't. I can't just sit here and let this happen."

"Yes, you can, Elsa. Remember your promotion—and your parents' letter. Remember what happens to you if you fail in this duty: you'll go back to prison, or worse. This will all be over in a few hours. Look, over there, why don't you go into that pharmacy? I'll stay here and keep an eye on things. Just go in and make sure they aren't hiding any Jews in there that are subject to this deportation. Check everyone's paperwork. And take your time about it."

"No, I should stay here."

"Go. It will be okay. I'll take care of things out here."

Elsa took a deep breath and then hurried away toward the pharmacy. She was embarrassed about her reaction, and wanted to turn back, but at the same time she was relieved by the chance to get away, at least for a little while. And this was an important task too, wasn't it? What if they *were* hiding Jews away inside the pharmacy? She reached the door and pulled it open, stepping inside. She was met with startled stares. Three women stood behind the counter. In the lobby, there were about a dozen people. Two were in line, but the rest were standing or sitting against the walls.

"Can I help you?" one of the women asked her in German. She stepped over and opened a little gate, letting herself out into the customer space.

"Who are you?" Elsa asked.

"I'm Irena Drozdzikowska."

"Is this your pharmacy?"

She shook her head. "The pharmacy is owned by Tadeusz Pankiewicz."

"And where is this Pankiewicz?"

"He's . . . not here today."

"Show me your papers," she said, trying to sound as stern as possible.

The woman reached inside her coat and pulled out a document, handing it to Elsa. She inspected the paper. It was an official German document giving her permission to work at the pharmacy inside the ghetto.

"You're a Pole?"

"Yes, my entire staff is—save one. We have a Jewish assistant, but she's not here today."

"And who are these people?" Elsa asked. As she spoke, she heard another gunshot and a scream outside. She flinched but tried to quickly recover.

"These are our customers. They are all here on official business."

"I'll have to check their papers as well, Irena. There are people in hiding."

"Of course you can," said the pharmacist, but she thought she saw a look of doubt crease her face for just a moment.

Elsa started with the people in line. Both of them had the little blue Blauschein sticker. She then turned to the people standing or sitting against the wall. The first person, a man, had the sticker as well, but the last seven did not. One of them, a man in his sixties, looked like he might try to run, but Elsa raised her club and stepped toward the door, blocking his way.

"Everyone without a Blauschein must come with me," she ordered.

"Please," said Irena. "Please, couldn't you look the other way?" she asked. "These aren't numbers. These are people. They aren't causing any problems. They aren't criminals. They just want the right to stay behind here in the ghetto."

"What would the point be?" she asked. She knew she shouldn't even respond to this Pole, but she couldn't force herself to be quiet. "Even if I walk away, they'll be caught by others. And if not today, then tomorrow. They don't have the Blauschein."

"Yes, maybe so. But an hour of life is still life. Please, leave them here. If they must be taken, let it be someone else's responsibility."

She realized it was her demeanor and her hesitation that let this Irena talk to her so. She should give her a beating with the club, and drag these others out. But she couldn't bring herself to do so. She stared at her for a moment, then turned to leave, feeling a coward and a fool.

Before she reached the door, however, it opened. She was shocked to find Klaus there, pistol in hand. His eyes widened when he saw her. "Elsa, what a wonderful surprise. I was just coming in to ferret out any Jews that might be hiding here. But you've already been here before me. Have you checked these people?"

She nodded.

"Do they all have Blauscheins?"

A burst of machine-gun fire erupted near the door. Elsa heard screaming and shouts in German. Klaus turned and grabbed the door. "You take care of things in here! Bring anyone out who doesn't have a permit!" He sprinted out the door, leaving her alone.

She turned back to them. She steeled herself to take them out. But she just couldn't do it. Taking a final look at the pharmacist, who gave her a grave smile, she turned and rushed out of the building, heading back toward the square. She was shocked by what greeted her. There were bodies everywhere, at least a dozen. Soldiers were rushing this way and that, chasing men and women who were rushing away, trying to escape. Klaus was nowhere to be seen. Elsa stared, dazed, shocked by what she was seeing. She looked around and found Rachel walking toward her through a hazy cloud of gunsmoke.

"What happened?" Elsa managed to ask.

"A few men in the middle here stormed the guards. They managed to knock two men down and steal their weapons. Other SS came up to stop them, but they rushed out, firing and trying to escape. A couple of them made it. The rest are there," she finished, pointing in the direction of the bodies.

"Is everyone okay from our unit?"

Rachel nodded. "They weren't involved. And look who's coming up now."

Elsa turned to her right and saw Klaus marching toward them, a grin on his face. "That was good sport," he said. "I almost missed the whole thing, checking on my girl. Did you bring those Jews out, Elsa?"

She was about to answer when she saw the door of the pharmacy open. An SS private was coming out of the store, the seven Jews without Blauscheins marching in front of him, arms in the air.

"Ah yes, you handled it. Wonderful job, Elsa. Tonight, we have to celebrate. Eight o'clock, at the same bar."

"We'll be there," said Rachel. "And bring a friend this time. An accommodating one."

Klaus laughed. "No problem. You had a couple of admirers last night, although you may not have known it."

"I noticed."

"It's a date, then. But I've got to go for now." He winked at Elsa and then turned, running back down a side street.

"He's lively, that one," said Rachel.

"I don't think I can go tonight," said Elsa. "I'm going to be sick."

"No surprise with what you're observing out here. It's not my first time seeing a dead body, or a wounded one calling out in pain for that matter. But for you, I'm sure this is a shock. You're doing wonderfully. Just hang in there. This will all be over soon."

But it wasn't over quickly. The day dragged on, far worse than the last. There were no more wholesale murders in front of them, but the families kept coming, one after another, to be carted off to who knew where by the Germans, then the square filled up again. Elsa watched it with eyes glazed over, becoming numb to the pain, the fear. She just wanted to slink off and drown her agony with liquor.

Finally, it was over. The operations were continuing in the ghetto, but their shift was up. They returned home, bathed to wash the sweat, dirt, and blood off their bodies, changed into fresh uniforms, and headed out to the bar. When they arrived,

Elsa ordered an entire bottle of schnapps. She took the cap off as they settled into their table, and took a deep drink directly, gulping at the fiery liquid until she choked.

"Easy there," said Rachel. "A little at a time." She handed Rachel some glasses, and Elsa poured out generous portions to both of them. But she didn't slow down. She drank a full glass, then another, until the alcohol dulled the pain.

Klaus arrived a half hour later with a companion. They took a seat at the table and Klaus filled all their glasses with a second bottle of schnapps he'd procured. Elsa helped herself to some more. Her head was spinning now.

"Let's get out of here," she said to Klaus.

"You're drunk," he said.

"Take me out of here now."

Klaus looked to Rachel, but her friend nodded in agreement. Klaus left her friend and his companion behind, helping Elsa to her feet. They stumbled out with his arms supporting her. When they were outside, she turned and grabbed the back of his head, kissing him deeply, violently. "Get us a room," she ordered.

"I told you—"

"I'm not asking."

He smiled at her. "All right, then." He led her half a block down within the square until they came to the backside of a little hotel. He sat her down at an outside table and then went within and purchased a room for the evening. They went upstairs and when the door was closed, she tore his clothes off with angry movements, and they made violent love on top of the covers. She clung to him, seeking escape from the horrors of the day, the dead, the desperate and the crying. When they were finished, they got under the covers, smoking a cigarette together, her head on his chest.

"It's not so easy, what we do," he said, his voice gentle, understanding.

"Those Jews. Where are they going?" she asked.

"You don't want to know."

She tensed at the words, but she had to know—had to find out what became of those seven Jews she'd half-heartedly tried to save. "Please, tell me. What will happen to them?"

"They are going to Bełżec," he said. "It's a camp."

"Is there work there?"

"For some, for a while."

"What do you mean?"

"Are you sure you want to know?"

"Yes."

"Nobody works there forever. Eventually, everyone is sent into a building for sanitation and inhalation. But it's not disinfectant that comes out. It's gas. Carbon monoxide. It's humane. I've heard it only lasts a few minutes."

"You mean they're murdered? All of them?"

"Yes. I'm sorry. But you wanted to know. It's a difficult thing, Elsa, but we've been tasked with ridding Europe of the Jews. Our grandchildren will celebrate us for it. But it's not easy. Even for me. And I've been at it for a while."

She lay there after that, eyes closed, crying a little. Those seven Jews were going to die. All of the seven thousand removed from the ghetto were going to die. She'd been here. She'd been responsible. The alcohol fought down her emotions. She was safe here, safe in his arms, away from the terror and the guilt, at least for this night. But a little part of her knew that she'd crossed a boundary today. Whether by choice or not, she had marched today into hell, and she could never go back.

Chapter 22

Podgórze District

Krakow
Occupied Poland
June 1942

Natalia rose before dawn and prepared for another day of searching. She'd spent the day before walking the streets of the ghetto, looking for her brother and her mother. She had been so sure she would find them, that someone would have seen them, but her efforts were in vain. Shocking, too, had been the pharmacy closure. She'd gone first thing to her work, hoping they would have some news, but it was locked up. When she'd gone inside, she'd found Jewish Policemen combing over the supplies and moving from room to room. She had backed out without drawing attention to herself. What had happened to her friends? She had decided she would have to worry about that later. Natalia had continued searching, risking everything to be out here in the open without the new permit. She'd thought of going back to the Judenrat and pulling Mr. Badowski out, so she could at least secure her own documents, but she couldn't expect him to take two trips for her, so she considered it prudent to find her family first.

And now it was another day. She hoped she would find answers out there, would locate her family and discover what was going on in the pharmacy. But before she could leave her apartment, she heard the sharp crack of a rifle, then another and another. The guttural bark of German commands echoed through her window. Looking out into the street, she saw SS everywhere, running together in teams. It was an *Aktion*. The Germans were cleansing the ghetto and Natalia was sure they would be after everyone who had not been granted a Blauschein. She had thought she would have more time, that there would be more days with tables and stamps. But apparently the Germans had issued as many permits as they intended, and it was already too late.

What was she to do? She didn't have a Blauschein. Was it too late now, even for herself? She decided she had to see Mr. Badowski. There was no point in searching for her family if she was deported herself. She would have to hope and pray that they would be safe, at least for a little while, and she could find them and secure permits before they were taken.

Natalia stepped out of her apartment into a fiery maelstrom. There were bodies lying in the street just outside her door. People were running this way and that. She heard shots, the vicious barking of German dogs, and the heavy clomp of booted feet rushing down the road. Hoping to escape notice, she adopted a casual pace and strode toward the Judenrat. She hoped that any German who saw her would assume she must have a Blauschein, for what sane person would stroll down the pavement during this *Aktion* without one?

Her theory worked. She was passed several times by groups of Germans. They ignored her, instead rushing down the street after more desperate prey. Irena made it to the Judenrat and pushed her way through the panicked throng. She rushed up the stairs before anyone could stop her and found Mr. Badowski's door open, and Sylwia with him.

"Natalia, you're safe!" her friend exclaimed, rushing into her arms. "We thought you were deported, or worse."

"No, I'm all right. But I haven't been able to find my family. I need that Blauschein, and I hope it's not too late."

"It's not too late for any of you," Sylwia's father said. "I managed to secure permits and Blauscheins for all of you, even without having them present."

"How did you manage that?"

He winked at her. "I'm not without a certain influence around here, even among the Germans." He handed the documents to her. "Those cost me a pretty penny," he said.

"I'll never be able to repay you," she said.

"Yes, your tab just keeps growing," he joked. "But go now. Go find your family and get them their papers."

"Thank you again," said Natalia, moving around his desk and giving him a kiss on the cheek.

"Stop it," Badowski said in mock distress. "You'll embarrass me."

"Do you want me to go with you?" asked Sylwia.

"Absolutely not. It's murder out there. You stay here, safe with your father."

Mr. Badowski nodded. "I agree. There is no sense in endangering both of you."

Natalia hurried out of the building and back onto the street. She now had their precious permits, but what was she to do with them? She still had no idea where her family might be. She decided to check back at her apartment. She arrived a few minutes after but it was as empty as it had been that morning. Where now? she wondered. She decided she would check the pharmacy again. She hoped it would be open, and she could find out if they'd heard anything, and also what had happened to them the day before.

She started out toward the pharmacy, thankful it was less

than two blocks away. The air was thick with smoke. Bodies lay on the street, blood pooling around angry wounds. She turned her head away from a boy, no more than eight, with a gunshot to the head. She made it the first block and turned to her right, heading toward the square.

"*Halt!*" a voice shouted. She turned to see an SS soldier rushing up to her, rifle in hand. He raised it, taking aim.

"I have a Blauschein!" she yelled, reaching into her coat. The man didn't seem to hear her, to understand. She crouched and an explosive roar tore at her ears. Looking up, she saw the soldier working the bolt of his rifle. She fumbled with her fingers, finding her permit. She ripped it out and flashed it at the soldier. "Blauschein!"

He glared at the document, raising his rifle again. She closed her eyes, waiting for the bullet that would take her life. She heard a growl of anger. Opening her eyes, Natalia watched the soldier rush forward and slam the butt of his rifle against her shoulder. She felt a fiery pain and she fell back, crashing hard against the pavement. The soldier stood over her, a demonic mask of anger scowling down at her. He spit on her face, kicked her in the stomach, and ran out of view.

Natalia lay there for some time, unable to move. But she knew she had to get up. To stay here was certain death. Taking a few deep breaths and battling down the pain in her shoulder, she pulled herself to her feet and started back toward Plac Zgody. She made it a few minutes later. The space was full of families, sitting packed together in the already baking sun. The area was surrounded by SS, some of them women. Natalia made her way around, skirting the edges of the square, keeping her even pace, eyes forward, as if she was strolling through the park.

She made it to the pharmacy. Tearing the door open, she stumbled in and collapsed on the floor. She heard a gasp and then hands on her. "Natalia!" It was Irena's voice. She looked up to find her friend there, crouching over her. "What's happened to you?"

"The Germans nearly killed me. A soldier fired at me and then he hit me on the shoulder with his rifle."

"Are you all right?"

"I think so. I just need to catch my breath. I need to lie down for a little while."

"Aurelia, Helena, help me!" ordered Irena. Natalia heard footsteps and the other women were there, helping her gently to her feet. Surrounding her, they led her behind the counter and up the stairs into Tadeusz's makeshift bedroom. Irena placed her on the bed, and then sent the other women back to the front.

"You'll be all right here, for a little while at least. But I don't know if you should stay. We've already had SS in here today. They took a group of people away who didn't have Blauscheins. They didn't search the back, but that might not be true next time."

"I have my permit now. Mr. Badowski obtained it for me."

"That's wonderful. Then you can just stay here and rest."

"What happened to you?" Natalia asked. "Where were you all yesterday?"

Irena's face darkened. "We were arrested, all of us. By Spira. We spent the night in jail, and most of yesterday."

"What did they want? Did they torture you?"

Irena shook her head. "Spira said it was for our own protection. But that's not the worst news. The Gestapo arrested Tadeusz. We haven't seen or heard from him since."

"Oh no. What are you going to do?"

"What can we do? We have to keep going here and do what we can."

"You should leave the ghetto, Irena. Helena has been right all along. If you all stay, they'll kill you at some point. This isn't a haven for the Jews. It's not even a jail. This is a tomb."

"We can't leave. I can't. I have to see this through. Now I must get back to work. I want you to stay here and get some rest. Stay for the rest of the day. At the end of the shift, we can talk more about what's happened and about the future."

"I can't stay. I have to find my mother and brother. Mr. Badowski obtained Blauscheins for them as well. If I don't find them, they will be taken away. I looked for them all day yesterday, but I haven't seen them since they disappeared from here."

"Do you want me to help you search for them?"

"I can't ask that of you, Irena. Tadeusz's arrest proves you are hardly safer here in the ghetto than we are—particularly at this moment. Besides, you need to stay here and take care of our customers. With the *Aktion* going on, there will be many people coming in for medicine and bandages. You're needed here."

"Well, be very careful out there," said Irena, taking Natalia's hand. "That German you just ran into proves that even the Blauschein is no guarantee of safety."

"I will. But I have to go, I have to find them."

"I understand." Irena squeezed her hands and then rose. "Can I get you anything?"

"Thank you, but no. I'll only be here a little while. I need to catch my breath, and then I'll be gone."

"Farewell, my friend. And hurry back."

Irena departed and Natalia lay back with her eyes closed, calming herself down. She found herself drifting off to sleep, but she fought the sensation, rising again after only a few minutes. As much as she would have liked to stay here, in the protection of these walls, she had no more time to risk. She stood up, a little unsteadily, and shuffled toward the door. Stepping out to the counter area, she stopped to watch her friends for a moment. They were all helping customers, and there were another dozen people in line. She observed how caring the three of them were, the gentle words, a kind gesture. She loved these

women, loved what they were doing, what they were sacrific-
ing. She owed them so much more than her life. As she owed
Tadeusz. Taking another breath, she walked around the counter
and then moved to the door, not looking back. She feared if she
hesitated, if she looked back for support from Irena, her courage might falter and she might never leave.

Back out in the square, she watched the chaos as Germans
led groups of Jewish families into the cobblestone space, forcing them down, shouting at them, sometimes beating them. She
turned and moved quickly away, her head down, pace steady.
She made it away and turned left on Targowa Street and then
right on Jozefinska. She thought she should try the Jewish hospital on Jozefinska and Wegierska. She stepped into the lobby
and froze. There were bodies on the floor and blood everywhere. The Germans had come here and apparently decided
that the patients were too burdensome to deport. So they had
just shot them out of hand. Stepping back in terror, she pushed
the doors open and fled back onto the street, her heart racing,
her body shaking. Natalia stood there for a few seconds on the
pavement, trying to collect herself, wondering where she should
go next.

She decided she should try the apartment again. She knew it
was unlikely they would return there after all this time, but she
had to do something, and she didn't know where else to look.
She cut down to Limanowskiego Street and turned left, heading
past the Optima factory toward the Jewish Police station and
ghetto prison where Irena had been kept the day before.

As she walked, she heard the sound of footsteps coming
rapidly up behind her. She increased her pace, trying to get
away, already reaching for her papers, hoping she would have
time to show them before she took a bullet in the brain. A hand
grabbed her right arm, pulling her to a stop. "I have a Blauschein!" she shouted.

"Quiet!" a man's voice ordered. "Come with me."

She ventured a look at the person who was holding her. It was a man she recognized: Dolek, the head of the resistance.

"What do you want from me?" she asked.

"Shut your mouth," he ordered, looking around. "Come with me immediately."

She tried to pull away, but it was impossible. He was far too strong. She turned and walked with him, his hand a vise, never losing its grip. She felt a sharp pain in her shoulder, where the rifle had struck her earlier. "You're hurting me," she whispered.

He looked at her, still moving. He loosened his hold but kept his hand on her. Leading her forward, he stepped up to an apartment building and opened the front door. They shuffled inside and he turned to the right, leading her down a long hallway with doors on both sides. He stopped near the end and stepped up to an apartment door. Looking both ways again, he knocked three times quickly, and then a few seconds later, two times. There were footsteps at the door, and then it was opened. A face stared at them through the crack. It was a man she'd never seen before. Dolek leaned forward and whispered something, and the door was opened. Natalia was led inside. Sitting on a sofa were her mother and brother.

Her brother rose and rushed into her arms. Her mother smiled, recognizing her, although her stare was vacant. "You made it," Stefan said. "I thought you were dead."

"Where have you been?" Natalia asked. "I've been looking for you for days."

"We were in hiding. First at a friend's flat, then here. Dolek tried to find you at the pharmacy yesterday, but it was closed. So he went out in search of you today."

"Yes, the pharmacy was closed yesterday. Dolek, Tadeusz has been arrested by the Gestapo. Irena and the others were detained by the Jewish Police, but they were released after an overnight stay in the prison, and they were able to reopen the pharmacy today."

"Tadeusz was arrested?" Dolek said. His face paled. "I wonder if I had something to do with it?"

"What do you mean?"

Dolek told her about his visit, about the request to Tadeusz.

"I don't know. But the Germans are always watching us. We have black market items we distribute to the poor—food and medicine. Any one of our customers could be informing on us. It's impossible to know what happened. Is there anything you can do for him?"

"We can make some inquiries. I'll get to work on that right now." He turned to Stefan. "I'll leave you to it," he said.

Stefan nodded. "Thank you again for hiding us."

"You're welcome. You've done us great service over the past few months, and that must be repaid in kind. Farewell," Dolek said, taking Stefan's hand. The leader nodded again to Natalia, then he and the other resistance member left the apartment.

"You've been working with the ŻOB?" asked Natalia. ŻOB was the Żydowska Organizacja Bojowa: the Jewish Combat Organization in Poland.

"Yes."

"What were you thinking? You could have been killed!"

Stefan laughed, cocking his ear to pick up the sounds of gunshots in the distance. "And you are safe?"

"There are always risks, but we have our contacts and Mr. Badowski."

"Badowski is a criminal. A traitor. They all are."

"How can you say that? He's done so much for us. And look," she said, retrieving the Blauscheins from her coat. "He's done yet more. I've obtained Blauscheins for you and Mama. We are saved."

Stefan scoffed. "You think those will save you? They might

delay things for a season. But the Germans are here to extermi-
nate all of us. The only way to deal with them is to resist."

"You're fourteen, Stefan. You're a boy. I got you a work
permit, and a job at the Schindler factory. You'll be safe now. I
forbid you to continue."

"Forbid me?" he laughed. "You're not my mother. And you
can't tell me what to do."

"Mama, tell him," urged Natalia, but Aleksandra kept looking past her, eyes glazed, lost in whatever world she'd been living in since Jakub was taken from them.

"She's not going to tell me anything," said Stefan. "We are
on our own."

"Well, we can sort out your resistance work later. For now,
let's get back to our apartment. We'll wait for the dust to settle
on this *Aktion* and then you can report to work."

"I'm not going to use that Blauschein. None of us are."

"What are you talking about?"

"I told you. Those permits are a death sentence. Now or
later. I've arranged a much better path for us."

"What do you mean?"

"I'm getting us out by the sewers."

"Out? By the sewers? Are you crazy?"

"I'm not. I've used them many times already. I come in and
out of the ghetto, bringing in food and weapons. I've made
arrangements through Dolek for a Polish family in the countryside to take us in. We're leaving tonight after dark."

"What are you talking about? We have no papers that would
identify us as Polish. Stefan, it's not safe in the countryside.
Jews are fleeing *into* the district. They've been coming *into* the
ghetto to try to save themselves."

"Sure, there might be some instances, but those people are
fools."

"Be that as it may, your plan assumes we could even make it.
Mama can't go through the sewers, and neither can I. I won't.

I've already solved our problems. We have everything we need. You need to take this permit and help me get Mama home."

"You're not listening to me. Mama can make it. She shimmied out of a second-story window with me to escape that pharmacy. She can make it through the sewers. You have to listen to me, Natalia. We need to get out before the Nazis liquidate this ghetto and send everyone to the death camps."

"The death camps are only rumors."

"No, they are not. We've had people come back from Bełżec and a new camp just west of here, at Auschwitz. They are gassing people, Natalia, whole trainloads. The idea of essential workers is a myth. They intend to kill all the Jews. The sooner you realize that the better."

Natalia shook her head. "That would be madness. They are committing terrible atrocities, I agree. But they aren't fools. And there will always be an elite that is protected. That's always been how it goes. We have the connections we need to weather the storm. I can't drag Mother through the sewers. She'd never make it. And if she did, what would we do in the country? Look at her, Stefan! She needs to stay here. Here I can protect her, I can watch her. She has a permit, she has protection. Out there, she'd be spotted. The Jew catchers would turn her in. And then she will be killed. Her only chance is in here."

"I'm not staying. And I'm taking her with me. Even if you refuse to go," said Stefan.

"No, you're not. You'll never get her through the sewers without my help, and I won't help her. Don't make me go to Badowski."

He stared at her, his anger rising. "You would betray me to the Judenrat? Your own family?"

"I'm not going to let you lead our mother to her death. If you don't want the Blauschein, fine, but I'm not going with you, and neither is she."

Stefan stared at her for long seconds. "Fine," he said. "Take your chances in the ghetto. But if she is deported, her life is on you. Now get out of here."

"Here," said Natalia, reaching out with the Blauschein. "Take this, just in case."

He shook his head. "I don't want it, and I don't need it."

"But if you're caught?"

He laughed. "They haven't caught me yet."

"What will you do?" she asked.

"I don't know. I'm more use here than in the country. I was only going to take Mama—and you, of course. But if you are insistent on staying here, I may stick around, and fight the Germans."

She stepped over and took his hands. "Be careful, Stefan. This isn't a schoolyard game. The Nazis play for keeps. If they catch you, they will kill you."

"You take care of yourself, too, big sister. Don't rely on Badowski too much. He's not who you think he is. And besides, any semblance of authority and stability in the ghetto is an illusion. It's all going to collapse on top of you."

"We shall see. Will you come back to the apartment? I won't stop you from coming and going."

He shook his head. "It's too dangerous there. I've got my hiding places."

She put her arms around him. "Be safe," she said, kissing his cheek.

"Go with God, sister. I hope you're right about Mama. If something happens to her and she missed this chance, I won't forgive you."

Natalia turned to her mother. "Let's go." Aleksandra still sat there, staring ahead. She moved over to her mother and pulled her to her feet. Leading her out of the apartment, they arrived back out on the street. It was starting to get dark now. The screams and gunshots were dying down. She couldn't see any

Germans in sight. She hoped the *Aktion* was over, and they would be able to get on with life.

Natalia led her mother down the street toward their own flat. They had to weave past the occasional body. She feared Aleksandra might scream at the horrors around them, thus attracting unwanted attention, but she was as stone-faced and unemotional as ever. "It's all right, Mama," she reassured her. "We're almost home now. Everything is going to be all right."

"Stop right there, Jews!" a voice screamed at them. Natalia looked up to see a German soldier rushing up to them. "You're late for the platform!" he screamed. "The trains are waiting for you!"

"But sir," Natalia said, "we have Blauscheins. We are essential workers." She reached the papers out to him.

"Quiet, you whore!" the soldier screamed. He knocked the papers out of her hands. "Get moving."

"But—"

The soldier shoved Natalia hard with the barrel of his gun. Stunned, she started marching, dragging her mother along. She wanted to protest, to say something to the man, but she'd shown him their precious permits, and he'd ignored them. Worse, he'd swatted them into the gutter, and she had nothing more to show anyone.

They reached Plac Zgody Square. Even in the falling light, Natalia could see it was packed with families, waiting to be marched out of the ghetto. The SS were there too, of course, along with Ukrainian auxiliaries. The soldier behind Natalia jammed his rifle into her back again. "Get going!" he ordered.

She took her mother's hand and stepped onto the cobblestones, finding a seat for the two of them on the edge of the square. At least it was near evening. The day had been blistering hot and she was sure those forced to wait here for hours in the afternoon had suffered terribly from the heat and from thirst.

"Mama, are you all right?" she asked. Her mother nodded, without looking up. "Do you need anything?" She wasn't sure there was anything she could give her mother, but the words had come automatically.

"Natalia!" She heard the voice and couldn't believe it. She looked up. Tadeusz was there, seated a dozen yards away.

"Tadeusz," she said, rising and moving to join him. "What are you doing here?"

"The Gestapo brought me. A half hour ago."

"But you're a Pole."

"They told me since I want to live with the Jews, I can die with them."

"I don't understand. Isn't there anything anyone can do? The pharmacy is right there."

"And a dozen SS between us and them. Even if I could reach it, what could they do for me? I would endanger all of their lives. What are you doing here?"

Natalia told her what had happened.

"Your brother wanted to take you out by the sewers. Perhaps he was right."

Natalia shook her head. "My mother would never have made it. I don't know if I could have made it. The idea of going down into the darkness, with everyone's waste—and Germans lurking everywhere, ready to pounce. I don't think I could do it."

"You could, Natalia. You're braver than you know. But I guess that doesn't matter anymore."

"Then you believe the rumors?"

He nodded. "They more or less confirmed them at the SS prison. These deportations are a one-way ticket."

"I suppose there's nothing we can do, then?"

"I don't think there is."

He took her hand and led her back over to her mother, taking a seat beside Aleksandra. "Good evening, Mrs. Wajcblum." Her mother gave him a wan smile, then turned away.

Natalia took a seat next to them. She'd barely sat down when a group of Germans stepped up and commanded all of them to rise. There were screams from the crowd as the SS moved in, clubs and weapons at the ready, shouting and prodding. Natalia and Tadeusz helped her mother to her feet, and they started moving along, heading west toward the far gate of the ghetto. The column moved slowly despite the constant attention from the Germans. Natalia wondered where they were going but guessed they would be taken to a rail platform and put on to trains. She'd heard rumors about that too—cattle cars stuffed with so many people that there wasn't room to sit down, barely room to breathe. She was claustrophobic at the best of times, and she felt the panic rising in her at the prospect of hours, perhaps days, in a confined, dark space.

It seemed like it took an hour or more to reach the other end of the ghetto, although she couldn't be sure in the surreal, terrified atmosphere. They were almost at the gate when her attention was diverted. To her right, Mr. Badowski and Symche Spira were standing, scanning the crowd. She called out to them and the Judenrat member caught her eye, then turned to tug violently on Spira's coat. She saw Spira step over to an SS officer who was supervising the traffic through the gate. Spira spoke to the man, then handed him some documents. The officer looked them over and then peered into the crowd toward Natalia. He stepped over with Spira and the two of them walked into the mob, directly up to her.

"What are you doing?" the officer asked. "Get your ass out of the line!" He was speaking to Tadeusz.

"These two aren't supposed to be here either," he said.

"Shut your mouth!" the officer screamed, slapping Tadeusz across the face. "Out now! *Raus! Schnell!*"

Tadeusz looked at Natalia.

"Go," she said. "Just go."

The officer grabbed Tadeusz and jerked him out of the line, shoving him toward Spira. As Natalia watched, Tadeusz hur-

ried over to Spira and Badowski, turning and pointing franti-
cally toward the line. The officer started arguing with them,
pointing at the paperwork. Finally, he turned and marched back,
pointing at Natalia. "You! Get out of the line and bring your
bitch mother with you!"

Natalia dragged her mother out of the slow-moving mass and
hobbled over to Spira and Badowski, the officer close in tow.
"Are these the two you're looking for?" he asked.

"*Ja*," said Spira. "They are essential workers. They have
Blauscheins."

"Let's see them," said the officer.

"A soldier knocked them out of my hand," said Natalia. "We
don't have our permits."

"Lieutenant Schueller," said Badowski, "I can vouch for
these people. I secured the Blauscheins for both of them."

"And where are they supposed to work?" asked the lieutenant.

"Natalia works with me," said Tadeusz. "She has for more
than a year."

"And the mother?"

"At Madritsch's," said Badowski. "She's just starting."

Natalia couldn't believe their fortune. They'd been saved by
Badowski again. And this time with Spira's help. They weren't
going to go off with this mass to their deaths. She felt a vague
tinge of guilt—that they would survive while these others perished. But what could she do about it?

"Well, let's not tarry out here," said Badowski. "I know the
lieutenant is very busy. Let's get inside the Judenrat and we can
have some tea and take a little rest before you all get back to
work."

"Too old," said Schueller.

"What?" asked Badowski.

"The mother bitch is too old for a Blauschein." He reached
into his holster, drew his pistol, and shot Aleksandra in the

forehead. Natalia watched the whole thing in slow motion, unable to move, unable to speak. Her mother's head snapped back, and her body crumpled to the ground. She hit the pavement, eyes wide open, a neat hole in the middle of her forehead. A pool of blood formed behind her head, growing by the moment. Her mother was gone. All of her influence had been for nothing. The Blauscheins were for nothing. Her brother had been right. She'd gambled her mother's life on these documents, and they'd failed. Her mother was dead, and it was all her fault.

Chapter 23

Podgórze District

Krakow
Occupied Poland
Under the Eagle Pharmacy
March 1943

Irena stood at the counter, her hands shaking as she read the note in the little girl's hands. She wasn't more than ten years old and had escaped the mass deportations of the summer and fall by hiding. Now she was here, as so many were, because of the rumors swirling around the ghetto. She was here, on her parents' behalf, requesting not medicines for healing or sickness, but for death. The crumpled paper she'd handed to Irena was asking for cyanide pills.

She excused herself and went into the back. She found the container she was looking for and loaded a brown paper bag with three pills, one for the child and one each for her parents. They had been smuggling in these tablets for the past few months. They were now their most popular commodity. The truth of it was they had very little else to give. The black market had dried up for most products—at any price. As the war wobbled endlessly on, and the Germans drained the Polish economy for food, medicine, lumber, and labor, there was almost nothing left to secure.

As such, the pharmacy had taken on a new character since last June. It had become a meeting place for families, for the resistance, for the Jewish Police, for informants, the SS, and Gestapo agents—at times all together, warily circling each other for information, rumors, even a strange socialization. It was as if with the death of the ghetto imminent, all the actors had become bonded, associated, sharing a mutual experience with each other.

Rumors were rampant that the end was near. For weeks now, Irena had heard talk that the final *Aktion* would occur to clear out the ghetto. All of the remaining population of Jews would be relocated to the new camp at Plaszow that had sprung up the past fall—relocated or perhaps liquidated before they even made it there. Nobody knew what the purpose of this camp was, or why the Germans wanted to close the ghetto. All they knew was that the information filtering through double agents, resistance contacts, and even half-mentioned comments by Germans right there in the pharmacy indicated that the Jewish District was coming to an end.

Irena stepped to the back for a few moments, the tears running down her cheeks. How could things be coming to this? They had battled for two years to defy the Germans, to take care of the people here. Now the Germans were going to take them all away? Murder them, grind them up in their camps? And all they had left to support their friends, this remnant of the population still here, was poison pills.

"Irena, what's wrong?" asked Tadeusz, noticing her as he came out of the kitchen.

"I can't do it anymore," she said, her voice trembling. "I

can't issue cyanide pills to that little girl out front without imagining her and her parents taking them, gasping for breath, and dying in some lonely apartment—all by my hand. It's against everything we were taught, all of our oaths."

"You're right," he said. "It's not difficult, it's impossible. But we are in impossible times. Think about the alternative. Would you want that little girl shoved into a cattle car? Standing in the darkness, in the freezing cold for days while her train slowly rattled along. Only to be ripped out and sent to a gas chamber? This is the only thing we have left to give them. We can spare them suffering. The Nazis have taken everything else away. We must be brave, Irena. For them."

She nodded. "I know you're right. But I—"

"Don't worry," he said, taking the little brown bag. "I'll take care of this right now. You go to the back and pour yourself some coffee. Close your eyes, take a break. Think about whether you want to be here for the next few days. I've been thinking about this very issue. If the last *Aktion* is coming, I have wondered if you and the other girls should just stay home. I can keep shop until those beasts are done with their work."

"Tadeusz, I can't let you do that, and I know everyone will feel the same way. We've traveled this long road together. All of us. And we will see it through, whatever the consequences."

"Even your life? Remember what happened last time. They almost took me to the trains. If it hadn't been for Badowski and Spira, I wouldn't be here right now. We can't depend on that happening again. The Germans could clear us all out, taking us with the rest—or they might simply step in here and shoot us all down."

"What about Klaus and his friends? Wouldn't they protect us?"

"I don't trust Klaus a bit. Oh, he's polite enough these days. But he'd slit our throats without a second thought if he was ordered to do so. So would that Rachel. She might be the most heartless of the three."

"And Elsa?"

"Yes, Elsa might be another matter. It's just a feeling I have. Nothing she's done, nothing she's said. But there's something else inside that one. I wish we had more time to cultivate it. If my instincts are correct, she could have been a valuable ally."

"Yes, I've felt it too. But it's too late."

Tadeusz nodded. "Yes. It's over now, and nothing left but the closing curtain. So, what will it be? Do you want to go home? I could send all of you."

"I told you, Tadeusz, we won't. Whatever happens, we're all in this together. We will see this through."

Tadeusz held up the little bag. "Yes, even if we are but gentler angels of death."

Chapter 24

Wawel Castle

Krakow
Occupied Poland
March 1943

Elsa, Klaus, and Rachel sat at the corner café, finishing their early breakfast. Elsa was washing it all down with a substantial glass of schnapps. They were discussing their jobs and the state of the war.

"Have you heard any news at headquarters?" Elsa asked. Klaus had been promoted and spent half of his time in the Wawel Castle complex, as an aide to a lieutenant colonel there.

"We've got the Eastern Front shored up after the fall of Stalingrad," he said. "And we've made some progress against the Americans in North Africa."

"Any talk of another offensive against the Russians?" Rachel asked.

Klaus shook his head. "I don't think there will be one. We've taken massive casualties, and the lines are razor thin. My understanding is they've shifted to just holding what we've already taken."

"But if we don't conquer Russia, won't that mean we've lost?" asked Elsa.

"Don't talk that way!" Klaus said, but then he smiled and patted her hand. "I just don't want you to get into trouble, my dear. Defeatist talk is treasonable. No, I think the Russians will come to terms with us, leaving us with almost all of European Russia. That includes Ukraine, which besides the oil fields is the only thing worth having. Don't you worry, we'll get the farm we've talked about after the war. Either in Poland or in Russia."

Rachel laughed. "I can't imagine the two of you as farmers. Klaus, with your service record, I imagine they'll want you for more than that."

Klaus shook his head. "I want a farm, and a place for Elsa and me to have a family. I don't need anything more than that."

"I do," said Rachel. "And I'm going to get it."

"You and Lieutenant Schueller?" asked Elsa. "He should have a secure place in the Reich when this is all over."

"He's a distraction for me," said Rachel. "Something to keep me from getting bored. No, when this is over, I'll latch on to some colonel or another. I want a big house, and servants, and all the money I can spend in a lifetime."

Elsa laughed. She knew her friend was serious. And she believed her. Rachel, despite her background, despite her diminutive size, always got what she wanted. Schueller, for example. One day she had simply informed him they were to be lovers. He scoffed at first—there were regulations against such things. But soon enough he found himself in her bed, despite his protests. They'd been together for six months now, and he was devoted to her—talking of their future together after the war. A future Rachel apparently did not intend to share with him.

"What about news closer to home?" Rachel asked. "Anything about these rumors concerning the ghetto?"

"They aren't rumors," said Klaus, taking another crust of bread. "They are fact. The ghetto will be liquidated, and soon."

Elsa bristled at this. Since that *Aktion* in June, she'd found ways around the deportations. She'd either scheduled other duties for the events, or feigned illness. Only Rachel understood what she was doing. Her friend had protested at first, but apparently had given up. They never talked about it, but Rachel had stopped badgering her friend about things. Now, though, there was going to be the biggest *Aktion* of all, and Elsa was sure there would be no excuse that would get her away from it.

"When is it going to happen?" asked Elsa.

Klaus shrugged. "No official word yet. But it has to be soon." He checked his watch. "Time to go, ladies."

They rose and started to leave. A waiter hurried up, handing Klaus the check. He simply stared at it, then handed it back, daring the man to insist on payment. The waiter looked as if he would say something, then bowed and walked away.

"The effrontery of that man," said Klaus. "I thought I was going to have to teach him a lesson."

"*Paying* for breakfast is traditional," said Rachel. "You can hardly blame him."

Klaus reached up and turned his collar to her. "*This* is my payment," he said. "Speaking of money, it's Friday. Let's swing by the pharmacy and pick up my zlotys. We can fish around for some news as well."

The Under the Eagle Pharmacy in the ghetto had become a regular stopping place for the three of them. They would waltz in, collect Klaus's payment, and usually linger at the counter for a glass of vodka and to hear any gossip they could extract out of Tadeusz or his assistants. Elsa knew that they terrified the Poles, and that everything they were told was probably a lie, or at least heavily altered, but still, it was a warm place to linger, and the staff wasn't so bad. Irena and the rest of them. Even the Jew Natalia was polite enough to visit with.

They stepped into Klaus's car. He rated one now as a senior sergeant. And they drove out of Old Town, heading south toward the Vistula bridge and the Jewish Quarter. Guards checked their papers at the bridge, and again at the gate. Klaus parked his car on the edge of Plac Zgody Square, and they swaggered into the pharmacy. Klaus was wearing his firearm, and Elsa and Rachel had their black cudgels swinging from their belts.

The lobby was mostly empty, with a single customer at the counter. Irena was there, helping some Jew or another, and Natalia was standing next to her. The assistant looked up and Elsa saw the color drain from her face when she saw them. She nudged Irena and whispered in her ear.

"Irena will be right with you," said Natalia.

"I don't think so," said Rachel. Her friend stepped up to the counter, jerking the customer around to face her. "Come back later," she ordered. It was a woman in her midforties, and she lowered her head and stumbled out of the store.

"Rachel, why did you bother the poor woman?" said Elsa. "We could have waited a moment."

"We're not waiting for Jews," said Rachel.

"Good morning, Irena," said Klaus. "Is Tadeusz around?"

Irena nodded. "Certainly, Klaus. Give me just a few moments." She stepped back from the counter and into the back.

"Natalia, how are you today?" asked Elsa.

"I'm fine, thank you," she said, keeping her eyes down.

"Any news in the ghetto?"

"Nothing." She looked up. "Well, there is something. There are stories going around that the ghetto is going to be liquidated."

"Nonsense," said Klaus. "There are always those kinds of rumors. Why would we do that? Where would we put all of you? There are factories here, and Schindler just a little way away. What good would it do to relocate all of you?"

Elsa felt badly that Klaus was lying to this woman. But of course he had to. If they told the truth, there would be a panic. Not only that, but everyone would go into hiding, making all of their lives more difficult. No, it was the right thing to do. These Jews were like children. It was better that they didn't know what was in store for them.

Tadeusz appeared a moment later, Irena in tow. He gave Klaus a grim smile. "Good morning, Sergeant. You're here early."

"Yes, I thought we'd come collect before the day got too far along. Do you have my payment?"

Tadeusz nodded and handed him an envelope. Klaus opened it and thumbed through the contents. "This is only one hundred zlotys. The price is two hundred."

"What do you mean?" the pharmacist asked. "It's always been one hundred."

"The price has gone up, my friend. War shortages, you know."

Elsa saw the frustration on the pharmacist's face. But what could he do? The man shrugged and stepped into the back again, returning a few minutes later with another handful of bills. "Here you are," he said. "I trust there won't be any more increases."

"Don't trust to anything," snapped Rachel. "You're lucky we let you operate at all. Now bring us some vodka, it's cold out there."

Tadeusz reached under the counter and pulled up a bottle and three glasses. He poured them each a glassful. Elsa drank hers in a couple of gulps. She was grateful for the warmth, and for the dulling of her emotions.

"Any news, Tadeusz?" Klaus asked. The pharmacist shook his head, looking down. Elsa was sure he was frustrated about the doubling of the protection money that Klaus collected each week. Her boyfriend finished his drink, belching. He slammed the glass down hard on the counter. "All right, Poles and Jews! We've got a busy day in front of us. You mind you watch yourselves while I'm gone. And no funny business in here, or we will shut you down." Klaus turned and strolled out the door, Rachel on his heels.

Elsa stood there a moment. She turned and looked behind her, and then stepped up to the counter. Reaching into her coat, she pulled out two packages of cigarettes, placing them on the counter. "This should make up the difference," she said.

"Thank you, Elsa," said Irena, taking the packages and sliding them under the counter.

"I would do more if I could."

"I know you would. Elsa, *are* they going to liquidate the ghetto? We've heard the rumors."

Elsa hesitated. She wanted to tell them, but she knew it would only create chaos. Still, they had a right to know. "They—"

"Elsa. What are you doing?" She heard Klaus's voice behind her. He'd opened the door back up and was standing in the entryway, eyeing her.

"Nothing," said Elsa. "I was just telling this Jew to watch herself."

Klaus smiled. "Good girl. She *should* watch herself. As should all of them."

Elsa turned and walked out of the pharmacy, her face flushed, hoping he wouldn't ask her more about what had transgressed inside.

"Where to now?" she asked when they were outside.

"Let's walk around a bit and see what's going on."

They strode through the square, heading west. Elsa remembered all the families packed in here last June. The sweltering heat, the calls for mercy, for water, and then the endless lines of them loading into the waiting cattle cars just outside the gates. All the undesirables of the ghetto being transported to Belżec to be gassed. She felt the tug on her conscience. How could she justify the wholesale murder of these people? But they were subhumans, weren't they? Lice-ridden vermin carriers who polluted the German people. So she'd been taught growing up, and so the posters and pamphlets spread all over Krakow told the populace. But did she believe it? Did Natalia seem like a vermin carrier? A subhuman? She'd chatted with the Jewish assistant a number of times. She was a college graduate. On her way to medical school before the war started. The daughter of some wealthy lawyer. Her family was all gone now, according to Natalia. Disappearing like much of the ghetto population, either by bullets or disease, starvation or the gas chamber. And all for the good of the Fatherland. Klaus believed it. And so did Rachel—or at least her friend didn't give a lick what happened to these people. Elsa had tried to be strong like them, but she couldn't drive the images of suffering away, although she could dull them with a wash of alcohol as she did almost every night. It was the only way she could sleep.

They marched together now, down the half-deserted streets of the ghetto. They were linked arm in arm, strolling as if through the park. Anyone who saw them rushed quickly away, or stood, hat off, head facing the ground, trembling before them. They were gods, or at least the next best thing. She felt that too. Incongruent with her other emotions. The rush of power, of importance, but most importantly of acceptance. She had a home in the SS, a part of something she'd never had before. It was worth the pain, the guilt, the moral dilemmas—or at least she told herself. And she'd managed to avoid the worst of it, through her own cunning actions. She prayed for some way out of this upcoming *Aktion*, some way to avoid it all.

"What will be next for us?" she asked. "After the last operation is finished?"

"We will be reassigned," Klaus said.

"I hope we'll all be together."

"It's a little out of our hands," said Klaus.

"I'll make sure we stay close," said Rachel. "I've already been working on things with my little mouse Schueller. I'll bat him around a bit more and he'll do what I want him to do. Or I'll cut off his little thingy."

Elsa laughed. "You're impossible, Rachel. I don't know how you do it."

"We all have to make our sacrifices. And you will too, my friend. Eyes will be watching all of us with the coming *Aktion*. There will be new people coming into town. People with experience in these kinds of bigger operations. They will be watching all of us, evaluating our abilities, our futures. When the time comes, it won't do you any good to have a cold."

Elsa felt the shame wash over her. So Rachel hadn't been fooled by any of it. And now she was giving her a clear warning. Friendship or no, she had to do her duty this time.

They kept up their march, arriving at the Judenrat building. The usual lines were there, shorter than they used to be because of the lack of population. Klaus collected here each week as well. They had to have their drinking money, after all. They pushed their way through the front door, Jews scurrying this way and that to avoid them. Klaus stepped up to the base of the stairway, where a woman sat at a table—a receptionist of sorts. Elsa had seen her many times in the past.

"May I help you?" the woman asked, eyeing them warily.

"I don't know if you can help us," said Klaus. "I'm here for my envelope."

"Of course, Sergeant, let me see now . . ." The woman shuffled through her paperwork, fingers fumbling through the documents. "I'm sorry. I don't seem to see it. Could you come back later?"

"Come back later?" said Rachel. "The cheek of these people. No, we can't come back later. Find the envelope now, you little shit."

"I can't leave my desk," she said. "Usually, the envelope is here. But it's not today. If you could just come back in an hour . . ."

Rachel stepped forward and brought her cudgel down on the woman's head. She recoiled from the blow, her head lolling around. It looked like she might fall out of her chair, but she grasped the table with both hands, her head facing the table, eyes closed.

"I'm sorry. If you could just give me a few seconds . . ."

"I don't think so," said Klaus. "We don't wait for Jews." Klaus pulled out his pistol.

"Don't! Please!" said Elsa.

Klaus looked at her. "I love you, my dear, but Rachel is right. We must do our duty."

He shot the woman in the head.

Elsa covered her eyes with her hands. She heard the body hit the ground. Her boyfriend had just killed a woman right in front of her. There was no way to hide from this, nothing she could do but let the death fill her ears, her nostrils, her soul.

Chapter 25

Podgórze District

Krakow
Occupied Poland
March 1943

Natalia and Sylwia sat sipping ersatz coffee at the pathetic little ghetto restaurant. It was the last of its kind, and over the previous months, Natalia had seen the menu dwindle until it served an acorn coffee, and little else. Perhaps a loaf of bread could be had for an exorbitant amount of zlotys. If so, Sylwia would pay out of her seemingly inexhaustible supply of money. How her family had held on to so much money when they came into the ghetto, Natalia often wondered—but it was not the kind of thing you asked a friend, and certainly not one whose family had saved your life more than once.

"How is the pharmacy?" Sylwia asked her.

"It's not too bad. But we're just like this restaurant. We're down to nothing. A little aspirin and a plentiful supply of cyanide. That's about it."

"I've heard about the cyanide," said Sylwia. "It's understandable, I suppose. For those without our connections. I feel badly sometimes, don't you?"

"I try not to think about it too much. The pharmacy has been a haven for me. I've been able to practice medicine, at least in a little way. The medical books Tadeusz gave me have got me through endless nights of boredom. Without Irena and the rest, and of course without your friendship, I would never have survived. Particularly after . . ."

"You don't have to say it," Sylwia responded, taking her hand. "I don't know how you survived what happened to Aleksandra. What you saw right in front of you." They'd never talked about the tragedy this past June. Natalia still wasn't able to do so, or even to think about it.

"Let's talk about better things," she said, smiling as best she could.

"Have you heard anything about Stefan?"

Natalia shook her head. "I told you, *better things*, Sylwia. But of course, I hope that he made it out, that he's in the countryside somewhere, or in the forest with the partisans. I should have listened to him. I should have gone with him. If I had, my mother would still—"

"No. There's no way you could have known. And the sewers were a death sentence for dozens of our Jewish friends that day, Natalia. Not that Stefan—"

"Yes, I've worried that he didn't make it. But I've never heard anything. I think if he had died, the resistance would have told me at some point."

"Couldn't you ask them if they know his whereabouts?"

"I would if I knew who to ask. I've looked for Dolek. Even asked for him. But in all this time I haven't seen anything, or anyone connected with the ŻOB."

"I could have my father make some inquiries."

"You're too kind. He's got too much on his plate."

"That he does. But I have good news for you, Natalia. He's been negotiating with the Germans. When they liquidate the ghetto, we will all be transferring to a new location at that camp we've been hearing about in Plaszow. The Judenrat will be receiving their own barracks, separate from the rest of the prisoners. They still want the council to govern the new camp, along with some of the Jewish police officials. Father says the conditions will be better—more blankets, more food, no hard labor. Anyway, he said he has put in a request for you to join us—that you would run the camp pharmacy for the Germans."

Natalia couldn't believe it. She would survive the *Aktion*. She would be put in better housing, with better food. And best of all, not only would she continue to work in a pharmacy, but she would be the head pharmacist.

"Is this possible?" she said. "I'm not licensed."

"The Germans don't care about all that. Besides, Father can swing it. If he says it will happen, it will happen."

"I can't believe it, Sylwia. I don't know what to say. Your family has saved my life over and over. And now you're doing it again."

Sylwia raised her hand and a waiter came over.

"A loaf of bread," she said.

"Madam, we don't have any bread."

"Yes, you do. And I want one. A whole loaf."

"But it would cost you a thousand zlotys."

Sylwia reached into her coat and pulled out a roll of notes. She counted off some and handed it to the waiter. "Bring it, now."

"Yes, madam."

"A thousand zlotys. But why, Sylwia?"

"We need to celebrate. If not the end of the ghetto, at least to our new beginnings."

The waiter brought out the bread, an enormous loaf, and white bread at that. Natalia hadn't eaten white bread since her arrest by the Gestapo two years before. Her hands trembled as Sylwia tore the loaf in half, handing her one of the sections. She took a bite, then another, struggling to slow down, to enjoy the flavor. She closed her eyes, relishing this veritable feast.

They lingered there, eating their food, chatting about life before the war, and about the new camp. They hoped conditions would be better there than in the ghetto. They would be together, able to live in peace, she hoped, sharing a table with other Judenrat members. Natalia asked what medicines she would be allowed and Sylwia promised to ask her father. It was growing dark when they finally separated.

"Thank you again, my friend," Natalia said.

"Of course. You've done as much for me as my father has done for you. Without you, I wouldn't have survived here."

Natalia departed, feeling full for the first time in months. She'd been fed consistently from Irena and the others at the pharmacy, but just like medicine, the black-market costs had skyrocketed on food items and she'd had a difficult time keeping any weight on. She hoped at the new camp, in their special barracks, there would be enough to eat. She wondered if she would have her own pharmacy building, or whether she would have to operate within the German administrative facilities. If she was in her own building, she might have the ability to trade items for food and other luxuries. It would be harder if she was under the thumb of the Nazis. She made a mental note to ask Sylwia about it when next they met.

She turned on her street, starting toward her flat. She'd acquired a novel from Sylwia a week ago and she was halfway through it. She'd had a hard time concentrating on the words, with worries about the upcoming *Aktion*, but now that she knew her future was assured, she would relish the book tonight. Perhaps she would even start over, so she could enjoy the entire book from the beginning. She reached the door to her apartment. The ghetto was so quiet these days, with so many having been carted off to the camps. She thought of her brother, as she did many times a day. She wished there was some way to know what had happened to him, that he was safe.

She entered into her building and was surprised by hands grabbing her from behind. "Who are you?" she asked.

"Quiet and go up to your flat."

She moved with them, her heart beating out of her chest. She reached the door of her apartment and then opened it. She was shoved inside. She turned to see two men she didn't recognize. They were both in their late twenties or so, thin with dirty clothing. She had feared the Gestapo, but these weren't Germans. They were Jews.

"What do you want from me?" she asked.

"I told you to shut your mouth." The man who spoke stayed with her, while the other one swept through her apartment. She could hear drawers being opened; clothing upended. She wondered what on earth they might be looking for. The other man stepped into her other bedroom, continuing his search.

"There's nothing in there," she said. "That was my mother's room. And my brother's. My brother Stefan, you must have known him. He was in the resistance—and I assume that you are too."

The man closest to her stepped over and backhanded her, sending her spinning onto the couch. "I told you to shut your mouth."

Natalia lay there on the cushions. She tasted blood and she could feel her lips swelling from the blow. What did these men want with her? They must be part of the resistance, and yet if so, why were they troubling her? She was only helping the other Jews. She had all this time at the pharmacy. She wanted to speak up again, to say something to these men, but she was afraid to do so.

The search continued, now in the kitchen. They both joined in now, opening her cupboards, checking under pots and behind plates. One of the men fished out a little chunk of sausage. It had been a gift from Irena.

"What do we have here?" he asked.

She explained where she got it.

"SS sausage. Very interesting."

"I told you, it came from the pharmacy. If you would only talk to them, they would tell you that I'm innocent."

"The pharmacy, is it? Yes, we know you work there. We also see Spira in there almost every day. And the SS. What have you been telling the Germans?"

Natalia was shocked by the statement. "How can you believe that?" she asked. "Tadeusz and the others have risked their lives for the Jews. They stayed behind when the Germans wanted them out. Tadeusz has worked with the resistance. He worked with Dolek."

"Dolek is dead," said the man. "Ambushed by the Germans. So much for working with Tadeusz."

"You can't believe that," she said. "How can you possibly question me about that?"

"We're the ones doing the questioning," he said. "How much contact do you have with the SS? We see a trio of them going inside almost every day."

"No contact at all. At least not by our choice. They do come in. An SS sergeant and two women. But it's nothing we want. They extort Tadeusz. A hundred zlotys a week. And they just doubled it."

"He pays a bribe to the Germans? What else does he give them to stay in operation?"

"I don't understand this," she said. "I told you he would never betray the Jews. They work with the resistance. You must know that. And my brother. He was with Dolek. But I haven't heard from him since June. Do you know anything about him?"

The door opened behind her. "He is well."

She turned and, to her surprise, Stefan was there. He was older, and taller than her now. And his face had grown careworn. He looked twenty, even twenty-five. "Stefan!" she shouted, rushing toward him. But he pushed her away.

"I'm not here for a reunion," he said. "I'm here for something else."

"But what's happened to you?" she asked, taken aback.

"Nothing has happened to me. It's what's happened to you that concerns me."

"Nothing is different, Stefan. Everything is the same. Please, I'm your sister."

"My sister died to me the day she took my mother to her death. I warned you of what was going to happen, but you didn't listen to me. And now she's dead, like our father before her. I told you I would hold you responsible. And I do."

"Please, Stefan. You have to understand. I had the Blauscheins—you saw them. They should have saved her. It wasn't my fault. We were unlucky."

"And I told you that the Blauscheins are useless. And so they are. The ghetto will be liquidated soon—perhaps in the next few days. And when that happens, everyone in this ghetto will be liquidated with it."

"That's not true, Stefan. The new camp. Plaszow."

"It's the final ending for everyone. They intend to work everyone there to death. Those they don't shoot outright during the upcoming *Aktion*."

"I can't believe that. I'm going to be with the Judenrat, Stefan. They are going to let me set up my own pharmacy. Why don't you come with me? I'm sure I could arrange things. Put this foolishness aside. Do you intend to fight? If so, with what? They'll kill you, Stefan. The only way out is by connections. The way it has always been. Just like Father said."

"Father. Where did his connections land him? And Mother? Your connections took her to her grave too. But you refuse to listen, sister. You still think your connections will save you.

That privilege means something in the ghetto—would mean something in that camp where they will grind us all to dust. But I'm glad we're talking connections, because that's what I'm here for."

"What do you mean?" she asked.

"We're here for Badowski. You're going to lead us to him, and we're going to kill him."

Chapter 26

Wawel Castle

Krakow
Occupied Poland
March 1943

Elsa slept fitfully that night. After the shooting, she had refused to talk to Klaus or Rachel. Elsa had gone up to her apartment and straight to bed. She'd felt exhausted, dejected, but sleep eluded her. The vision kept galloping through her mind—the woman reeling from the blow Rachel had given her, and then Klaus, drawing his revolver, ignoring her protests, and shooting the poor woman in the head. She finally drifted off to sleep and woke at first light, sandy-eyed and depressed.

As she was getting ready for the day, Elsa heard a knock at the door. She answered and Klaus was there, holding flowers in his hand. She let him in and took the flowers, placing them in a glass she retrieved from the cupboard. She made some coffee, still not speaking to him.

"Do you want to talk about it?"

"Talk about what? About you murdering some poor woman right in front of me for no reason at all? You know how I feel about those things, Klaus. We've talked about this before. You promised you would let others do these things, that we would try to keep ourselves untainted as much as possible—for our future."

"Elsa, we're in the SS. I have a job to do. Part of that job is setting examples. That woman defied me. I had to act. I don't like it any more than you do."

"She didn't defy you, Klaus. She couldn't find your bribe. That's hardly an act of rebellion." She poured him some coffee. He tried to take her hand, but she jerked it away. Pouring herself a cup, she slouched down into a chair across from him at the kitchen table.

"That woman didn't have a future, Elsa. None of them do. We've been through this over and over. I don't like it any more than you do. But we don't get to decide. Besides, it will all be over soon enough. Another year or two, and all the Jews will be gone from Europe. Our kids and their kids will thank us for it. And we can go on with our life, our farm, our future."

"They're people, Klaus. I know the propaganda says they aren't. But I don't believe it. I look into their eyes. They smile like us, they weep and beg and cry like us. They hold their children in their arms like us. This thing that we are doing, it's wrong. And there's going to be some terrible retribution for it. I feel it in my bones. We have to distance ourselves as much as we can. That's what we discussed and that's what we decided. And then you went and did this."

"You're right," he said, putting his hand on her shoulder. "I was wrong. I shouldn't have lost my temper. But I've been under a lot of pressure lately. It's this damned promotion. The new responsibilities are double what I had before. I'm thankful for the grade, and the pay. And it will make a difference in our future. Our land allotment will be larger. I might be selected for a government post of some kind where we settled. I'm doing this for our future, Elsa. And I know I'm not perfect."

"Promise me you won't do that again."

"I promise. Unless I'm directly ordered, I won't commit a random act like that. Now, can we forget the whole thing? The next few days are going to be a nightmare. I can't go through it with you angry with me as well."

"Yes. I forgive you. Let's just put the whole thing behind us."

There was a knock at the door. "Who could that be?" asked Klaus.

"It must be Rachel. She went out for some exercise. I bet she forgot her key." Elsa stepped over to the door and opened it. She was surprised to find not Rachel, but an SS sergeant she'd never met before.

"Elsa Baumann?" he asked.

"Yes?"

"I've been instructed to bring you with me."

"Now?" Elsa felt her blood freeze. What was this about?

"Yes, now."

"What's going on?" asked Klaus, getting to his feet. "Who are you and what are you here for?"

"Who I am is none of your concern. But I'm here on behalf of the new camp commandant of Plaszow. He's made a special request to see Corporal Baumann. I've already cleared this with Lieutenant Schueller." He reached inside his coat and removed an envelope. "Here are the orders."

"But why would the commandant want to see me?" Elsa asked. "I don't know him. And I've never been to Plaszow."

"He didn't say. But you're to come with me immediately."

"Can I see that?" asked Klaus, stepping forward.

"Certainly."

Klaus opened up the envelope and pulled out a single sheet of paper. He reviewed the contents and then handed the letter to

Elsa. "It's official," he said. "Although it doesn't say why he wants to see you."

The bedroom door opened, and Rachel stepped out, still in a bathrobe. "What's going on?" she asked.

"I've been summoned to Plaszow."

"What? Why?"

"I don't know," said Elsa. "But look." She handed the orders to her friend.

"Strange. Do you want me to go with you?"

"That is not allowed," said the sergeant. "I only have orders to transport Corporal Baumann."

"Well, I guess you'll have to go," said Rachel. "I wish I could come with you. I haven't seen the camp. And there are new SS men there by all accounts. I wouldn't mind getting to see if there are any worth my attention."

Elsa laughed in spite of herself. "I'm sure you'll get your chance. For now, I need to go."

Klaus stepped forward and took her hands. "You'll be all right. Get dressed and get going."

Elsa changed into her uniform quickly and fixed her hair. A few minutes later, she found herself in the back of a staff car, rolling through the streets of Krakow. They drove past the ghetto and then through the outskirts of town. "How far are we going?" she asked.

"It's about ten kilometers to the camp."

They arrived at Plaszow fifteen minutes later. The entire space was surrounded by wire fencing, with guard towers spaced out around the perimeter. A series of wooden buildings, likely barracks for the prisoners, dotted the interior of the camp, along with larger buildings that Elsa couldn't guess at. The camp was set in a valley between two hills. On the hill to her right, there was a series of houses overlooking the complex.

Their car was met at the gate, and an SS private approached the window, and then checked their papers. The vehicle rumbled into the interior of the camp and came to a stop a short space within. The sergeant stepped out of the passenger seat and opened the door for Elsa. She looked around. There was a buzz of activity including the sounds of construction everywhere. Shouts rippled through the confined space. She observed several work crews of what were obviously Jews, carrying wood and stone to locations, and some working to erect an unfinished barracks. She looked down at the road and was surprised to see it was made up of gravestones.

"From the Jewish cemetery," the sergeant said. "Finally, a good use for them, no?"

She didn't answer. The sergeant led her past a building to her left and then up the stairs toward a house on the hill.

"Where are we going?" she asked.

"Up to the commandant's house," he answered. "He's running a little late today."

She climbed up the steps with him, a little out of breath as they reached the top. They entered the house, and the sergeant motioned for her to take a seat in the entranceway. He disappeared through a door, arriving back a few minutes later. "The commandant will see you now," the sergeant said.

Elsa was led through a door and into an office. The commandant was there behind a large mahogany desk. He rose and Elsa was surprised by the man's looming height. He had light brown hair and piercing blue eyes.

"Heil Hitler," said Elsa, using the traditional greeting.

"Heil Hitler. I'm the commandant, Amon Göth. And you must be Corporal Baumann," he said, looking down at a document he had in front of him. "Would you like some tea? Have you had breakfast?"

"Tea would be nice," she said. She didn't feel like eating. She wasn't even sure what this was about.

"Excellent. I'll order up some now." He stepped out of the room and then returned. "That should be along any minute."

"Sir, thank you for inviting me," began Elsa, wanting to take back a little control in the situation. "It's very nice to meet you, but I must inquire why you wanted to see me."

Göth smiled. "A little spark of courage, I see. I like that. Where are you from, Baumann?"

"From Breslau."

"Ah. I like Breslau. I've been there a number of times. I'm from Vienna. Not so far away from Breslau, really. A half day's drive on a lazy Sunday."

She smiled but didn't answer, so he continued. "Well, to business, then. I was appointed some time ago to organize the camp here at Plaszow. I've been here with a unit of SS since February. We imported a number of Jews from Krakow over the past month. I'm sure you saw some of them working when you arrived."

"Yes."

"They've been laboring for some time now, constructing barracks for the camp. We also have a number of industrial sites we've been putting together, for Madritsch, Schindler, and the like. Do you know Schindler?"

"I don't, sir. I've heard the name, of course."

"I'll have to introduce you to him. A raucous fellow. He's generous, and a real rogue. In any event, I'm sure you've heard that we are moving toward liquidating the ghetto."

"Yes, sir. Do you know when?"

"Soon," said Amon, with a wink. "In any event, I've been working with your Lieutenant Schueller about some staffing issues. He told me a curious thing about you."

Elsa felt her stomach fall. He must have told her how she shirked her duties before every *Aktion*. That she'd been promoted early but had turned out to be somewhat of a disappointment. She was sure she would be dismissed from service or sent out on some terrible assignment away from Klaus and Rachel.

"Yes, Lieutenant Schueller had a lot to say about you."

"I'm sorry, sir, but what did he say?"

"He said you've been a staunch and loyal NCO for him. That you and your friend Rachel have been the core of the women's unit in Krakow. He recommended you for service here in Plaszow. But that wasn't the thing that sparked my interest. What he also told me is that you are an accomplished typist."

That caught Elsa by surprise. How did he even know that? Then she remembered that early on, Schueller's assistant had fallen ill at the end of the month, and he had called her in to assist with his reports to Berlin. "Yes, sir, I took typing in high school. I'm not really good at much of anything to be honest— not naturally talented at life. But I found typing to be easy, and I excelled in my class."

"Show me," he said, gesturing at a small desk to his left. A typewriter was there. She stood up, feeling nervous, and moved over to the machine.

"Are you ready?" he asked.

"Yes, sir."

Göth then began dictating at a rapid pace. It had been some time since Elsa had typed anything, and at first, she had difficulty keeping up. But then her nerves settled, and her fingers began dancing on the keys, the old familiarity and confidence soaring through her. Göth went on for several minutes, and then finished. He stepped over and removed the paper, reading through it.

"You made a mistake, just there," he said, pointing to the paper.

"I'm sorry, sir."

He continued on. "Just one mistake, on the whole page. And this is your first time working with me. I'd like to offer you a position," he said. "I need a personal secretary. You would be on staff here and work closely with me. I know it might feel like a downgrade, and of course you don't have to accept. It would be pulling you away from all of the action. If you're not interested, I can find you something else in the camp. You could be in charge of some of the women's barracks. But if you do accept, I can promise you a warm place to work, extra food, a comfortable place to sleep, and a ration of vodka each month. If you serve me well, I'll make sure you receive another promotion, and I'll give you a glowing reference for after the war."

"Yes, sir, I accept."

"You don't want to think about it?"

"No, sir. I would love to work with you in that capacity."

Göth smiled. "Thank you, Corporal. You've made me very happy. Paperwork is not my favorite part of this job, and my last assistant was an absolute disaster. It will be a real pleasure to have someone competent in your role. Not only that, but you've served in the ranks. You are SS, and you know what it's like to be out there. That gives me confidence in you, and it will also help in you formulating reports, and understanding my perspective on things."

"When can I start, sir?"

"Is tomorrow too soon?"

"No. I would love to start tomorrow."

"Excellent. I'll have the sergeant get you back to Wawel, and you can pack up today. I'll send a car round in the morning. Have your things ready then."

"Thank you, sir."

"Thank you."

Elsa rode back in a state of euphoria. Göth seemed the ideal boss—kind, sensitive, and caring. She was going to be able to serve the rest of the war in an office, warm and safe. She wouldn't have to be involved in any more *Aktions*, or even have to witness any atrocities. She hurried up to her apartment and spent the day packing up her items. She couldn't wait to tell Rachel, although she felt a little sad about moving out. But that wouldn't last long. Rachel and Klaus would be over right after the *Aktion*, and they would all be together as usual—and all in jobs that suited them perfectly.

She finished her packing and then sat, trying to read a book, waiting impatiently for her friends to finish their shift. The hours ticked by slowly. She thought about walking down to the ghetto, seeking them out, but it was already late afternoon, and they would soon be home. She intended to take them out to celebrate.

Finally, when she thought she could wait no more, a key jingled in the lock and the door opened. Rachel and Klaus were there, stepping into the apartment. She rushed into Klaus's arms, kissing him and holding him tight.

"Your trip to Plaszow must have gone well," said Rachel dryly.

"You won't believe it," said Elsa. "Come sit at the table, both of you, and let me fill you in on what's happened." They all sat down and she told them all about Plaszow, about Göth, the interview, and her new duties.

"So, you've secured a new position," said Rachel. There was a strange quality to her voice and Elsa was surprised by her reaction.

"What's wrong?" she asked. Elsa had expected elation, excitement from her friends, but they were both regarding her with somber expressions.

"Do you want to tell her or should I?" asked Rachel.

"Go ahead."

"You weren't the only person to receive new orders today," Rachel said.

"What do you mean?"

"Klaus and I both were pulled into Schueller's office, back-to-back. I'm being reassigned to Auschwitz after the *Aktion*, and Klaus to Gross-Rosen."

"That can't be true," Elsa said. "Schueller wouldn't do that to you, Rachel."

"It seems he's soured on our relationship and must be looking for a way to get rid of me."

"How can that be? And you, Klaus. Why aren't you both being sent to Plaszow?"

"That camp is already filled with the commandant's men. At least that's what Schueller told me," said Klaus. "They don't have room for all of us. Don't worry, we'll all be within a few hours of each other. Things will be all right."

But Elsa knew those words were a lie. With the intense war schedules they were under, they wouldn't have leave to visit each other except a couple of times a year perhaps. Her best friend and her boyfriend were being pulled away from her. All of her joy fell away, as she contemplated facing the war alone.

Chapter 27

Podgórze District

Krakow
Occupied Poland
March 1943

Natalia stood in utter shock as the words poured over her again. "Kill Badowski? How can you say that? He's on the Judenrat. He's helping the Jews. He's saved my life several times, Stefan. He tried to save yours and Mother's. He's the one that issued the Blauscheins I tried to give to you. You should be fighting the Germans. Why are you talking about killing my best friend's father?"

"Because he's been growing rich on the backs of Jews. He sells out families to the Germans. He extorts zlotys from workers and organizations for his alleged protection. He works with the Germans, helping to draw up the lists of who goes, and who stays. Now, with the liquidation coming, he'll be prepared to sell out anyone and everyone to assure his position in the new camp. He's an enemy to the people, Natalia. He's not your friend or your ally. He's the devil."

"You've got the wrong man. Please, I'm begging you. Go with me to talk to him. Confront him about what you're saying. I know he's not who you think he is."

"You're naïve, Natalia! You've had your head buried in the sand at that foolish pharmacy—giving out gumdrops and hope when you should have been watching, learning, and preparing to fight."

"To fight who? Our own people? The Germans are our enemies, Stefan, not the Judenrat. Think about it. They are in an impossible situation. The Nazis are the ones who have done the deportations, not the Judenrat. If they've required the council and the police to identify who the essential workers were, and who they weren't, how is that their fault? This is a madness of our occupiers, not our leaders. If you were in his position, how could you do different?"

"I wouldn't take that job. I would fight."

"And you would die. If you refused, the Germans would have shot you out of hand, as they would have Badowski."

"Then I would still have my honor."

"That's a child's answer."

"I'm not a child. Not anymore. Not after everything I've seen and done. But I'm not like you, Natalia, I'm not trying to maintain my standard of living and privilege. I care about all the people, not just those with the right credentials."

"Say what you will. I'm not going to help you kill Badowski."

"You disappoint me, Natalia. And I begin to wonder now about your connections to the Germans yourself. That little pharmacy you play at has become quite the hotbed of German activity."

"You can't believe that about Tadeusz and the rest of them. They've done nothing but help the people here. It's not their fault that the Germans come in. There's hardly a place left in the ghetto to congregate. Our lobby has become a place to meet. It's warm, and as safe as any place in the ghetto. The Germans over time have realized the same thing. But we don't encourage them. Dolek liked having them come in. He told Tadeusz that himself. It gave resistance agents a chance to eavesdrop on conversations they had over a glass or two of vodka. To see whom they met with, what their attitudes were. Who might be a more gentle soul, a sympathetic figure for use in the future."

"A lot of good it did him," said Stefan. "The Germans found his hiding place and killed him, along with half of his group. Dolek was dealing in subtleties. We felt the same way at one point, that we should watch and learn, that we should gather our resources and see what would happen. But those days are over, Natalia. We are out of time. Now we are going to fight, and we are going to get retribution not only against the Germans, but against those who have lined their pockets at our expense and saved their little skins by betraying their fellow Jews. And your Badowski is at the top of the list."

"I'm telling you, you have the wrong information. You have the wrong man. I'm begging you to go with me to talk to him. He wouldn't betray me. Look at this," she said, stepping over to the far wall. She moved her hand behind a bookcase and pulled a latch. A door swung open to reveal a false wall, with a narrow space. "He had this built for me. A hiding place in case I need it. It cost him a thousand zlotys. He didn't get anything from me in return. I'm not sleeping with him. I haven't helped him with the Germans—not that I could. He did this out of the goodness of his heart."

"Saving one friend doesn't make him a saint. Even the Nazis look after their own. It's the same old game, Natalia. Privilege looking after privilege. Perhaps that's all right in peacetime. But when it comes at the expense of the lives of hundreds or thousands of others—then it's inexcusable. No, you won't change my mind. I want you to go to the Judenrat and invite him on a pretext to take a walk with you. Tell him it's about that little whore of a daughter you are friends with. That you're worried about her. Get him out on the street, walking past the aid society. We want it to be right after work, at twilight, when the light is falling. You get him there and we'll nab him. If you cooperate, we won't ask anything else of you. Not only that, we'll help get you out of the ghetto."

"By the sewers? That same old promise. And to where? Some farm where the Polish family will sell me to the Gestapo for a Christmas ham? Stefan, I won't do it. Badowski has promised to keep me safe. He's going to move me to the new camp with him and let me live in the Judenrat barracks with him. They're going to let me run the pharmacy in Plaszow. That is a real future, Stefan, if a future exists for any Jew in Krakow right now. Please, leave him alone. If not for his sake, then for mine."

"You're a fool, big sister. A fool who is going to get herself killed in the end."

"We're all facing death right now. And we're all facing impossible circumstances. I'm begging you to give me a chance. To leave my friends alone. To give me a future."

Stefan shook his head. He walked over and stood near one of his men. They held a hurried, whispered conversation. Natalia strained to hear what they were saying, but she couldn't make out the words. They kept at it for several minutes, then Stefan stepped back over to her.

"I think you're making a tremendous mistake, Natalia. But if this is the course of action you're choosing, then for the sake of our father and mother, I will leave Badowski alone."

"Oh, Stefan. Thank you, thank you so much! You don't know what that means to me. I'll prove to you that you were wrong about him. You'll see. He's going to save me. You're giving me a chance for life."

"I think you're going to your death. But that's your own choice. But I'm not doing this for free. There's a cost for everything in the ghetto, dear sister. If you want Badowski's life, you're going to have to pay for it."

"What do you mean?"

He told her.

"I can't do that," she said.

"You will, or we'll kill your friend without your help. And we'll keep you locked up here until he and his daughter are dead."

"I don't see how I can assist."

"I don't care how you do it. Just make it happen. It's your choice, Natalia."

She didn't want this, didn't want to be responsible for anyone's death. But she had no choice. It was this or betraying her best friend's father, her savior.

She nodded.

"Good. That's the right decision. So, listen, this is what we are going to do . . ."

Chapter 28

Plaszow Labor Camp

Occupied Poland
March 1943

Elsa rode quietly toward her new job. She had a little suitcase with all her worldly possessions. She stared out the window blankly, still stunned by the news she'd heard the night before. She arrived at Plaszow a few minutes later. Her driver led her to her new housing. She was assigned part of a house overlooking the valley of the camp. Her escort explained that she would share it with a couple of other women NCOs, but they had not yet been assigned to the camp, so for now, she had the entire place to herself. Under other conditions, she would have been ecstatic about her new housing. It was nicer than any place she had ever lived. She had a full bedroom to herself, and there were spacious living areas and even a balcony that looked out over the camp. She would be able to sit out there in the mornings and drink coffee in peace before her days began.

But today she couldn't think of such things. She put away

her things, went to the bathroom and checked her hair and makeup, and then walked down with her escort to the SS administrative building where she would work each day. She was shown to a little desk in a side office, another thing she would have normally celebrated: having her own office. She settled herself in and opened up the drawers, making a mental inventory of where the paper and pens were, and making a short list of additional supplies she thought she might need. As she did so, there was a gentle knock on the door. She looked up and saw Göth there, leaning against the doorframe.

"Good morning," he said.

"Good morning, sir."

"All settled in, then?"

"Yes, sir."

"Excellent. Well, I hate to put you straight to work, but I have a memorandum for you to prepare."

And thus, Elsa found herself typing out the detailed instructions for the liquidation of the ghetto, which was to occur the following morning. Amon went on for nearly an hour, giving information about the number of troops involved, the sections to be cleared and in what order, escorts for the groups to the trucks that would bring them to Plaszow, or for those who would be sent straightaway to Auschwitz. He dictated requisitions for ammunition, and where additional ammunition and food would be kept for the SS during what would surely be a very long day. He gave detailed instructions about the operations that would occur after all of the willing volunteers left. The search of each apartment and building—and that all those who had not cleared out of the ghetto during the day would be summarily shot. She fought back her nerves and a wave of nausea as she filled out these instructions. She knew each street he described, and she could imagine the people, rushed out into the street, some killed as they went, shot down by the random whims of trigger-happy soldiers who would be whipped up by bloodlust and drunk on vodka. She thanked God that in her new position, she would not have to witness the end, and would not have to be involved in the operation to end the district, and so destroy so many lives.

Finally, he was finished. She'd typed more than twenty pages. He sat down in a chair across from her, seemingly exhausted from his efforts. He offered her a cigarette and took one himself. Puffing away, he read through the pages several times through. "You did a brilliant job, Baumann. Schueller was right to recommend you. Not a single mistake. And I was going so quickly."

"Thank you, sir."

And even though Göth did not know her, he must have seen something in her expression, in her failure to beam at his approval. "Is something wrong?" he asked.

"I don't want to bother you with it, sir."

"Nonsense, tell me."

"It's just that my best friend and my boyfriend both received news yesterday as well. I was sure they would be moving into Plaszow after the upcoming *Aktion*, but they both received orders yesterday that they were being relocated to other camps. To Auschwitz and Gross-Rosen."

"Are they good people?"

"The best."

"Well, I can't have my new secretary in a foul mood every day, can I? Don't you worry your little head one more moment. Just give me their names and ranks, and I'll get them transferred here."

"Really, sir? Can you do that?"

"As easy as this," he said, snapping his fingers. "Now tell me who they are."

She gave him the information and he wrote it down in a little black book he carried. "I'll take care of this today, and you can even let them know."

"How would I do that? I don't have any way into Krakow."

"You do today. I'm sending you with a copy of these orders to Lieutenant Schueller. Take some extra time to track down your friends and let them know."

"Thank you, sir. Thank you so much. I'll never be able to repay you."

"Just keep up the good work, Corporal. Now let me escort you out to the car."

They walked together into the camp yard. Göth opened the car door for her. "Thank you, again."

"Take your time out there today. Tomorrow, I'll need you in the office early. I may have to call in memorandums to you from time to time."

He closed the door behind him. The vehicle moved up to the gate. She heard a commotion behind her and some shouting. Göth was standing near one of the barracks, shouting at a Jewish worker who was sitting near a pile of bricks. As she watched, Göth drew his pistol and shot the man in the head. She whipped her head away and pressed back in her seat, eyes closed. She couldn't believe what she'd just seen. Göth had seemed incapable of any unkindness. If anything, she'd wondered how effective he might be in running a labor camp. Now she realized she didn't know the man. Perhaps he was different from what she had supposed. Well, it didn't matter. As Klaus had said, a war was on, and they had orders. She would be in her little office, insulated from what happened inside the camp. She could survive that way—a typist away from all the horror. So she told herself.

The driver dropped her off at the ghetto, by the gate near Plac Zgody Square. She showed her identification and the order memorandum she had for Lieutenant Schueller. The guard informed her that the lieutenant was at the Optima factory, conducting an inspection. That was likely where Klaus and Rachel would be as well. She stepped through the gate and started toward the square. She'd only gone a few steps before she stopped. She felt an internal war going on in her mind. She knew she should just keep going, but something was stopping her. Taking a deep breath, she turned to her right and headed toward the pharmacy. She opened the door and found Irena and Natalia manning the counter.

"Elsa, good morning," said Irena, a touch guardedly.

"Good morning," said Elsa. She stepped up close to the counter. "Can I talk to you for a moment? Alone."

"Certainly," said Irena. "Natalia, could you excuse us for a minute?"

The Jewish girl looked at the two of them, and then stepped into the back. Elsa couldn't help but feel Natalia had given her a strange look, one she'd never seen before on the woman's face, but she didn't have time for that right now. She turned back to Irena. "I have to tell you something," she said.

"What is it?"

"I am risking my life in giving you this information. So, I must trust you not to tell anyone it came from me. The *Aktion*, it will be tomorrow. They are liquidating the whole ghetto."

Irena's face paled. "The whole thing? We've heard rumors of another deportation, but we'd hoped it would be a limited scale. They're taking everyone?"

"Yes, everyone."

"Where to?"

"I can't. I can't tell you that. But I think you should stay home tomorrow. All of you. I'm not sure you will be safe."

Irena looked stunned. "I don't know if we can. I know Tadeusz, he will want to be here."

"I don't think you should be. But if you do decide to come to work tomorrow, I'll talk to my friends, to Rachel and Klaus. I'll see if they can keep an eye on you."

"Thank you, Elsa, thank you for telling me this. You're a good person. I've known that for a long time. I don't know how you ended up in the SS. How you can stand doing what you do."

"That's a story for another time. Perhaps I will tell you some day. But you're right, Irena. I'm not suited for this. But I've had good news. I've been hired as a typist away from all this. I won't have to be directly involved anymore."

"Well, that's something—for you at least. I wish there was something I could do for all of these poor people here."

"I do too. If I could save them, I would. But I don't have any power. If there's anything I can do for them in my new job, I will. But for now, they have to go through this crucible, and there's nothing you or I can do."

"How about Natalia? Is there something you can do for her?"

Elsa shook her head. "No, but tell her to come to the pharmacy and stay there. Don't try to hide in her apartment—they'll shoot everyone they find hiding. But stay in the pharmacy until things settle down a little. I'll have Rachel come collect her and escort her personally to the trucks. I'll make sure she gets sent somewhere safe—as safe as any place for Jews these days."

"Thank you, Elsa, thank you for everything."

"Goodbye, Irena. I don't know when I'll be back in Krakow. But if I get a chance again, I'll come and visit you."

"Goodbye."

Elsa stepped out of the pharmacy and headed toward the factory. She felt better than she had in a long time, since before the first *Aktion* she'd endured. She knew she had just betrayed her country, her people. She'd put her life in danger. And yet she finally felt like she was doing the right thing. She didn't know if she would have any power in Plaszow, any opportunity to help the Jews in the camp. But she resolved to do so to the best of her ability.

She arrived at the Optima factory a few minutes later. She delivered the orders to Lieutenant Schueller, and he told her where Klaus and Rachel could be found. She tracked them down a few minutes later, inspecting a set of machines.

"Elsa, what are you doing here?" asked Rachel.

"I have news," she said.

"What kind of news?"

"The *Aktion* is going to happen tomorrow."

Klaus nodded. "I'm not surprised. I thought it would have already happened by now. I guess we're going to have to go out and celebrate when it's over; we're not going to have much more time together."

"Yes, we will," said Elsa. "I've fixed that too."

"What do you mean?" asked Rachel.

Elsa told her about Göth's promise to transfer them both to Plaszow.

"Ah, but how delightful," Rachel said. "And how clever of you to win favor with the commandant so quickly. What is he like?"

"He's been so kind to me. He's cultured, attractive."

"How attractive?" asked Rachel.

"Attractive enough that I'll bet he's your newest project."

Rachel smiled. "Good. I'm tired of Schueller, and apparently he's tired of me as well. I need something new to distract me."

"I thought he might be sensitive for the job, but then he shot a prisoner just as I was leaving this morning. It really disturbed me."

Klaus shrugged. "I told you, Elsa, there is a job to do. Don't blame the man for doing it."

"I suppose you're right. But I don't think I'll ever get used to it."

"I know that, Elsa. And I love you for it. I'm so delighted you have this typing job now. And that we'll be together in Plaszow." He took her hands. "Look at us, the three musketeers."

"Four musketeers, once I snag Göth," said Rachel.

They were interrupted by a woman hurrying up to them. She was Jewish and she came to attention, bowing her head and looking at the floor as was required.

"What is it?" Klaus asked with annoyance.

"I'm sorry, sir, but I have a message for Corporal Baumann."

A message? Who would have sent her a message through a Jew? Elsa took the note out of the woman's hands.

"Now shoo," ordered Rachel.

The woman scurried off without another word.

"What is it?" Rachel asked.

Elsa, perplexed, unfolded the message and read it. "Strange. It's from Natalia. She said she needs to see us immediately, all three of us."

"Who the hell is Natalia?" asked Klaus.

"The Jew. You know, the one that works at Pankiewicz's."

"How do you know her name?"

"I took the time to learn it."

"Why would she want to see us?"

"I don't know," said Elsa but she was worried it had something to do with the warning she'd given to Irena. What if they'd been overheard? What if she'd caused the Pole some kind of harm by telling her what was coming tomorrow? "I suppose we should go see what she wants."

"Why should we?" said Rachel. "We don't dance to the tune of some Jewish skirt. To hell with her!"

"Now, now," said Klaus, perhaps remembering their conversation from the last fight. "If Elsa thinks we should go, then we should go." He checked his watch. "We could waltz over there now if you'd like. This machinery isn't going anywhere, and I wouldn't mind a little coffee, laced with something stronger than that."

"Fine," said Rachel. "Since Elsa has lined us up with a new job, and me with a new boyfriend, I'll indulge her weakness for Jewish sentimentalities."

"I didn't guarantee he'd be your boyfriend," said Elsa. "He could be married."

"Hah! Like that's going to make a difference. I'll have him, all right. I just need to get through this *Aktion* and then I'll sink my claws in him."

They walked out of the factory and headed toward the pharmacy, chatting about the future. Elsa filled them in on what she'd seen and heard at Plaszow.

"What opportunities are there for me?" said Rachel.

"Göth mentioned that SS women would be in charge of multiple barracks," said Elsa. "He offered me the job if I wasn't interested in being his secretary."

"If I typed, I'd be his secretary, all right," said Rachel. "But running some barracks will suit me fine as well. There should be some opportunities to scrounge up gold and jewelry from the prisoners, in exchange for little favors. Yes, that position could be quite profitable indeed."

"I hadn't thought of that," said Elsa. "You're right, Rachel. We could make a mint working with the prisoners. A loaf of bread for a diamond. A sausage for a Swiss watch. Ten thousand zlotys to pull someone out of a line that is headed for Auschwitz. Yes, we can make our fortune there indeed."

They were nearing the pharmacy, walking past the last row of buildings before the square. Elsa heard a crack and her ears exploded from the thunder. Klaus jerked forward and fell to his knees. As she stared in horror, she saw a hole in his back. His green-gray tunic was filling with blood. Another crack and he tumbled to the ground, a second shot to his shoulder. His body was jerking, and blood was pouring out of his wounds, pumping in a froth fountain.

Another explosion, and Rachel stumbled against her, holding on to her arm. She thought her friend was trying to push her away, to get her out of whatever was happening, but Elsa saw that part of her jaw was missing. Rachel's eyes were glazed over and her throat was gurgling. Elsa tried to hold her friend up, but she collapsed to the ground. Another shot rang out and the concrete beneath her feet exploded in white powder. Without thinking, she turned, sprinting the way she had come. Another shot, and another. Somehow, they missed. Elsa made it to the intersection and rushed around the corner. She sank against the wall of a building, her breath coming in ragged gasps. She felt a fiery burning. Looking over, she saw that her right shoulder was wounded. Blood was running down her uniform. She took out a cloth she'd been carrying for a cold and pressed it against the hole. She heard screaming and the sound of boots on the pavement. Looking up, she saw Schueller sprinting toward her along with a couple of other men. She tried to call to him, but a dizziness erupted in her head, and she slumped to the pavement, the darkness overwhelming her.

She woke up in the hospital a few hours later. She'd been lucky, the doctor told her. The bullet must have gone through Rachel first. It had largely been spent and had only mildly punctured her shoulder. They'd removed it easily. There was no permanent damage.

Lieutenant Schueller was there. He was looking down at her with concern and sadness. "Are you all right?" he asked her.

"Yes. Yes, I think so."

"Göth will be along soon," he said. "He was very concerned."

"How are my friends?" she asked. "How are Klaus and Rachel?"

She saw the pain rush across his face. "I'm sorry, Elsa. There was nothing we could do. They're gone."

Elsa felt the rage tearing through her. She tried to rise, to get out of bed, but the lieutenant put his hands on her and gently laid her back down. "You can't go anywhere," he said. "You have to rest."

"I'm going tomorrow," she whispered, her eyes closed.

"That's impossible," he said.

She didn't answer him. She knew if she argued, he would talk to the doctor, and she would be restrained. She merely nodded, as if by agreement. But she knew one thing for sure. Nothing on this earth would stop her from entering the ghetto tomorrow. She had unfinished business there.

Chapter 29

Podgórze District

Krakow
Occupied Poland
March 1943

Natalia hid behind the false wall. All around her she could hear the familiar sounds of an *Aktion*, the screaming, the shots, the heavy boots running up and down stairs. She hadn't thought she would need this place, built at considerable expense by a carpenter secured by Mr. Badowski. She thought she would have waited out the *Aktion* with the Badowskis themselves at their three-floor townhome, dining on bread and perhaps a little cheese, waiting for the Germans to escort them and the rest of the Judenrat families in private vehicles to their new special barracks in Plaszow. But her plan to save her benefactor had gone astray. The resistance snipers had killed two of the SS who had pestered the pharmacy, but they'd missed the last one. Elsa, the kind one, who had always given her a little smile and who had warned Irena of the coming German operation. Natalia hadn't wanted to betray her. But she'd had no choice. The other two could go straight to hell as far as she was concerned, and they probably had. She had felt bad about including Elsa in the ambush.

However, they'd missed her somehow, and she had to assume Elsa knew she had set them up. Resistance members had spotted her slouching against the wall. She'd been wounded. They'd watched the SS cart her away in an ambulance. Perhaps she'd died of her wounds too? Although based on what was seen, the observers didn't think so. And thus Natalia, after consulting with Mr. Badowski, had settled on the idea of hiding in her apartment, to avoid a raid at the pharmacy or the Badowskis' home. If the Germans had failed to look for her by the end of the day, it would mean that Elsa likely had died from her wounds. She could then be safely collected by Mr. Badowski and she would still ride with them over to the new housing at Plaszow. If the Germans were seeking her out, then he would obtain forged papers for her. He would arrange for someone to come over and give her the papers, and also cut her hair and dye it a different color. She wouldn't be able to join them in the Judenrat under those circumstances, but they should be able to get her into Plaszow and hopefully away from Elsa permanently. With thousands of women working there, and her hair altered, there was every chance Elsa would never find her. They hadn't really talked that many times after all.

She thought of her brother. She hadn't gone to him. They were intent on staying and fighting. She was sure they would all be dead before dawn tomorrow. She felt a flicker of pain about that, but then he'd rejected her—forced her to betray these Germans, almost forced her to betray the man who had done so much to save her. No, she couldn't depend on him.

So now she stood in the darkness, wedged between two walls with a bare eighteen inches of space. The area was dusty and freezing cold. There was nothing to sit on, nothing to do.

She had to simply stand there in the darkness, listening and waiting.

The hours passed with a continuous roll of screams, shouts and gunshots. Natalia was thankful she didn't have to face what was going on in the streets below. She leaned her head against the wall, half dozing. But the bricks were too cold, and every time she started to sleep she jerked off-balance and caught herself in a panic. So she simply stood there, letting the seconds tick slowly by, hoping it would be dark soon and Mr. Badowski would come and fetch her.

She heard footsteps coming down the hallway. That might be him now. But then she realized they were speaking German. There was a sharp knock at her door. She took a deep breath, trying to hold the panic down. She heard a crash. They must have kicked down the door. The boots clomped on the floor, her floor. What were they doing in there?

"So, the Jew bitch is hiding here somewhere? *Ja?*"

"Yes. There's a false wall."

"Did you happen to ask where?"

"No."

"*Idiot.* I don't want to spend all day in here."

"She's the one from the pharmacy, I heard."

"That's what he told us."

"And he gave her up to save himself? And his family?"

"Not even that. He's been giving up names all over the ghetto, at a hundred zlotys apiece. This one cost us five hundred, though. A special case. Apparently loads of people trusted him, and he instructed them to set up these false locations. The bastard kept a list of them, can you believe it? His own people."

Natalia couldn't believe what she was hearing. After all she'd been through. After all the things he'd done for her, Badowski had betrayed her for a little money. Her brother had been right about him. He was a snake, a traitor to his people. And she'd saved his life.

She heard knocking on the walls. The Germans were searching for the false space. They were in the bedrooms right now. She wondered if she could get out and escape before they came back out. But the latch was loud and the internal hinges creaked. She'd meant to oil them but then the need for this space had passed from her mind and she'd failed to tend to it. No, there was no way out. They moved to the other bedroom. They were chatting away like they were on a Sunday stroll. She knew the second they found her, they were going to shoot her. The Germans made no exceptions for those who tried to evade them.

They were in the front room now. It sounded like they were starting on the far wall. It was minutes, perhaps seconds, until they would come to this side and discover the hollow space. She closed her eyes and thought of her mother and father. She could see their faces smiling sadly down on her. She thought she would run the pharmacy in the new labor camp, and live a life of comparative luxury, safe from the killings and the hard manual labor of the general population. But that had all been a lie. Had he intended to betray her all this time? Or perhaps it was because of the botched assassination? Yes, that must be it. She'd become too much of a liability for him. She realized if this had not happened, she would have gone with the Badowski family to her new life, without ever knowing all the people, all the families he had betrayed.

And now she was moments from discovery. She closed her eyes, trembling in the darkness, waiting for the end.

A thunderous crack rang out, followed by another and another. She heard screams and the sound of bodies hitting the floor. There were footsteps on the hardwoods of her room. Then two more shots. Her ears rang and the smell of acrid gunpowder filled her nostrils. She heard a knock on her door. She didn't answer. There was another knock.

"Sister. I've taken care of the Germans. I followed them here."

"Did you hear their conversation? Mr. Badowski—"

"Betrayed you? Yes. I heard it. I told you about him, but you didn't believe me. I can't stay here long."

Natalia unlocked the latch and pushed the door open, stepping out into the room. There were two SS privates on the floor of the apartment, neat gunshot wounds to each of their foreheads. She stared down at them for a moment, and then looked at her brother. "What now?" she asked.

"You have your choice," he said. "If you want, you could join us. We're going to fight here, die here. We're going to make a stand and show the world that not all of the Jews went like sheep to the slaughter. That the butchers can't conquer us all."

"Stefan, I can't. I'm sorry, I don't know how to shoot a weapon. I've had no training. There's no time."

He smiled at her. "I know. I understand. Then you should go to the pharmacy if you can make it. Ask Irena to hide you there. I'll let my people know. If any of us survive the night we'll try to get you out of the ghetto. I'm afraid I still can only offer the sewers to you."

Natalia would have preferred to simply accept her fate and head to the mass loading up for the new camp. But she didn't know if the Germans were after her. She might be shot on the spot. Her brother was right. "That's what I'll do," she said.

He stepped forward and took her hands. "Try to survive," he said. "You're the last of us. Please forgive me for blaming you about Mother. You were right. We could never have gotten her out. She wouldn't have made it in the countryside. She'd already given up. But you, you can make it. Find some hole in that pharmacy and stay there, today and tonight. Someone will be by tomorrow to get you out, if any of us survives."

"Why don't you come with me?" she said. "We can get out together."

He shook his head. "I have Germans to collect. These two aren't my first, but I'll notch some more before they get me. But remember me, sister. Remember what we did here."

She embraced him, holding on tight, tears running down her face. "I will, Stefan. I promise."

There were shouts in the street. Stefan looked up. "We have to go," he said. "Get to the pharmacy, however you can." He reached down and picked up the pistols from both of the soldiers along with their ammunition belts. Tucking them into his coat, he gave her a final smile and then departed.

Natalia stood there for long minutes, unable to move. Then, steeling herself for what was ahead, she stepped out of the apartment and out onto the street. She wasn't prepared for what she saw. The road was littered with bodies, dozens of them. There was luggage everywhere, some spilled open as if it had been flung from the windows above. She looked left and right, and there was nobody in sight. She turned and started walking toward the pharmacy, her gait steady and her head held high, falling back into her strategy that she was supposed to be there, that she had a purpose in her path.

She passed the first block and then the second, she could see the square in front of her now, the pharmacy poking out in the distance on the far side. Now there were Germans, and the familiar mass of families, pressed together for warmth, eyes wide with fear and uncertainty. Natalia stepped into the outskirt of the square and began making her way around the edges, still striding along as if she was running late for another day of work. Her heart raced as she walked right past two soldiers that were guarding a group of women. One of them glared at her, talking to the other and pointing her direction, but she ignored them as if she had not a care in the world, and kept her measured pace toward the pharmacy. She was a hundred yards away and then fifty. A gunshot erupted in the square, and another. Screams and shouting assaulted her ears. By some miracle she reached the front door and opened it. She stepped in and found the whole staff there, standing behind the counter.

"Natalia!" shouted Irena. She rushed from behind the counter and into her arms. "You're alive! You're supposed to be in hiding!"

"The Germans were in my apartment. Mr. Badowski gave away my hiding place. He betrayed me, Irena, and he betrayed others."

Irena gasped. "I'm sorry, Natalia, I'm so sorry. These are terrible times, and it's led good people to do terrible things."

"He's not a good person," said Tadeusz. "He's been taking money for years. Money that the Judenrat donated to us to keep the flow of medicine."

Natalia looked up. "Why didn't you ever tell me?" she asked.

"I didn't want it to get back to him. And you were so close to his daughter, so close to him. I didn't want to alter the way you saw him. And remember, Natalia, he did save your life, several times, and mine as well."

"We don't have time to keep talking," said Helena, looking around. "The Germans could come in at any moment."

"She's right," said Irena. "We have to hide you."

"Can you?" said Natalia. "My brother said if I can stay here until tomorrow, he will get me out of the ghetto through the sewers—if any of the resistance survives the night."

"Yes," said Tadeusz. "We can hide you. Although if the Germans come looking, they will find you."

"And if they find me, they'll kill all of you as well," said Natalia. "I can't have that. I'll find somewhere else."

"There is nowhere else," said Tadeusz. "Besides, you're not the only person we are hiding. Come with me." He led her up the stairs and to his bedroom. Unlocking it, she saw there were a dozen people already there, crammed into the space. "This is all I can do for you," said Tadeusz. "If the Germans search us, I'm afraid they will find all of you. But I have vodka and bread out front. I know a lot of these characters and if they come in, I'll do everything I can to keep them up front. I wish I had a better hiding place for you, Natalia. I should have invested in something along the way, but for some reason, it never occurred to me that they would liquidate the ghetto, that I would need a place to put people."

"Don't feel badly, Tadeusz. You've done so much for all of us. This pharmacy has been a haven for me. Without it, I would never have survived. I must admit, I've had selfish reasons for being here. While all of you have helped the people, I just wanted to play at doctor. I've lived in a dream world where I was better than other people, that my family connections and my background would give me privileges and save me in the end. Mr. Badowski was an extension of that belief. Now I realize I was wrong. I'm not any better than anyone. Not more deserving of life, or a future. I realize now that privilege is an ugly illusion. That my motives were selfish."

Tadeusz took her hands. "Don't be so hard on yourself," he said. "You've helped thousands of people while you've been here. You gave me someone to mentor, a little distraction and joy for me amidst all this pain and suffering. Sometimes we have the wrong motives but the right results. Sometimes we fall into grace."

"Thank you, Tadeusz, thank you for everything."

He nodded and closed the door behind him. The room was completely dark. The window above was open to allow for more air and the space was frozen. She crowded in with the rest of the people, standing in the silence, huddled for warmth, listening to the gunshots and the cries of the wounded and the dying as the long final day of the ghetto continued.

Natalia was half dozing when she heard it. A shout and screaming much nearer. She realized she recognized the voice and her heart sank. Tadeusz was shouting back, joined by Irena. They were talking fast, trying to protect her. But she knew there was no point. Elsa was there, and she was demanding to search the pharmacy. She could only have one purpose, to find her and to exact revenge. The shouts ramped up. Natalia knew she only had moments left. She thought of the people with her now. She thought of the Jews in the ghetto who had lived with her and starved and died with her these past two years. These people whom she had largely ignored while she worked at the pharmacy, enjoyed her spacious flat, and ate dinners at the café and at the Badowski home.

She knew what she had to do. Turning, she unlatched the lock and stepped out into the hallway. Closing the door behind her, she rushed down the stairs and to the front, arms in the air. She took in the scene in a moment. Elsa was there, her right arm in a sling, her left hand holding a pistol. Her face was mottled and tear streaked. She was screaming at Irena, pointing the barrel her direction.

"I'm here!" Natalia shouted. "Elsa, I'm here!"

The woman turned her eyes to Natalia. "You!" she shouted. "You murdered my boyfriend and my best friend. Get out here now!"

Natalia complied. Stepping out from behind the counter, her arms still in the air, she stepped between Elsa and Irena.

"On your knees!" Elsa screamed.

Natalia dropped down, lowering her head, waiting for the bullet that would end her life.

"Elsa! Don't!" shouted Irena. "Please, don't do this! I know you. You've always been kind to us. If you do this, it will haunt you forever!"

"I don't care about that!" Elsa shouted, her voice cracking between sobs. "She took everything away from me!"

"I know she did! But you have a chance. A chance to redeem yourself. Think of what you belong to. What the SS represents. But that's not you, Elsa! I could tell that from the moment I met you. I've watched you. I've never seen you do anything in anger to the Jews. I've noticed your absence during all of the *Aktions*. You came to me and told me about the liquidation of the ghetto! Now you have the chance to prove who you are. If you kill Natalia, it will haunt you for the rest of your life. But you have a chance to save her, to spare her life. If you do that, you will know you showed mercy—that will be your legacy. Please Elsa, please do the right thing."

"I can't. I can't," Elsa repeated. She put the barrel to Natalia's head.

"Don't do it, Elsa. Not for her sake, but for your own."

Elsa let out an animal shriek of despair. She pulled her arm back and brought the pistol down on Natalia's head, knocking her to the ground. Natalia reeled, her mind spinning, sharp agony burning through her head. She felt a hand in her hair, pulling her to her feet. "Move, now, before I change my mind!" Elsa shouted.

She stumbled forward, the pistol in her back. Elsa led her out into the square and shoved her into the mass collected for transport to Plaszow. "Don't move from there or I *will* shoot you," she said. "I don't want to see you ever again, don't want to hear your voice. You took everything from me!" Elsa spat in her face and kicked her hard in the back. Turning, she stumbled away, marching toward the ghetto gate.

Natalia huddled with the rest of the crowd, shivering in the cold, waiting for the next wretched chapter. The nameless mass of Jews. One people, battling desperately to survive.

Chapter 30
Podgórze District

Krakow
Occupied Poland
March 1943

The acrid stench of death clung to the air as Irena pressed her palm against the cool glass of the pharmacy window. Her eyes swept over the desolate square, a graveyard of abandoned lives strewn across the cobblestones. There was luggage everywhere. SS soldiers walked here and there, some bending over to rifle through the bags, looking for cash and valuables. As Irena watched, one of the men straightened up and held a gold ring to his eye, squinting to look it over closely. He turned the object over in his fingers, then with a quick look around, he shoved it into his pocket.

"I can't bear to look," she whispered, her voice trembling. "But I can't look away either."

Tadeusz stood beside her, his jaw clenched tight. "We must bear witness, Irena. For those who no longer can."

A child's doll lay face down in a puddle, its once-bright dress now stained dark. Irena's heart clenched. How many children had she helped, their tiny hands reaching for medicine? Now, silence reigned where laughter once echoed. She thought of the cyanide they'd distributed over these last days. She wondered how many families now lay in their apartments, dead from the pills they'd administered. Still, after what they'd witnessed that last day and night, she knew that Tadeusz had been right. As horrible as it was, they had given some of the residents of the ghetto another way out, perhaps a better one.

"Look," Tadeusz murmured, nodding toward another group of SS soldiers picking through the debris.

Irena's breath caught in her throat. The soldiers moved with predatory grace, their black uniforms a stark contrast to the gray desolation.

"Vultures," she hissed, surprising herself with the venom in her voice.

Tadeusz placed a gentle hand on her shoulder. "Careful, Irena. Even walls have ears these days. And we have to remember that we aren't out of this yet. We still have one more secret to protect."

She nodded, forcing herself to take a deep breath. The soldiers were so close, just beyond the thin barrier of glass and brick. One wrong word, one misplaced glance, and their sanctuary could crumble.

"How do we go on?" Irena whispered, her scientific mind grappling with the senseless brutality before her. "How do we continue our work in the face of . . . this?"

Tadeusz's blue eyes met hers, filled with a mix of sorrow and determination. "We go on because we must. Because every life we save, every moment of comfort we provide, is a victory against this darkness."

Irena nodded, drawing strength from his quiet resolve. She

thought of the hidden Jews upstairs, of the countless others they had helped. It wasn't enough—it could never be enough—but it was something.

A sharp crack echoed across the square. Irena flinched, her heart racing. An SS officer had fired his pistol into the air, laughing as his comrades scrambled for a piece of jewelry.,

"We should get back to work," Tadeusz said softly, his hand still on her shoulder. "There's inventory to be done, and we must be prepared for . . . whatever comes next."

Irena nodded, forcing herself to turn away from the window. As she moved toward the shelves of mostly empty bottles, she allowed herself one last glance at the desolate square. *We will remember*, she vowed silently. *We will bear witness. And somehow, someday, we will make this right.*

The pharmacy door swung open with a sudden, jarring creak. Lieutenant Schueller's polished boots clicked against the worn floorboards, each step a thunderclap in the oppressive silence. Tadeusz's spine stiffened, his face a mask of practiced neutrality as he greeted the officer with a polite nod.

"Herr Lieutenant," Tadeusz said, his voice steady despite the tension coiling in his gut. "What brings you to our humble establishment today of all days?"

Schueller's cold eyes swept the room, settling finally again on Tadeusz. "I bring news, Herr Pankiewicz. Good news for you. These ghetto walls," Schueller continued, his tone as detached as if discussing the weather, "will be coming down. This area will be cleansed of the last vestiges of the Jewish disease, and then will be repopulated with Poles." He paused, a cruel smile playing at the corners of his mouth. "A return to normalcy, one might say."

The words hung in the air, a stark counterpoint to the grim tableau visible through the pharmacy window. Tadeusz struggled to maintain his composure, acutely aware of the lives hidden just above their heads.

"I . . . see," Tadeusz managed, his throat suddenly dry. "And what has happened to the current residents?"

Schueller's laugh was devoid of humor. "Surely you jest, Herr Pankiewicz. You must mean the *former* residents. The Jews are gone. You've seen that yourself, have you not?"

Tadeusz nodded mechanically. "Of course, Herr Lieutenant. I simply meant that the Jews must have gone somewhere. I hope somewhere better than here. Somewhere safe."

"Leave that to us," Schueller said, his gaze sharpening. "Your only concern is to continue operating this pharmacy. The new residents will need your services, after all."

The Nazi officer prepared to depart. Irena found herself trapped between relief and dread. The immediate danger had passed, but what new challenges lay ahead? How long could they maintain this fragile sanctuary?

Irena held her composure, her eyes fixed on a spot just past Schueller's shoulder. She had to remain calm, passive, as if nothing was wrong. Her heart thundered so loudly she was certain the Nazi officer would hear it. Every word he spoke sent a fresh wave of terror through her, images of the hidden Jews upstairs flashing through her mind.

"A new era for Krakow," Schueller continued, his voice dripping with false optimism.

Irena forced herself to nod, her face a mask of polite interest. She could feel beads of sweat forming at her hairline, and she prayed they wouldn't betray her.

Tadeusz cleared his throat, drawing Schueller's attention. "We appreciate the update, Herr Lieutenant," he said, his tone measured and calm. "Naturally, we'll continue to serve the community as needed."

"Excellent," Schueller replied, his eyes narrowing slightly. "I trust you'll report any . . . irregularities you might encounter?"

Irena's breath caught in her throat. She glanced at Tadeusz, marveling at his composure.

"Of course," Tadeusz assured him, his expression betraying nothing. "We're here to help maintain order, after all."

As Schueller turned to leave, Irena's mind raced. How long could they keep up this charade? How many lives depended on their ability to lie convincingly?

The door closed, and for a moment, the only sound was their ragged breathing.

The click of the door latch echoed like a gunshot. Irena exhaled sharply, her shoulders sagging as the tension drained from her body. She gripped the edge of the counter, steadying herself.

"That was too close," she whispered, her voice trembling.

Tadeusz nodded grimly. "We can't afford any mistakes. They're watching us."

Irena's mind raced, calculating risks and necessities. "I'll see to our guests. I don't know when the resistance will show up, if they do show up. In the meantime, they'll need food, water, and reassurance," she murmured, more to herself than to Tadeusz.

Without waiting for a response, she moved swiftly to the back of the pharmacy. Her hands, usually so steady when measuring medications, shook slightly as she gathered bread and a canteen of water.

Irena climbed the stairs. She was as quiet as possible. She didn't want to alert any Germans who might be listening for unusual noises. Tiptoeing down the hallway, she carefully opened the door to Tadeusz's bedroom. She was hit by a foul stench as she entered the space—the smell of unwashed bodies and excrement. The room was in total darkness, and she strained to see the outlines of the Jews who were hiding there.

"What's happened?" a woman asked.

"It's over," said Irena. "The ghetto has been liquidated. There's nothing out there but the dead and the Germans."

"What about our rescuers?" a man asked.

"They should be along any time now," Irena said, praying she was right. If they had all been killed, she didn't know what they would do. Turn them over to the Germans? She couldn't do that. But she knew nothing of sewers or secret passages. She would worry about that later. "I have a little food," she said. "And some water. I'm sorry it's only one loaf."

A hand reached out and greedily took the bread. "Thank you. This is more than we could expect. I'll divide this equally and make sure everyone gets a share."

She handed over the water also. "Is there anything else I can bring you?"

"No. Thank you again. Thank you for everything you have done."

"It is nothing," she said, tears welling in her eyes. "I wish we could have done more."

"This pharmacy has been a light of hope for us. An island of sanity. You're saints. All of you."

Irena didn't know how to respond to that. "Take your meal and then please stay here and remain quiet. The Germans are still around. One of them was just in the pharmacy. I'll be back as soon as the resistance arrives."

She returned downstairs to find Tadeusz busy at work inventorying the mostly empty bottles on the shelves. "What are we going to do if the resistance is all gone?"

He looked at her. "I don't know, Irena. We will have to cross that path if it comes."

"Would the Polish resistance help?"

"They might. But it will be some days, I suspect, before things will settle down enough to get into contact with them."

"What's going to happen to everyone they took away?"

A sadness passed over Tadeusz like a shadow. "Most of them will never come back. I think even this labor camp, this Plaszow, is just a depot on the way to Auschwitz. I don't understand it, Irena. To murder people on a production line, like some kind of industrial factory. And why? Because of their race? Their faith? I've worked with Jews my whole life, and my father before me. They are just people, like you and me."

"I hope Natalia will make it."

"I do too. I worry about her. She's lost Badowski's protec-tion—if such was ever a real thing to begin with. And I don't know about Elsa. You saved Natalia's life with your words, Irena—at least for that moment. But will she stay true to that when nobody is around? I fear for Natalia's life, and not just because of where she is headed."

"Elsa won't kill her. The moment has passed. I've seen enough of that woman. In her heart, she is one of us. She would have helped these people, in another life, another situation. I would have liked to have known her better. I think we could have been friends—in other circumstances."

"Yes, it's important to remember these Germans are people too. At least some of them. It's this war—and the insanity of their leader, that has led them to this."

"And will this war ever end, Tadeusz?"

"I think it is already ending. Not right away, mind you. But the Germans have shot their bolt in Russia. They are losing ground there, and now the Americans and British are nipping at their heels. It might take years, maybe a generation, but I think in the end they will lose. And then we will be Poland again and have our lives back."

"It will never be the same."

"No, it won't. The Jews, for one. There won't be many of them left. And those that survive won't want to stay here. We've lost a rich piece of our culture forever. And our govern-ment? I don't think it will ever be the same. Nobody wants the old nationalist government, and the Socialists are on the rise. Not only that, but I can't imagine the Americans will reach us here. It will be the Russians. And they will bring a new set of problems."

"What will you do, Tadeusz, now that the ghetto is gone?"

"I will stay here, like I always have. And I want you to stay too, Irena. You and the rest. That Schueller fellow said only one thing that I agreed with: When the wall comes down, we will have access to many of our old customers. The Poles that were left outside the walls, who didn't have access to our services anymore. We will have a chance to take care of them again, and if new people move into the neighborhood, we will be able to help them too."

"He also said the Germans would supply us with medicine again."

Tadeusz shook his head. "I don't care if it breaks me. If it takes my last zloty. I won't accept anything from the Germans. We will get what we need on the black market. It will cost our customers a little extra, but they'll understand. Just like our Jewish friends did."

The door rattled and opened. Irena had expected to find another Nazi, but it was a young woman, clothes in tatters, face smudged, a hunted look on her face.

"Can I help you?" Tadeusz asked cautiously.

"You're Pankiewicz?" the woman asked.

"I am."

"I understand you have a package for us."

"A package?"

"Yes, something you want taken to the other side."

"I do," he said, smiling at Irena. "So, some of you survived."

The woman nodded. "Not many. But we did good work last night. A dozen Germans are out there amongst the stones and the rubble. They won't harm anyone again."

"What will you do now?" Tadeusz asked.

"I will get your friends to the countryside first. Then we're going to the forest. There are Jews out there too. Jews willing to fight."

"Thank you," Tadeusz said. "Thank you for that."

"No, Pankiewicz. All of the thanks go to you."

Chapter 31

Soviet Prison

Krakow
Soviet-Occupied Poland
August 1945

Elsa Baumann sat at the table in the interrogation room, her wrists and ankles shackled. The door opened and Irena stepped into the room, followed by a Russian soldier. The man took position at the door, as if Elsa might somehow spring out of her irons and escape.

"Irena, thank you for coming."

"It's good to see you, Elsa. I tried to bring you some food. I had it with me. But they took it away from me at the front desk."

"That's kind of you. How is the pharmacy? How is Tadeusz?"

"We're still there. After the ghetto was liquidated, they tore down the walls and allowed Poles to move into the neighborhood. With the wall done, we were better able to secure some supplies and medicine, which enabled us to return to a more normal operation. A lot of our old Polish customers returned to us, and of course the new ones. But our Jewish ones—"

"Are all gone. Yes, we saw to that."

"What happened to you after the liquidation? I thought I would see you again, but I never did."

"I kept on working at Plaszow as Göth's secretary. He turned out to be a monster. Maybe the worst human I've ever met. He committed random murders all over the camp. Daily. Even Jews in our administrative office. He would kill for the slightest mistake, or even on a whim. I tried to help those around me. I gave them what food I could, and cigarettes to trade. But I couldn't save them. When the camp was shut down this last summer, everyone was shipped to Auschwitz. They all perished, as far as I know. I was kept here at Wawel as a secretary in the SS administration. There was a chance to evacuate when the Russians drew closer, but I chose to stay behind."

"What happened to Natalia? Do you know?"

Elsa shook her head. "I refused to look at her, to talk to her. I came across her a few times in the camp, but I'm sorry, Irena, I couldn't bring myself to do it. I did send her some food a few times. Only never directly. I just couldn't face her."

"I understand. But even helping her a little—that took real courage and integrity. But why did you remain behind? Surely you knew what that would mean?"

Elsa nodded. "Yes. I stayed behind to pay for my sins. To be punished as a German."

"But you helped people. You were never involved in the killings. I can speak to the authorities. Tadeusz too. They should know."

Elsa shook her head. "I don't want you to. Someone has to pay for what happened. It's not enough to have looked the other way. To have slid a loaf of bread to someone now and again. I was part of all of this. Part of the horror. I can't escape responsibility, and I refuse to do so."

"What is going to happen to you?" Irena asked.

"I've been sentenced to death. By hanging. I must admit to you, Irena, I'm afraid. Afraid to die like that. I asked them to just shoot me. A merciful bullet in the back of the head. But they refused. They said I had to suffer more than that, for what I had done. I am terrified of hanging. But they are right. I don't deserve their mercy."

"What if Tadeusz and I wrote declarations asking that they give you a more merciful death? Please let me do that for you."

Elsa shook her head. "It wouldn't be fair. Not to the thousands who died here while I typed away, hiding from everything going on around me. I'm afraid of the death that is awaiting me, but I deserve it, and I will endure it."

"Is there anything I can do for you?" she asked.

"Can you write my parents, and tell them what has happened to me? They won't let me send a letter."

"Of course. Can you give me their address?"

Elsa did so. "Irena, you should be proud of yourself. You, Tadeusz, and all the rest. You were the opposite of me. You actively resisted when you didn't even have to, you helped those people in the ghetto for years, at the risk of your own life. People will remember you for what you did. For me, I am just thankful that I will be forgotten."

"I don't know about all of that, Elsa. But don't be so hard on yourself. You could have chosen to be one of the butchers. Like Göth. Frankly, like Klaus. But you didn't. And you helped those around you, at risk to yourself."

Elsa smiled. "Thank you for that. I try to remember that too. But I'm not upset about my fate—although I'm terrified of the end. I stand for Germany here, and I hope my death will pay a small part of the price that we owe to the Jewish people, and to the world."

Chapter 32

Podgórze District

Krakow
Soviet-Occupied Poland
Under the Eagle Pharmacy
August 1945

Irena stood at the counter helping the last customer of the day. He was an elderly gentleman whom they had served before the war, before the ghetto. She gave him a smile and handed over the little brown bag with his medicine. A moment later he was out the door and Aurelia stepped around the counter to lock it.

"Well, we made it," Irena said. "Another week in the books."

"By the skin of our teeth," said Aurelia. "We've almost nothing left to give out. These Communists are as bad as the Nazis."

"Quiet!" said Helena. "We have no idea who might be listening."

"And that too feels the same," said Irena.

"What can we do about it? At least they aren't threatening to shut us down or shoot us."

"They've shot plenty of people," said Irena. "And more have disappeared. And we've all been questioned time and again about our involvement with the Germans—as if we were fascists. The Nazis wouldn't even sell us medicine, but here we are, having to defend ourselves. I want our old Poland back."

"It's gone forever," said Helena. "And the more we adjust the better. I don't have it in me to defy another government. If this is what we have, then this is what we will live with."

Tadeusz stepped up from the back. He gave them all a smile. "Discussing our new glorious government, I hear."

"We're all just acclimating ourselves," said Irena. "And Helena is right. It's better than the Nazis."

"Well, we have another adjustment to make," said Tadeusz. "I received this in today's post." He waved an envelope at them.

"What is that?" Irena asked.

"It's a notice from the head administrator in Krakow. Oh, and he's occupying Wawel Castle too, ironically."

"What does it say?"

"It says that as of September first, the workers and peasants of Poland own the pharmacy."

"No," said Irena. "They can't take it from you. After all you've been through."

"It's not a punishment," said Tadeusz. "I think after my eleventh interview with the secret police, they've decided we aren't Nazi traitors. But I am a traitor of a different sort. I'm a business owner, a capitalist. And all capital in the country is passing into the ownership of the people—or more accurately, of the government."

"Are they offering you a fair price?"

Tadeusz laughed. "The fairest price of all. Zero."

"You can't mean it," said Aurelia. "Is there no way to appeal?"

"Appeal to who? The workers and peasants? Again, I've been

expecting this. Although I thought they would pay me something."

"Oh, Tadeusz, we're so sorry," said Irena. "What's going to happen to you? To all of us?"

"Ah, that is the silver lining. They are graciously allowing us all to keep our jobs here. I will be the manager—at least for now. There will be an inspector who will come by each week, to check the books and make sure every last pill is accounted for. Zlotys in, zlotys out. I was assured in the letter that any discrepancy will be assumed to be a black market transaction, and that the penalties will be severe. So, we'll have to be very careful with our accounting. In this, I must appreciate our German friends. They expected a little bribery and black marketeering and were willing to look the other way."

The door rattled and there was a knock. They all froze. Who could be coming at this time of night? Had they been heard talking after all? "Don't worry," said Tadeusz. "I'll get it." He stepped over to the door. Peering through the glass, he tore open the door. "I can't believe it!" he shouted.

Irena looked up. Natalia was there. Tadeusz swept her up in his arms, lifting her off her feet and spinning her around. "You're alive," he said. "You're alive. I can't believe it." He set her down and she shuffled toward the counter. Irena couldn't help but notice that as thin as she'd been in the ghetto, Natalia had lost a tremendous amount of weight. She also walked with a pronounced limp and her hair had thinned and was streaked with gray. She rushed around the counter and embraced her friend.

"You're alive," she repeated.

"Yes," said Natalia, "if only barely."

"What happened to you?" Irena asked. "I tried to reach out to you at Plaszow, but they weren't letting any letters in or out. I couldn't even find out if you were all right."

"I weathered Plaszow as well as anyone could. I was marched

out with the last group from the ghetto. When we arrived we were split into men and women, and the camp was divided by electric wire. The barracks they assigned us to were drafty and poorly heated. We slept two and sometimes three to a bunk. They forced us to work twelve hours a day, sometimes sixteen. There were random executions. Worst of all was the commandant. Göth would sit up on his balcony with a sniper rifle. He would shoot anyone who was resting, or not working at the speed he wanted. Sometimes it seemed he shot people just for fun."

"How terrible," said Irena.

"I was lucky, though. I was assigned to work in Madritsch's factory inside Plaszow. The work was hard, but Madritsch was kind to us. He snuck in extra bread and sometimes oatmeal. Because of him, we were able to keep some of our weight on, when everyone else in the camp was starving to death."

"What happened to Badowski and his daughter?" Irena asked.

"I was lucky there too. The Germans betrayed the Judenrat and the Jewish Police. Badowski, Sylwia, Spira, all of them were taken up the hill where that old Austrian fort was and shot. It's the same place where they buried all the victims shot in the *Aktions* and the liquidation of the ghetto. Later they dug them all up and burned them. The smell was horrible and the ash fell like snow on us."

"It even fell here," said Tadeusz. "We thought it was snow at first, then we realized it was something else."

Natalia nodded. "We kept hearing rumors that the Russians were growing closer. We hoped and prayed that they would overrun the camp, and we would be saved. But no such luck. Last summer, they closed the camp down and we were all evacuated to Auschwitz. Because of the condition I was in, I was given the tattoo and allowed to keep working. Many people from Plaszow went right into the gas chambers. But in Auschwitz we Madritsch Jews no longer had access to extra food. I lost weight and grew sick. I thought every day that I might die or be selected for the ovens."

"I can't believe all of this," said Aurelia. "Of course we've seen the pictures now of Auschwitz. God forgive the Germans."

"God may, but I never will. The Russians grew closer to our camp. The Germans shot a lot of people out of hand and left many others who were too sick or weak to simply die. I was marched out with tens of thousands of others through the snow. No transportation, no food, no winter clothing. The Germans shot anyone who fell out of line. Thousands perished. We finally made it to some little camp in Germany. I don't even know the name. They didn't even try to work us anymore. They just kept us in barracks under lock and key. There was no heat, almost no food. Dozens of people perished each day. And then one day we woke up and the Germans were gone. I was so weak I didn't even understand what that meant. The Russians arrived a little while later. I was taken to a hospital. For weeks I floated between life and death, but I gradually began to improve and gain weight. I was released a few weeks ago and made my way back here. On foot."

"Natalia, I'm so sorry," said Irena. "Please come sit down. Have some food, have some vodka."

Natalia gratefully took a seat. Aurelia brought her some bread and sausage, and a little fermented cabbage. She ravenously consumed the food, not looking up or talking until she was finished. "Thank you," she said at last. "I haven't had any food for two days."

"Why did you come back?" Tadeusz asked. "Are you going to live in Krakow again now that this is over? If so, you can have your old job back. If the Communists will let me give it to you."

Natalia shook her head. "That is kind of you, Tadeusz, but I could never live here now. I can't live in Poland. I came looking for my brother. Have you had any word of him? Did you hear anything about him after the ghetto was liquidated?"

"I'm sorry, Natalia, but we haven't," said Irena. "The only thing we know is that the resistance fought bravely. They killed a number of Germans. But most of them perished in the fighting. One of them showed up here looking for you. Because you were gone, she took the group that had been hiding in Tadeusz's room. They made their way out of the sewers and as far as we know, they were placed with families in the countryside. Because of you, Natalia, because of your brother, lives were saved. But that's the last we heard anything about the resistance, or about your brother."

"He must have died in the fighting, then," said Natalia, a look of sadness creasing her worn features. "I had hoped for a miracle."

"What will you do now?" Irena asked. "Will you at least stay with us for a while?"

"I would be grateful to stay with you, Irena. At least for a week or two while I make inquiries about Stefan. After that, I intend to make my way into the American lines, and eventually to the United States. I have relatives there, my aunt on my mother's side. She moved away when I was just a little girl. She lives in New York somewhere. I am going to try to find her."

"Of course, you're welcome to stay as long as you wish," said Irena. "I'll take some time off and we will search for any record of your brother." She paused. "I saw Elsa, by the way."

Natalia started in surprise. "When? Why?"

"She's in a prison here in Krakow. She's been sentenced to death and she's awaiting execution. She told me she sent food to you in Plaszow."

Natalia nodded. "Yes, that's true."

"I'm glad to hear it. She said she allowed herself to be captured by the Russians and she told them what her role was. She wants to be punished."

"There was always something to her. Something more than the others. She still must atone for her sins. But she treated me properly in Plaszow, and she had no reason to do so. All of you, on the other hand, deserve far more than you've received. I expected to come back to find you heroes, with banners of celebrations and articles about you in the paper. But there's nothing."

"Our new hosts seem unimpressed by our efforts," said Tadeusz, smiling. "And we didn't do any of it for recognition. I wish we could have done more."

"When I get to the Americans, I'm going to tell them what you did. And I know others will, as well. The word will get out. You will be remembered, all of you."

"I will simply be content if it never happens again," said Tadeusz.

"Let us pray this was the last."

Chapter 33
Plac Zgody Square

Krakow
Soviet-Occupied Poland
August 1945

Stefan Wajcblum watched Natalia enter the pharmacy from across the square. He was elated to see her. He'd watched the pharmacy for weeks now, hoping for a miracle, a chance that his sister had survived. He would contact her soon, if everything turned out all right.

He thought of his own existence since the ghetto fell. He'd spent that last day fighting the Germans, killing three more of them, the last with his bare hands. In the morning, he'd sent an associate to the pharmacy, hoping to get Natalia out, but she was gone. At Tadeusz's request they'd taken a group of Jews hiding in the pharmacy. Stefan had led them through the sewers under the wall and then out of the city, placing them with trusted contacts in the countryside under false papers. Every one of them had survived the war. Through his contacts, he'd

312 James D. Shipman

found out that Natalia had survived the purge and was in Plaszow. He'd paid to have her transferred to Madritsch's factory and paid yet more to make sure she was watched and protected. Of course, all of that had fallen apart when the camp itself was shut down—but he'd done everything he could to shelter and protect her. Now he knew his efforts had produced fruit. He had a family still, a future.

He walked out of the square and north, passing through what was once a ghetto gate and moving across the Vistula. The bridge was open to traffic now—there were no Germans to guard it. Stefan kept a wary eye out for Russian soldiers and police. He hadn't registered with the new regime. He suspected the Russians might make him disappear for his role in the resistance—a strange quirk of the new administration was that they were punishing those who had resisted the Nazis, for being aligned to the old Polish government or some such nonsense. In any event, he had no intention of staying in Poland. He would travel to Palestine as soon as his business here was over. He hoped to take Natalia with him.

Stefan worked his way through the Kazimierz district and into Old Town. He found a café in the big square and enjoyed a meal of Kielbasa and a thick black bread, washed down with plenty of vodka. The young Polish waitress flirted with him outrageously. He got her name and found out what time she was getting off work. His plans for the later evening were set, assuming all went well.

When he was finished, he paid the tab and checked his watch again. It was five minutes to seven. Perfect timing. He rose from the table and hurried down the street. A couple of blocks later he stopped in the shadows of an alley, staring across the street at a building. He checked his watch again. One minute to spare.

The door opened. A middle-aged gentleman waltzed down the steps, an umbrella on his wrist, whistling a tune. Stefan had watched for weeks now. He was right on time. The man turned right and moved down the street. Stefan hurried now, crossing the road, and turning to his left, following thirty meters behind him. The man turned to the right, down an empty street, moving toward his car that was parked as always halfway down the block. Stefan hurried now. He only had a few moments. Looking this way and that, he made sure there were no cars coming, no pedestrians watching. The man arrived at his car. Fumbling for his keys, he was already reaching for the lock.

Stefan was on him in an instant. He wrapped his left hand around the man's mouth, pulling him backward and cutting off the ability for him to scream. With his right hand he drew his knife up to the man's neck.

"Hello, Petre. It's Stefan Wajcblum. I've come to repay you for your kindness to our family." He ripped the knife across the man's neck. His throat gurgled as Stefan severed the artery. He shoved the man against the car, staring down at the figure as it writhed and moaned, eyes wide. He peered down, smiling, then gave the betrayer a wink. Rising, he turned and walked quickly down the street, looking around to make sure he hadn't been spotted. Making his way around the corner, he walked another three blocks, wiping the knife clean with a handkerchief and then depositing the weapon in one trash can and the bloody cloth in another a block down.

Stefan stepped into a bar and ordered a drink. He checked his watch. The whole operation had taken less than fifteen minutes. He sipped the vodka, relishing his victory. He had avenged his father and his mother. Tomorrow he would go to Tadeusz and collect Natalia. Tomorrow, their future would begin.

Historical Notes

(The source of these notes is drawn from Wikipedia, the Yad Vashem website, and other sites.)

Tadeusz Pankiewicz

Tadeusz Pankiewicz (1908–1993) was a Polish pharmacist whose courageous actions during World War II saved many lives. Pankiewicz studied pharmacy in Krakow and took over his father's Under the Eagle Pharmacy in the Podgórze district of Krakow.

After the Germans occupied Poland in 1939 and subsequently outlined a Jewish Ghetto in 1941, Pankiewicz found that his business was located within the confines of the new quarter. He decided along with his three female pharmacists—Irena Drozdzikowska, Helena Krywaniuk, and Aurelia Daner-Czortkowa—to remain within the ghetto to take care of the Jewish population. These actions were unpopular with the Germans and they kept a close eye on the pharmacy, with Gestapo agents and SS visiting regularly.

The pharmacy served not only as a place to dispense medicine, but as a social gathering place within the ghetto. Many of the leading intellectuals and artists amongst the Jewish community became close friends with Pankiewicz, and he also worked closely with the Jewish and Polish resistance, often acting as a conduit between the two.

As the life of the ghetto progressed, Pankiewicz and the female pharmacists smuggled food and medicine into the ghetto, and also provided hair dye for people to look younger and cough syrup for parents to administer to children to keep them from alerting the Germans when the families were in hiding.

After the war, Pankiewicz continued to operate his pharmacy. He also published a book, *The Krakow Ghetto Pharmacy*, where he outlined his experiences during the war. This book was one of the earliest Holocaust memoirs, and it provided firsthand information about the Krakow ghetto, the mass deportations, and the people living within.

Pankiewicz faced challenges under the Communist regime, but continued his career in his pharmacy in Krakow. In 1983, he was recognized by Yad Vashem, Israel's official memorial to Holocaust victims, as one of the Righteous Among the Nations for his heroic efforts to aid Jews during the war.

Irena Drozdzikowska

Irena Maria Drozdzikowska (1913–1994) was one of the three Polish women pharmacists who worked under Tadeusz Pankiewicz at the Under the Eagle Pharmacy in Krakow during World War II. Irena completed her pharmacy degree at the University of Krakow in 1935, and started working for Tadeusz in 1939.

Irena, along with her colleagues Helena Krywaniuk and Aurelia Danek-Czortkowa, played a critical part in working with the Jewish community during the war. Irena directly saved the life of one Jewish woman who, when interviewed after the war, said she let her hide under the counter during one of the German *Aktions*.

After the war Irena kept working at the pharmacy, even after the Communists nationalized the business in 1951. The pharmacy eventually closed in 1967.

Natalia Wajcblum

Natalia is a fictional character, although she represents many characteristics of a Jewish Holocaust Survivor from Poland. The Jewish population in Poland contained many people who were educated and non-religious. They often spoke Polish and German, and didn't speak Yiddish, the common tongue of more traditional, Orthodox Jews in Europe.

Natalia and her family are shocked and confused by the restrictions imposed on them when the Nazis invaded. There had, of course, been reports of German laws and even atrocities in Germany, but the Jewish population in Poland was mistrustful of the Polish government, and did not necessarily give full credence to the information. After the Germans came into power, they quickly stripped the Jews of their rights. For a family like Natalia's this would have resulted in the loss of their jobs, the loss of access to education, and the freezing of their assets. But wealthier, more influential Jews would still have had options. They might have overseas accounts or money owed to them from others. They would have jewelry, and potentially cash reserves or reserves of gold and silver. And, at least in the first year after the invasion, they would have likely held on to their housing.

This would have the Wajcblum family in the position of believing they could weather the storm. They had money left to buy food and special items on the black market, and would have felt that, between the influence they had before the war and the ability to pay bribes, they had a decent chance of surviving the war right where they were. There was also a long Jewish tradition of responding to periods of persecution in just this way. By bending but not breaking, by buying influence and protection, they could wait out periods of violence and restriction, until more sensible people came back in charge and realized, as always, how important a part of the population these educated, skilled Jews really were.

Then came the ghetto. This would have come as a nasty surprise for the Wajcblums. Now they were losing their homes, and would be forced into cramped living spaces in one of the poorest sections of Krakow. It would not be surprising at all for them to attempt to buy their way out of the requirement, or even out of the country. Many Jews did, and some even made it to other countries, although many were betrayed along the way, much like the Wajcblums were.

Once in the ghetto, the intellectual and wealthy families would have been confused by the German system of classification. Those with literature, history, English, and music degrees were denied the life-giving worker permits. The Germans weren't interested in the intelligentsia. They only wanted essential trade workers, and even those only for a limited period of time. Still, those with money and influence were often able to bribe and buy their way into work permits. Not only this, but there was a concerted effort amongst the Judenrat and members of the Jewish community to protect the most educated portion of the population, toward some hopeful future after the war.

Natalia had the attitude that her education and her family placed her in an elite position. Her job at the pharmacy, and access to food and influence both from her employment and her friendship and connection with the Judenrat, perpetuated her feelings of superiority. Only at the end, when she was betrayed, and when she realized that all of the Jews in the ghetto were in the same position, did she understand that she was an equal with everyone there, that she should sacrifice herself to protect others.

Elsa Baumann

Elsa Baumann is also a fictional character. But just like Natalia, she represents a common theme amongst Germans before and during World War II. Elsa came from a working-class family that had been devastated by the depression and the hyperinflation experienced in Germany in the 1920s and early '30s. The

German people, already devastated by the loss in World War I, saw their jobs, their homes, and their life savings ravaged by economic forces outside their control.

Elsa, wracked with her own tragedies, finds hope and a sense of purpose when she joins the SS. The concentration camp section of the SS often recruited soldiers who had been disgraced or jailed, giving them an opportunity to redeem themselves through difficult duty. That is not to say all of the members were in that position. The SS also attracted some of the most educated, privileged people in the nation, for Heinrich Himmler's private organization was held to be one of the most elite parts of Hitler's new Germany. The rise of Hitler himself restored German confidence in their nation, and as he rearmed and defied the rest of Europe, he renewed the pride of Germans in themselves and their nation's future.

Once Elsa reported for duty, she was faced with the horrors of the Holocaust. Mixed up in this reality were the requirements of duty, love of country, years of propaganda about Jews as secondhand humans, and also the fear of consequences and reprisal for refusal to perform—not only to the individual, but potentially to their family as well.

Elsa took the hard road at the end of the day. Not only did she maneuver around direct atrocities, but she also accepted responsibility after the war and accepted the consequences of her actions. There were some real people in Germany who did the same. But they were depressingly few. It is difficult to stand up to tyranny, to have the moral and physical courage to defy everything you are being told, and to risk your life for what you believe is right.

Oskar Schindler and Julius Madritsch

Oskar Schindler and Julius Madritsch were two German industrialists who employed Jewish laborers during World War II. Both of them were responsible for many heroic acts that helped save a number of lives. They were striking in this, as they were almost the only industrialists who acted thus.

Schindler operated his Deutsche Emalia Fabrik (DEM) in a neighborhood of Krakow not far from the ghetto. At first he was largely working for his own profit, but he gradually began conducting acts of kindness, including buying additional bread and furnishing better soup to the employees of his factory.

Schindler was arrested several times by the Gestapo and interviewed for his activities, both for kindness to the Jews and also for black marketeering. But he was so well connected he was able to secure his release quickly in each instance.

As conditions in the ghetto worsened, Schindler stepped up his activities. When the ghetto was liquidated and the inhabitants moved to Plaszow, Schindler arranged at great expense to build a sub-camp connected to his factory. At this camp the food was much better, and the SS guards were not allowed on the factory floor.

Late in the war, Plaszow was shut down, and all of the inhabitants were to be moved to Auschwitz or other extermination camps. Again at great expense, Schindler built a camp for his workers in Moravia, and had them transported there (not without some obstacles). On arrival, he again refused to let the SS on the floor and he shepherded the Jewish population through the end of the war. This Schindler's List was about 1,100 members, and almost all of these people survived the war.

After the war was over, Schindler was arrested by the Americans but later released and celebrated as a hero. He later failed in his marriage and a number of businesses, but was supported by his former workers and was ultimately named a Righteous Among the Nations by Yad Vashem in Israel.

Julius Madritsch was an Austrian businessman who operated a textile firm in the Krakow ghetto. He and his manager, Raymond Titsch, worked together to provide better working conditions and more food for his workers. They also forged fake documents for Jews hiding in the Aryan portion of Krakow and in the countryside.

When the ghetto was liquidated, Madritsch moved his factory inside Plaszow, where he continued to sneak in black market bread and other food and provided a safer, protected place for the Jewish prisoners who worked with him. Madritsch was approached by Schindler to relocate his entire worker population to Moravia. Madritsch considered the proposal but ultimately declined. Despite this, he saved many lives by maintaining the health of his prisoners, and thus the majority of them were assigned to work details within Auschwitz instead of being selected straightaway for the gas chambers.

The Judenrat and the Resistance within the Ghetto

Judenrats were set up by the Germans in all of the Jewish ghettos. These ruling councils were placed in an impossible position, as they tried to manage ever more restrictive and demanding requirements by the Nazis. At first, they were involved in finding food and housing for the Jewish populations, along with work permits. But over time, they were required to make lists of Jewish individuals and families for deportation. This was impossible enough, but inevitably, the members took steps to protect their own families and friends. Some of the members were also withholding food and trading on the black market during the course of the ghetto, amassing fortunes. None of these efforts proved fruitful: the Judenrat members and the Jewish Police, while the last to be deported from their respective ghettos, were almost uniformly liquidated by the Germans, to erase prime witnesses to the atrocities that had been committed.

Plaszow Labor Camp and Auschwitz/Birkenau

Plaszow Labor Camp was constructed in the latter part of 1942 and into the winter of 1943. The Krakow ghetto population that was not directly deported to Bełżec and Auschwitz was sent here. The camp was about ten kilometers from the outskirts of Krakow, and was newly constructed in a valley between a number of houses and buildings, and the ruins of an Austrian Fort. This fort, situated on a hill, became the scene of mass shootings, including of the Krakow Judenrat and police force, as well as many influential figures from the ghetto, and later, masses of people from the influx of prisoners from other areas. An estimated 65,000 bodies were buried in the immediate area of the fort, which created a massive problem later when the Germans ordered that the bodies be exhumed and burned. The camp was liquidated in the summer of 1944, and the population deported primarily to Auschwitz, where the vast majority of the survivors perished.

Auschwitz, or Auschwitz-Birkenau, located in southern Poland, was the largest and most infamous Nazi concentration and extermination camp during World War II. The camp was created in 1940 on the grounds of a former Polish barracks. The original Auschwitz, Auschwitz I, is a small camp where the first shipments of prisoners were sent. Eventually, a crude gas chamber and crematorium was constructed. These are the only ones that survive today.

The much larger Auschwitz II, Birkenau, was constructed a few miles out of town in 1941. This camp initially had two tiny gas chambers in former cottages known as the "little white cottage" and the "little red cottage." Later, four huge gas chambers/crematoria were constructed in a segregated area of the camp itself. Birkenau was capable of killing ten thousand people a day, although it did not typically reach those numbers.

The entire Auschwitz complex was not exclusively a killing center, however. Approximately fifteen percent of those coming out of the cattle cars were selected to work in various industries spread over miles of countryside. Many of the prisoners were marched out and had to walk miles to and from work each day, along with working twelve hours or more of backbreaking labor. The average calorie allotment for the prisoners was six hundred per day, and the average prisoner, without help, would perish in six weeks. Many prisoners did survive through connections within the camp network, which had access to extra food and also valuables from the camp warehouses in a section called Canada that housed the clothing and luggage of the prisoners who had been murdered on arrival.

Auschwitz was also the site of macabre medical experiments by the likes of Joseph Mengele, who would operate on twins, freeze people to try to find better solutions for naval personnel submerged in the ocean for long periods of time, and conduct other unethical and terrifying procedures in the name of Nazi science. Mengele escaped from Germany after the war, and died in the 1970s in a swimming accident in South America.

The camp was evacuated on the approach of the Russians in January 1945, and the 75,000 survivors forced to march miles into Germany, in frozen conditions, often without food. At least 1.1 million people, mostly Jews, perished there.

Both Auschwitz I and Auschwitz II have survived at least partially to today, and are the site of museums and tours. This author has visited the site, as have millions of others, and it is a sobering, somber experience, but one that every person should try to make at some point in their life, to remember what humans are capable of doing to each other, on an industrial scale.

Krakow Today

Krakow today is a beautiful city, largely preserved after the horrors of World War II and the difficult Communist occupation years thereafter. A number of guides and sites on the internet reference that if one wants to see what Warsaw looked like before the war, then one should visit Krakow. The old city with the huge city square is breathtaking, with shopping, hotels, and many outside restaurants facing the interior of the space available to visit.

Wawel Castle, where Hans Frank was headquartered as the head of Occupied Poland, is a phenomenal medieval castle, with many original works of art and furnishings. The castle by itself is worth at least half a day on a tour.

The Jewish Ghetto district and the Jewish Quarter are well preserved. The Under the Eagle Pharmacy is still there, but it is now a Holocaust Museum. Just outside the pharmacy is the Plac Zgody Square, where now there are seventy empty chairs, representing the Jewish Ghetto population that was extinguished during the war.

Schindler's Factory also still exists, and is another Holocaust Museum well worth the visit. Krakow was also the original home of Pope John Paul II, and there is his home cathedral and other interesting places to visit related to his time there.

While Poland is not necessarily a frequent place to visit on many people's travel list (Americans at least), it is well worth the time. The cost of travel is less than in Western Europe, the food is phenomenal, and the people friendly. There are so many things to see, to enjoy, and so much history and architecture. There are river cruises also available on the Vistula, if one wants to visit a number of Polish cities in one trip. Krakow was one of this author's favorite places to visit ever, and he looks forward to coming back again to revisit the sites, and to spend more time in Poland.

Acknowledgments

I'd like to thank as always my wife, Becky, for her support and advice during the writing process. Also my intrepid writing group of Catherine, Sarah and Jeff, who always have great advice and edits. Finally, to my agent, Evan Marshall, and editor, John Scognamiglio, for all of their support and faith over the years.

CROSSING THE LINE

ABOUT THIS GUIDE

The suggested questions are included to enhance your group's reading of James D. Shipman's *Crossing the Line*!

DISCUSSION QUESTIONS

1. Why did the Wajcblum family attempt to flee Poland? Were there alternatives to this course of action they should have considered?

2. Why did Tadeusz Pankiewicz and the rest of the pharmacy staff remain in the ghetto? Would you have the courage to make the same decision if you were faced with it?

3. Why did the Polish population of Krakow not rise up and tear down the ghetto walls? Why did this not occur with any of the ghettos throughout Poland during the war?

4. Why was it so difficult for the population of the Krakow ghetto to accept the information that they received about the horrors of Bełżec and Auschwitz, even when there were first-person eyewitnesses who managed to make their way back to the Jewish District?

5. The members of the Judenrat and the Jewish Police force both attempted to work for and with the Jewish population in the ghetto *and* also with the German authorities to protect themselves and their families. What were the moral and ethical elements of this situation?

6. If you were Elsa Baumann, what would you have done differently?

7. Did Natalia conduct herself correctly throughout the book? Is there anything she should have done differently?

8. Oskar Schindler and Julius Madritsch were industrialists in Krakow profiting from slave labor. However, they also took steps, often at considerable risk, to properly feed

and protect their Jewish workforce. Were they heroes or criminals?

9. After the war there continued to be rampant anti-Semitism against the Jews in Poland. Why is this the case?

10. The world in 2026 is heading back toward authoritarian governments. How is today's time different from what existed in the 1930s? If America becomes an authoritarian state (either liberal or conservative), how would you act differently from the people in Europe during World War II?